THE SPEAK OF THE MEARNS

James Leslie Mitchell (pen-name Lewis Grassic Gibbon) was one of the finest Scottish writers of the twentieth century. Born in Aberdeenshire on 13 February 1901, Mitchell's boyhood in a small rural community shaped his ideas and imagination throughout his life. He was a brilliant school pupil, although less successful as a journalist in Aberdeen and Glasgow. In 1919 he joined the Royal Army Service Corps and served abroad. In 1925, he married Rebecca Middleton, a childhood friend, and four years later he became a full-time writer. The couple lived in Welwyn Garden City until the writer's premature death in 1935, of peritonitis, at the age of thirty-four.

He was a prolific writer of novels, short stories, essays and science fiction, and his writing reflected his wide interest in religion, archaeology, history, politics and science. His major published works are: *Hanno: or the Future of Exploration* (1928); *Stained Radiance: A Fictionist's Prelude* (1930); *The Thirteenth Disciple* (1931); *The Calends of Cairo* (1931); *Three Go Back* (1932); *The Lost Trumpet* (1932); *Sunset Song* (1932); *Persian Dawns, Egyptian Nights* (1932); *Image and Superscription* (1933); *Cloud Howe* (1933); *Spartacus* (1933); *Niger: The Life of Mungo Park* (1934); *The Conquest of the Maya* (1934); *Gay Hunter* (1934); *Scottish Scene*, a collaboration with Hugh MacDiarmid (1934); *Grey Granite* (1934); and *Nine Against the Unknown* (1934).

Ian Campbell is Professor of Scottish and Victorian Literature at the University of Edinburgh. He has worked with the Lewis Grassic Gibbon estate (now in the National Library of Scotland) and the Grassic Gibbon Centre in Arbuthnott.

LEWIS GRASSIC GIBBON

The Speak of the Mearns

with selected short stories and essays

Edited and introduced by Ian Campbell

Short stories introduced by Jeremy Idle

First published in 1982 by The Ramsay Head Press.
This edition published in 2007 by Polygon,
an imprint of Birlinn Ltd

West Newington House
10 Newington Road
Edinburgh
EH9 1QS

9 8 7 6 5 4 3 2 1

www.birlinn.co.uk

ISBN 10: 1 84697 020 2
ISBN 13: 978 1 84697 020 7

British Library Cataloguing-in-Publication Data
A catalogue record for this book
is available on request from the British Library.

Typeset by Hewer Text UK Ltd, Edinburgh.
Printed by Creative Print & Design, Wales

Contents

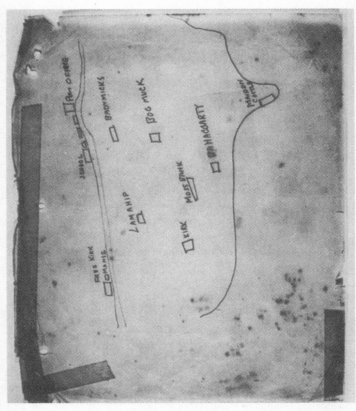

Sketch map of the area from Lewis Grassic Gibbon's notebook

Introduction

It is easy to see why *Sunset Song* has achieved the popularity never quite attained by the other novels in *A Scots Quair*. *Cloud Howe* and *Grey Granite*, while still heavily autobiographical in content, give little of the immediate gratification of belonging to a living community which is the characteristic of any first reading of *Sunset Song*. Bitter and backbiting it may be – Grassic Gibbon's parents were to complain that he had made them 'the speak of the Mearns' with his all-too-recognisable portraits and sardonic references – but *Sunset Song*'s Kinraddie is a living community of farmers and traders, minister and dominie, a kailyard village without the kailyard traits of finish and excess of good sentiment. Small wonder Chris Guthrie has ambivalent feelings about the neighbourhood she grew up in; small wonder that her creator was careful in the last paragraphs of *Sunset Song* to ensure that not only Chris's husband Ewan, but also the whole village he was part of, had effectively been killed by a war fought unseen in the distance, touching Kinraddie only tangentially when the finest of its men were killed – yet effectively killing the whole community. There would be no more bothies, no more small farms to ensure the close networking and the harvest and new year festivals which make *Sunset Song* a living record of a vanishing Scotland. The world of *Cloud Howe* is one of large and increasingly mechanised farms, the populations drifting to the small town and then the city, in search of work increasingly scarce as the Depression years begin to bite. When the minister unveils the monument to the four Kinraddie men killed in the Great War, he is quite right to say that it was the Old Scotland that died with them: when Chris months later (in *Cloud Howe*) takes the minister back to Blawearie, by now as his wife, the farm has all but vanished and with it the world of Chris

Guthrie's youth. Blawearie, as they now see it, is peopled by sheep and by the ghosts of memory.

> She could smell the winter smell of the land and the sheep they pastured now on Blawearie, in the parks that once came rich with corn that Ewan had sown and they both had reaped, where the horses had pastured, their kye and their stock.

A Scots Quair is the record of the author moving on: moving from the Arbuthnott of his youth to Stonehaven and school, to Aberdeen and Glasgow for a disastrous period of journalism. The fiction has little to say of the experience beyond, which was to take Grassic Gibbon in his service days to the Middle East, to Egypt and to Persia, to a wider world which could never allow him to drop back into the Mearns of his youth, even had it been still there. The autobiographical essays he was to publish in 1934 (the year of *Grey Granite*) are eloquent of the mixed emotions with which he looked back on these early Arbuthnott experiences, above all in the plangent writing on Spring and Autumn in the country, though even in Winter he writes with passion of the Land, semi-inanimate, and the people who work it, as much a part of the land as the acres of clay (he remembered them as 'hungry') of his father's croft, Bloomfield, which haunted Grassic Gibbon's mature imagination. For it is Bloomfield he writes about in the *Quair*, and Bloomfield and its neighbours in *The Land*, in *Clay, Greenden, Sim* and *Smeddum*. When he longs in distant cities for the sounds of his youth, it is the peewits of Bloomfield which haunt him: when he reads sentimentalised versions of life on the land (he particularly detested Chesterton's) it is the bitter memory of life on a 60-acre croft, on the edge of poverty, which sharpens his creative pen. When he seeks a style to embody these childhood experiences, to transmit a vanishing Scottishness to an audience which may never have known it at first hand, it is the speechforms and rhythms of Arbuthnott which are at the basis of his extraordinary style.

A Scots Quair, then, is very much an act of memory. James Leslie Mitchell (1901–35) was to compress a lot of writing into a brief artistic career, a long apprenticeship of short stories and rejection slips before his last wonderfully creative and productive years, culminating in the *Quair* (1932–34) before his collapse and death in early 1935. As James Leslie Mitchell he would become known as a prolific and professional writer of fiction (including historical fiction of a high order, *Spartacus*) as well as an amateur geologist and archaeologist whose passionate interest in the history of civilisation produced non-fiction (*Nine Against the Unknown*) as well as science fiction (*Three Go Back, Gay Hunter*). Film criticism, book reviewing, publishers' reading, editing – all was grist to his busy pen, for these were lean years and the Mitchell family was growing in Welwyn Garden City. 'Lewis Grassic Gibbon' was his distant cousin, a convenient fiction who could produce work alongside Mitchell's without alarming the public at the speed with which he wrote: he was someone to be quoted, to be referred to genially, a persona in which Mitchell could write the fiction from memory which is the *Quair*, the splendid Scottish short stories and essays of *Scottish Scene* (which he co-authored with Hugh MacDiarmid in 1934), and a name under which he was still writing vigorously in the closing months of his life.

Mitchell was a scrupulous, organised writer – he solicited work, tried to bargain up the offered fees, organised republication in the USA of his successful titles. He also typed his work and kept it neatly, so that when he died his papers were there to be preserved by his widow as his memorial. Now in the National Library of Scotland, they are a testament to his astonishing energy: a testament, too, to the possibilities had he survived, to fulfil the promise of these productive early 1930s. *The Speak of the Mearns* was never published in his lifetime: like much else, it was still on the anvil when Mitchell died in February 1935, neatly put away, unfinished but ready to take up again when it reached the top of the pile. In fact it was not to see print till the Grassic Gibbon archive reached Edinburgh and the National Library of Scotland, when it was pieced together from an unfinished typescript and published by the Ramsay Head Press in 1982.

The Speak of the Mearns (the title was not his, but his modern editor's) was an ambitious project to recreate the success of *Sunset Song*. There are significant differences.

First, he shifts the scene of the novel from Arbuthnott to Kinneff, nearer the North Sea, a setting almost visible from Bloomfield (the Blawearie of *Sunset Song*) and very much within the range of the youthful Mitchell's cycling expeditions. His passion in these early years was amateur archaeology, and he cycled for miles in pursuit of Roman and pre-Roman remains. Ruins were a particular pleasure, and in the early decades of the century the ruins of the castle near the Old Kirk of Kinneff – not the modern Free Kirk alongside the main road from Aberdeen to Dundee, but the ancient kirk buried in the trees near the seashore, – were still plainly visible. Today a map is needed to follow their outline, but the setting for *The Speak of the Mearns* is immediately plain to the visitor who leaves the A92, perhaps visiting the Grassic Gibbon centre in Arbuthnott first, then down to the sea shore. There, even without the map Grassic Gibbon had drawn to help him with names, the setting is plain: the castle, the rocky coast with its cliffs and ruined cottages, the close-packed farms within sight of one another, the network of farm roads which made passage of goods and people – and gossip – an easy matter. *The Speak of the Mearns* starts in the larger field of Montrose, but rapidly narrows to Kinneff, the ancient parish and above all the narrow coastal plain where castle and Kirk dominated.

Thus the new novel would be within a long arrow shot of the first in setting, but with a whole new cast of characters and possibilities. For Kinneff had its own gossip, its own characters, and while Gibbon may not have known it as he knew Arbuthnott, there is no indication that he was slow to draw the same kind of picture of rural life in Kinneff that had made his parents the speak of the Mearns – and made of *Sunset Song* a vividly alive Scottish rural community. Significantly, Kinneff has its old Kirk at its heart as Arbuthnott had: the character of the minister was to be pivotal in both.

Second, the experience of *The Speak of the Mearns* was to be mediated through a male, rather than a female character. Despite its success, *Sunset Song* remains the conception of a masculine mind imaging a feminine imagination: his success has to be balanced with the inevitable limitations of the technique. With

Keith, he was more immediately autobiographical, and we can surmise that the vividness with which the school scenes, the memory of farm life with his brothers, memories of illness and hard-working parents whose presence on the croft is inescapable, come from his own early years at Bloomfield. We know he was a sensitive and often lonely boy, given to reading rather than football, averse to the drudgery of the farm when he could avoid it, essentially an outsider and a watcher rather than an uncomplicated participator as Keith's brothers seem to be. The pose of Lawrentian observer would well have suited Gibbon as the novel proceeded, the rural community (and the rural school) vividly captured as Keith's adolescent imagination absorbed the impressions crowding in from the rural community, the gossip, the inevitable pain and restriction as well as the joy. One of the less developed characters in *Sunset Song* is Chris's brother Will, fiercely opposed to his father and sexually thwarted by him, glad to escape from Blawearie to a freer existence overseas, dismissive on his return of the idea of settling back to the drudgery of Blawearie. Will has travelled by now, travelled as a soldier in the war, seen something of the world: he knows, as Chris does not yet, how dead Blawearie really is, how little room there is in a modern Scotland for Kinraddie.

> Chris said *But you'll come back, you and Mollie, to bide in Scotland again?* and Will laughed, he seemed still a mere lad in spite of his foreign French uniform, *Havers, who'd want to come back to this country? It's dead or it's dying – and a damned good job!*

Keith in *The Speak of the Mearns* would no doubt have shared Will's trauma, but also his keen perception of a world slipping away from him in the 1910s and 1920s even as James Leslie Mitchell moved ever further from an Arbuthnott he could not dismiss from his mind, but could not revisit with any comfort for more than a few days after his roots had been planted in Welwyn Garden City, and a writer's London.

Nevertheless, *The Speak of the Mearns* is more than reworking, a busy writer's re-cycling of earlier material. It urgently reminds the reader of today of the wealth of communities which existed in the early years of the century, when James Leslie Mitchell was attending the village school in Arbuthnott and the Mackie Academy in Stonehaven, when his bicycle would be encountering increasing numbers of the motor cars which had been the cause of John Guthrie's move to Kinraddie from Echt, the same motor cars which would destroy the local railways Chris used for school and leisure travel in Kinraddie, which today link the surviving and increasingly scattered farms required for the reduced labour force of an agriculture which would be unrecognisable to Grassic Gibbon's father – or to Keith's. The Great War did indeed savage the community of Kinraddie: it took its leading characters (Chae, Rob, Ewan) who went, with various degrees of enthusiasm, to the front and to death while the more calculating stayed behind to profit from the extraordinary commercial possibilities of war-time. But more, it took away the system of bothies and labour-intensive small farms: John Guthrie's Blawearie would have been unworkable after the Great War, even had Guthrie survived – too small, too under-mechanised, too dependent on the labour force no longer available in quantity and at low wages.

    None of this takes account of the terrible image with which Grassic Gibbon sums up – from memory – the rape of the countryside of his youth. The stripping of the forests which protected the fields of Arbuthnott from the East wind, ordered in the name of war emergency by a distant government with no understanding of the fragile systems which governed local agriculture, effectively made the kind of farming John Guthrie and Chris regarded as normal impossible. After the war, sheep would be the main crop along with others which could survive without the cover the trees had provided. The Old Scotland which perished in the war was human, was inanimate, was unmeasurable – the world of bothie ballad and song, of festival and community, a continuum of oral tradition which manifests itself regularly in the first novel of the trilogy, but is brutally elbowed out in the later ones by urban values, by an increasingly Anglocentric society, finally by the banality of Gibbon's version of the changes brought to Scotland by Hollywood. When Chris and her son Ewan face one another at the end of *Grey Granite*, it is to decide what to do.

And Ewan sat with his jaw in his hand, the briskness dropped
from him, the hard young keelie with the iron jaw softening
a moment to a moment's memory: *Do you mind Segget
Manse and the lawn in Spring?*

Chris said that she minded, and smiled upon him, in pity,
seeing a moment how it shook him, she herself beyond such
quavers ever again . . . Rain tomorrow, Ewan said from the
window, rotten for the march, but they'd got those boots . . .

Plainly, there is no going back: Chris goes finally (at the end of *Grey
Granite*, after her Aberdeen years) not to Blawearie but to her
parents' Echt, while Ewan goes (like his creator) to the distant
South where influence and political decision lie, where the future is
being written.

All this is implicit in the shape with which Gibbon began *The
Speak of the Mearns*, the concentration on the small community
and the deep roots put down by the central character, a tight and
narrow vision just being disturbed by school and by a growing
awareness of the adult world around. It does not take much of an
act of the imagination to read 'Autumn' (from *The Land*) alongside
The Speak of the Mearns, and see Grassic Gibbon himself looking
back on a sequestered youth, and trying to link it to his much more
travelled manhood.

That change, inevitable, brutal, but necessary, is the theme of
story and essay, of the *Quair*, of the fragment of *The Speak of the
Mearns* which survives. Chris in *Sunset Song* realises the inevitability and the necessity of change, even as it hurts her: Keith is
beginning the same discovery at the end of his story.

Grassic Gibbon, as we have already seen, was a historian of
culture. By choice he was a diffusionist, someone who believed
mankind to have become 'civilised' only at a terrible cost in
personal freedom compared to his free, uncomplicated, nomadic
ancestors who had roamed the world without possessions or social
structures, without religion or king or master or slave, unashamed
of body or sexual urge, without possessions or the need to guard
them. Such, for the diffusionist, is the golden age compared to the
horrendous 'civilisation' of the Depression years, product of cen-

turies of repression and increasingly structured societies which protected property for the few, exploiting the labour of the many, threatening punishment on this earth or vague promises of a better world in the next. Grassic Gibbon accepted this analysis of the sickness of his own society – his essay on *Glasgow* is eloquent proof of that – and he incorporates his diffusionist theory in *Spartacus* and in the science fiction utopia of *Three Go Back* and the dystopia of *Gay Hunter*. The same civilisation which threatens those worlds exploited the labour force of Kinraddie, stretched and embittered the small farmers like John Guthrie, drove Jean Guthrie to suicide and her husband to a kind of sexual perversion justified by his pseudo-religious pretence. The unseen civilisation of London and the larger world, while it will have a dreadful impact, is simply not interesting to Kinneff and Arbuthnott in Grassic Gibbon's fiction. Chris Guthrie's response to the outbreak of the Great War is typical:

> Sugar was awful up in price and Chris got as much as she could from the grocer and stored it away in the barn.

Her husband Ewan has no more time for the War in distant Europe than Chris: *Oh, to hell with them and their hell both, Chae! Are you going to the mart the morn?* But Chae – and soon Ewan himself – is shortly to see the hell of the war at first hand, the war which kills them both (and Long Rob), which cuts down Kinraddie's trees and changes the rules of farming and trade effectively to destroy the Old Scotland.

There is no standing still in Grassic Gibbon's Scotland, and this more than anything else sets him apart from the kailyarders who had been popular a generation earlier, and whose sentimentalised rural pictures of Scotland he despised. As the kailyarders reassured their readers that Thrums and Drumtochty were still there, somewhere off the beaten track, they gave readers the sense that somehow Scotland could maintain or recover those values which seemed threatened by the change of the wider world with its wars and commotions. No such reassurance comes from *A Scots Quair*, where Grassic Gibbon recreates the beauty of his childhood Scotland only brutally to dismantle it at the end of *Sunset Song*,

and then to draw the reader on to the changing face of a countryside struggling in *Cloud Howe* and *Grey Granite* to come to terms
with the twenties and thirties.

Even in *The Speak of the Mearns* the theme of change is at the
forefront in the part which Gibbon managed to write. The farm
of Maiden Castle is not known territory, but new: the castle itself
is a daily reminder that once vanished Scots watched over these
fields, and worked them as now Keith's family do. The whole
tenor of *The Land*, likewise, is change: change in the community,
change in the farming, in birth control, in urbanisation, change
against the backdrop of the unchanging fields, the unchanging
certainties of The Land. Young Keith is slowly growing to this
perception in Gibbon's novel: all the characters of the Scottish
short stories in one way or another face the same problems of
adaptation as Keith's family does, against the exigencies of the
clay soil, the claustrophobia of Greenden, the sheer survival
pressure that brings out the smeddum in his characters. Gibbon's
whole life-story was onward, and it takes only the briefest of
readings of *Stained Radiance* or indeed these essays to see how
little attraction the changed life of Kinraddie would have for its
author in the 1930s.

The other essays in this collection should be read with the shape
of *Scottish Scene* (published in 1934) in mind. For Gibbon's *Antique
Scene*, MacDiarmid provided a modern equivalent: for Gibbon's
Glasgow and Aberdeen, MacDiarmid provided a Dundee and an
Edinburgh. There were deliberate jokes, jokes of overstatement and
repetition, the joke of a book put together by two contributors who
deliberately did not consult during writing, separated as they were
between Welwyn and Shetland. Some of the essays are free-stand-
ing, and in few places does Grassic Gibbon reveal his ideas on his
contemporary Scottish writers more openly than in 'Literary
Lights', adding at the same time the celebrated definition of his
own style which has not been bettered: 'to mould the English
language into the rhythms and cadences of Scots spoken speech,
and to inject into the English vocabulary such minimum number of
words from Braid Scots as that remodelling requires'. Clinically, he
then goes on (*Grey Granite* as yet unpublished when he writes this

self-analysis) to a joke and a self-gibe typical of this assured journalist. Wrting of 'Lewis Grassic Gibbon', Mitchell says:

> His scene so far has been a comparatively uncrowded and simple one – the countryside and village of modern Scotland. Whether this technique is adequate to compass and express the life of an industrialized Scots town in all its complexity is yet to be demonstrated; whether his peculiar style may not become either intolerably mannered or degenerate, in the fashion of Joyce, into the unfortunate unintelligibilities of a literary second childhood, is also in question.

What is typical of the Gibbon who wrote his share of *Scottish Scene*, and indeed put together the final project for the publishers, is the sense of self-assurance. Just as he could handle autobiography in *The Speak of the Mearns*, and plan ahead, blending memory and fiction for the unwritten section, so he can handle self-insult and outside insult in *Scottish Scene*. He took pleasure in gathering the insults of the reviewers, indeed urged MacDiarmid to do the same so that they could republish them in their collection, the reviews looking very foolish indeed in such company. The narrow vision and literary insensitivity of the 'Newsreel' section they thus assembled are shocking: out of context, what sort of Scottish scene is reflected by quotations from *The Scotsman* 'Whether you have toothache, bad roads, or bad weather, the remedy is a Scottish Parliament', or 'To us the family, and even the name, means much more than it does south of the Tweed'? But what of the reviews of *Sunset Song* and *Cloud Howe*?

> Mr Gibbon must surely confess the distortion to his own heart (*The Scotsman*)
>
> It is a story of crofter life near Stonehaven; but it is questionable if the author, or authoress, is correct in the description of crofter girls' underclothing of that period (*Fife Herald*)
>
> The 'Kailyard' writers of a generation ago gave us pictures of Scottish life at its best. The tendency today is to go to the

other extreme, and, in dealing with rural life in particular, to
gloat foully (*Kirriemuir Free Press*)

Easy targets. But influential attitudes, particularly when in his own
homeland Gibbon could be accused of making his family 'the
speak of the Mearns'. What his essays, his short stories, his
unfinished novella bring to this problem is the outsider's eye,
the writing of the Scot who has moved on, co-operated with the
inevitability of change, acquired the outsider's vision and the
outsider's ability to combine the loved with the hated which
characterises Chris throughout *A Scots Quair*. The same Chris
who survives the plot and its vicissitudes, who has the money in the
first novel, the social status in the second and the anonymity in the
third to leave her native North-East and make a new life, chooses
to separate the loved from the hated, and learns to live with both.
This, essentially, is her creator's achievement very much exem-
plified in the work of this selection.

Nowhere is the outsider's eye more clearly shown than in
Gibbon's essay on religion, a reminder of his fairness (his acknowledgement of the difficulties faced by the Kirk of his time, and the
good people in it) and the breadth of vision he brought to the
description of Colquohoun in *Cloud Howe*. Aberdeen obviously
retains a nostalgic pleasure for him – though not, so far as we can
see, a Glasgow spoiled by memories of difficult journalism and a
failed suicide attempt. While the society of the Antique Scene
ruined the Scotland of today, that same Scotland as depicted in the
four parts of *The Land* leads him to the realisation that, whatever
his outsider's eye and the journalistic skills it gives him, he is still
rootedly 'Scotch', 'how interwoven with the fibre of my body and
personality is this land', even though his home is in the South in
'seasons of mist and mellow fruitfulness as alien to my Howe as the
olive groves of Persia'. The similarity to Robert Louis Stevenson's
own position is striking: situated at a distance from the source of
nostalgic recollection, he cannot get it out of his creative mind, and
inevitably he turns back to it in imagination (in *The Speak of the
Mearns*, describing a countryside he can hardly have visited at any
length for over a decade and a half) or even – briefly – in the flesh

in his desperate visit to Aberdeen and the Barmekin Hill to finish *Grey Granite*. Perhaps this explains Gibbon's amused but appalled response to Ramsay MacDonald in *Representative Scots*:

> There is hardly a Scotsman alive who does not feel a shudder of amused shame as the rolling turgid voice, this evening or that, pours suddenly from his radio. We have, we Scots, (all of us) too much of his quality in our hearts and souls.

The first person plural explains a lot in that last sentence. Much of the writing in this collection is intensely autobiographical, and we can surmise that young Keith Stratoun's story might have become even more so. 'We' Scots are an obvious target of these stories and essays, yet the dust jacket of *Scottish Scene* deliberately showed the authors at the edge of Scotland, North and South, training tele-scopes on a distant country. The rollcall of authors – Stevenson, Douglas Brown, Buchan, Gibbon – who wrote from a distance shows that distance is no barrier to the understanding of a Scotland still in the grip of a kailyard image which stood between it and the outside world. No critical reading of these short stories and the splendid journalism of Gibbon's *Scottish Scene* articles could retain the crudest kailyard premise that all is best in the best of all possible Scotlands untouched by the advances laying waste uncivilised lands to the South. Better by far to be the Speak of the Mearns than accept this premise. Gibbon, after all, had lived the kailyard (as had Douglas Brown) and wanted as little to do with it as Brown did in creating the Barbie of *The House with the Green Shutters*.

Yet just as Brown dedicated his counterblast to the schoolmaster who, kailyard-like, had fostered Brown's growth and escape from poverty in Ochiltree to Glasgow and Oxford – acknowledging a debt while yielding to the artistic imperative to write against the kailyard – so Gibbon throughout *A Scots Quair*, throughout these stories and essays, in every part of *The Speak of the Mearns* indicates that while loving his past and cherishing the memory of his youth, he resolutely moves on to a separate artistic stance which has no room for uncritical reminiscence. This is the work of a professional journalist, Southern-based, independent, self-aware, sardonic, sharply in control of a developed technique which (whatever his protestations) was well up to the challenge of depicting the strains and change at the heart of contemporary Scotland. It was his ability to be inside the Mearns, as well as outside, which gained him notoriety, and ensures his lasting ability to write critically. His work deserves to be widely read, for his reputation can only gain by the recognition of how originally and how skillfully, he wrote of the Scottish Scene of the mid nineteen-thirties.

Ian Campbell
August 2007

Ian Campbell is Professor of Scottish and Victorian Literature at the University of Edinburgh.

THE SPEAK OF THE MEARNS

BOOK I

When the Romans came marching up into Scotland away far back in the early times they found it full up of red-headed Kerns with long solemn faces and long sharp swords, who rode into battle in little carts, chariots they called them, of wicker and wire, things pulled by small ponies that galloped like polecats and smelt the same, scythes on the hubs; and the deeper they marched up through the coarse land and less they liked it, the Italian men. And by night they'd sit down inside their camps and stare at the moving dark outside, whins and broom, hear the trill of some burn far off going down through Scotch peats to the sea, and wish to their heathen Gods that they'd bidden at home, not wandered up here. And next morning they'd dig some more at the camp and pile up great walls and set up a mound and mislay a handful or so of pennies and a couple of bracelets and a chamber pot to please the learned of later times, and syne scratch their black Italian heads and make up their minds to push further north.

Well, the further they got up beyond the low lands the wilder and coarser the wet lands turned, the Caledonians had wasted the country and burned their crops and hidden their goats far up in the eyries, even sometimes their women, though women weren't nearly so valuable as goats, all that you needed to breed a fresh woman was a bed and a loan of your neighbour's wife, long faced and solemn as yourself. So the Romans jabbered at the women they got, and built more camps and felt home-sick for home, Rome, and its lines of wine shops, till they came in the lour of a wet autumn day up through the Forest of Forfar, dark, pines lining the dripping hills in a sweat, and saw below them the Howe of the Mearns, along dreich marsh that went on and on and was some-times a loch and sometimes a bog, the mountains towered north, snow on their heights eastwards, beyond the ledge of more hills, came the grumble and southwards girn of the sea . . .

. . . their creash into the red Mearns clay as it well became the lowly-born, pointed by God to serve the gentry.

By then the long Howe was drying up, here and there some little tenant of the lords would push out a finger of corn in the swamps, and dry and drain and sweat through a life-time clearing the whins and the twined bog roots, working his wife and bairns to the bone, they'd not complain, there wasn't time, from morn to night the fight would go on, at the end of a life time or thereabouts another three acres would be hove from the marsh and a man would be easing his galluses, crinkled and bent and half-blind, and just be ready to go a slow stroll and take a look at the work of his life: and the canny Mearns lairds would come riding up 'Oh, ay? You've been reclaiming land here?' And the tenant would give them a glower, 'Ay.' 'Then you know that all lands reclaimed in this area belongs to the manor?' And the tenant if he had any wisdom left from the grind and chave of his sweating day would 'gree to that peaceful and pay more rent; if he didn't he was chased from the land he held and hounded south and out of the county, maybe strayed to Fife and was seized on there and held a slave in the Fifeshire mines, toiling naked him and his wife and bairns, unpaid, unholidayed in the long half-dark. For that was the Age of God and King when Scotland had still her Nationhood.

And here and there a village rose, with a winding street and a line of huts, each fronted by a bonny midden-pile, along the coast rose St Cyrus, Johnshaven, Bervie, Stonehaven, Stonehaven's middens the highest and feuchest, in the days of the Spanish Armada a lone and battered ship of that fleet crept up the North Coast on a foggy night, the Santa Catarina, battered and torn; and maybe she'd have escaped to her home and her crew got back to their ordinary work of selling onions up and down the streets but that she came within smell of Stonehaven and sank like a stone with all hands complete.

But about the times of the Killing Time the castle of Dunnottar was laid seige by the English, men of that creature Cromwell came up, him that had warts on his nose and his conscience, and planted great bombards against Dunnottar where the crown and the sceptre of Scotland were\ hidden. And George Ogilvie was the childe in command, he said he wouldn't surrender, not him, though the heavens fell and the seas should yawn, he was ready to sacrifice his men, the castle, the land, Kinneff itself, rather than yield an inch to Cromwell. And the English, aye soft-headed by nature, prigged at him to yield, they didn't want blood, only the crown and the sceptre, that was all. But while they were prigging he'd those fairlies lifted and carted off to another place, the minister's wife, Mrs Grainger hid them, carting them off in the hush of one night to the Headland of the Howe, soft laplap went the sea in the dusk as she rowed the boat in under a crumbling wall and ruined dyke lone and pale in the light of the moon, here Maiden Castle once had arisen. And as she climbed up the eyrie track and over the long deserted walls, something moved queer in her heart at the sight, she turned and looked from the walls to the sea and the moon sinking low and wan; and made up her mind she would mind that place till the time she died.

She did the minding before that came. The English grew tired of besieging Dunnottar and brought up their bombards and trained them and fired them; and George Ogilvie gave a skirl of fear and surrendered at once and the English came in and ransacked Dunnottar from top to bottom, not a trace of the regalia stuff; and not a trace had any for years, till the Restoration came and the King and the Graingers howked the regalia stuff from the place where it had lain under the floor of the kirk; and when they came to ask for reward Mrs Grainger asked that she have the land where Maiden Castle stood by the sea.

Now the Grainger woman had been a Stratoun, she was big and boney with black thick hair, a bit like a horse, only not so bonny, and she planned to settle her goodson Grant in Maiden Castle, could they get it re-built, and plough up the tough land on the landward side and get him to do a bit fishing or smuggling or stealing or a bit of pirating and keep himself in an honest way. So with the little she'd saved in her life, her man the minister a fusionless old gype mooning and dreaming and thinking of God and rubbish like that instead of getting on, she set up Grant in

Maiden Castle, they built a fine Scotch farm-house, half that and half a laird's hall it was; and Grant she had alter his name to Stratoun; and there was laid the beginning of folk who sweated a three hundred years in that parish douce and well-spoken, if maybe a bit daft. The littlest of lairds in changing Kinneff, they would lift their heads as the years and the generations went by and see changes in plenty come on the land, it broadened out from the old narrow strips into the long parks for the iron plough, horse-ploughing came and at last a road, driving betwixt Bervie and Stonehaven, filled with the carriages of the gentry folk; and here and there a new farm would rise, to spoil the lands of the little crofters. And by then Kinneff had two kirks of its own, and a schoolhouse and a reputation as a home for lairs so black it would have made a white mark on charcoal.

Stonehaven had grown the county town, a long dreich place built up a hill, below the sea in a frothing bay, creaming; and it had a fair birn of folk in it by then, bigger it had grown than any other Mearns place, even Laurencekirk with its trade and its boasting; and a Stonehaven man would say to a Laurencekirk man: 'Have you got a Provost in Laurencekirk man?' and the Laurencekirk childe would say 'Aye, that we have; and he's chains'. And the Stonehaven gype would give a bit sniff, 'Faith, has he so? Ours runs around loose'.

Bervie had mills and spinners by then when the eighteen eighties opened up; and it was fell radical and full up of souters ready to brain you with a mallet or devil if you spoke a word against that old tyke Gladstone. It lay back from the sea in a little curve that wasn't a bay and wasn't straight coast and in winter storms the sea would come up, frothing and gurling through a souter's front door and nearly swamp the man setting by his fire, with the speeches of Gladstone grabbed in one hand and Ingersoll under his other oxter.

Now these were nearly the only towns that the folk of the Howe held traffic with, they'd drive to them with the carts for the market, cattle for sale, and bonny fat pigs, grain in the winter, horses ploughing through drifts, and loads of this and that farm produce. And outside it all was an antrin world, full of coarse folk from the north and south.

The Howe

I

Now here was the line of the curling coast, a yammer of seagulls
night and day, the tide came frothing and swishing green into the
caves that curled below; and at night some young-like ploughman
childe, out from his bothy for seagull's eggs, swinging and showding from a rope far down would hear the dreich moan of the
ingoing waters and cry out to whoever was holding the rope: 'Pull
me up, Tam. The devil's in there.'

But folk said the devil maybe wasn't so daft as crawl about in the
caves of The Howe when he could spend a couthy night in the rooms
and byres of Maiden Castle, deserted this good ten years or more,
green growing on the slates and a scurf from the sea grey on the
windows and over the sills. The last Stratoun there had been the laird
John who drank like a fish, nothing queer in that, a man with a bit of
silver would drink, what else was there for the creature to do if he was
a harmless kind of man? But as well as that his downcome had been
that he swam like some kind of damned fish as well, he was always in
and out of the sea and the combination had been overmuch, one
night his son, John was going to bed when he heard far low down
under the wall a cry like a lost soul smored in hell. He waited and
listened and thought it some bird, and was just about to crawl under
the sheets, douce-like, when the cry rose shrill again. It was summer
and clear, wan all the forward lift over the sea; and as young John
Stratoun ran down the stairs he cried to his mother 'There's a queer
sound outside. Rouse the old man.'

His mother cried back the old devil wasn't in his bed to rouse
but out on some ploy, John should leave him a-be, he'd come on
all right, never fear the devil aye heeded to his own. And with that

the coarse creature, a great fat wretch, she could hardly move for her fat, folk said, a Murray quean, they aye run to creash, turned over and went off in a canny snooze. The next thing she knew was John shaking her awake. 'Mother, it's faither and I'm feared he's dead.'

So she got from her bed with a bit of a grunt and went down and inspected the corpse of her man, ay, dead enough, blue at the lips, he'd filled himself up with a gill of Glenlivet and gone for a swim, and been taken with cramp. And folk told that the Stratoun woman said 'Feuch! You were never much, Sam lad, when you were alive and damn't, you're not even a passable corpse.'

But folk in the Howe would tell any lies, they'd a rare time taking the news through hand, Paton at the Mains of Balhaggarty said the thing was a surely a judgement, faith on both the coarse man and his coarse-like wife, the only soul he was sorry for was the boy. And at that the minister to whom he was speaking, nodded his head and said 'Ay. You're right. Then no doubt you'll have no objections, Mr Paton, to contributing a wee thing for the creature's support? They've been left near without a penny-piece.' So Paton pulled a long sad face and had to dig out, and it served him well.

They didn't bide long in the place after that, the stock and the crops and the gear in the castle were rouped at the end of the Martinmas, the Stratoun woman would have rouped Maiden Castle as well but she couldn't, it descended to John the son. So instead she left the place stand as it was, no tenant would take it, and went off to the south, Montrose, or foreign parts like that, to keep the house for her brother there, him that was a well-doing chandler childe. And sleep and rain and the scutter of rats came down on Maiden and there had bidden for a good ten years, till this Spring now came, a racket of silence hardly broken at all but that now and then on a Sunday night when the minister was off to his study for prayer and the elders prowling the other side of the parish and the dogs all locked up and even the rats having a snooze, after their Sunday devotions some ploughman lad and his bit of a lass would sneak into the barn and hold their play and give each other a bit cuddle, frightened and glad and daft about it: and if maybe they thought they saw now and then some bogey or fairley peep out at

them there was none to say that the thing wasn't likely Pict ghosts
or the ghosts of the men long before peeping from the chill of that
other land where flesh isn't warm nor kisses strong nor hands so
sweet that they make you weep, nor terror now wonder their
portion again, only a faint dim mist of remembering.

II

Now the nearest farm to Maiden Castle was the Mains of Balhaggarty along the coast, you went by a twisty winding path,
leftwards the rocks and the sea and death if you weren't chancy and
minding your feet, right the slope of the long flat fields that went
careering west to the hills to the cup of the Howe, and, bright in
Spring, the shape of Auchindreich's meikle hill. The Patons had
been in Bahaggarty a bare twelve years and had done right well
though they were half-gentry, old Paton an elder, precentor, he
stood up of Sabbath in the old Free Kirk and intoned the hymns
with a bit of a cough, like a turkey with a chunk of grain in its
throat, and syne would burst into the Hundreth Psalm, all the
choir following, low and genteel, and his wife, Mistress Paton,
looking at him admiring, she thought there was no one like Sam in
the world.

Folk said that was maybe as well for the world, Paton was as
mean as he well could be, he'd four men fee'd, a cattler and three
ploughmen, and paid them their silver each six month with a groan
as though he were having a tooth dug out. But he farmed the land
well in a skimpy way, with little manure and less of new seed, just
holding the balance and skimming the land, ready for the time
when he might leave and set himself up in a bigger place. He'd had
two sons, or rather his wife, you'd have thought by Paton's holy-
like look his mistress had maybe had them on her own, the elder
would never have been so indecent as take a part in such blushful
work. The one of them, William, was a fine big lad, a seven years
old and sturdy and strong, with a fine clear eye that you liked, he'd
laugh, ''Lo, man, Losh you've got a funny face.' And maybe then
you wouldn't like him so much, queer how fond we all are of our
faces. But he was a cheery young soul for all that, aye into mischief

out in the court, or creeping into the ploughmen's bothies and hearkening to the coarse songs they'd sing, about young ploughmen who slept with their masters' daughters and such like fairlies, all dirt and lies, a farmer's daughter never dreamed of sleeping with a ploughman unless she'd first had a look at his bank-book.

The second son Peter, a six years old, you didn't much like the look of, faith dark and young and calm with an impudent leer, not fine and excited when you patted his head but looking at you calm and cool, and you'd feel a bit of a fool in the act. But you never could abide those black-like folk, maybe they'd the blood of the Romans in them or some such coarse brood from ayont the sea. The wife, Mistress Paton, was an Aberdeen creature, she couldn't help that nor her funny speak, she called *buits beets* and *speens* for *spoons*, they were awfully ignorant folk in Aberdeen.

Well, that was the Mains of Balhaggarty, and outbye from it on the landward side lay the little two-horse farm of Moss Bank, farmed by a creature, Cruickshank the name, that was fairly a good farmer and an honest-like neighbour except when his temper got the better of him. He was small and compact and ground out in steel, blue, it showed in his half-shaved face, with a narrow jaw like a lantern, bashed, bits of eyes like chunks of ice, he'd stroke his cheeks when you asked his help, at harvest, maybe or off to the moors for a load of peats, and come striding along by your side to help, and swink at the work till the sun went down and the moon came up and your own hands were nearly dropping from their dripping wrist-bones. And if your horse might tread on his toes with a weight enough to send an ordinary man crack and make him kick the beast in the belly, he'd just give a cough and push it away, and get on with his chave, right canty and douce. And at last, when the lot of the work was done he'd nod goodbye, not wait for a dram, and as he moved off call back to know if you'd want his help the morn's morning?

You'd think 'Well, of all the fine childes ever littered give me the Cruickshank billy, then' and maybe plan to take a bit rise out of him and get him neighbour-like, for more work. But sure as God in a day or so some ill-like thing would have happened between you, a couple of your hens would have ta'en a bit stroll through the dykes to his parks and picked a couple of fugitive grains and laid an egg as return, genteel, and turned about to come away home. And Cruickshank would have seen them, sure as death, given chase and caught them, and a bird in each hand stood cursing you and the universe blue, might you rot in hell on a hill of dead lice, you foul coarse nasty man-robber, you. And just as the air was turning a purple and the sun going down in a thunderstorm and all the folk within two miles coming tearing out of their houses to listen, he'd a voice like a foghorn, only not so sweet, had Cruickshank, he'd turn and go striding back to his steading, a hen in each hand, with a soulful squawk, and clump through the oozing sharn of the court, heavy-standing, deep-breathing his bull would be there with a shimmer and glimmer of eyes in the dark. So into the house and brush past his wife and cry 'Hey, bring me a pen and some paper.' His wife, a meikle great-jawed besom, nearly as big and ugly as Cruickshank, and of much the same temper, would snap back 'Why?' And he'd say 'My land's being ruined and lost with the dirt that let loose their beasts on me. Me! By the living God I'll learn the dirt – hey, where's that paper?' And that paper in hand he'd sit and write you a letter that would frizzle you up, telling you he held your hens, and you'd get them back when you came for them yourself and paid the damage that the brutes had made. And for near a six months or so after that when he met you at kirk or mart, on the turnpike, he'd pass with a face like an ill-ta'en coulter. There was no manners or flim-flams about Cruickshank at all, and sometimes you'd think there was damn little sense.

They'd had two sons, both grown up, the one Sandy bade at home with his father and ran a kind of Smithy at Moss Bank, coulters and pointers and the like he could manage, not much more, the creature half-daft, with a long loose mouth aye dribbling wet, and a dull and wavering eye in his head like a steer that's got water on the brain. He'd work for old Cruickshank with a good enough will a ten or eleven months of the year and then it would come on him all of a sudden, maybe shoeing a horse or eating his porridge or going out to the whins to ease himself, that something was queer and put out in his world, and you'd hear him give a roar like the bull and off he'd stride, clad or half-clad, and Moss Bank mightn't see him for a month or six weeks, the coarse brute would booze his way away south and join up with drivers off to the marts, and vanish away on the road to Edinburgh, and fight and steal and boast like a tink. And then one night he'd come sneaking back and chap at the door and come drooling in, and the father and mother would look at him grim and syne at each, other, and not say a word, real religious the two of them except when cursing the Lord Himself for afflicting decent honest folk that had never done Him any harm with a fool of a son like this daftie, Sandy and a wild and godless brute like Joe.

Now Joe had been settled in Aberdeen in a right fine job with a jeweller there and was getting on fine till the women got him, next thing there came a note to Mossbank that Joe would be put in the hands of the police unless his thefts were paid to the hilt. Old Cruickshank near brought a cloud-burst on the Mearns when he read that news, then yelled to his mistress to bring him his lum-hat and his good black suit. And into the two of them he got like mad, and went striding away down the road to Stonehaven, and boarded a train, into Aberdeen, the jeweller said he was very sorry, what else could he do, Joe was upstairs, and the sum was twenty five pounds if you please. And old Cruickshank paid it down like a lamb, if you can imagine a lamb like a leopard, and went up the stairs and howked out Joe and hauled him down and kicked his dowp out of the jeweller's shop. 'Let me never look on your face again, you that's disgraced an honest man.'

Joe was blubbering and sniftering like a seal by then, 'But where am I going to go now, Father' and old Cruickshank said to him shortly, 'To hell,' and turned and made for the Aberdeen station.

Well, he went there, or nearly, it was just as bad, he joined the army, the Gordon Highlanders, full up of thieves and ill-doing men, grocers that had stolen cheese from their masters and childes that had got a lass with a bairn and run off to get-out of the paying for't, drunken ministers, schoolmasters that had done the kind of thing to this or that scholar that you didn't mention – and faith, he must fairly have felt at home. So off he went to the foreign parts, India and Africa and God knew where, sometimes he'd write a bit note to his mother, telling her how well he was getting on; and

Cruickshank would give the note a glare 'Don't show the foul tink's coarse scrawls to me. Him that can hardly spell his own name, and well brought up in a house like this.'

For Cruickshank was an awful Liberal man, keen to support this creature Gladstone, he'd once travelled down to Edinburgh to hear him and come back more glinting and blue than ever, hating Tories worse than dirt, and the Reverend James Dallas worse than manure. Now, the Reverend James Dallas was the Auld Kirk minister, the kirk stood close in by the furthest of the Mossbank fields, huddling there in its bouroch of trees, dark firs, underneath were shady walks with the church of pine cones pringling and cool in the long heats of summer and in winter time a shady walk where the sparrows pecked. Within the trees lay kirk and manse, the kirk an old ramshackle place, high in the roof and narrow in the body, the Reverend James when he spoke from the pulpit looked so high in that narrow place you'd half think sometimes when the spirit was upon him he'd dive head first down on your lap. And all the ploughmen away at the back would grunt and shuffle their feet, not decent, and the Reverend James would look at them, bitter, and halt in the seventeenth point in his sermon till the kirk grew still and quiet as the grave, you'd hear the drone of a bumble bee and the splash of a bead of sweat from your nose as it tumbled into a body's beard. Then he'd start again on Hell and Heaven, more the former than the latter for sure, and speak of those who came to the Lord's House without reverence, ah, what would their last reward be in the hands of GED? For the Lord our Ged was a jealous Ged and the Kirk of Scotland a jealous kirk.

You thought that was maybe true enough, but it wasn't half so jealous as the Reverend himself, he'd a bonny young wife new come to the Manse, red-haired and young with a caller laugh, a schoolteacher lass that he'd met in Edinburgh when he was attending the Annual Assembly; and he'd met her at the house of her father, a minister, and fairly taken a fancy to her. So they'd wedded and the Reverend had brought her home, the congregation raised a subscription and had a bit concert for the presentation and the first elder, Paton, unveiled the thing, and there it was, a brave-like clock, in shape like a kirk with hands over the doors and scrolls all about and turrets and walls and the Lord knew what, a bargain piece. And the Reverend James took a look at it, bitter, and said that he thanked his people, he knew the value of time himself as the constant reminder of the purpose of Ged; and he hoped that those that presented it had thought of time in eternity. And some folk that had paid their shillings for the subscription went off from the concert saying to themselves that they'd thought of that, he needn't have feared, and they hoped that he would burn in it.

If he did folk said he would manage that all right if only he'd his wife well under his eye. For he followed her about like a calf a cow, he could hardly bear to let her out of his sight though while she was in it he paid little attention, cold and glum as a barn-door. She'd laugh and go whistling down through the pines, him pacing beside her, hands at his back, with a jealous look at the cones, at the hens, at the ploughmen turning their teams outbye, at Ged himself in the sky, you half-thought, that any should look at his mistress but him.

Well, that was the Reverend James Dallas, then, and his jealousy swished across the Howe and fixed on the other kirk of the parish, the wee Free Kirk that stood by the turnpike, a new-like place of a daft red stone, without a steeple and it hadn't a choir, more like a byre with its dickie on, than a kirk at all, said Camlin of Badymicks. The most of the folk that squatted in it, were the shopkeeper creatures that came from the Howe villages and the smithies around and joineries. The kind of dirt that doubted the gentry and think they know better than the Lord Himself. The only farmer in its congregation was Cruickshank of Mossbank sitting close up under the lithe of the pulpit, his arms crossed and his eye fixed stern on the face of the Reverend Adam Smith, shining above him in the Free Kirk pulpit like a sun seen through a maiden fog.

The Reverend Adam was surely the queerest billy that ever had graced a pulpit, in faith. He wasn't much of a preacher, dreich, with a long slow voice that sent you to sleep, hardly a mention of heaven or hell or the burning that waited on all your neighbours, and he wasn't strong on infant damnation and hardly ever mentioned Elijah. Free Kirk folk being what they are, a set of ramshackle radical loons that would believe nearly anything they heard if only it hadn't been heard before, could stick such preaching and not be aggrieved, especially if the minister was a fine-like creature outside the kirk and its holy mumble, newsy and genial and stopping for a gossip, coming striding in to sit by the fire and drink a bowl of sour milk with the mistress. But the Reverend Adam neither preached nor peregrinated, your old mother would be lying at the edge of death and say 'Will you get the minister for me? There's a wee bit thing that I'd like explained in the doctrine of everlasting damnation; forbye, he might put up a bit of a prayer.' And off you'd go in search of the creature, and knock at his door and the housekeeper come, and she'd shake her head, he was awful busy. You'd say 'Oh? Is he? Well, my mother's dying,' and at last be led to the Reverend's study, a hotter and hotch of the queerest dirt, birds in cages and birds on rails, and old eggs and bits of flints and swords and charts and measurements, a telescope, and an awful skeleton inside a glass press that made your fairly grue to look on. And the Reverend would turn round his big fat face and peer at you from his wee twink eyes, you'd tell what you needed and he'd grunt 'Very well' and his eyes grow dreamy and far away and start on his scribbling as before. And you'd wait till you couldn't abide it longer: 'Minister, will you come with a prayer for my mother? She's sinking fast' and he'd start around 'Sinking? What? A ship off the Howe' – the fool had forgotten that you were there.

And when at last he'd come with the prayer and you'd take him along to your mother's room and she'd ask him the point about burning forever, instead of soothing her off, just quiet, with some bit lie to soothe the old body and let her go to hell with an easy mind, he'd boom out that there were Three Points at least to look at in this subject, and start on the Early Fathers, what they'd said about it and argued about it, a rare lot of tinks those Fathers had been, what Kant had said, and a creature Spinoza, the views of the Brahmins and the Buddhists and Bulgarians, and what that foul creature Mohammed had thought, him that had a dozen women at his call and expected to have a million in heaven. And while he was arguing and getting interested your mother would slip from under his hands, and you'd pull at his sleeve. 'Well, sir, that'll do. No doubt the old woman's now arguing the point with Kant and Mohammed in another place.'

Faith, it was maybe more that and a chance, folk said, that the
big-bellied brute was keen on Mohammed. What about him and
that housekeeper of his, a decent-like woman with a face like a
scone, but fair a bunk of a figure for all that. Did he and her aye
keep a separate room, and if that was so why was there aye a light
late in hers at night, never in his? And how was it the creature could
wear those brave-like clothes that she did? And how was it, if it
wasn't his conscience, faith, that the Reverend Adam was hardly
ever at home? instead, away over Auchindreich Hill, measuring the
Devil's Footstep there, or turning up boulders and old-time graves
where the Picts and the like ill folk were buried in a way just as
coarse as Burke & Hare.

East, landwards of the Free Kirk rose Auchindreich, spreading and
winding back in the daylight, north along the road was the toun of
the Howe, and south-east before you came to it two small crofts
and a fair sized farm. Now the childe in the croft of Lamahip was a
meikle great brute of a man called Gunn, long and lank with a great
bald head and a long bald coulter of a red-edged nose, he farmed
well and kept the place trig and his wife and three daughters in a
decent-like way. And, faith, you'd have given him credit for that if
it wasn't he was the greatest liar that ever was seen in the Howe or
the Gowe. If he drove a steer to the mart in Stonehyve and sold it
maybe for a nine or ten pounds, would that be a nine or ten
pounds when he met you down in the pub at the end of the day?
Not it, it would be a nineteen by then, and before the evening was
out and the pub had closed it was maybe nearer twenty-nine; and
he'd boast and blow all the way to the Howe, staggering from side
to side of the road and sitting down every now and then to weep
over the lasses he had long syne, the lasses had aye liked him well,
you heard, and he'd once slept with a Lady in Tamintoul, she'd
wanted him to marry her and work their estate, but he'd given it all
up, the daft fool that he'd been, to take over the managership of a
forest in Breadalbane – had you heard about that? And you'd say
'God, aye, often,' and haul him to his feet and off along the road
again, up over the hill that climbs from Stonehyve in the quietude
of a long June night, you looking back on the whisper and gleam of

Stonehaven, forward to the ruins of Dunnottar Castle, black and immense against the sky, the air filled with the clamour of seagulls wings as they pelted inland from a coming storm.

His wife was a thin little red-headed woman, canty and kind and maybe the best cook that ever yer had been seen in the district, she could bake oatcakes that would melt between your jaws as a thin rime of frost on the edge of a plough, baps that would make a man dream of heaven, not the one of the Reverend Dallas, and could cook that foul South dish the haggis in a way that made the damn thing nearly eatable, not as usual with a smell like a neglected midden and a taste to match, or so you imagined, not that you'd ever eaten middens. And she'd say as she put a fresh scone on the girdle 'But they're not like the fine cakes you had from your Lady, are they now, Hugh,' with a smile in her eye, and he'd answer up solemn, No, God, they weren't, but still and on, she did not so bad. And she'd smile at the fire, kneeling with the turning fork, small and compact, and keeping to herself, you couldn't but like the little creature.

Faith, that was more than the case with the daughters, the oldest, Jean, had a face like a sow, a holy-like sow that had taken to religion instead of to litters as would have been more seemly. But God knows there was no one fool enough in the Howe to offer to bed her and help in that though she'd seen only a twenty-three summers and would maybe have been all right to cuddle if you could have met her alone in the dark, when you couldn't see her face, you don't cuddle faces. But she never went out of a night, not her, instead sat at home and mended and sewed and read Good Works and was fair genteel, and if ever she heard a bit curse now and then from old Hugh Gunn or some lad dropped in to hear the latest or peek at her sister she'd raised up her eyes as though she suffered from wind and depress her jaws as though it was colic, fair entertaining a man as he watched.

But her sister Queen was a kittler bitch, dark and narrow with a fine long leg, black curly hair in ringlets about her and a pale quiet face but a blazing eye. She was a dressmaker and worked the most of the day above the shop down there in the Howe, sewing up the bit wives that wanted a dress on the cheap without the expense of going to Stonehyve, or needed their lasses trigged out for the kirk, or wanted the bands of their frocks let out when another bairn was found on the way. And Queen Gunn would sit and sew there all day and at night would sit and just read and read, books and books, birns of the dirt, not godly-like books or learned ones, but stories of viscounts and earls and the like and how the young heir was lost in the snow, and how bonny Prince Charlie had been so bonny – as from the name you had half-supposed. And in spite of her glower and that blaze in her eye she'd little or no time at all for the lads; and the Lord alone knew what she wanted, the creature.

Now the second of the crofts in that little bouroch was Bady- micks that stood outbye the land of Cruickshank, a little low dirty skleiter of place, the biggings were old and tumbling down, propped up here and there with a tree or so, or a rickle of bricks or an old Devil Stone brought there by Arch Camlin from one of his walks. He was the only Camlin that had come in the Howe and faith, folk said that that was as well, one of the breed was more than enough, the Camlins were thicker in the Howe than fleas, farmers and croppers and crofters and horse-traders, horse-stealers, poachers and dairymen, and the Lord knew what, if a Camlin stole your watch at a fair and you cried on a bobby to stop the thief it was ten to one, in Fordoun or Laurencekirk, the bobby would be of one of the Camlins too, and run you in for slandering a relative. Well, Arch was maybe the best of the lot, a forty years or so old, swack and lithe, with a clean-shaven face and meikle dark eyes. He'd married a second time late in life, a creature from the way of Aberdeen, she'd come to Badymicks a gey canty dame, with fine fat buttocks and a fine fat smile, she'd been a maid to a couple of old women that had worn away through a slow slope of years as worms wear off from sight to a grave. They'd left her a couple of hundred pounds and just as she was wondering what to do with it along came Arch Camlin on some ploy or other and picked up the two hundred in his stride, so to speak, and the poor lass with them and carted the lot away to tumbledown Badymicks. And there for a while it had been well enough, Arch was land-mad, at it all day criss-crossing his plough- ing with a sholt and a cow and planning the draining of the sodden fields, he could work the average man near to death. And coming from the fields to his supper at night he'd dally with the woman and give her a squeeze and she put on a fine dress and smile at him soft, and all had been well for a little time.

But Arch had been married long afore that, his first wife had died and left a wee lass, Rachel, that Arch had put out to suck with an old widow woman in a village of the Howe. So now Arch brought this quean Rachel home, short and dark with a sallow skin, black-haired, black-browed, with a bit of a limp, and her eyes wide with a kind of wonder, you couldn't make up your mind on the lass, but Mistress Camlin made up hers at once, she couldn't abide her and would hardly heed her, the little lass would follow Arch all day long out in the fields, in the flare of sun, in dripping rains on autumn's edge, keen and green on a morning in Spring you'd hear her cry him into meat. She was only five when she came to Badymicks and the next year the new family started to come, first a loon and then a lass, and there was every sign in this year as well that another bairn was hot on the way. And no sooner had the first put in its appearance that the gentility went from poor Jess. She grew whiny and complainy and bunched in the middle and seemed hardly to ken her head from her feet, and even if she did what to do with either, and she'd stare at Eda, Bogmuck's house-keeper, and shake her head and wonder aloud how any women could get pleasure out of *that*.

Bogmuck was the second biggest place in the parish, and the man that had ta' on it on the new thirteen years' lease was a well-set up and well-doing childe, Dalsack the name, from a bothy in Bogjorgan. He was maybe a forty, forty-five years old, with whiskers down the side of his face, decent, and aye wore a top-hat on Sundays, an elder at the kirk, and a fine, cheery soul. He made silver as some folk made dirt or bairns, Dalsack had had over much sense for the latter, he'd never married and never would, over shy to be taken in by any woman. He was a knowledgeable and skilly man, cheery-like and the best of neighbours if maybe a wee bit close with his silver. And why shouldn't he be? It was only dirt that brought themselves to paupers' graves that would fling good money about for nothing. Well, God, if that was the case, as they said, there was little chance of Dalsack a pauper, he'd smile, big and cheery but careful to the last bit farthing there was, as he

paid out the two fee'd men of Bogmuck or the money the
housekeeper wanted to pay for groceries and the like brought
up from Bervie. For a good six years he'd had a housekeeper, a
decent young woman though awful quiet, that did right well and
never raised scandal, no fear of that with Dalsack about, he must
nearly have fainted with shyness, you thought, when first he found
himself in his mother's bed: in the bed of another woman, faith,
he'd dissolve into nothing but one raddle of a blush.

So things were canty and quiet enough till the January of 1880
came in, and then the housekeeper left of a sudden, nobody got to
the bottom of it, she packed her bag and went trudging away, folk
saw her come past the houses of the village with her face white and
set, could it be that she had the belly-ache? And one or two cried to
her to come in and sit her down for a cup of tea – was she off to
Stonehyve then, would it be? But she just shook her head and went
trudging on and that was the last of her seen in the Howe.

And faith, Dalsack didn't meet her marrow. Instead, he fee'd to
Bogmuck a quean whose capers were known all over the Howe,
Eda Lyell, a shameless limmer, she came from Drumlithie, a bonny
like quean, but already with three bairns on her hands and each of
them by a different father. Folk shook their heads when they heard
of her coming and the Reverend Dallas went to Dalsack and told
him bitter that the parish would be tainted and riven with sin if he
brought this woman to Bogmuck, a foul insult in the face of Ged.
But Dalsack just gave his nose a stroke and smiled and said canny
that he didn't think so. And come she did in a week or less, trailing
over the head of Auchindreich hill with her three weans clinging
on to her skirts, half-dead with the voyage through the whins and
broom; and the whole of the village made a leap for its windows
and stared at her as she panted by, the foul trollop that she was,
said all the women, and the men gave a bit of a lick at their lips,
well, well, fine buttocks and a fine like back.

But she'd more than that, some thought it clean shameful, for
before she had been a three months in the Howe Eda was a
favourite with every soul, big and strapping with a flushed, bonny
face and hair like corn, ripe corn smoothed out in flat waves in sun
under the ripple of a harvest guff, and a laugh that was deep and

clear and snell, snell and sweet as a wind at night. There wasn't a
more helpful body in the Howe, or more obliging, she worked like
a nigger indoors and out – ay, Dalsack had fairly a bargain in her.
Near the only creature that still looked down on her was the
Reverend James Dallas, as you may well have guessed, he met her
out in the parks one day, her spreading dung under the coming of
April, a white-like morning, dew about, and the peewits wailing
and crying like mad. And he said to her 'Are you the woman of
Badymicks,' and she nodded to him blithe, 'Ay, sir, I am that.'
'Then see there are no more fatherless bairns brought into the
world by you to your shame. Give you good-day' and he went
striding off, leaving Eda staring after him, big and tall and sonsy
and flushed, frozen a minute, a ploughman was by and heard every
word and told the tale. And when folk had heard they said it was
shameful, who was he to slander the poor quean like that? Maybe
he was mad that for all his trying and the guarding of that
Edinburgh wife of his he couldn't bring a single bairn in the
world, let alone a healthy bit three like Eda's.

Now the village was hardly a village at all, long lines of houses
fronting the road and across that the tumbling parks of the farms
and the crofts, the rigs of Badymicks, the curving whin lands
seeping to Bogmuck, beyond that far and a two miles off the sea
and the high roofs of Maiden Castle. One end of the village was the
school and school-house where old Dominie Moncrief lived with
his daughter, him an old creature near to retiring, her a braw lass
awful keen on the lads. Betwixt was the line of the cottar's houses
for roadmen and folk of like ilk and bang at the other end of the
line the village shop and post-office in one, a fine big place where
you'd buy anything, tow and tea and marmalade, and gingham
strips and crinolines and baps and bags of peasmeal and rice and
hooks and eyes and needles and stays, boots for the bairns for
going to the kirk, and anything from a flea to a granite gravestone.
The Munros were the folk that ran the place, father and son, and
old Munro, that was Alick, was fair dottled by then and mixing up
time and space and all, he'd come peering behind a bale to serve
you, his runkled old face in the light of the crusie looking like one
of the salted fish the shop sold in such stores for the winter's

dinner. He aye wore a nightcap upon his head and fingerless mittens on his hands, poor stock, and he it was the postmaster, Johnnie his son carried round the letters. Folk had made a bit rhyme about old Munro –

> He wears a nightcap on his head
> And muggins on his han'
> And every soul that sees him pass
> Cries Mighty, what a man!

But he'd never heard that, the thrawn old tyke, and thought himself right well respected, and would read any letter that came to you all over from back to front of the envelope with a sharp like look as much as to say 'And who are you to be having letters and disturbing a man at his real work, then?' So he knew all the things that were going on, some said that he and his son, young Johnnie, steamed open every letter there was, God knows they got little for their pains if they did.

Young Johnnie was a bit of a cripple, like, thin and souple, but his right leg twisted on back to front as though he'd made up his mind to go back and never come into the world at all. But faith, Mistress Munro had beaten him at that, out into the world he'd come at last, a thirty years before that time, and his mother had taken a look at him and then turned her face and just passed away. And Munro was once telling that tale in the shop and a ploughman childe said he didn't wonder, it was the kind of face to turn even a mother. And Johnnie the cripple foamed with rage and went about swearing for days what he'd have done if that ploughman had stayed – he was awful for thinking himself a terror, poor Johnnie.

Well, whether or no it was true that they steamed the letters it was from the post office that the news spread round, a two months before the Lammas came in, that the Stratouns were coming back to the Howe, to Maiden Castle down by the sea that had lain lost and empty ten years. John Stratoun the son was coming back, he'd a wife and three bairns and was coming from Montrose to farm the land and put it to right and establish the Stratouns on the land again.

The Stratouns

I

Alick was eight and Peter five and Keith just turned a three years
old the spring when John Stratoun left Montrose and carted the
family and gear he had to Maiden Castle. He'd been foreman for
the contractor in the new drains they were laying in Montrose, had
father, he'd been doing that kind of work for years, but never much
satisfied, he thought little of towns; and never he could take a walk
on a Sabbath outside the town through the greening parks but that
he would stop and dawdle and peer down at the earth and test the
corn-heads and nod his own head at the nodding corn, 'Aye, God,
but it's canty stuff to look at.'

Mother would say in her sharp-like way 'Don't swear like that in
front of the little 'uns' and father would say ' 'Od, lass, did I swear?
Well, well, they would hardly know what I meant' and give Alick's
hair a bit of a tug, or make out he was thrappling Peter's long
throat; but you were only a baby then, Keith, and he'd pitch you up
in the air, high, suddenly the fields rose high, you saw Montrose
and the gleam of the sea, flat and pale, and gave a scream, not
frightened, you liked it, just couldn't help the scream. Mother
would give another snort, such awful conduct on a Sabbath, this,
what ever would the neighbours say if they saw?

Well, the stay in Montrose came suddenly to an end, Granny
that bade at the other end of the town, in a little house like a lop-
eared hare, died at last at her kitchen table one day, with a meikle
bowl of brose before her and a coarse-like book spread out on her
lap. She'd fair been a right fine granny, Keith thought, she never
come into the house but she brought a man sticks of candy to suck
right to the end and make himself sick, but Mother you thought

didn't like her much, you'd heard her say to father once that of all the coarse creatures she'd ever set eyes on his mother, she thought, was nearly the worst.

Father had just said in his quiet-like way, ' 'Od, lass, and maybe you're right, 'od, aye' and mother had looked mad enough to burst, if there was a thing that she couldn't abide worse than somebody to argue with her it was somebody who gave in all the time. And she'd skelped Alick's ear for leaning over the fire, and swooshed Peter out of her way from the table, and no doubt would have given you a shake as well if it hadn't been you were sitting good as gold, in a corner, cuddling the big cat, Tibbie. 'Right? Ay, I'm right. And a bonny look out to think that such blood runs in the little 'uns.' You wondered what kind of blood it was, Granny's, you thought it blue, not black, her hands were white and skinny and thin and you could see the veins when they lay at rest; maybe Mother thought blue blood awful coarse.

Well, Granny died and all the house in Montrose was fair in a strew for a day or so, mother coming and going and weeping now and then, loud out she wept, just like yourself, 'Oh, it's awful, awful, poor creature, poor creature,' she meant Granny, and father patted her shoulder 'Wheesht, lass, wheesht, she's safe and at rest.' But Mother just wept a bit more at that, and Alick that was making a face behind her, making on he was weeping as well, real daft, was so funny that you and Peter burst out in a laugh. And at that Mother stopped from her greeting at once and wheeled round and smacked Alick one on the ear, and you and Peter got a bit of a shake. 'Think shame of yourselves, you coarse little brutes. Laughing and your granny new in her grave. Whatever would the neighbours say if they heard?' And father said quiet and bit wearied-like 'Och, they'd just say it was Granny's coarse blood.'

But syne Father found he'd been left nearly three hundred pounds, he'd never suspected, neither had Mother, that Granny had nearly as much as that, and they sat up half the night whispering about it, Mother loud out saying 'Yea' and 'Nay', father in a canny whisper, low, so that you and Peter and Alick wouldn't waken in the meikle box bed ayont the fire – you were all three awake and hearing each word and tickling each other under the sheets. And whenever father might raise his voice a wee, Mother would whisper fierce 'Wheesht! You'll waken the bairns, man' herselfloud enough to waken the dead.

And what they were arguing and bargying about was whether or not to leave Montrose and trail away up through the Howe to some place that father called Maiden Castle. Mother was just as keen as father, but she wouldn't let on to that, not her, she'd to be prigged and pleaded with half that night and most of the next day, and again next night till at last father said with a bit of a sigh 'All right, lass. Then we'll stay where we are.'

At that Mother flared up 'Stay here in a toun when you've a fine farm away in the Howe? Have you no spunk at all to try and make you improve yourself?' and father said nothing, just smoked his pipe, and mother started singing a hymn-tune, loud, she aye did that when blazing with rage; so you knew that father had won the battle.

II

Father was a meikle big man with a beard, or so you aye thought, but Alick didn't, he said the old man wasn't bad, but only a wee chap, and couldn't fight a bobby. But father had fought worse than bobbies in his time, when Granny came down to live in Montrose he'd gone to school and grown tired of that and then worked in a flax-mill and tired of that, till Granny had asked him in the name of God what did he think there was to turn his useless hands to, then? And father had said 'The land' and Granny had said that was daft, he couldn't be a ploughman, the Stratouns had a name to keep up in the Howe. So father had borrowed some money from had and emigrated to a place called America, awful wild and full up of buffaloes and bears and wolves that at night came snuffling under the doors of the sheds where father and others slept, snuffle, snuffle in the moonlight. If they peered through the cracks they'd see the glare of the eyes below. But father said he hadn't been feared when he'd tell you the stories, and you knew he hadn't, he'd just thought 'Ay, losh, but the poor beasts are famished' and turned over to sleep in the other side. There was an awful queer lot of men

there, Germans and Poles and such-like folk, father hardly knew a
word they said, that wouldn't have scunnered him, the farming
did. For it wasn't real farming at all, he told, just miles and miles of
sweet damn all, prairie and long grass and holes in the horizon, and
a bleak, dull sky night and day, hardly a tree and at night a moon so
big and red it seemed to a man the damn thing would come
banging down on the earth. And the ploughs were the queerest and
daftest things, the cattle were scrawny and ill-kept beasts; and after
six years John Stratoun looked about and decided he'd just have a
look at Scotland. And off he set and home he had come, in a cattle-
boat, with ninety pounds of his savings tied up in a little pock
under his arm-pit, awful safe, but when he got into Glasgow he'd
forgot to keep out any change and nearly had to take all his clothes
off in the railway station to pay for his ticket.

Well, he got back to Montrose, still the same, the feuch of it he
smelt from the railway carriage, he'd never much liked the place,
you knew, though father had a good word for near everything,
every place, every soul, he ever had known, he'd have said that the
devil wasn't maybe so bad, it was just the climate of hell that tried
him. But as the train came coasting the sea and Montrose was
below father looked out, it was harvest time, they were cutting the
fields, a long line of scythemen and gatherers behind, and one of
the gatherers straightened up and looked at the train and father at
her, and it was mother, though she didn't know it, father did, he
made up his mind at that minute, he would say, that she was to be
mother (and Alick in bed would snigger about that, and say funny
things and you couldn't but laugh).

She wasn't much taller than father was, but well-made, a fine-
covered woman with flaming red hair and sharp blue eyes and full
red lips and white strong teeth; and father thought her the bonniest
thing he'd seen in all the days of his life. And he'd hardly got into
Montrose with his things and knocked up Granny, she'd said 'Oh,
it's you? Shut the door John, I can't abide draughts' than he was
out of the place again, and bapping away back by the railway track
through the long haycocks that posed to the sun and over soft
stubble and so to that park.

And he made himself acquaint at the place, and got a fee there

and wedded mother. And they finished the feeing and came into
Montrose, to work at contracting, and that father stuck till Granny
was carried at last to her grave, she's a stone above it; and years
after that Keith once had a spare hour on his hands, autumn,
dripping with rain and a sough of the soft and slimy sea wind from
the sea of Montrose was a scum on the roofs, and he wandered into
the graveyard, dark, and looked for that stone and found it and
read, queer and moved:

Ann Stratoun.

Aged 89.

'And still he giveth his beloved sleep.'

III

It was late in the jog of an April day when our flitting of Montrose
came through the Howe, over the hill of Auchindreich and into the
crinkly cup of the village, shining weather, far up all day as we came
rode little clouds like lost feathers, high, as though some bird were
lost in the lift, moulting maybe, and beyond it the sun, and clear
and sharp all about the roads the tang and whiff of the suntouched
earth, warm and stirring, little mists riding them by the Luther
bridge, and the teeth of a rainbow came out and rode the seaward
hills by Johnston Tower. I couldn't see it though Alick held me up
and pointed it out from the back box-cart. And then I was sleeping
to the chug and sway of the horses' hooves and the moving cart and
on the three carts rumbled along together, father sitting in the lead,
behind him the gear he'd gotten for his farming and a dozen hens
locked up in a coup, and two ploughs dismantled and loaded up
and high towering about it all the bit of the furniture that wouldn't
go into the second cart, a great oak wardrobe from Maiden Castle
carted away from there thirty five years before when Granny
moved from the place to Montrose.

And there was Laurencekirk all asleep, with its lint-mills and its
meikle bobbies about, with their big straw hats and their long-
falling beards. Now and then we met in with some creature
traipsing along the turnpike, a tink with bare feet and hardly a

stitch, his rotten sark sticking out from his breeks, behind him his wife with a birn of bairns, they'd cry out for silver and father would nod ' 'Od, aye we can surely spare you a something.' Mother was mad and said it was wastery, what would tinks like that do with your bawbees that you'd earned yourself by the sweat of your brow? Spend it on drink, the foul stinking creatures. And Father said agreeably 'Oh ay, no doubt' giving his long brown beard a bit wipe, his brown eyes, mild, lifted up to the hills, his hands soft on the reins of the new mare, Bess.

Alick came behind with the second cart, awful proud and sitting up there like a monkey, chirking away at the gelding, Sam, Sam paying no heed but flinging his legs fine and sonsy and switching his tail and stopping now and then to ease himself, the tail switched up in Alick's face. The furniture and gear was piled in that cart and the meat we'd need when we'd gotten to Maiden, and all our clothes and the like of things, Mother as well, sitting up genteel, dressed in best black and her eyes all about, sharp and clear on everything, only her hair was just like a flame that didn't seem somehow to go with the eyes, said Geordie Allison, our new fee'd man. And he said Ay, God, she no doubt led old Stratoun a dance and fairly believed that she wore the breeks.

Geordie Allison himself drove the last of the carts, a well set-up and stocky man with a long moustache and a long red neck, he'd worked for father once in Montrose though he was a ploughman and like father couldn't stick a job that wasn't out on the land. He was awful old, we all of us thought, maybe thirty or forty or nearly a hundred, Mother didn't like him much, we were sure, she'd been awful shocked by the way he spoke to the minister man outbye from Mondynes.

We'd newly come through the wee toun of Fordoun when we met the minister, out for a walk, with his black flat hat and his long black clothes, he stood to the side of the road, and father lifted his hat to him and mother bobbed, as folk had to do when they met in with a minister childe. The minister held up his hand and father hauled at the head of Bess and the whole three carts came showding to a halt while the minister ran his eyes over us all, wee pig eyes and not very bonny, and asked where we were going, where we'd come from, what were our ages, were we godly folk. And father just sat and looked at him douce, but mother bridled and answered him short, and at last Geordie Allison cried out from the back 'Are we standing all day with this havering skate? If he's no place to sleep let him take to the ditch, we've to get to Maiden afore the sun sets.'

Mother had been awful ashamed and red, she said after that she was black affronted, whatever would the minister say about them? them that had aye been decent folk. But father just chirked to make Bess get up 'Ay, no doubt he'll have a bit tale to tell, the lad had a nasty look in his eye. But ministers aye are creatures like that, they've nothing to do but stand and claik.' And Mother said wheesht, not to talk that way and her trying to bring up the bairns God-fearing. And Geordie Allison muttered at the back there was surely a difference between fearing God and fearing the claik of a flat-faced goat with a flat bottom bulging out his black breeks.

Then we came to a ridge between the hills, early afternoon, Peter only asleep, snoozing dead to the world, so tired, on the shelvin lashed to the back of the cart. And father said 'Well, we'll stop a while here and have a bit feed,' and Mother said no, she wouldn't have folk think they were tinks, they could eat a piece as they went along. But father just gave his brown beard a stroke and led the carts in by the side of the road, a burn flowed and spun and loitered below, minnows were flicking gold in the shadows, far up over Geyriesmuir hill there were peewits crying and crying, crying, the sound woke Peter and he cried as well, lost and amazed a minute, in the midst of the bright, clean, shining land where only far off in other parks were the moving specks of men at the harrows. And Mother came running and lifted him down and nursed him and said that he was her dawtie, he didn't much like it, Alick was sneering 'Aye, mammy's pet' and I was grinning, he could sleep his head into train oil, Peter.

But Geordie Allison was out and about, gathering broom roots and hackles of whins, and coming striding back for the kettle and tearing off down to the burn with it and setting it loaded over the fire, tea hot steaming in a mighty short while, all sitting around to drink from the cups, and eat the fine oatcakes. Mother could make better oatcakes and scones than any other soul in the Howe, or so she was to think till she got to the village and heard of the reputation of Mrs Gunn. We'd brought a great kebbuck of cheese as well, old and dried, full of caraway seeds and with long blue streaks out and in, all crumbly, and we all ate hearty, father sitting by mother and as he finished he gave her a smack on the bottom as she stood to pour him another cup 'Faith, creature, you can fair make a tasty meal, even though it's only by the side of a road.'

Mother said 'Keep your hands to yourself and don't haver. What would folk say if they saw you, eh?'

' 'Od, they'd go blue at the gills with envy. Let them see, let them see. Well, Keith my man, what do you think of the Upper Howe?'

But you just yawned and were sleepy again and a little bit frightened of the horses, the place, the clear cold crying of the long grey birds, all this business of going to a farm where Alick said there would be great big bulls to gore you to death, and swine that ate men, a swine had once eaten a man in Montrose, and maybe lions and wolves and bears, in an awful old Castle full of ghosts and golochs and awful things. But you chirped up 'Fine, faither' and he said you were a gey bit lad, a man before your mother all right, and then as your face grew all red and flushed he rose and carried you away from the rest, round the corner behind the whins. Other men didn't do that kind of thing, but father did, he hadn't any shame. Mother said it sometimes left her just black affronted the woman-ish things he could turn to. But you liked it, you gripped his hand coming back, and he patted your head, his eyes far way, forward and upward to the cup of the Howe.

And the horses were bitted and the cart-stands let down and father and Geordie lighted their pipes, blue puff-puffs, and mother smoothed down her dress, looking this way and that, with sharp, quick eyes, in case a neighbour might be looking on, though there wasn't one within twenty miles. And you all piled into the carts again and went on through the long spring afternoon, hardly it seemed it would ever end, down past Drumlithie, white and cold and sleeping under the Trusta hills, here the Grampians came marching down, green-brown, towering in snow far in the peaks, beyond as you turned by the farm of Kandy, far up and across through rising slopes, rose Auchindreich all dark and wild with the winding white track that climbed by Barras to the end of our road.

Bunches of firs in long flat plantations, the road all sossed where they grew each side, and then you were through the Fiddes woods and turned up right to tackle the hill, the sun going down and greyness coming over the hard, clear afternoon. Mother got down from the second cart and came and wrapped up the bairns, tight, in plaids, they could hardly move, Peter didn't care, just snored on, he snored with his mouth wide open and you would sometimes watch the waggle of a thing inside like a little red frog, to and fro, and think what an awful thing was a mouth, you'd queer-like fancies even then.

And looking out from the plodding carts as the last of the little farms passed you saw the dark was following you along the road and between the whins, like a creeping panther or a long black wolf, pad-pad in long loping shadow play, what if the thing were to catch you here? And as you thought that it rushed and caught, the carts were in darkness, slow thump, thump, hares were running and scuttling across the deeps of the road and far away, miles off in some lithe sheltered peak a cow was mooing in the evening quiet. Then lights began to prink here and there as they rose and rose, to the roof of the world as it seemed, though only the lip of the Howe, up and up to the long flat ridge where in ancient times the long-dead heathen had built their circles and worshipped their gods, died, passed, been children, been bairns and dreamed and watched long wolf-shapes slipper and slide about their habitations in dark, unfriended, unguarded by such a one as Geordie Allison with a fine long whip and a fine long tongue; he wasn't frightened at anything, Geordie, the dark or a horse or even Mother.

You went rumbling through the Howe in the dark, father striding ahead with a lantern, mother following leading Bess. Bess hungry and dribbling soft at her hand, Mother saying 'Feuch, you nasty brute' as the mare wetted her fine Sabbath gloves; and then was sorry in the way she would be, 'Poor lass, are you wearied for your stable, then?' At that Bess nibbled some more and snickered, then shoved down her head and went bapping on, no meat till the end of the road, she knew.

Father hadn't been down that road since nearly a thirty five years, last time running and sobbing up this brae, past Badymicks to the village to send for a doctor to come look at his father dead and spread out by the barn of Maiden. But he hadn't forgotten it, striding ahead, the lantern gripped sure and canny in his hand, no fairlies vexed him minding that last time, there was nothing from the other world ever vexed a decent man if he minded his own business and hurt no one, he would face up to God at the Judgement Day, Father, and knock the shag from his pipe; 'Ay, Lord, this is fairly a braw place you have,' kind and undisturbed and sure as ever, sometimes there was something in that surety of his that half-frightened Mother, was there ever such a man? And she'd cease to scold him and fuss around, seeing to his boots or his breeks or his meat, and creep against him, alone at night, and his arm go round her corded and strong 'Well, lass, tired lass?' Oh – a fine lad, John, but she mustn't be a daft, soft fool and think that.

And Mother gave Bess's reins a tug, Bess heeded nothing, swinging along, past Badymicks and the smells of Bogmuck. Father sniffed at the smells of the midden, ay, they'd fairly a fine collection of guffs, fine for the crops, fine for the crops. And already he was half-impatient to be home and settled in and get on with the work – God, man, what a smell was dung at night thick and spread on the waiting land!

But now a new smell was meeting the carts, sharp and tart and salt in the throat, the smell of the sea, and then its sound, a cry and whisper down in the dark as you wound by an over-grown rutted lane, a weasel came out and spat at Father and once the long shape of some sheep-killing dog snarled at him from the lithe of a hedge, but he paid no heed, going cannily on. He'd fallen to a wheeber, soft and quiet, a song he'd often sing to the lads:

> 'Oh, it's hame, dearie, hame, fain
>   wad I be,
> Hame, dearie, hame, in my ain
>   countree,
> There's a gleam upon the bird
>   and there's blossom on the tree,
> And I'm wearin' hame
>   to my ain countree.'

And suddenly, great and gaunt, owl-haunted, Maiden Castle.

*   *   *

The boys were never to forget that spring, it wove into the fabric of their beings and spread scent and smell and taste and sound, till it obscured into a faint far mist all their days and nights in the town of Montrose. And it seemed they had bidden at Maiden forever, and would surely bide there forever. Alick would say By God he hoped not, he would rather bide in a midden, he would.

The three loons slept in the meikle box bed set up in the kitchen of the windy Castle, so long and wide with its clay floor and its low wood beams, all black and caked, that at night when you looked out from the blankets it seemed you slept in the middle of a park, far off across its stretching rigs the fire gleamed low by the meikle lum, the grandfather clock by the little low window was another door and the moonlight crept and veered and flowed on the ground, nearer and nearer, you could hear it come. And above that sound, unending, unbegun, the pelt of the tide down under Maiden, soft and whispering, where dead men were, fishes, and great big ugsome beasts, without feet or faces, like giant snails, they crept out at night from the caves in the rocks and came sniffling, sniffling up the rocks, sniffling and rolling, they'd get in at the window, you could hear the slime-scrape of a beast on the walls. And you'd bury your head below the bed-clothes and cuddle close to the sleeping Peter, he in the middle, Alick far at the side. You were only little and had to lie in the front, no defence. And Peter would stop in his snoring a minute and consider, and give a grunt and a torn groan, and start in hard at his snoring again till you'd think in a minute his head would fall off, clean sawn through – Losh, how he could sleep!

And at last so would you, curled up and small, and the next thing you know that the morning was come, five o'clock and father and mother up, a windy dawn on the edge of the dark, the dark rolling back from the sleeping Howe parks like a tide of ink, a keen Spring wind breenging and spitting in from the sea, gulls on its tail – ay, rain to-day. And Father would button up his jacket and grab a great horn lantern in each hand, and cry up the stairs, 'Are you ready, Geo man?' and Geordie Allison come clattering down and out they go to tend to the cattle, the horses, the pigs, tackitty boots striking fire from the stones in the close as they waded through the

midden over to the dim sleeping cattle court, frosty in steam from
the breath of the kine.

Behind in the kitchen Mother, a scarf wrapped round her
flaming hair, would be shooting to and fro and back and about
and up again, collecting pails and sieves and pans, and oilcake for
the calves and a little dish to give the cats that bade in the byre, five
of the brutes, a taste of milk. And at last, with a guano sack about
her, as an apron, and her frock kilted up high, she'd go banging out
of the kitchen door; and Alick would groan from the far side of the
bed: 'The old bitch would waken Kinneff Kirkyard,' he was funny,
Alick, aye fighting with Mother.

Father and Geordie would be meating the horses, four of them
now, fat and neighing, waiting their corn and straw steamed with
treacle, as Mother opened the door of the byre and went in to the
hanging lantern there, and banged down her pails on the calsay
floors. The cats would come tearing out to meet her, mewing and
purring, and mother would say 'Get out of my way, you orra dirt!'
and kick them aside, but not very hard, and get the leglin down
from the wall and stride over the sharn to the big cow Molly. 'Get
over, lass,' and Molly would get over, and down Mother would sit
and start to milk, slow at first, then faster and faster, the milk
hissing, creaming, into the pails, the five cats sitting in a half-circle
below, watching, or washing their faces, decent, and now and then
giving a little mew, and the kittens dabbing at the big one's tails.

Father would bring in bundles of straw and throw them in the
stalls in front of the kine, 'A fine caller morning with wind in the
loft. We'll need to take advantage o't. Can you hurry up the
breakfast, lass?'

Mother would turn her head from the cow, 'Hurry? And what
do you think I'm doing now? Having a bit of a sleep in the greip?'

' 'Od no, you're fine. But just have the breakfast right on time.
We're beginning the meikle Stane Field to-day.'

So mother would be tearing down to the house in less than ten
minutes, skirts flying, pails flying, nearly flying herself, crying to
the boys 'Aren't you up yet? Think shame of yourselves lying there
and stinking. Out you get, Alick and Peter.' Peter would grumble
'Well, you told us to lie and not mess about in your road in the

morning' and Mother would snap as she shot to the fire and stirred in handfuls of meal in the pot: 'None of your lip, you ill-gotten wretch,' and Alick would mutter 'And none of yours,' but awful low, Mother was a terror to skelp.

So out the two of them would get from the bed, gey slow, Oh God, it was awful, just a minute longer and they wouldn't have felt as though their faces would yawn from their heads. They'd have mixed up their clothes the night before as they went to bed, Alick would have lost his breeks or his scarf, Peter had kicked his boots under the bed, and they'd have a bit of a fight while they dressed, and Peter would say from his solemn fat face 'Punch me again and I'll tell mother.'

'Oh, aye, you would, you mammy's pet. You're worse than Keith.'

'I'm not.'

'You are. Who's feared at the kine? Who's feared at a punch? Even Keith could make you greet if he tried.'

Mother would cry 'None of your fighting. Alick, get out and open the hen-rees, and mind that you don't chase the chickens. Peter, come and give the porridge a steer. Are you wakened, my dawtie little man?'

You would whisper from the bed 'Ay mother, whiles' it was true enough, sometimes you'd hear and see for a minute, then there came a long blank, you were swimming about, down into darkness, up into light of the cruse-lamp above the fire. But now Mother had dowsed that, it was nearly daylight, through the kitchen window you could see far off the parks all grey in that early glim, waiting and watching like tethered beasts, with a flick of their tails the line of seagulls rising and cawing in by Kinneff. And Mother would pull out the meikle table, well-scrubbed and shining, and get down the caps, big wooden bowls with horn spoons, and lift the porridge pot off the fire, black and bubbling, pour out the porridge, set the great jug of milk in the middle and breakfast was ready and out on the close was the sound of the feet of father and Geordie coming for it, and behind them Alick, he'd let out the hens, nobody looking and shooed them and tried a new swear-word on them, and slipped into the stable, given Bess a pat, taken a draw at Geordie's pipe left alight in the top of a girnel, been nearly sick, walloped a calf that looked at him nasty-like in the byre, and eaten a handful of locust beans he'd nicked from the sack in the turnip-shed. And now he came looking as good as gold and quiet, and Mother said 'That's my man. You're fair a help. Sit into the breakfast.'

Then father would bow his head above the table, big brown beard spread out on his chest in tufty ends, and say the grace, decent and quiet:

> Our Father which art in heaven
> Hallowed be thy name
> And bless these mercies for our use
> For Christ's sake, Amen.

But the boys didn't know that these were the words and for years after that you would sit and wonder what God was doing with a chart in heaven and why father should swear at the end of the grace, folk only used the name of Christ when a horse kicked them head first into a midden or they dropped a weight on their toes and danced, or a flail wheeled round and walloped them one as they flung up an arm at thrashing-time. Only you knew Father couldn't be swearing, not really, else Mother would have been in a rage, instead of sitting there perky and quick, flaming hair, Geordie Allison said if ever fire failed them here in the Maiden they could warm their nieves at the mistress's hair.

'So you're tackling Stane Park this morning then?'

Father said 'Ay we'll be at it all day. Can you send out the dinner at twelve, would you say?' and Mother said couldn't he come home for it, like a decent man, he'd be tired enough, her eyes upon him in that way that she sometimes had, it made you ashamed that anybody should look at father, like that. But father shook his head, no time, they were far behind with the season as it was, must hash on ahead and try and catch up. 'Ready, Geo?' and Geordie would nod 'Faith, nearly, when I've sucked down the last of the brose. Right, Maiden, then, I'll be following you,' he called father Maiden and it sounded queer till you learned that all the farmer folk were

other hand and stand on one leg and wheel round about, making fun of the Howe and Maiden Castle, the teams in the parks and the sun in the sky, he was fairly a nickum was Alick, said Geo Allison.

Father once caught him doing that and said ''Od, laddie, is your nose so ticklish?' Alick said that it wasn't, but father said it must be and caught Alick under his oxter, gentle, and upended him and rubbed his nose in the earth, to and fro and Alick howled and father dropped him and stroked his beard: 'I'll ay be pleased to help you, Alick.'

Alick stood up and went away grumbling, but he said he didn't mind the old man, if it had been Mother caught him at that she'd have deaved the backside from a sow about it, him-disgracing-the-house-and-taking- the-Lord's-name-in-vain,just-awful-and-what-would-the-neighbours- say-about-it.

When they'd gone it was your chance to ransack the place and play the devil, and climb down the rock with hands holding the grass, down and down to the water's edge, the tide going out, far on the rocks shells and fine things littering the beach, fill all your pouches, there was a seagull, 'Shoo away, creature' slow flap-flap it rose, yourself up the rock and round the mill-course and spread out your shells in the sun. By then the cats would have crept from the byre and come round in a circle to watch you a while, but whenever you'd your house with the shells built up they'd mew through the middle and knock it down, they were awfully ignorant creatures, cats.

You'd weary a while of the playing then, and lie flat on your back and look up at the sky, pale-grey, and wan in the slight spring sun, rooks cawing about the firs, high and far, caw-caw, unending; and there, a blink on the edge of the day, a thing like curtains sweeping on Maiden. You'd seen it before and knew what it meant and would race for the shelter of the cart-shed and watch, the curtain would wheel and the sun shine through, there rainbows glimmer and then the wash of the rain was pelting the roofs and sweeping up inland across the Howe, drooking the parks a minute, passing. Father and Allison wrapped a minute in the flay and sweep of the water, shining out next minute not hurted at all. It must be fine fun to be a man.

At eleven o'clock Mother would have made the dinner, porridge again, or stew of a rabbit, and loaded that into a pail and that into a great big basket with plates, four spoons, a bit of the kebbuck of cheese, a flask of the ale that she made herself; and slung the basket over her arm and cried 'Come on, Keithie, we'll away with the dinner.'

You hated her to call you Keithie, but trotting beside her her hand was kind, helping you up the chave of the road and on to the track that led to Stane Park. Father would see the two of you coming and draw in the horses at the tail of a drill, and Geordie Allison follow him in that, they'd loosen the harness and wipe down the horses and then come and sit under the lithe of the broom while mother dished the dinner out, sharp and quick with her scornful eye and her big red face and her thick-lipped mouth. 'Ay, well, it doesn't look as though the two of you've done much in spite of all your haste to be out.'

' 'Od, woman, I'm sure we haven't been idle. What think you, Geordie?'

'Well, damn't, man Maiden, you must speak for yourself. Maybe you lay down and had a bit snooze, I didn't or else my memory's going.'

'That'll do, Geordie Allison. Here, here's your plate. Fill up your gyte and give's less of your din.'

And they'd all sit and eat, the horses nibbling grass, the sun flaring, the team in the other parks would have loosed and going swinging up to their biggings far off in the bothy of Bahaggarty some childe would be singing as he made his brose:

> And Jean, the daft bitch, she would kilt
> 　up her coat
> From her toes to her knees, from her
> 　knees to her throat
> And say to her lad, as blithe as you
> 　please—

And Mother would say it was just disgusting, those tinks of ploughmen and the things they sang, bairns hearing them too.

You wished that you could have heard what the lass said, but father just nodded and said 'Od, aye, he'd never seen much fun in singing that kind of stuff about your lass, even though she's been as kind and obliging as the singer said, there was a time and place for these kind of pleasures, and the time to sing about them was when you were having them.

Mother would turn redder than ever at that and said 'For shame, Maiden, you brute,' and father give his beard a slow stroke and say 'Well, lass, I've sang with you, and you with even less on your back than the lass in the song of that bothy billy.'

Father was sore behind with his fields, but he was winning as the Spring drew on, the Stane Field at last had been ploughed and harrowed, and a day came when bags of the new manure were carted from Stonehaven down to Maiden and from there out along the top of Stane Park and edgeways on to the long moor fields, two of them and the narrow one that fronted the sea and was needed for turnips. Father planned to manure the lot, the land had lain fallow in fine condition, but a touch of manure would kittle it up. And you would come out and watch them at it, still Spring, and still the fine weather holding, father swinging the hamper in front and broadcasting the manure with swinging hands, Geordie Allison toiling behind him and the sacks with a pail in each hand to replenish the hamper, the manure flying out in white clouds as they worked, shrill and queer down by the sea the clamour of the tide returning again, to you it seemed sometimes those afternoons would never end, on and on, till the sun at last, wearied with manure, sunk half-way down and looking out on the winding track that led to the Howe you would see two specks that moved and loitered and halted once a little way and stopped and considered, a long half-hour, Peter, Alick – coming home from school and digging out their boots from the ditch where they'd hidden them as they set out for school, Mother had intended them to be decent but at school the scholars had laughed at them, they went barefoot day in and day out and Mother would sometimes see their feet, at night and say 'Well, God be here, however did you get your soles scratched like that?' And Alick would say 'Och, we just had a game. Mother, can I have some supper now.' And Mother would

say 'Supper at your age? Away to your bed, let's have no more of
you.'

But before that came had come loosening time, the four horses,
unyoked from the harrow or ploughs and brought champing in
through the cobbled close, caked with sweat, father in the lead as
they stopped and drank at the meikle stone trough. 'Steady on,
Bess. Don't drink so fast,' he was as careful of a horse at the tail of
the day as he was of one at the early morning. But Geordie Allison
would be crabbed and tired: 'Come on, you old brute' he would say
to Lad, 'God Almighty what are you standing there doing. Pray-
ing?' and gave him a clap in the haunch that would send old Lad
through the close at a trot and breenging like a one-year old into
the stable. Father never said a word, for he knew Geo tired, as some
folk could be, he himself never. So the two would meat the beasts
in the half twilight and rub them down and water them, and
straighten up and look at each other, and take down their jackets
from the stable door.

'Ay, man, well, I think we'll away in for supper.'

'Faith, Maiden, I think we've half earned it.'

Summer and the cutting of the short wild hay, there'd be no time
to lay down clover, Father got out a couple of heuchs and he and
George Allison were at it all day on the long salt bents that rose
from the sea beyond the peaked curl of the castled Headland. Then
came broiling weather and the water failed inside the yard of
Maiden Castle, the well went lower and lower each day till at last
father had the roof taken off and he and Mother and Geordie
looked down, the thing was old and green-coated, far down the
water shone in half-mirk. Father took off his coat and went down,
Mother watching, white faced, crying to him not be a silly-like
gawpus now, as he usually was, and not spoil the water.

She and George Allison lowered pails while Father stood to the
knees in mud and loaded the pails and had them pulled up, pail
after pail through a long summer day, when he came up at last he
was caked with dirt but canny and kind and calm as ever. 'Aye,
well, we'll tackle the rest the morn.'

And tackle it they did, father again went down with a spade and pails and moiled in the half-dark and cleared out the mud and stones and dirt that clanjamfried the bent of the well. Geordie Allison pulled them up to the top and flung out each pailful over the dyke, spleitering out in the long wide arc to the boil and froth of the sea below, you thought it fun and at every throw let out a scream till Mother came running, flame-hair and red face gone white, and thrashed you because you had feared her so. And Geordie said when she'd gone to the house never to fear, you'd grow up yet and be able to thrash a woman himself, that would be some consolation like for the aching doup that you had at the moment.

So they cleared out the well and the water started slow to come in, Geordie Allison was made to load barrels in a cart and go up to the village and borrow there while father stayed and watched the well. And at first the water was a dribble, slow and then it came in jets and bursts, and father went down the rope to taste it and came back with his face a bit sober like. And he cried out 'Lass,' and mother came. 'The water in the well – just have a look in.'

So mother looked in and you did as well and nearly fell head first over the coping, seeing the pour and spray of it. And Father told Mother the water was salt, the sea had got in and the well was finished.

They sent off that night for a ploughman childe that sometimes worked on Balhaggarty, an old, slow stepping, quiet-like man, and he came down that evening as the light grew dim and chapped at the door and spoke to Father. And he said 'Well, well, it's my were bit stick you need, I doubt,' and drew out a moleskin case from his pouch, the three boys crowding round to look. And inside the case was a bit of wood, no more, Alick said aloud what was the daft old gype thinking he was doing with that.

But he and Father went out from Maiden and walked slow up and down in the park out from the Castle where the headland rose. And after a while the ploughman childe pointed at the stick he held in his hand, it was wriggling about like a snake alive. 'You'll find water here, and not over-deep. And my fee'll be five shillings, man.'

Father said there was nothing else for it; and they dug the well through the month that followed, whenever they managed to get back from the work, digging and hafting in the evening light, Geordie Allison swearing under his breath by God when he fee'd he'd fee'd as a ploughman not as some kind of bloody earth-mole. But Father was the queerest man to work with, he never answered, just looked at him kind, with far away look that was somehow fey, and made a body fell silent to wondered, and felt ashamed to have vexed the man – aye, God, a queer character, Stratoun of Maiden.

And when at last the well was finished and sweet water flowing in Father said that they'd have a day off, what would Geo Allison do with the money if he had a ten shillings given him? Geordie said that apart from fainting with surprise he'd take the lot into Aberdeen and have such a real good blinding drunk he wouldn't know a known man's face. Father brought out his wallet and counted ten shillings into Geo's hand, Geo standing with his lower jaw hung down like a barn door that was badly used. Then he habbered 'Well, Maiden, well man, this is fine,' and turned and went off to the bothy room. Mother had seen and heard it all and she was in an awful rage at Father: 'You heard what the creature said he would do?' And father gave his beard a bit stroke and mother a bit of a clap on the bottom '.'Od, aye, lass, I heard, as I'm not very deaf. And what for no? Let every man follow the gait of his guts.'

Mother said she never heard such coarse talk and father should be ashamed of himself, how would his bairns grow up to behave if they heard him say the like of that? Father said they'd no doubt trauchle long; and he didn't expect that Geo, sonsy man, would be as daft as behave as he'd said.

But faith, that was just what Geo did, next morning he wasn't to be found in Maiden, and the long red farmer childe of Bogmuck was out in the seep of the autumn morning, taking his ease, he'd had an awful night with eating over meikle salt fish to his supper, when he saw a man going over the hills, bapping it away Stonehaven way. And that man was Geo Allison and no other, he walked the whole way to Aberdeen, canny-like, to save his silver, through the Dunnottar woods of Stonehaven that scent in green all the countryside, Stonehyve itself was asleep as he passed but for a stray cat or so on the prowl and a couple of lasses that lay in the gutter, mill-lasses caught and ill-used by the fishers the night before, with their petticoats torn and their breasts sticking out, a dirty disgusting sight, Geordie thought, why couldn't the foul slummocks have stayed at home? They were just beginning to waken up but he paid them no heed and went shooting through, up the long road by Cowie and Muchalls, through Newtonhill with never a rest, the sun had risen and the teams were out, blue rose the smoke from the morning pipes as the scythemen bent in rows to the hay, here and there Geo Allison would meet with a tink or a gentry creature in a fine bit gig, and he paid heed to neither rich nor poor and near two o'clock in the afternoon looked down and there under his feet was the grey granite shine of Aberdeen, smoke-clouded, with the smoke of the sea beyond, a gey fine place though awful mean, and as full of pubs and cuddlesome whores as the head of a Highlander full of fleas.

And Geordie started on the first pub he came to and worked on canny into Aberdeen, outside the fifth pub was a cart and horse and Geo jumped in and drove off in the thing, careering over the calsays a while till he tired of that and the folk all shouting, so he halted the thing in a quiet-like street and went into another pub, near and convenient, and said to the man 'A nip of your best.' And when the man drew the nip and set it down Geo of a sudden took a scunner at his face and gave the barman one in the eye to waken him up and teach him better than carry a face like that in public. It took the barmen and three other folk to throw Geo out on his head on the calsays, it did Geo no ill, he staunched the blood and crept round the back of a shed for a sleep, he woke up just as the dark was coming and counted his change, he still had four shillings. So he started in through the lighted street, and had here a drink and there a cuddle, pubs and whores as thick as he'd thought, then it all faded to a grey kind of haze, he'd a fight with a sailor, and he and a lass had gone and lain on a heap of straw, a gey fine lass though she thought him drunk and tried to rape his pouches for him, he'd given her a cure that cured her of that, and syne the mist had come down again, he'd argued with a policeman, and held a horse and stood in front of a stall for a while, singing, till they told him he'd better move on; and at last, in one of the last of the pubs, or thereabouts, he'd suddenly thought how full up this Aberdeen was of Tories, the scum of the earth, the dirty Bees. So he started telling the pub about it, and next time he woke up the stars were fading, a windy dawn grey over Aberdeen, he was lying in a puddle of urine in the street, and he'd been so thrashed and kicked about he thought for a while he could hardly walk. But faith, he could, and turned him about, and picked out the north star, and turned his back, and started on the road for home again.

And that was Geo Allison's day in Aberdeen, Father laughed when he told him the tale, ''Od man, you got little for your silver, I think.' Geo Allison said that Maiden was mistaken, he'd got a change, and changes were lightsome as the monkey said when he swallowed the soda.

By September the Maiden Parks on the uplands were rustling in long green-edged gear that every evening lost some of the green and turned a deeper and deeper yellow, though Stane Hill loitered behind the rest and scratched at its rump and slept at its work and wouldn't waken, a real coarse Park. Father went the round of them and looked at the earth in the evening light, the crumbly sods and the crackling corn and the rustle far down through the forest of stalks as some hare lolloped off, filled up, to its bed. Above the sky a shining bowl of porcelain, flecked and tinged in blue, Father stroking his beard and nodding eyes far off on the shining slopes where Auchindreich climbed up purple into the coming of the darkness's hand. 'We'll start the cutting the morn's morn.'

They hired a band of tink creatures from Bervie, ragged and lousy and not over honest, they'd nip in the hen-houses and steal mother's eggs if she weren't looking, the clothes from the line, the meal from the barn, and the dirt from under your fingernails. And Alick going in in the quiet of an evening to steal a handful of locust beans came tearing out with his face all red 'Father, the spinners have been stealing the beans,' in a fury about it, but Father not. He took Alick's ear in his right hand, soft, ''Od, have they so? And not left some for you?' – Mornings, right on the chap of six, the bouroch of tinks were in Maiden close, waiting for the master the Geo Allison and the man they had hired from the village, warm, a cool wind up from the sea drifting through the clouds of the warmth as the lot set off for the Tulloch Park, or Joiner's End or at last Stane Muir.

And Father would halt inside the gate, the lot behind him, and take off his jacket, roll up his sleeves, and whet his scythe, the ring of it echoing up through the half-light, all the ground grey and dry and waiting, scuttle of little birds deep in the corn, Geo Allison whetting his scythe behind him and the man from the village with a spit and growl using his whetstone and telling the tinks to stand well back if they had the fancy to keep their legs. Then Father would bend and swing out slow, and cut and the sheaf of corn would swish aside, quicker and quicker, till at last he got the pace for the bout, behind him the other two following, uneven at first till they got the rhythm, the gatherers following, gathering and binding, quick and sure, their thin white faces straining and white, gasping as they flung the sheaves aside. Behind, if they looked up a dizzied moment they'd see on all the parks of the Howe the glitter of far scythe-blades, shining, gleaming, ay, man a fine sight, a real good harvest and the weather holding.

You would come out with Mother whiles when she brought the pieces for the harvesters, oatcake and ale and a bite of cheese for the gatherers, they called her Mem to her face, what they called her behind her back she never guessed, you did, you heard one and your heart nearly stopped, frightened and angry and wanting to cry. But for Geo and Father there were white sheaves and scones, milk and great yellow dollops of butter, Alick and Peter were on school holiday and would come tearing in about as well and sit and stare and look fearfully starved, Mother didn't heed, if they couldn't stay and help in the parks they could wait for their dinners at the ordinary times.

Then one noon a great black cloud like the hand of a man fast-clenched in rage rose up above the shining humps of the Grampians far way in the east, across the haste of the harvesting Howe, folk stopped and stared at the thing and swore, it wheeled and opened and gleamed in the sun, bonny you thought it, only a kid, you didn't know better, Geo Allison swore 'God damn't, that's the end of harvest to-day.' The hand was unfolding and

whirling west, a little wind went moaning in front like a legion of
kelpies, the devil behind, over the hill of Auchindreich, the sun
went, bright and shining a minute, dark the next, then the swish
of the rain. Father cried to you 'Run for the house, my man,' you
ran, legs twinkling in and out, fun to see your own legs twinkling,
fell twice, didn't cry, too brave, you'd show the damned rain,
couldn't catch you, there was the barn door and Peter and Alick
standing inside crying 'Come on, Doolie,' they called you Doolie,
and you them Bulgars under your breath, an awful word you
mustn't let mother hear.

It rained for nearly two days and nights, the sea well frothed over
and out of the streaming windows of the tower the sea looked like
the froth of a soup tureen, far away as the evening closed the fisher
boats of Stonehyve and Gourdon reeled into safety with drooked
sails, the fog horn moaned down by Kinneff and the gatherers all
went back to Bervie. Father sat in the barn, twisting ropes out of
straw, Geo Allison or Alick fed the straw, father twisting, fun to
watch, when you grew up you'd do that as well and be a big farmer
and have a brown beard and marry mother and sleep with her and
give her a smack in the bottom, like that, when she was in a rage
about something or other.

You thought that the harvest was finished then, you'd stay in the
barn day on day and twist up ropes, lonely playing, and listen for
rats, Towser and you, he wagged his tail and cocked his ears and
looked at you, sly, you the same, squeak the rat, the dirl of the rain
swooping over the byres, go on for ever and when next Spring
came you'd be a big man and go to school. But then the rain
cleared off in a blink, late in the evening, father went out the round
of the parks, you hung on his hand, still all the fields except that up
in Balhaggarty a bothy childe was singing clear, to the soft drip-
drip of the bending corn-heads.

The whins were a dark green lour in the light and father stopped
and looked up at them, and smelt the wind, and looked down the
fields at the glisten of the sea as it drew into dark and pulled its
blankets over its head. And just as the two of you stood and
listened there came a thing like a quiet sigh, like a meikle calf that
sighed in sleep, grew louder, the wet head of the corn moved round

and shook, father nodded. 'Ay, fine, it'll be dry ere the morning, Keith.'

And next day they started in on the harvest again, and got through it afore October was out, all cut and bound and set in stooks, great moons came that hung low on the plain above the devils stones in the old Stane Park while Geo Allison and father led by moonlight driving out Bess with an empty cart through the scutter and flirt of the thieving rabbits, the brutes came down in droves from the hills and ate up stooks and riddled the turnips, through the plaint and wheesh of the peesies flying, dim and unending through the moon-hush, to the waiting lines of the sound-won sheaves. Then they'd pack the carts full and plod back to the close and set to the bigging of the grain-stacks there, the harvest moon lasted nearly a week and one Sunday night Father looked at the sky and said they'd better take advantage of the grieve weather that lasted. Mother was in all her Sabbath clothes, she said to Father 'Think shame of yourself. Lead on the Sabbath, there would come a judgment on us.' Father said 'Well, lass, maybe there will. But it's work of necessity and mercy, you ken,' and mother said it was no such thing she was sure, but just clean greed, and whatever would the neighbours say?

But 'od, the creatures had no time to say a thing, the scandal of that night was soon all over the Howe, no sooner did dusk come down that Sabbath over all the touns than canny folk who had been to the kirk and stood up there right decent by the sides of their women, snuffling the Hundredth Psalm right godly, took a taik indoors and off with their lum hats and their good black breeks and their long coats with the fine swallow tails and howked on their corduroys and their mufflers and went quet from their houses out to the stables, and yoked up the horses, whistling under-breath, and took out on the road to the waiting stooks. And all that night the Howe was leading, ere morning came there wasn't a standing stook in the Howe, all the harvest in and well-happed and bigged; and a man had time to sit down with his paper and read of the Irish Catholics, the dirt, them that wanted Home Rule and the like silly fairlies, the foul ungodly brutes that they were.

The potato harvest was next on the go, Geo Allison said to

Father, 'Maiden, if we want to be clear of the rot this year we'll need to howk up and store fell early, I can feel in my bones a wet winter's coming.' Father said Faith then, he was sorry about the bones, but it was real kind of them to give the warning, he and Geo would tackle the potatoes the morn. And so they did, Alick and Peter and Mother to help, you yourself ran up and down the drills and looked at the worms, big ones, pushing their heads out of holes and watching the gatherers, you liked worms, but Mother said 'Feuch, you dirty wee brute' when you showed her your pockets full up of them. So you took them away to the end of the park and laid them all out on a big flat stone, they wriggled and ran races, fun to tickle them, but they wouldn't speak to you, they were awful sulky beasts, worms, when they were offended, like.

Geo Allison said that of all the foul coarse back-breaking jobs ever invented since Time was clecked potato-gathering was surely the worst, he'd a hole in his back above his dowp where his spine and his bottom had once joined on. Mother turned right red when she heard him say that and told him 'None of your vulgar claik', but father just said Geo must bear with the thing and fill up on fried tatties throughout the winter, funny man, father, Alick said he was daft, messing about with the drills at the end and going all over the land again and making as sure as a sparrow with dirt that there wasn't even a little wee tattie left, when Alick was big he wasn't to stay at home here, he was going to grow up and get a fee as a farm-servant on a place down the Howe, and drive big Clydesdales and every night go and sleep with a lass at the back of a stack, same as the Reverend Adam Smith did with his housekeeper.

That was at the end of the potato harvest he said that, the three of you sitting round the tattie pits, sorting out rotten tatties from the fresh, clean ones, a snell wind blew. And Alick boasted some more about what he would do, Peter listening half asleep as usual, you yourself began to speak as well, you said you wouldn't sleep with any body, ever, when you were big, but alone by yourself, and you'd be a cattler and look after bulls. And Alick said 'Go away and not blether, Doolie,' Alick was a cruel beast and you thought sometime when you were grown up, maybe ten or eleven, you'd get him alone you with father's gun, and blow off his head right, with a bang, and that would teach him, that would.

But you caught a cold out by the pits that afternoon on November's edge, it closed and choked about your wind-pipe, Mother cried that God, the bairn was smoring when you sat at supper and caught you up, something red with a long forked tail seemed running and scuttling up and down your throat and then you saw father rise from the table, face all solemn, and cry to Geo Allison. Then you were taken off to bed, Mother's room, mother carrying you, sometimes you didn't like her at all, now – only with her safe and alone, if only she would hold you all the time, in darkness you woke and screamed for her and she held you close, funny texture her breast, smell of it, long hair about you, but the devil was back, fork-tailed, racing up and down your throat, low in the hush of one night you woke with the blatter of sleet on the window-panes, sudden in that hush the cry of an owl.

So you saw little or nothing of that year's end, Hogmanay for you was blankets, hot drinks, father's grave face, did he think you'd die? You closed your eyes a little and waited and then the funniest thing started to happen, the room and chairs began to expand and explode all about you, growing bigger and bigger, you looked at your arm, like the leg of a horse, you could see it swell and swell as you looked till it filled the whole room and blotted out everything, then Mother reached down shook you, 'Keithie, here's your broth.'

So Hogmanay went by, you heard skirling in the kitchen, somebody singing, somebody laughing, whistle of strange sleet one morning as you woke and looked out and there it was snowing white, ding dong out and across the happed lands, through the wavering pelt you could see from the window the smoke rise far from Balhaggarty, from the bouroch of trees that hid the kirk, black things, the crows, flying above it, oh, winter had come and you couldn't go out, you'd wanted to play in the snow.

Father said to the Doctor will the little'un die? and the Doctor was big and broad and buirdly, he'd ridden from Bervie on his big fat sholty, he shook his head 'Faith no, not him. He's spunk in him, this bit son of yours, But he'll gang a queer gait by the look of him.' Father asked how and the Doctor said 'Faith, have you never used your eyes on him? He's as full up of fancies and whigmaleeries as an egg of meat, he's been telling me his dream and his fancies, – faith, that's a loon that'll do queer things in the world.' Father said 'Well, well, if he' does no ill, he may do what he fancies, I'll not bar his way.'

But after that Father and Mother were queerer, they'd look at you queer now and then and syne nod, and you hear the story about the doctor and couldn't make out what they meant at all you'd just had a dream, every body had dreams. But you were growing up, oh, that was fine, a bairn no longer, to school next year, this first year at Maiden Castle put by.

BOOK II

Schooling

As the New Year came blustering into the Howe, folk took the news of the parish through hand, standing up douce and snug in the bar and watching the whirl and break of the flakes that the wind drove down from the hills to the sea like an old wife shake the chaff from a bed. Ay, God there hadn't been a winter like this, said Gunn of Lamahip, since 'yt, he minded it well, he was fee'd at that time up in a place in Aberdeen, called Monymusk, one morning he woke and looked out of the bothy window, b'god, the farm place had vanished entire, nothing about but the shroud of the snow. So he'd louped from his bed and gotten a spade and hacked his way from the bothy door and set to excavating the lady, gey rich and stuck up, that owned the place. Well, he chaved from morning nearly till noon and at last got a tunnel driven through, and reached the front door and broke down that. And the lady said she'd seen many a feat, but never that kind of feat before, and raised his wages right on the spot and hardly left him a-be after that, maybe running in to see him in the bothy, he got scunnered of her after a while, though a gey soft keek and canty to handle–

Arch Camlin of Badymicks had come in, he said 'God, Gunn, are you at it again? Cuddling the jades'll yet be your ruin.' Gunn gave his great big beard a bit stroke, 'Faith, man, it might once, but I've gotten by that. Did I ever tell you of that sawmill place that was owned by a countess creature in Angus. Well, one day she said to me, "John, man"'

Young Munro, the nasty wee crippled thing said 'Faith, she was making a doubtful statement,' and Gunn turned round and said 'Faith, and what's that?' and Munro said 'That you were a man. Ay, God, Lamahip, you can fairly blow.'

That was a nasty one for Lamahip, folk sipped their drams slow

and squinted at them, and wondered if Gunn would take the
crippled creature a bit of a bash on his sneering face to teach him
better manners, like. But he couldn't well do that with a cripple,
and God, it was doubtful if he'd understood the nasty bit insult of
the nasty creature, he went stitering on with the tale of his women,
folk yawning and moving away from him and watching from the
window a childe or so coming swinging up from the storm-pelted
road into the shelter and lights of the bar. There was Dalsack of
Bogmuck that fine-like childe, his boots well clorted up with sharn,
he'd been spending the day mucking out the cattle-court and came
in now eident and friend-like and shy, and said to Craigan back of
the bar 'A wee half, Jim. Faith, man, but it's cold. Have you heard
the newsy-like tale from Moss Banks?'

Folk cried out 'No, what's happened down there?' and Dalsack
took a bit sip at his dram and told them the tale, folk crowding
about, God damn't, now wasn't that fairly a yarn? The poverty laird
of Maiden Castle had got a right nasty clout in the jaw.

His horses had near gone off their legs with standing about the
winter in the stable, snuffling at the scuffle of rats in the eaves and
tearing into great troughs of corn, gey sonsy beasts, and he fed
them well, him and that tink-like man of his, Geo Allison, ay, that
was his name. Well, yesterday, when the snow cleared up, the
Stratoun man had made up his mind to let out the horse for a bit of
a dander, frost on the ground and a high, clear wind, and Geo
Allison had set about the bit job, with the midden loons clustering
at the stable door. The big mare had been led out by Allison, and
the man was standing chirking at the door to cry out the others, all
patient and fine when one of the loons, that big one Alick, had
stuck a bit thistle alow the mare's tail. No sooner she felt that than,
filled up with corn, her heels rose off the ground in a flash and
planted themselves on Geo Allison's chest. He sat down saying un-
Sabbath-like words, and b'god the world was full of horses' legs,
the rest of the brutes, unloosed in the stable, no sooner heard the
clatter of the mare's flight than they themselves tore like hell from
the stable, scattering the two Stratoun loons like chaff, and
careering round the court like mad, nearly running down Mistress
Stratoun in the clamour. She cried to the brutes weren't they black

ashamed, but damn the shame had one of the horses, they found the close gate and went galloping out, nearly tumbling head first down the old well, syne wheeling like a streek of gulls for the sea, gulls above it, cawing and pelting, Geo Allison scrambled up to his feet and tore after the beasts, crying to them to stop, the coarse Bulgars that they were and get their bit guts kicked in. Well, the mare was in the lead and she stopped and took a bit look out over the sea and syne another back to Geo Allison and kicked up her heels and took a bit laugh and turned and went racing across the ley field, making for the moor, the others behind her, and so vanished like the beasts with the chariot of fire, Geo Allison pelting like hell at their heels, folk living up here in the clorty north had only themselves to blame, the fools, instead of biding in the fine warm south.

Well, the horses fairly enjoyed themselves, they went over the moor of Balhaggarty and took a bit keek in at the kitchen window where Mistress Paton was making the sowans, she thought it was one of her churchyard ghaists and gave a yowl, and at that the mare gave back a bit nicker and showed her teeth and turned round, fair contemptuous-like and rubbed her backside against the window and ate a couple of flowers from a pot, and seemed to ponder the next bit move. Well, b'god, she'd soon a flash of inspiration, and raised up her head and looked over the hill to where the lums of Moss Bank were smoking, far away, a smudge by the tracks. And she gave another neigh and set off, the douce black plodding at her heels, gey quiet, the old gelding and the young mare skirting behind, stopping now and then to kick up their heels and look back at the figure of Geordie Allison, no more than a blue and blurring dot, far across the snow and turning the air blue as he cursed all the horses from here to Dundee, the daft-like dams that had given them birth and the idiot stallions that fathered them.

Well, you all know the kind of a creature Cruickshank is when he'll sight just one of your hens taking a bit of a stroll before breakfast and maybe casting one eye on his land. He was out at the tattie pits when he heard the coming of the Maiden horses like the charge of the cavalry at Balaclava, he looked up and cursed and turned white with rage. His wife heard the grind and clatter as well

and came running out to stand beside him, the two of them just
statues of fury, watching the mare nose round the close and nibble
the hay from one of the stacks, and kick down a gate and look over
at Cruickshank, one ear back and the other forward, a devil of a
horse if ever there was one, just putting her fingers to her nose at
him. But Cruickshank was fairly a skilly childe, he came out of his
stance of sheer amaze and ran for the house and a pail of hot water
and dosed it well with treacle and brought out slow across the close
and put it in the middle of the cattle court. The smell was enough
for all four of the horses, a bit thirsty and cold-like from their
winter caper, they trotted nickering into the court and Cruickshank banged up the gates behind them and nodded, 'Ay, well,
when you next get out, it'll be with your owner's written apology.'

Mistress Cruickshank cried 'Ay, and his pay for the damage,'
and Cruickshank said 'Get into the house. When I need your
advice, I'll maybe ask for it' and they stood and glowered one at the
other, frosty and big, fair matches for each other, till they both
sighted Geo Allison coming dandering in about on the look-out for
the Maiden horses. He cried out to ask if Cruickshank had seen
them and Cruickshank glunched at him, Ay, oh, ay, he'd seen the
coarse foul stinking beasts, where had the dirt come from, would it
be?

Geo Allison was a bit ta'en aback ay that and said that they'd
come from Maiden's, of course, where the hell else, out of the sea?
At that Cruickshank told him he wanted none of his lip, but he
could take home this message to his master: If he wanted his foul,
mischievous beasts he could come and get them, he'd not get them
else.

Faith, Geo Allison didn't like the look of him and tailed away
home with his tail 'tween his legs, and was hardly at Maiden than
back came Maiden himself from his tear away over to Bervie. No
sooner was he back than he heard the story, a funny devil Stratoun,
and worth the watching. And all that he said was 'Well, well, we'll
see,' and set out himself for the toun of Moss Banks.

The two of them met in the cattle court, Cruickshank had a
straw skull full of neeps and was carrying them up to the door of
the byre, big and squash, the sharn rising brown under his boots,

when Maiden cried to him canny to stop. So he stopped and set down the skull, face black as thunder, and started in with hardly a pause for breath to ask what the hell he meant by it? Was this the way to treat an honest man, the stinking, half-gentry dirt that he was? Mistress Cruickshank came tearing out to watch, and all three looked at Stratoun and they thought him gey feared, he stood stocky and quiet, giving his beard a bit stroke, and syne nodded 'Well, well, I'm sorry for that. But I doubt I'll need my horses back again.'

Cruickshank said. 'You'll get them back when you pay for them,' and Maiden just stood and shook his head, 'Faith, no man, I'll take them back just now,' and sure as death there'd have been murder then, Cruickshank was just taking off his coat and Maiden was fairly a sturdy billy, but that Alick, the biggest of the Maiden sons, came tearing through the yard at that minute, crying 'Father, father, you'v got to come home. Keithie's ill again, and spewing up blood,' his mother had sent him, he'd run all the way. Stratoun turned round and went striding out of the close and across the hills, the loon at his heels, forgetting everything about the horses.

Geo Allison would have tailed out after him but that Cruickshank cried 'Hey, what's your hurry? You can surely lead a pair of them back yourself. I'll take the other pair back for you.' And while Geordie Allison stood and gaped b'god Jim Cruickshank lead out the horses that he'd sworn he wouldn't part with at all, and got ropes to lead and followed Geo, and they sludged back douce across to the Castle, and stabled the horses up slow and quiet, not to raise a din with the bairn sick. And when he had finished with doing that Cruickshank went down to the kitchen door and lifted the sneck and went cannily in and asked Mistress Stratoun was there anything he could do, they hadn't a sholt here at Maiden, should he drive down to Bervie and bring up the doctor?

And what thought you of that of the Cruickshank childe? For off to Bervie b'god he had driven, as anxious to help with the saving of the loon as he'd been to knock John Stratoun's teeth down his throat a bare half hour afore. Faith then, when he'd broke down the ice there would maybe other folk go down to Maiden, an ill-like thing with the bairn dying, 'twas said he wouldn't last out the week.

III

Drift and coloured clouds and a long queer time that you tripped and stumbled, shamble and slip, down a long cave that was littered with bones, dead men here, dead men there, thick air so you couldn't breathe, choking and stumbling for lack of breath down and down to the dark of the cave. And then you were out, for a minute up, and opened your eyes, and there was mother, funny man beside, with a basin all blood, awful stuff blood, it must be the doctor, they did coarse things to little loons, you screamed and screamed while they held you and soothed you, and you fought some more and went back to the cave.

Alick and Peter, as they told you later, could hardly sleep for the din you raised, like a calf with the scour, and them both so sleepy. And they couldn't get to their beds that night, anyhow, for the gallons of hot water that had to be boiled on the open fire, Mother flying about the place with her skirts kilted up and her face all red, flinging the furniture out of her way, not safe to be anywhere near the daftie, Alick had whispered low to Peter. Father had just sat down in the chimney-corner, Geo Allison over at the other side, there was nothing they could do and they took it calm, but mother was all in a fash that when the doctor came down he could wash his hands and the blood from the knives he'd been cutting you with, and not find the place looking like a bit of a barn. Father gave her a pat on the bottom 'Don't fash, it'll come to all the same in the end. We've all of us got to pass some time, and he's the only one that we've lost.'

Mother rounded on him in an awful rage: 'Who've we lost? He'll outlive you all, and do things in the world you'll never do.' Father said 'Well, well, if that's the case, why are you getting ready to rub down the corpse?' and Mother told him not to be a daft fool, this wasn't for a corpse, but the doctor man.

And when he came down he was washed and fed and said he thought you'd maybe survive, and Geordie Allison trying to be newsy, struck in 'Och, ay. There's a lot of killing in a kyard,' and mother gave him a look that nearly blasted him, you were always Mother's pet, yes you were.

Well, it was that night while you were sleeping and the snow was on again, that the village began the first of its visits, Dalsack and his Edith, the housekeeper lass, came down from Bogmuck, stitering through the drifts, Dalsack with a load of a kebbuck of cheese, for the invalid, like, and Edith with a pot of jam, Mother had heard all about her, a Real Coarse Quean, and was maybe a bit short when they were shown in. But losh, Peter thought her awful bonny, he'd sleep with her when she'd grown up, she'd red hair and fine round legs and arms, and she sat down and hoisted up her skirts and warmed herself at the fire and spoke and Mother thawed out, and sat down for a rest. And no sooner had she done that than Edith herself jumped up to her feet and started getting a meal ready for them all, Mother that wouldn't let another help gave her a nod, 'Oh ay, if you like'. Dalsack and father were at it on the land, about the best time to muck it and the short-eared corn, would it be a decent crop in the Howe? And just as they were getting on fine there came another scuffle at the sneck and in came stamping the Cruickshanks of Moss Bank, Father and Mother and another one. Mother would hardly speak to them at first and she and Mrs Cruickshank eyed one the other like a couple of hens about to fight, Mrs Cruickshank big as Bess, gey near, and with an awful face to match; but Father cried her into a seat and they all sat down, and the third one from Moss Bank, a young-like childe, was introduced, awful exciting, you couldn't guess who he was . . . You said yes you could, and Alick said you couldn't, you were lying upstairs all cut up with knives and dripping blood like a new killed pig. So you couldn't guess, see? . . . And the man was the son of the Cruickshanks, William, that had been a jeweller up in Aberdeen and had run away and joined the soldiers and fought all over the world, Blacks, and Chinese, awful brave, when Alick was grown up he'd do the same, steal things from jewellers, only he wouldn't be such a fool as get caught. So *he* sat down as well, and the old Cruickshank cuddy and Mrs Cruickshank, hell, what a face, and they claiked and claiked till they wearied the lads, Mother wouldn't let them go to their beds in the corner, it wouldn't have been decent, though they were nearly yawning their heads off with sleep and pulling up the corners of the blind and squinting out at the ding of the snow, the squeege of the sea worse than ever that night, like the kind of daft beast you'd said it was like.

Father had cried out to Peter to ask ''Od man, you're gey white about the gills. What it's that's got you?' and Peter, the fool, had told the story you'd whispered in bed, before you were ill, of the ill beasts without eyes, great slimy worms, who rose from out the sea in the night, wet squelch and scuffle over the Maiden walls, snuffling blind hungry, a grue in the dark. And all the folk in the kitchen listened, and looked a bit as though they'd grue themselves, Mistress Edith gave a shiver and covered her eyes and old Dalsack even took a keek over his shoulder at the rattle and smoulder of the black night wind snarling outside the kitchen door, for a minute they all listened, even father, to the whoom of the storm in the lum, beneath it, below it the surge of the water rising up from the caves of the sea, even Mother had her red face queer a bit, with its flitting eyes and that nasty smile frozen on her jaws, and the Cruickshank fright neighed out it wasn't canny, a laddie like that, not much wonder he was lying up ill. But Father just smiled placid at his pipe and so did Jim Cruickshank, they didn't fear anything, Alick thought it was a pity they hadn't had that fight he'd stopped when he brought the news of your illness, they'd plenty of guts for a fight the both of them.

Then William Cruickshank, that was sitting by Dalsack's housekeeper, Edith, started to tell of the queer fairlies he'd seen and heard in India, an awful antrin place, the creepers came down and moved at night with things like hands of flesh, if a man was caught in a jungle alone those coarse-like plants would strangle him. And he told of the heat and the thirst of the days, the pallor at night like spilt buttermilk, buttermilk sprayed on a summer midden, full of ill smells, about the trees watching and waiting, the thump of your heart nearly sickening your stomach, and far off down the bit track you had took the thump and thud of following feet, following quick and sharp on your track through the glow and flow of the moonlight, daren't look back, could only go on, maybe a tiger, maybe worse, he himself had once been tracked that way, he could hear the pad of the beast close behind and at last he swung round and faced and God –

And Soldier William stopped when he got to there, cheery and buirdly, but his voice now solemn, you'd have heard a pin drop, and Mistress Edith behind him was gripping his arm, he looked down at her hand and then at her face and gave the hand a pat, she mustn't fash, guess what the bloody thing was after all? Only a wild pig, a sow at that, maybe tame once and grunting at his heels in the hope he'd have a bit offal to give it? But Jesus, it nearly had turned his wame!

That was a fine enough story, eh? but his father that silly old sumph, Cruickshank, God who would have him for a father, said sharp 'Ay, maybe you've had your adventures, that's no reason to take the Redeemer in vain. If you've come home to bide at Moss Bank with us you'll bide as a well-favoured, God-fearing lad.' And even Peter and Alick felt shamed, Moss Bank speaking that way to a grown-up man like his son, but he didn't seem shamed, just laughed and said in his English-like way 'Don't worry, father, I feared God enough that night when I thought the tiger was with me.' And then he told another story that mother and Cruickshank both thought right fine, about a soldier in his regiment, a decent-like chap, who'd said he was an atheist, didn't believe in God. Well, he caught a fever and was taken to a hospital and his last words were 'Give me the Book.' And when he asked 'What book' he said 'There's only one Book – my bank-book, of course,' and then laughed at them, the coarse devil had known they expected he'd say the Bible. And he'd died right like that, an awful warning.

Mother said 'Yes, the foul stinking swine', Alick said she would like to cut folks throats for Jesus, so would Moss Bank, they both looked as solemn as hens choked on dirt, but Alick took a look at the soldier, William, and he was looking at Mistress Edith and just at that minute he gave her a wink, and Alick looked at the others then, Father was staring up at the couples, Geo Allison was blowing his nose gey loud, Alick said to Peter in bed later on he thought that that soldier Bulgar was just making fun of Mother and Moss Bank. And whether that was true or not he'd no right to look at Edith like

that, Alick himself was to have her for his lass when he'd grown up
and robbed some jeweller and pushed mother off the Maiden cliff,
so he would sometime, he was sick of her nagging, and owned
Maiden himself when Father was dead, so he would, Peter and you
would be just his ploughmen, he was the eldest.

Well, they'd all had a late bit supper then and Mother gone up to
have a look at you, and Mistress Edith with her, tall, and ruddy,
you'd opened eyes to the dazzle of light, stopped your blowing of
little red bubbles, to stare at the woman beside Mother, bigger,
with her fine face and laugh, she whispered 'Poor man, oh, poor
were man' and you stared and stared and tried to speak and then
tumbled in to the cave again. But Mother had thought you were
getting on fine, and taken Mistress Edith down again, a meikle
supper spread in the kitchen, ham and oatcakes and some of the
Dalsack cheese, and father sat in to say his grace and they all ate up
and had a claik, Dalsack said with his shy, fine smile 'That must be
an extraordinary laddie, your youngest, Mistress Stratoun,' and
Mother said 'Och, just ordinary, ordinary' she didn't want folk to
think you queer. But Geo Allison said b'god you weren't that, with
the queerest havers and stances and answers, a funny bairn, no
doubt you'd get on, into a daftie-house, maybe in the end. Father
said 'No fear of that. Though, faith, I will say he's a queer-like
nickum. He'd speir the head from a Devil Stane or a creel of fresh
herring back into the sea. 'Od, he'll be a handful to the teachers, I
warrant, when we send him up to the village school this Spring.'

You'd always remember till the day you died that queer, quiet
evening in middle March that father took you out to the fishing,
the first evening you'd been letten out, pale for a breath of air,
Father wrapped you up in a blanket and carried you, rod and tackle
over one arm, you over the other, the sun had gone down saffron
behind except for some tint on the verge of the sea, it was sleeping
in a little foam of colour and far away on the dying edge of the
white wings of the Gourdon fleet went home, you stared and stared
at it all, at the quietness that was rising a dim wall in the east,
creeping up the sky and overtaking and drowning in blood the
lights behind the fisher boats. Father set you down and stepped in

the boat, tucked you up, and sat down and picked up the oars.
'Fine, Keith lad?'

You said 'Ay, father,' and looked over the thwarts to the little
hiss of the water, out, down to the shag and sway and green gleam
of the bottom of the sea where the fairlies bade. But there were
none to be seen at this, it was clear and open and you looked up
and saw far along the fringing cliffs the place where the seagulls
wheeled and cried out over the brinks from Dunnottar Castle it
came on you this was maybe the sea, the beasts only silly dreams
after all, light and the gulls and white hiss of the sea. Your stomach
still felt awful funny inside you, as though Bess the mare had
stepped on it, the smell of the sea made it turn a wee, but you
didn't let on, Father would have turned and taken you back.

Instead he took the boat out to the point, beyond it, suddenly,
the evening wind came, it blew a little spume in your faces, your
nose and cheeks stung to its touch, a little smother of blood on the
sea, soaking and pitching under the keel, Way way way! the gulls
crying. You said 'Father, why do they aye cry that?' and he stopped
and listened from unlimbering the tackle, 'Cry what, my mannie'
and you told him 'That – Way, way, way!'

Father said well, 'od, he didn't right know, the beasts and birds
had funny-like cries, it was maybe some kind of speaking of theirs.
You said 'Oh. But have they all lost their way?' and father gave you
the funniest look, he said that you were a gey queer lad, and bent to
his tackle and then straightened again, listening to the gulls and
stroking his beard, the sunset behind him on the sea.

You drowsed a bit then and opened your eyes, father was pulling
a fish aboard, a great gaping brute that blinked at you and worked
its jaws and floundered and gasped, you drew up your legs away
from it, Father didn't notice, the beasts were coming in bourochs,
fast as he let down the lines for them, blue and grey rising out of
the sea, fluttering and flicking, paling and dying, now the great wall
behind the horizon's edge had blackened and blackened as though
some Geordie Allison out there with a pail and tarbrush in the
other hand had mistaken the sky for the barn wall, through the tar
there came a glimmer of a star funny things stars, lights far away,
God lighted them at night with a spunk from the box in a pocket of

his breeks, striding backwards and forwards the roof of heaven, he'd a long brown beard like Father's just, but he wasn't so fine, sometimes you were dead feared of him. Father turned round 'Not cold are you then,' and you said you weren't, neither you were, just frozen in a wonder looking at the sky, arching and rising in the coming night. What if God made a bit slip some time and cracked the sky and came tumbling through, box of spunks still gripped in his hand and splashing the water so high from the sea it went pelting high up across the Howe –

And then you were feared, you held your breath, tight, there was the crack, growing wider and wider, a splurge on the lift, the dark behind, light in front, the splurge blue and yellow, the gulls had stopped that daft crying and crying and the wind had stilled, why didn't father see, He was coming, He was coming.

Boom!

Something flickered from the crack, and father raised his head.

' 'Od, we'll need to be holding back. There's the thunder, Keith, it'll frighten your Mother.'

That thunder-pelt was the beginning of the wettest Spring that had come on the Howe for many a day, all that night it thundered and rained, in turn, when one had finished with splitting the sky and scarting its claws along the earth and over and through the dripping parks, the other came down in blinding pelts, the swash of it warping through roofs and walls, the cattle court of Balhaggarty was flooded out and half the stock drowned, at Moss Bank Sandy the dafty had come home gey late from a boozing ploy and gone into the smiddy where the coals still glowed and sat him down for a bit of a warm before sneaking up the stairs to his bed. And faith if he didn't fall fast asleep and was woke with a smack of cold water in his face, the smiddy swirling with a thing like a wave, he thought between the coals and the water he was surely in hell at last, not fair and went yammering out of the place to the kitchen door of Moss Bank to beat and clamour till letten in by his brother William who'd been the soldier. William asked what the hell was he up to, the fool, screeching around like a sheep half-libbed, and Sandy yabbered and dribbled and shook and said that coming by

Dalsack's, he minded, he'd heard an awful commotion and cry and decided the devil was in there at last, getting at Dalsack for sleeping with his housekeepers, but he'd never thought Auld Nick would follow him here.

William said 'Here, what's that that you say. Dirty lout,' and near bashed him one. Mistress Edith a fine and upstanding girl that wouldn't look at a rat like Dalsack. But Sandy only moaned and yabbered some more, and at last Will put on his breeks and leggings and his reefer coat and set out for Moss Bank, near blind with the flare of the lightning sizzling and pelted with a slow dry wind that blew steady and strong, 'twixt the gusts of rain. In the Bogmuck kitchen a light was shining, he chapped at the door and went in and found out then what the commotion was about, Dalsack had had water taken in his kitchen, with a fine pipe and the Lord knew all the arrangements, and been a bit proud at being civilised: but early that night as they went to their beds the whole damn arrangement had burst in the rain, that was the commotion that Sandy had heard, the bed of the bairns in the kitchen drenched, Dalsack had come tearing down in his sark, naught else, and tried to light a candle, and the bairns had thought that he was the devil, coarse tinks creatures to think that of the man because he had whiskers like a yard of broom, syne Edith had come and tried to comfort them, and stop the flow of the water from the pipe, from them, an awful soss. Well, William was a skilly man with his hands, he'd learned in the Army to do all kinds of things from mending a pipe to cutting a throat, he shot about and stopped the flow, and took a sly look at Edith in her nighty wet, it stuck to her bonny chest with the points of the nipples sweet and showing, wet hair down her back like a Viking maid, by God, he made up his mind at that moment he'd get her and have breasts, hair and all, though the whole of the Howe was to be one long howl. Dalsack smiled shy through his whiskers and sark and said he was awful obliged to him, a fine childe, Dalsack, he dug out the whisky they sat drinking that till the morning came and William would stride back again to Moss Bank, through a Howe that was just a soss and a puddle and under the lour of a sky like lead.

And going back he followed the ridging track and went round

and through by the Auld Kirk lands, and there a gey antrin sight met his eyes as he looked over into the old kirkyard where the folk of the Village had been laid in earth since ever the memory of man began, there ere old stones there that leaned this way and that, with daft-like inscriptions and curlicues, stones from the days of Christ's Covenant, one with a picture graved in the stone of an old-time brig in full sail, fair daft, that had been the ship of a Captain Stratoun; and the grass grew high and rank and dreich, choked round with the flat, bland blades of docken, a fine kirkyard and seldom disturbed except for the hares that had their holes there, maybe lairing there young in some coffin place in the bones of a woman once young and bonny, as Geddes Munro, the cripple, had once said, the foul young beast, so William remembered, he'd said it no doubt for a spite of the fact he'd never lair *his* body in any woman's. But now as William Cruickshank looked over the wall under the drip of the dreich dark yews, it looked like a hotter in a cattle shed, stones had been flung down here and there and a tide of water swashed through the place, flinging up the end of a new-buried coffin, that would be the coffin of a joskin man from the Home Town back of the village. In the thin wet glimmer of the March morning it looked an evil and fervid place, and Will Cruickshank shivered and turned in a half-run till he saw something that near made him sick, the figure of a woman over by the church wall, pressed up against it, a woman in white, in a nighty, hair down about her shoulders, bonny-gleaming, and weeping and weeping as though her heart would break. God damn't, what was she doing there? For it was the Reverend James Dallas's wife.

Well, he nearly stept over to question her on't, and was just giving his soldier's mouser a twist afore he did that, a fine figure of a man, when she turned and went out of the place by herself, bare-footed, he saw the gleam of her bare feet, she passed down into the shelter of the avenue trees, the morning was hardly breaking, white, he stood with a prickle of skin and stared after, had he really seen her or was it a fancy?

So he went back to Moss Bank and told the tale of the riven kirkyard, but not of the weeping minister's wife, he kept that till later, and Moss Bank said it was the just the kind of a thing that would happen in a proud and sinful place like an Auld Kirk, you'd not find the like of that in the field where the Reverend Adam Smith buried the Free Kirk men. And just as he said that the postie came in about, young Munro with his white, sneering face, and asked if they'd heard the news from the Howe? They hadn't, and so he began to tell them – they knew of that daughter of Gunn of Lamahip, Queen, the dressmaker, so dark and stuck-up, a Gypsy-like bitch with her quiet airs? Well, where do you think she had spent the night? – at her shop in the village, not going home, she said that coming on of the storm had stopped her. Faith, maybe so it had, but did that account for the fact that as the morning broke and the Dominie's servant lassie, Kate, was getting up with a wearied yawn and taking a keek down the street she saw the door of Queen's shop slide open and who should come out, rubbing his eyes, unshaven, with a gey dreich look on his face, but the Reverend Adam Smith himself, that fat coarse ill-living Free Kirk loon. – Cruickshank of Moss Bank said 'G'way with your lies,' but young Munro just sneered at him coarse. 'Lies? Fegs, there was lying enough there last night – your Free Kirk man in the bed of Queen Gunn.'

And afore that Saturday was done the news of the ploy was all over the parish, men meeting one another on the top of boxcarts cried it out, they cried from hedges and stacks, and the tops of barns they had set to repair, at Balhaggarty Mrs Paton greeting in her dairy where all her cheese had been spoiled by the water and the eggs piled up like a ready made omelette, dried up to listen to her servant lass, and then ran to carry the news to the elder, Sam Paton, solemn, rubbing his stomach, he's awful pains below his waistcoat this morning, he said it was just the kind of thing he expected to have happened to a Free Kirk minister, and rubbed his stomach some more and looked round, and went down to Maiden to see how they were, so he said, but really just to pass them the news, awful kind of him, Mrs Stratoun said, ay, God, a right handsome bitch of a woman and had brought three fine sons intil the world, though they said that the youngest one was a daftie.

The storm had nearly missed Maiden Castle, except the loft where Geo Allison bade, Geo said that it smote in on him at midnight like the angel of God, by the look of his face he and the angel weren't on good terms, he sat and shivered the day by the fire. When he heard the story of the two bit kirks, the auld one with its dead in resurrection and the Free one with its minister acting spry and quick, he said he expected that from ministers, did they ever work like other folk and use up their juices and go tired to bed? – Not them, they'd had to be randy to live. John Stratoun said 'Od, that might be so, but he hardly saw that the fact would account for the Reverend James Dallas at the least getting out of his bed in the middle of the night and tearing up a coffin or so, just to prove that he was a vital man. And Sam Paton gave his stomach a bit rub, and a glower at Geo Allison, sour as his wame, and said he'd no liking for blasphemy. And Geo Allison mumbled 'Your stomach won't stand it,' but not over loud, he was only a joskin and not a gey big farming man.

The only place in the Howe that day that hadn't heard the two scandals till late was Archie Camlin's at Badymicks, the couples of the byres had tumbled in and nearly killed a couple of his kye, and Arch was up in the roof giving them a mend with wee dark Rachel standing below, carrying the nails and her eyes on Arch as though on Elijah coming from the clouds when Sandy Cruickshank took a wamble in there and cried up the news, teething and dribbling and mouthing. Arch said b'god he saw nothing in that, couldn't the Reverend Adam have a sleep where he liked or the dead in the kirk of the Reverend Kames go out a bit stroll if it took their fancy? 'Get away home, Sandy, man, to your bed, and not blether that kind of dirt to me with the lassie there standing by and listening.' Sandy looked at Rachel and mouthed and yammered 'She over-young to understand' and Arch called down 'Away home with you. Bairns ken well enough from the womb, I think, all the ways that got them there. And I've little fancy for her growing up to snigger and sniffle around every tale of every auld childe that sleeps with a woman.' So off poor Sandy had to waddle through the glaur, all the thanks that he got for his story, and what did Arch Camlin mean by his say, would he have the quean Rachel grow up a fair heathen and not know the difference between right and wrong?

Next day there was such a power of folk in Free Kirk at ten as hadn't been there since the news of Balaclava, near, the Reverend Adam climbed into the pulpit and peered down at them over his stomach and the two-three chins he wore over his collar, and puffed, and then drew out his great hankie, and blew a blast on it like the Last Trump's blast, and then preached them a sermon from Numbers, fegs, all about figures and descents and ascents and a creature called Jeanie Ology, would she be one of his lasses, would you say? It was more than likely, but heard you ever the like, him introducing into the pulpit the name of another lass after that night he's spent in the cuddles of Queenie Gunn.

The Auld Kirk itself was nearly toom, the Reverend James Dallas preaching bitter on the traipse that creature Lot had had when he went out of the City of Sodom, there was hardly a soul in the pews that day, pine shadowed, the sun shone through flying blinks of rain, forward under the pulpit head the choir sitting upright, genteel, behind them the pew of the Badymicks folk, Arch Camlin there with his little lass, and God she had a right unco stare, her with her boots and her funny limps and her dark-like skin, like a nigger's near, you couldn't wonder if the mother in law wasn't so keen about the bit creature. Midway was the pew of the elder, Sam Paton, with his wife prinked out in all her braws and jingling when she moved like a horse at a show, and behind that the seat of the Lamahip folk, would you believe there was Queen Gunn sitting there distant and quiet and dark, her eyes staring out of her face like live lumps of coal, only quiet coal, up at James Dallas as he preached from the pulpit, down from him to the seats in the corner where sat the folk from the manse themselves, the mistress and her bit maiden Ella, and further back still in their gentry's pew, the folk from Maiden, John Stratoun himself and his red-faced wife her head bent genteel but her eyes sharp and flitting on everything about her, their three weans beside them, all dressed up and starched. And over and above them all there thundered the tale of that creature Lot, his life, his death, and the coarse thing she'd done with that daughter of his in a bit of a cave. Folk put up their hankies to hide their yawns and poked their bairns to keep them awake, all except Arch Camlin with his dark quean Rachel, her head had fallen forward on the desk in front, sleeping the creature and over the way the youngest of the Stratouns sleeping, as well, that laddie that had nearly died a month back.

Ah well, they were gey young for the kirk. They were going to school inside the next week, and fegs that would waken them up for good.

You thought it an awful funny place, the school, the Dominie was big and bald and thin, with glasses perched on a long thin nose, he stood in the playground between the two walls that separated the lasses' playground from the lads', and rang a bell and afore you could blink there were scholars tearing in from all directions, out of the hedges and over the walls, and tearing out of the lavatories where they'd been drawing funny pictures and up from the post-office tattie-pit where they had been throwing things at the post office, big loons and little ones and medium ones, and lassies with long plaits and legs, didn't like it, thought you'd maybe cry for a bit, and felt awful lost till you sighted Peter. You ran to him and took his hand but he was ashamed and pushed you away and said 'Your place's with the bairns, see?'

So you'd to line up last of all the lines and were awful ashamed, they put a lassie beside you, little and dark, and she looked at you queer and you stared down at your boots, fine boots, Mother had brought them in Bervie for you. And minding mother you nearly cried again, till you thought of the piece that you carried in your bag, for dinner, bread and butter and jam and a big soda scone with treacle inside it. So maybe you'd like the school after all.

Inside Miss Clouston took the little ones, she was awful thin and stern and fierce and the scholars said she wore red drawers and kept her strap in brine to pickle, she wasn't young, and looked about a hundred, and if one of the little ones messed up the floor she'd flush up red and say 'Dirty, go out' and near frighten a little 'un out of its life. But she didn't with you, she liked you from the first and was awful kind and took you to the fire and you warmed up and newsed with her and told her of the fish father catched in the sea, and had she ever seen the Maiden Mare Bess, losh, yon was a horse, last month you were ill, it was awful queer, the doctor cut you, you liked better sleeping on your own for all that, had the Missie ever slept by herself, did she ever hear the queer beasts at night that came creeping up out of the sea, snuffle and slide, Father said they weren't real, hadn't that loon a funny face, 'My brother Peter says you wear red flannel drawers'.

Miss Clouston said sharp 'Well, that'll do, Keith. Now sit down here beside this wee girl, her name's Rachel, and see you don't fight.' So down you'd to sit beside a lass, fight, you wouldn't fight with a quean, and you said right out that Alick said a quean couldn't fight a kipper off a plate, they were over weak in the guts. And there was a snicker of laughing all about and next minute you thought your head would fall off, Miss Clouston had smacked you so hard in the ear, she was a bitch and you cried a bit.

And while you were doing that and Miss Clouston, red faced, was taking the first of the lessons, singing, they'd all to stand up and she banged the piano and said 'Do Ray' and they all said 'Do Ray' the little quean Rachel tugged at your sleeve and said not to mind and not to be feared, she herself wasn't feared at any one. So you dried your nose on your sleeves and said you weren't feared, you weren't feared at anything, one night you were out, it was awful dark and a great big dog had come leaping to bite you, and you'd taken an axe and killed it dead, you were gey strong. Rachel said 'Oh losh, that was awful brave' and you told her some more of the things you'd done till Miss Clouston barked 'No talking there among the little ones,' that meant you two and you just sat wearied.

But syne she started lessons for you two and drew three funny pictures on the blackboard and told you to draw them as well, awful hard, they looked all wrong, one was a funny man called A, standing the way father sometimes stood, and another B, would that be the daft Bee that Geordie Allison would call the horses, the third was C, and was just daft, sea wasn't like that, oh, it was awful school, you minded sudden the sea and its greensy splurge out over the rocks and the gulls crying. But then you saw Rachel was drawing the daft-like stuff on her slate, so you had, and some more after that, and it wasn't so bad, though you fell asleep afore dinner-time.

At dinner you sat at the foot of the playground on the edge of the hedge and listened to Alick saying what he'd do to a lad, Jockie Elrick, that had said that he could fight Alick easy. And Alick finished his dinner quick and said to Peter 'Look after Ma's Pet' he meant you, and took out a great gully knife from his pouch and started to sharpen it on the sole of his boot, loons standing around and gaping at him, he was going to libb Jockie Elrick with it and then cut his throat from ear to ear, so he said, you cried out 'Ay, hurry up,' for you'd never seen that done afore to anyone. And over at the other side of the playground Jockie Elrick was sharpening his knife as well, the lads all said there'd be an awful lot of blood.

But the bell rung afore they could get to grips, and you'd the long afternoon to get through. Miss Clouston brought you a book of pictures, one was a train, you'd like to drive a train, and one was a beast that you didn't know, like a great big dog. Rachel knew more than you, she spelled it out and said it was a lion, her father had told her a lot about lions, they bade in a place called Africa and ate up black men, you asked why, it would surely be nicer to eat white, Rachel didn't know, that was just the way with lions. And then Miss Clouston called 'Children, you mustn't talk,' so you had a little bit sleep instead, and woke up with Alick shaking you awake, he'd come to take you home your first night.

The bairns were pouring out of the school and down in the playground going mad with delight at being freed from the Dominie and Missies, one had a kite, he'd let it high up, and two loons crept through the lower hedge and stole a handful of the Dominie's tomatoes, and Peter took out his knife again, sharp, and waited for Jockie Elrick, they circled round each other, knives all ready, Peter said that Jockie Elrick was a Bulgar, and Jockie said that Peter was another, see, and then they both nodded 'Wait till the morn' and separated, and you all held home, lasses trailing along in groups with their arms wound round one the other's shoulders, awful big, they petted you, you were over wearied to tell them you didn't like lasses, except maybe Rachel, she was fine.

She came down the Badymicks road behind you and Peter and Alick and you twice looked back, and saw her limp, and felt awful sorry, she looked dark herself in the fading light, would the folk in Africa that the lions ate be like her, would you say? And you looked back again and felt feared for her, and ran back to her side and took her hand, 'I'll take care of you if the lions come.' She said that was awful fine of you, but there weren't any in Scotland, she thought, you said 'Maybe no, but this is the Howe' and held her hand down to Badymicks, she put her arms round you and kissed you then, liked it, but Peter and Alick had stopped and looked back and started mocking you. 'Och, look at the lassies slobbering and kissing,' and the Bulgars tormented you all the way home.

Mother asked how you'd gotten on, and you said 'Och, fine' though you were so wearied, you fell asleep at the supper table and dreamt you were chasing Miss Clouston up the Howe with a gully knife in your hand, only it wasn't Miss Clouston but a great big beast, a lion from Africa, and it in its turn was chasing Rachel Camlin, pant and pant, you heard its great slobber, but you were gaining, gaining on it quick.

And then you woke up in the kitchen bed, dark in the early gliff of Spring morning, beside you Peter and Alick asleep, and far underfoot with shoggling surge the tide in the darkness taking its turn.

And still the rains of that Spring came down, at School every morning the bairns of the Howe sat and steamed like ill plates of porridge, and far and near through the tumbling runnels the water poured from the drooked lands to leave room for a fresh pelt coming at noon, piles of water tumbling and falling with a wheeling of rainbows and a cawing of gulls. To plough was to wade in mud to the knees, Arch Camlin digging up a bit of his moor fell into a bog and was nearly laired, he'd have died there but that Rachel was here, a Saturday, and ran for help to the figure of Dalsack across in his fields, ploughing and steaming with a blowing pair. Dalsack cried 'What? Well, well, thet's gey coarse' and came stepping canny across the fields and looked down at Arch Camlin pinned in the hole under a weight of lever and broom. 'Fegs, man, we'll need to howk you up out of that.' Arch Camlin said he was awful kind, but wouldn't he first like a draw at his pipe? So Dalsack was a wee bit nipper then, and howked out Arch, clorted up and down from head to feet and over his head, shivering with cold.

Dalsack would have let him stagger off home, but Edith had seen the whole play from the kitchen and came running out and invited

him in, 'Dalsack, you old Bulgar, help the man to tirr.' And she ran
and made him a hot berry drink while Arch stripped off every clout
he wore and got into a baggy old suit of Dalsack's, Rachel sitting by
with her staring eyes, Edith big and bonny bustling around, caring
nothing for naked men, seeing that Dalsack gave all his help. And
Arch Camlin, coming away a bit later, thought back on the way
that Edith behaved, 'od, yon was a funny-like way for a housekeeper to act with her lawful master, now.

He met in with Cruickshank from Moss Bank up the road and
stopped to pass the news of the day, and said what he'd thought
about Edith and Dalsack. Jim Cruickshank said 'Damn't, and
what's funny? She's a fine lass, Edith, but a whore for all. I'se
warrant she warms the old sinner's bed.'

Arch wouldn't have that, No, no, a fine lass, and Cruickshank
said she was fine enough, but a whore by nature, she'd burn yet. So
he drove off and Arch Camlin went home, Fannie trailing about
like a wee dish cloth. He told her the tale of his time in the moor
and all she said was 'Faith, did you then? Eh me, and now I'll have
to wash up your breeks and sark,' b'god that was all that worried
her.

So Arch took a bit of a stroll out that evening, walking canty
along the dripping paths, and came to the high still ridge in the
dripping silence of the cease of the rain, below the lights of Maiden
were twinkling, he'd take a bit taik in about there, he thought. In
the yard Geo Allison was watering the horses, the poor brutes
skirted up over their dowps, and they stood and had a bit news a
while till Maiden himself came out of the byre and cried 'That you,
Arch? Come away in.' And into the kitchen Arch Camlin stepped,
and who should be there, either nook of the fire than that Edith of
Bogmuck and the soldier-childe, William, the ill-doing soldier-son
of Moss Bank, looking chief as a cock and hen at each other, Mrs
Stratoun tearing around at her work, the lads all snuggled in their
beds already. Faith, it seemed the young Cruickshank hadn't the
objections to Edith that his ill-tuned father had.

But Arch thought that little business of his and started with
Maiden to take through hand the threshing mill that was coming
to the village in a week or so, to Badymicks first, Bogmuck, and

syne Maiden, then across the moor to Balhaggarty, from there along to Lamahip, Moss Bank said he would thresh his own. Edith and young Cruickshank sat and listened, young Cruickshank ignorant about things like this, he asked if they'd ever thought a time would come when a place like Maiden could drive its own thresher with electricity up from the sea? John Stratoun said ''Od, maybe we will, but we'll leave that over a year or two yet,' giving his beard a bit of a stroke, ay, a dry soul, Maiden, Arch Camlin thought.

So out at last he went taiking home, and young Cruickshank and Edith rose to go with him, outside the rain had passed, stiffly blustering a great wind was darting up the Howe, they'd to bend their heads to the tingle and blow and fight their way to the long hedge-dripping track. At the break of the roads that led east and south, Arch Camlin cried out he'd take Edith home, but young Cruickshank said 'Ho no, I'll come with you. Fine evening for a bit of a stroll, you know.'

Faith, if that was the thing that he wanted he ended up with a sappier touch, looking back when he parted with them outside Bogmuck Arch Camlin saw him with Edith close up, tight in his arms as though he would mince her and kissing her lips in a fashion not decent, was that the way to behave to a lass that was good enough, but just a plain whore?

Postscript

The novel, as the typescript was left, finishes at this enigmatic point. Already there are signs of haste in the typescript, signs like inconsistency of spelling and changes of mind, and near the end of the finished product, some signs of illness or inattention, words quite wrongly typed and not corrected. Pen corrections of the first-draft typescript are frequent in the early pages, then tail off completely towards the end.

What is interesting is not just the incomplete state of typescript, but the appendices which follow. If Gibbon had been composing at speed he could reasonably have been expected to go ahead full steam with his inspiration. Yet he finished the novel off neatly at the end of a sentence, and an episode, indeed those who write in this way will recognise the device of finishing at a point of interest where it will be relatively easy to bring the plot to life again after an interval.

There *are* signs that Gibbon meant the novel to be laid aside. The lack of corrections of the latter parts (work to be postponed till later), the frequent mistakes in typing not even back-spaced for obvious correction indicate haste and possibly poor health. But most significantly, the plot outlines which follow are all produced on the same typewriter, and cover incidents all completely outside the finished portion. These appendices were composed, we deduce, after the typescript was laid aside, as an indication of how work-in-progress was to be completed. They are not working documents, already partly incorporated in the plot, but all look to the future.

Two reasons suggest themselves. One, simply, is that Gibbon knew he had to put the novel in cold-storage (for reasons either of health or more pressing deadlines on other projects) and so jotted down in legible form some outlines of his original intentions, as a

guide when he came back to this typescript. It would be a wholly
natural thing to do.

Another, less obvious, reason is suggested by the fact that all the
incidents relate to as-yet-unwritten parts of the plot. We know
publishers were pushing Gibbon hard, and it is possible that in
putting this project aside, he was typing up a fair-copy list of this
kind to show to a publisher as a token of good intentions, and
proof that he had run out not of inspiration, but of time. This is
pure supposition, but the fair-copy nature of these postscripts does
suggest that they were meant to be taken along with the completed
portion to indicate a novel which could easily be brought to a
publishable state, given a little more time. It would be a practical
thing for a hard-pressed author in poor health to do, to buy a little
relaxation of deadlines.

The reader who has followed the typescript through the finished
and partly-corrected version will be struck with familiarity between *The Speak of the Mearns* and other Gibbon productions,
obviously *Sunset Song*, less obviously the short story 'Clay' and the
incident of breaking in the field (and finding the buried prehistoric
remains), the story 'Smeddum' and the masterful farmer's wife.
'The Land', the eloquent essay from *Scottish Scene*, finds much that
is attractive about Scotland that tallies exactly with Keith's exact
observations of the land, the birds, the seasons in Kinneff; Malcom
Maudslay remembers experiences very like Keith's at the school he
suffered in *The Thirteenth Disciple*. Yet the real similarities are to
Blawearie and Kinraddie in *Sunset Song*, the obsessive gossip and
interest in sexual peccadillo, the family of brothers with a quiet
father and red-haired, hyperactive mother, the quiet bookish
observer beside the more active brothers – whether as Chris in
Sunset Song, or Keith here, the author is drawing on autobiographical experience, his own experience in a crofting kitchen set
aside from the farming interests of brothers and family, aiming for
the school and the world outside, furthered by the energy of his
mother, and almost despite the opposition or the inertia of the rest
of the community, always excepting the teachers and the school
friends drawn very much from Gibbon's own childhood memory.
Memorable, too, is the *Sunset Song* style with its careful mixture of

Scots forms and English narrative base (defined by Gibbon in his 'Literary Lights' essay in *Scottish Scene*), and its unique drift from autobiographical *parole intérieure* to the mind of the person hearing what is being said, to the overall consciousness of the community. The same multiple viewpoints which give the reader such delicate apprehension of the mind of Kinraddie give the reader of these pages something of Keith's infant apprehension of his community, and at the same time an adult's apprehension of a community far beyond the understanding of young Keith, with his inexperience of the world and of the female sex.

The shape of the finished novel, obviously, would have expanded Keith's observations from the intimacies of farm and father, family and friends to the world of books and experience, archaeology and travel, the towns and cities, and the world beyond; like James Leslie Mitchell coming from the farms and village school of Arbuthnott to national fame as Lewis Grassic Gibbon, so the central intelligence of *The Speak of the Mearns* would have expanded as incident succeeded incident, and in this controlled way would have grown to match the community voice of experience, then to pass it as Keith moved beyond the limitations of Maiden Castle and its village. That expansion had just begun with his emancipation from home to school; the further development must be the reader's responsibility, guided by the scanty notes Gibbon left.

The Speak of the Mearns would not have made Gibbon much more popular in his native countryside than did *Sunset Song*. Scandalous incident can at least be suggested to be tied to gossip and real-life incident, but as in the earlier work the close-knit community of obsessive interest gives marvellous cohesion to the work. The reader never pauses to think that Keith's world could never encompass this richness; rather the reader learns to move effortlessly in and out of Keith's world, till Keith himself comes of age. The technique here is obviously that of a man with a proven success in *Sunset Song*, deploying the same methods towards a fresh success in this sequel. The text is imperfect (though it has been lightly edited to remove obvious belmishes) but it suggests the secure ability to recall and to adapt, to marshall and control the speed of development which would very probably have made *The Speak of the Mearns* a success very much like *Sunset Song* – fascinating to those involved in Scottish rural life but not offended by local incident and allusion, infuriating to friends and family, and curiously, compulsively readable to those non-Scots who tried through Gibbon's technique to gain some insight into a vanishing world of Scottish rural activity. The novel's unfinished state is a real loss to the history of popular twentieth-century fiction in Scotland.

I.C.

Appendix

Lewis Grassic Gibbon's notes left at the end of the novel

1. On the back of an envelope, Gibbon had scribbled:

Balhaggarty – Sam Paton & wife (Strachan) – two young sons, William & Peter

Moss Bank – Jim Cruickshank & huge wife. Two sons: Sandy the daftie & Joe the soldier

Auld Kirk – Rev James Dallas. Young, pretty wife

Free Kirk – Rev. Adam Smith. Housekeeper

Lamahip – Gunn; Bright wife; daughters Jean (religious) & Queen (mysterious)

Badymicks – Arch Camlin, his wife, & daughter Rachel

Bogmuck – Dalsack & Edith

Howl [a name he sometimes applied in the draft to the village near Maiden Castle] – Munros, The Postmaster & son.

2. *Development of Story*

Sam Paton and his wife BALHAGGARTY: Paton develops cancer. He was always full of wind and water. Mrs Paton sees more and more ghosts.

Jim Cruickshank and his wife of Moss Bank: They are drawn into the drama of Joseph's love of Edith, and finally flee the district. Towards the end, Cruickshank is out with a gun to kill Dalsack of Badymicks.

Reverend James Dallas of the Auld Kirk and his wife: The Rev grows more bitter and narrow, a sadist who ill-treats his wife and refuses her sexual intercourse. An afflicted imagination with the horrors of the Old Testament. Mrs Dallas ultimately consoles herself with young Munro of the Howe and his tormented sneers change to love.

Reverend Adam Smith of the Free Kirk summoned to console the mystic Queenie Gunn is confirmed in his dislike of all hatred not thoroughly dead. He goes digging in Stane Park and uncovers an ancient grave: the man done in with a blow at the back of the skull.

Stephen Gunn of Lamahip continues his lies. But in the end the old lair proves to have told the truth – some laird woman remembers him. At the Big House. Religious Jean with a baby. Queen goes to London and becomes a preacher.

Arch Camlin of Badymicks continues whistling and working. His complaining wife has another baby at which Mrs Stratoun attends.

Dalsack of Bogmuck and his housekeeper. Edith and Joe continue their firtation. Edith reveals the father of her child as Dalsack. Marriage with Joe.

The Paralysed Pinto of Adam's Castle: His forester, Johnson, his keeper, McGrath. Hatred between the Stratouns and Pintos.

3. *Incidents*:

(1) Steam-mill. All the people of the Howe there. Water carrying. Chaff. Hum of the engine. Sights out beyond.
(2) Wedding of Joe and Edith.
(3) The horse that tumbled over the cliff: Geo Allison and Bess.
(4) Annual Games and Dance.
(5) Sunday School Picnic.
(6) Prize-giving.
(7) Tree-sawing in the woods – steading trees.
(8) James Dallas's discovery of his wife in Munro's arms.
(9) The hanging of Stephen Gunn.
(10) Burns' Nicht supper.

New Characters.
The Laird
Forester Johnson
Keeper McGrath
Gunn of Lamahip as old Scorgie plus old Hodge.

ESSAYS

from *Scottish Scene* (1934)

The Antique Scene

The history of Scotland may be divided into the three phases of Colonization, Civilization, and Barbarization. That the last word is a synonym for Anglicization is no adverse reflection upon the quality of the great English culture. Again and again, in the play of the historic forces, a great civilization imposed on an alien and lesser has compassed that alien's downfall.

Few things cry so urgently for rewriting as does Scots history, in few aspects of her bastardized culture has Scotland been so ill-served as by her historians. The chatter and gossip of half the salons and drawing-rooms of European intellectualism hang over the antique Scottish scene like a malarial fog through which peer the fictitious faces of heroic Highlanders, hardy Norsemen, lovely Stewart queens, and dashing Jacobite rebels. Those stage-ghosts shamble amid the dimness, and mope and mow in their ancient parts with an idiotic vacuity but a maddening persistence. Modern research along orthodox lines balks from the players, or re-names them shyly and retires into footnotes on Kaltwasser.

Yet behind those grimaces of the romanticized or alien imagination a real people once lived and had its being, and hoped and feared and hated, and was greatly uplifted, and loved its children, and knew agony of the patriotic spirit, and was mean and bestial, and generous, and sardonically merciful. Behind the posturings of those poltergeists are the lives of millions of the lowly who wiped the sweats of toil from browned faces and smelt the pour of waters by the Mull of Kintyre and the winds of autumn in the Grampian haughs and the sour, sweet odours of the upland tarns; who tramped in their varying costumes and speeches to the colour and play of the old guild-towns; who made great poetry and sang it; who begat their kind in shame or delight in the begetting; who were much as you or I, human animals bedevilled or uplifted by the play of the forces of civilization in that remote corner of the Western world which we call Scotland.

All human civilizations originated in Ancient Egypt. Through the accident of time and chance and the cultivation of wild barley in the Valley of the Nile, there arose in a single spot on the earth's surface the urge in men to upbuild for their economic salvation the great fabric of civilization. Before the planning of that architecture enslaved the minds of men, man was a free and happy and undiseased animal wandering the world in the Golden Age of the poets (and reality) from the Shetlands to Tierra del Fuego. And from that central focal point in Ancient Egypt the first civilizers spread abroad the globe the beliefs and practices, the diggings and plantings and indignations and shadowy revilements of the Archaic Civilization.

They reached Scotland in some age that we do not know, coming to the Islands of Mist in search of copper and gold and pearls, Givers of Life in the fantastic theology that followed the practice of agriculture. They found the Scots lowlands and highlands waving green into morning and night tremendous forests where the red deer belled, where the great bear, perhaps, had still his tracks and his caverns, where wolves howled the hills in great scattering packs, where, in that forested land, a danker climate than to-day prevailed. And amid those forests and mountain slopes lived the Golden Age hunters – men perhaps mainly of Maglemosian stock, dark and sinewy and agile, intermixed long ages before with other racial stocks, the stock of CroMagnard and Magdalenian who had followed the ice-caps north when the reindeer vanished from the French valleys. They were men naked, cultureless, without religion or social organization, shy hunters, courageous, happy, kindly, who stared at the advent of the first great boats that brought the miners and explorers of the Archaic Civilization from Crete or Southern Spain. They flocked down to stare at the new-comers, to offer tentative gifts of food and the like; and to set on their necks the yoke under which all mankind has since passed.

For the Archaic Civilization rooted in Scotland. Agriculture was learned from the Ancient Mariners and with it the host of rites deemed necessary to propitiate the gods of the earth and the sky. Village communities came into being, the first peasants with the first overlords, those priestly overlords who built the rings of the Devil Stones on the high places from Lewis to Aberdeenshire. And the ages came and passed and the agricultural belts grew and spread, and the smoke of sacrifice rose from a thousand altars through the length and breadth of the land at the times of seedtime and harvest, feast and supplication. They buried their dead in modifications of the Egyptian fashion, in Egyptian graves. There came to them, in the slow ebb of the centuries, a driftage of other cultural elements from that ferment of civilization in the basin of the Mediterranean. They learned their own skill with stick and stone, presently with copper, and at last with bronze. But, until the coming of the makers of bronze that Archaic civilization in Scotland, as elsewhere, was one singularly peaceful and undisturbed. Organized warfare had yet to dawn on the Western World.

How it dawned is too lengthy a tale to tell here in any detail: how bands of forest-dwellers in the Central European areas, uncivilized, living on the verge of the great settlements of the Archaic communities and absorbing little but the worst of their practices, fell on those communities and murdered them was the first great tragedy of pre-Christian Europe. The ancient matriarchies of the Seine were wiped from existence and in their place, (and presently across the Channel) came swarming the dagger-armed hosts of a primitive who, never civilized, had become a savage. This was the Kelt.

We see his advent in the fragments of sword and buckler that lie ticketed in our museums; but all the tale of that rape of a civilization by the savage, far greater and infinitely more tragic than the rape of the Roman Empire by the Goth, is little more than a faint moan and murmur in the immense cañons of near-history. In Scotland, no doubt, he played his characteristic part, the Kelt, coming armed on a peaceful population, slaying and robbing and finally enslaving, establishing himself as king and overlord, routing the ancient sun-priests from the holy places and establishing his own devil-haunted, uneasy myths and gods through the efforts of the younger sons. From Berwick to Cape Wrath the scene for two hundred years must have been a weary repetition, year upon year, of invasion and murder, inversion and triumph. When Pytheas sailed the Scottish coasts it is likely that the Kelt had triumphed almost everywhere. By the time the Romans came raiding across the English Neck Scotland was a land of great barbaric Kelt tribes, armed and armoured, with a degenerate, bastardized culture and some skill in war and weapon-making. It was as capable of producing a ferocious soldiery and a great military leader like Calgacus as it was incapable of a single motif in art or song to influence the New Civilization of the European World.

Yet of that culture of those Picts or Painted Men, those Caledonians whom the Romans encountered and fought and marvelled upon, it is doubtful if a single element of any value had been contributed by the Kelt. It is doubtful if the Kelts ever contributed a single item to the national cultures of the countries miscalled Keltic. It is doubtful for the best of reasons: There is no proof that the Kelts, invading Britain, came in any great numbers. They were a conquering military caste, not a people in migration: they imposed their language and their social organization upon the basic Maglemosian-Mediterranean stock; they survived into remoter times, the times of Calgacus, the times of Kenneth MacAlpin, as nobles, an aristocracy on horseback. They survive to the present day as a thin strand in the Scottish population: half Scotland's landed gentry is by descent Normanized Kelt. But the Kelts are a strain quite alien to the indubitable and original Scot. They were, and remain, one of the greatest curses of the Scottish scene, quick, avaricious, unintelligent, quarrelsome, cultureless, and uncivilizable. It is one of the strangest jests of history that they should have given their name to so much that is fine and noble, the singing of poets and the fighting of great fights, in which their own actual part has been that of gaping, unintelligent audition or mere carrion-bird raiding.

The first serious modification of the basic Pictish stock did not occur until towards the end of the sixth Christian century, when the Northumbrian Angles flowed upwards, kingdom-building, as far as the shores of the Firth of Forth. They were a people and nation in transit; they exterminated or reduced to villeinage the

Kelt-led Picts of those lands: they succeeded in doing those things
not because they were braver or more generous or God-inspired
than the Pictish tribes, but because of the fact that they were
backed by the Saxon military organization, their weapons were
better, and apparently they fronted a congeries of warring tribes
inanely led in the usual Keltic fashion – tribes which had inter-
warred and raided and murdered and grown their crops and drunk
their ale unstirred by alien adventures since the passing of the
Romans. The Angle pressed north, something new to the scene,
bringing his own distinctive culture and language, his own gods
and heroes and hero-myths. About the same time a tribe of Kelt-
led Irish Mediterraneans crossed in some numbers into Argyllshire
and allied themselves with, or subdued the ancient inhabitants.
From that alliance or conquest arose the kingdom of Dalriada – the
Kingdom of the Scots. Yet this Irish invasion had no such
profound effect on the national culture as the coming of the
Angles in the South: the Irish Scots were of much the same speech
and origin as the Argyllshire natives among whom they settled.

With the coming of the Angles, indeed, the period of Colonization comes to a close. It is amusing to note how modern research
disposes of the ancient fallacies which saw Scotland overrun by
wave after wave of conquering, colonizing peoples. Scotland was
colonized only twice – once fairly completely, once partially, the
first time when the Maglemosian hunters drifted north, in hunting,
happy-go-lucky migration; the second time, when the Angles
lumbered up into Lothian. The Kelt, the Scot, the Norseman,
the Norman were no more than small bands of raiders and
robbers. The peasant at his immemorial toil would lift his eyes
to see a new master installed at the broch, at the keep, at, later, the
castle: and would shrug the matter aside as one of indifference,
turning, with the rain in his face, to the essentials of existence, his
fields, his cattle, his woman in the dark little eirde, earth-house.

The three hundred years after that almost simultaneous descent
of Scot and Angle on different sectors of the Scottish scene is a
tangle of clumsy names and loutish wars. Kings bickered and bred
and murdered and intrigued, armies marched and counter-
marched and perpetrated heroisms now dust and nonsense,

atrocities the dried blood of which are now not even dust. Christianity came in a number of guises, the Irish heresy a chill blink of light in its coming. It did little or nothing to alter the temper of the times, it was largely a matter of politics and place-seeking, Columba and John Knox apart there is no ecclesiastic in Scots history who does not but show up in the light of impartial research as either a posturing ape, rump-scratching in search of soft living, or as a moronic dullard, hag-ridden by the grisly transplanted fears of the Levant. The peasant merely exchanged the bass chanting of the Druid in the pre-Druid circles for the whining hymnings of priests in wood-built churches; and turned to his land again.

But presently, coastwise, north, west, and east, a new danger was dragging him in reluctant levies from his ancient pursuits. This was the coming of the Norsemen.

If the Kelts were the first great curse of Scotland, the Norse were assuredly the second. Both have gathered to themselves in the eyes of later times qualities and achievements to which the originals possessed no fragment of a claim. The dreamy, poetic, God-moved Kelt we have seen as a mere Chicagoan gangster, murderous, avaricious, culturally sterile, a typical aristocrat, typically base. The hardy, heroic Norseman uncovers into even sorrier reality. He was a farmer or fisherman, raiding in order to supplement the mean livelihood he could draw from more praise-worthy pursuits in the Norwegian fjords. The accident of his country lying at the trans-Baltic end of the great trans-Continental trade-route had provided him with the knowledge of making steel weapons in great number and abundance. Raiding Scotland, he was in no sense a superior or heroic type subduing a lowly or inferior; he was merely a pirate with a good cutlass, a thug with a sudden and efficient strangling-rope. Yet those dull, dyspeptic whey-faced clowns have figured in all orthodox histories as the bringers of something new and vital to Scottish culture, as an invigorating strain, a hard and splendid ingredient. It is farcical that it should be necessary to affirm at this late day that the Norseman brought nothing of any permanence to Scotland other than his characteristic gastritis.

Yet that cutlass carved great sections from the Scottish coasts:

presently all the Western Isles had suffered a profound infiltration of the thin, mean blood of the northern sea-raiders. In the east, the attacks were almost purely burglarious. The hardy Norseman, with his long grey face so unfortunately reminiscent of a horse's, would descend on that and this village or township, steal and rape and fire, and then race for his ships to escape encounter with the local levies. On such occasions as he landed in any force, and met the Picts (even the idiotically badly-led, Kelt-led Picts) in any force, he would, as at the Battle of Aberlemno, be routed with decision and vigour. Yet those constant raidings weakened the Eastern kingdom of the Picts: in A.D. 844 the Scot king, Kenneth MacAlpin, succeeded to the Pictish throne – it was evidently regarded as the succession of a superior to the estates of an inferior. Thereafter the name Pict disappears from Scottish history, though, para-doxically immortal, the Pict remained.

From 1034, when Duncan ascended the Scottish throne, until 1603, when James VI ascended the English throne, Scotland occupied herself, willy-nilly, in upbuilding her second (and last) characteristic civilization. Her first, as we have seen, was that modification of the Archaic Civilization which the Kelts overthrew; this second which slowly struggled into being under the arrow-hails, the ridings and rapings and throat-cuttings of official policy, the jealous restraints of clerical officialdom, was compounded of many cultural strands. It was in essentials a Pictish civilization, as the vast majority of the inhabitants remained Picts. But, in the Lowlands, it had changed once again its speech, relinquishing the alien Keltic in favour of the equally alien Anglo-Saxon. The exchange was a matter of domestic policy, a febrific historical accident hinged on the bed-favours wrung from his consort by the henpecked Malcolm Canmore.

The third of the name of Malcolm to rule in Scotland, his speech, his court, and his official pronunciamentos were all Keltic until he wedded the Princess Margaret, who had fled from the Norman invasion of England. A great-niece of Edward the Con-fessor, Margaret was a pious daughter of the Church and greatly shocked at the Keltic deviations from Roman dates and ceremonial incantations. She devoted her life to bringing the usages of the

Scottish Church into harmony with orthodox Catholicism. She bred assiduously: she bred six sons and two daughters, and in return for the delights of the shameful intimacies which begat this offspring, the abashed Malcolm refrained from any hand in their christening. They were all christened with good English names, they were taught English as their native speech, they lived to grow up and Anglicize court and church and town. Of the two great women in Scots history it is doubtful if the most calamitously pathological influence should be ascribed to Margaret the Good or to Mary the Unchaste.

Yet this Anglicization was a surface Anglicization. English speech and English culture alike were as yet fluid things: it meant no cultural subjection to the southern half of the island. It begat a tradition, a speech, an art and a literature in the southern half of Scotland which were set in an Anglo-Saxon, not an English, mould, but filled with the deep spiritual awarenesses of the great basic race which wielded this new cultural weapon as once it had wielded the Keltic. It was a thing national and with a homely and accustomed feel, this language in which Wyntoun and Barbour and Blind Harry were presently telling the epic stories of the great War of Independence.

The effect of that war, the unceasing war of several centuries, was calamitous to the Scots civilization in the sense that it permanently impoverished it, leaving Scotland, but for a brief blink, always a poor country economically, and a blessing in that it set firmly in the Scots mind the knowledge of national homogeneity: Scotland was the home of true political nationalism (once a liberating influence, not as now an inhibiting one) – not the nationalism forced upon an unwilling or indifferent people by the intrigues of kings and courtesans, but the spontaneous uprising of an awareness of blood-brotherhood and freedom-right. In the midst of the many dreary and shameful pages of the book of Scottish history the story of the rising of the Scots under the leadership of William Wallace still rings splendid and amazing. Wallace was one of the few authentic national heroes: authentic in the sense that he apprehended and moulded the historic forces of his time in a fashion denied to all but a few of the world's great political leaders – Cromwell, Lincoln, Lenin.

It was 1296. Scotland, after a dynastic squabble on the rights of this and that boorish noble to ascend the Scottish throne and there cheat and fornicate after the divine rights of kings, had been conquered, dismembered and ground in the mud by Edward the First of England. He did it with a cold and bored efficiency, as a man chastising and chaining a slobbering, yelping cur. Then he returned to England; and the chained cur suddenly awoke in the likeness of a lion.

'The instinct of the Scottish people,' wrote John Richard Green, 'has guided it right in choosing Wallace for its national hero. He was the first to assert freedom as a national birthright.' His assertion roused Scotland. The peasants flocked to his standard – suddenly, and for perhaps the first time in Scots history, stirred beyond their customary indifference over the quarrels of their rulers. Here was something new, a leader who promised something new. Nor did he only promise: presently he was accomplishing. At the head of a force that bore the significant title of the 'Army of the Commons of Scotland' Wallace met and routed the English in pitched battle at Cambuskenneth Bridge in 1297, was offered the crown of Scotland, refused it, and instead was nominated Guardian of Scotland, a great republican with the first of the great republican titles, albeit he called himself a royalist.

For a year it seemed his cause would sweep everything before it. The laggard nobles came to join him. Presently the Army of the Commons of Scotland was being poisoned by the usual aristocratic intrigues, though still the troubled peasants and townsmen clung to their faith in the Guardian. Then news came that Edward in person was on the march against Scotland. Wallace assembled all his forces and met the invader at Falkirk. The Scots cavalry, noble-recruited, noble-led, strategically placed to fall on the ranks of the English archers and rout them at the crucial moment, fled without striking a blow. Wallace's great schiltrouns of heroic peasant spearmen were broken and dispersed.

Wallace himself sailed for France, seeking aid there for his distracted country. In 1304 he returned, was captured by the

English, tried and condemned as a traitor, and hanged, castrated, and disembowelled on Tower Hill. This judicial murder is one of the first and most dreadful examples of that characteristic English frightfulness wielded throughout history against the defenders of alien and weaker peoples. More serious than Wallace's personal fate, it murdered that fine hope and enthusiasm that had stirred the Army of the Scots Commons on the morning of Falkirk. In a kind of despairing hatred, not hope, the Scots people turned to support the rebellions of the various shoddy noble adventurers who now raised the standard against the English. By intrigue, assassination, and some strategical skill one of those nobles, Robert the Brus, had presently disposed of all his rivals, had himself crowned king, and, after various reverses and flights and hidings and romantic escapades in company with spiders and Lorne loons, succeeded in routing the English at the Battle of Bannockburn. With that victory the Scots royalties came to their own again, however little the Scots commons.

Yet, in the succeeding centuries of wars and raids, dynastic begettings and dynastic blood-lettings, the commons of Scotland showed a vigour both un-English and un-French in defence of the rights of the individual. Villeinage died early in Scotland: the independent tenant-retainer came early on the scene in the Low-lands. In the Highlands the clan system, ostensibly aristocratic, was never so in actuality. It was a communistic patriarchy, the relation of the chief to his meanest clansman the relation of an elder blood brother, seldom of a noble to a serf. The guildsmen of the towns modelled their policies on those of the Hansa cities and Augsburg, rather than on the slavish subservience of their contemporaries in England. Presently the French alliance, disastrous from a military point of view, was profoundly leavening the character of Scots culture, leavening, not obliterating it. Scots built and carved and sang and wrote with new tools of technique and vocabulary to hand. The Scots civilization of the fifteenth and sixteenth centuries absorbed its great cultural impulses from the Continent; as a consequence, Scots literature in the fifteenth century is already a great literature while in contemporary England there is little more than the maundering of a poetasting host of semi-illiterates.

Despite the feuds and squabbles of noble and king, there came into being a rude plenty in Scotland of the fifteenth and sixteenth centuries. The reign of James the Fourth was, economically and culturally, the Golden Age of the great Scots civilization. Its duration was brief and its fate soon that which had overtaken the Golden Age of the happy Pict hunters three thousand years before.

The end of James the Fourth at Flodden in 1513, the dark end to the greatest raid of the Scots into England, plunged the country into fifteen years of mis-government, when this and that clownish noble attempted to seize the power through this and that intrigue of palace and bedchamber. The Golden Age faded rapidly as marauding bands of horse clattered up the cobbled streets of the towns and across the fertile Lowland crop-lands. By the time the Fifth James assumed the power Scotland was a distracted country, the commons bitterly taxed and raided and oppressed, the ruler in castle and keep a gorged and stinking carrion-crow. James, the Commons' King, the one heroic royalty in Scots history, faced a hopeless task with the broken and impoverished commons but half aware of his championship. He put down the nobles with a ruthless hand, defied the monk-murdering Henry VIII of England, established the Court of Session and the Supreme Court of Justice; he might well have re-established the economic prosperity of his father's reign but for the English invasion of the country in 1542. The nobles refused to join the army he raised – the pitiful Church army routed at Solway Moss. Dying at Falkland Palace a few days later James, God's Scotsman as he has been well called, heard of the birth of a daughter. 'It cam wi' a lass and 'twill gang wi' a lass,' he said, speaking perhaps of his own dynasty; unforeseeing the fact that it was the Scots civilization itself that that daughter was to see in early eclipse.

That eclipse was inaugurated by the coming of the tumultuous change in Christian ritualism and superstitious practice dignified by the name of Reformation. Into its many causes in Western Europe there is no need to enter here. Nobles hungered to devour Church lands; churchmen were often then, as later, cowardly and avaricious souls; the Church, then as often, seemed intellectually moribund, a dead weight lying athwart the minds of men. So, in apparent dispute as to the correct method of devouring the symbolic body of the dead god, symbolically slain, hell was let loose on the European scene for a long two hundred years. Men fought and died with enthusiasm in the cause of ceremonial cannibalism. In Scotland the Reforming party had been growing to power even in the age of the Fifth James. During the long minority of his daughter, Mary Queen of Scots, it was frequently in possession of the reins of power: in 1557 it gathered together its forces and signed a National Convention for the establishment of the Reformed Faith.

Two years afterwards the ecclesiastic, John Knox, returned from a long exile in England and on the Continent. Knox had served as a slave on the French galleys for eighteen months after the assassination of Cardinal Beaton in 1546, he had definite and clear beliefs on the part the Reformation must play in Scotland, and in the years of his exile he had wandered from haunt to haunt of the European revolutionaries (much as Lenin did in the first decade of the twentieth century) testing out his own creed in converse and debate with Calvin and the like innovators. Once again a Scotsman had arisen capable of apprehending the direction of the historic forces, and determined to enchannel those for the benefit of a Commons' Scotland. The nauseous character of his political allies in Scotland did not deter him from the conflict. In the triumphant Parliament summoned in 1560 the Protestants under his direction established the Reformed Church, forbade the mass, and practically legalized the wholesale seizure of Church property. Knox's intentions with regard to the disposal of that property were definite and unshakable: it would be used for the relief of the poor, for the establishment of free schools, for the sustentation of a free people's priesthood. But, though he had foreseen the direction of the historic forces thus far, history proved on the side of his robbing allies, not on his. The Covenant left the Commons poorer than ever and Knox an embittered and sterile leader, turning from his battle in the cause of the people to sardonic denunciations of the minor moral lapses of the young Queen.

He was a leader defeated: and history was to ascribe to him and his immediate followers, and with justice, blame for some of the most terrible aberrations of the Scots spirit in succeeding centuries. Yet Knox himself was of truly heroic mould; had his followers, far less his allies, been of like mettle, the history of Scotland might have been strangely and splendidly different. To pose him against the screen of antique time as an inhibition-ridden neurotic (as is the modern fashion) who murdered the spirit and hope of an heroic young queen, is malicious distortion of the true picture. The 'heroic young queen' in question had the face, mind, manners and morals of a well-intentioned but hysterical poodle.

Her succession by the calamitous Sixth James, who was summoned to the English throne in 1603, was the beginning of the end of the Scots civilization. That end came quickly. Not only had temporal power moved from Edinburgh to London (for at least a while) but the cultural focus had shifted as well. There began that long process of barbarization of the Scots mind and culture which is still in progress. Presently it was understood to be rather a shameful thing to be a Scotsman, to make Scots poetry, to be subject to Scots law, to be an inhabitant of the northern half of the island. The Diffusionist school of historians holds that the state of Barbarism is no half-way house of a progressive people towards full and complete civilization: on the contrary, it marks a degeneration from an older civilization, as Savagery is the state of a people absorbing only the poorer elements of an alien culture. The state of Scotland since the Union of the Crowns gives remarkable support to this view, though the savagery of large portions of the modern urbanized population had a fresh calamity – the Industrial Revolution – to father it.

Yet, though all art is no more than the fine savour and essence of the free life, its decay and death in Scotland was no real mark of the subjection and decay of the free Scottish spirit: it was merely a mark of that spirit in an anguished travail that has not yet ceased. Presently, gathering that unquenchable force into new focus, came the Covenanting Times, the call of the Church of Knox to be defended as the Church of the Commons, of the People, bitterly assailed by noble and King. That the call was justified we may doubt, that the higher councils of the Church government themselves were other than sedulously manipulated tyrannies in the hands of the old landed Keltic gentry may also be doubted. But to large sections of the Lowland Scots the Covenant was not so much a sworn bond between themselves and God as between their own souls and freedom. They flocked to its standards in the second Bishops' War, they invaded England. For a time the Covenanting Scots Army at Newcastle dictated English policy, ruled England, and almost imposed on it the Presbytery. Thereafter, in the sway and clash of the Parliamentarian wars, it suffered collapse under the weight of its own prosperity and rottenness. Cromwell forcibly dissolved the General Assembly of the Scots Church in 1653, incorporated Scotland in the Commonwealth, and marched home leaving a country under English military governance – a country chastised and corrected, but strangely unbroken in spirit. Scotland and the Scots, after a gasp of surprise, accepted Cromwell with a wary trust. Here, and again, as once in those brief days when the standards of the Guardian of Scotland unfurled by Stirling Brig, was something new on the Scottish scene – English-inspired, but new and promising. If they laboured under dictatorship, so did the English. If their nobles were proscribed and persecuted, so were the English. If their frontier was down, trade with England and the English colonies was free. . . . It was a glimpse of the Greater Republicanism; and it faded almost before Scotland could look on it. The Second Charles returned and enforced the Episcopacy on the Scots, and from 1660 until 1690 Scotland travailed in such political Terror as has few parallels in history.

The People's Church gathered around it the peasants – especially the western peasants – in its defence. At Rullion Green the Covenanting Army was defeated, and an orgy of suppression followed. Covenanters were tortured with rigour and a sadistic ingenuity before being executed in front of their own houses, in sight of their own women-folk. In the forefront of this business of oppression were the Scots nobles, led by Graham of Claverhouse, 'Bonny Dundee.' This remarkable individual, so much biographied and romanticized by later generations, was both a sadist and a criminal degenerate. He was one in a long train of the Scots nobility. He had few qualities to recommend him, his generalship was poor and his strategy worse. Torturing unarmed peasants was the utmost reach of statesmanship ever achieved by this hero of the romantics. Where he met an army – even a badly organized army as at Drumclog – he was ignominiously defeated and fled with the speed and panic of the thin-blooded pervert that he was. His last battle, that of Killiecrankie, he won by enlisting the aid of the Highlanders against those whom they imagined to be their enemies. His portrayed face has a rat-like look in the mean, cold eyes; his name has a sour stench still in the pages of Scottish history.

That last battle of his marked almost the end of the Church persecutions: the Kirk of Scotland emerged with the Revolution from its long night into a day of power and pomp. So doing, following an infallible law of history, it shed the enthusiasm and high loyalty of all generous souls. From 1690 onwards the history of the churches in Scotland is a history of minor and unimportant brawling on questions of state support and state denunciation, it is an oddly political history, reflecting the dreary play of politics up to and after the Union of the Parliaments, the Union which destroyed the last outward symbols of the national civilization.

Whatever the growing modern support for repudiation of that Union, it is well to realize that the first tentative moves towards it came from the side of the Scots Parliament, if not of the Scots people. As early as 1689 the Scots Parliament appointed commissioners to treat for an 'incorporating union,' though nothing came of it. Scottish trade and Scottish industry was very desperately hampered by the English Navigation Act, in which Scots were treated as aliens; and also by the fact that the Scots lacked any overseas dominion on which to dump their surpluses of wealth and population – though indeed, except in the farcical economics of that time (ours are no less farcical) they had surpluses of neither. The first attempts at Union came to nothing: the Scots turned their energies to founding a colony in Darien.

The attempt was disastrous: the Spaniards, already in possession, and aided and abetted by powerful English influences, beat off the settlers. News of the disaster killed among the Scots people any desire for union with the auld enemy; nor indeed did they ever again support it. The Union was brought about by as strange a series of intrigues as history is aware of: England ingeniously bribed her way to power. There was little real resistance in the Scots Parliament except by such lonely figures as Fletcher of Saltoun. On May 1st, 1707, Scotland officially ceased to be a country and became 'that part of the United Kingdom, North Britain.' Scotsmen officially ceased to be Scots, and became Britons – presumably North Britons. England similarly lost identity – impatiently, on a scrap of paper. But everyone knew, both at home and abroad, that what really had happened was the final subjuga- tion of the Scots by the English, and the absorption of the northern people into the polity and name of the southern.

There was a smouldering fire of resistance: it sprang to flame twice in the course of the first half-century. In 1715 the Earl of Mar raised the standard for the exiled Jacobite King. He received a support entirely unwarranted by either his own person or that of the puppet monarch whose cause he championed. At the strange, drawn battle of Sheriffmuir the Jacobite rebellion was not so much suppressed as suddenly bored. It was as though its supporters were overtaken by a desire to yawn at the whole affair. They melted from the field, not to assemble, they or their sons, for another thirty years.

This was with the landing of Prince Charles Edward in the Highlands in 1745. Scotland – Scotland of the Highlands, great sections of Scotland of the Lowlands – took him to her heart. The clans rose in his support, not unwillingly following the call of their chiefs. Here was relief from that crushing sense of inferiority that had pressed on the nation since the first day of the Union: here was one who promised to restore the Ancient Times – the time of meal and milk and plenty of the Fifth James; here was one who promised Scotland her nationhood again. In after years it became the fashion to pretend that the vast mass of the Scots people were indifferent to, or hostile to, this last adventure of the Stewarts. But there was no Scotsman worthy of the name who was not, at least at first, an enthusiast and a partisan.

Charles marched from victory to victory: presently he was marching across the Borders with an ill-equipped army of High- landers and Lowland levies, seeking the support promised him by the English Jacobites. He sought it in vain. To the English Jacobite, to all the English, it was plain that here was no exiled English king come to reclaim his throne: here was something long familiar in wars with the northern enemy – a Scots army on a raid. Charles turned back at Derby, and, turning, lost the campaign, lost the last chance to restore the ancient nationhood of Scotland, lost (which was of no importance) himself.

His final defeat at Culloden inaugurated the ruthless extirpation of the clan system in the Highlands, the extirpation of almost a whole people. Sheep-farming came to the Highlands, depopulating its glens, just as the Industrial Revolution was coming to the Lowlands, enriching the new plutocracy and brutalizing the ancient plebs. Glasgow and Greenock were coming into being as the last embers of the old Scots culture flickered and fuffed and went out.

There followed that century and a half which leads us to the present day, a century through which we hear the wail of children in unending factories and in night-time slums, the rantings of place-seeking politicians, the odd chirping and cackling of the bastardized Scots romantic schools in music and literature. It is a hundred and fifty years of unloveliness and pridelessness, of growing wealth and growing impoverishment, of Scotland sharing in the rise and final torturing maladjustments of that economic system which holds all the modern world in thrall. It was a hundred and fifty years in which the ancient Pictish spirit remembered only at dim intervals, as in a nightmare, the cry of the wind in the hair of freemen in that ancient life of the Golden Age, the play of the same wind in the banners of Wallace when he marshalled his schiltrouns at Falkirk.

Representative Scots (I)
The Wrecker: James Ramsay Macdonald

Language, that 'perfected crying of apes and dogs' at which Anatole France professed a whimsical astonishment in its ability to debate the profoundities of metaphysics, has never been merely a technique of expression for Mr MacDonald. Very early he was snared in the ancient debate between Nominalist and Realist and very early (albeit unconscious of the fact) took sides in that ancient argument. He has never succeeded in penetrating behind words to thought: there is, indeed, no evidence that he ever attempted this awesome feat. Even in elementary manipulation of English one is conscious of a curious phenomenon: he is a clever, if rather unintelligent child, engaged in lifting sentences piecemeal from some super-abacus frame and arranging them in a genteel pattern. He is not engaged in displaying either James Ramsay MacDonald or his reactions of awe or hate or wonder or love towards that bright glimmer between the shades of sleep that we call the universe. He is merely engaged in genuflection at the shrine of Words:

'Away to the north, across the Firth, rose the pale blue hills of Sutherland and Ross: to the south lay the fertile farms of Morayshire sloping up through green wood and purple moorland into the blue tops of the Grampians, with the ruined Palace of Spynie in the mid-distance; to the east swept the sea, bordered by a wide stretch of yellow sand bending away into the horizon, with hills in the background, the whole stretching out in peaceful beauty which has won for it the name of the "Bay of Naples". . . .'

Note both the cleverness and the rigid adjectival conventionality: pale blue hills and fertile farms and peaceful beauty. It is the kind of thing that the dux in a little Scots school pens while the

Dominie beams upon him (I know, having been such a dux myself, companioned by such a Dominie). It is pre-adolescent, it tells one nothing about either Mr MacDonald's countryside or about his feelings towards it. It is the kind of guidebook chatter which raises your ire against an unknown (and probably inoffensive) landscape.

So with that philosophy of Socialism which Mr MacDonald was wont to exfoliate in the days before, glancing downwards and backwards, he caught sight of the seemly shape his calves occupied inside the silk stockings of Court dress. Perhaps this Socialism had once a logic, as certainly it had once a fine, if anæmic, sincerity, a passionate pity if also an unimpassioned patience. In the mazes of Mr MacDonald's vocabulary it behaves like a calf in an amateurish slaughter-shed, dodging with frightened moos the impact of innumerable padded bludgeons:

'Biologically "the negation of the existing state of things," its "inevitable breaking up," its "momentary existence" is impossible. Here we find, as we find everywhere in the Marxian method, a lack of real guarantee (although there are many verbal guarantees) that change is progress. The biological view emphasizes the possibilities of existing society as the mother of future societies, and regards idea and circumstance as the pair from which the new societies are to spring. It gives not only an explanation of the existing state of things, but of its giving birth to a future state of things. It also views every form of existence on its actual process of movement and therefore on its perishing – very different from perishable – side. It lays the very slightest emphasis on its "critical and revolutionary side", because it is mainly constructive and the idea of "clearing before building" is alien to its nature.'

This is a waste of wind and water, a seeping marshland under a fog. Note the power of the word 'biological' in the mind of Mr MacDonald. It means one of a dozen things, and means none of them for long. Firstly, it is pure Darwinism in operation. Then it is Weismannism. Then (for all we know to the contrary) it is the epitome of the benign convolutings of Tantric Buddhism. We catch a faint glimpse through yellow fogs of verbosity of an idea that the great lizards of the Mezozoic suffered no deep or terrible calamity with the coming of the ice-caps. Did the stegosaurus

freeze in his swamps and pass from the world for ever? Not at all.
The stegosaurus looked about him and said: 'The cold comes on
apace. I must discard my scales and grow me some hair.' And this
the good stegosaurus did, mislaying scales, claws, reptilian intes-
tines and reptilian nature, and was presently a mammoth.

This – if ever he has possessed a view, not merely a vocabulary –
is Mr MacDonald's view of the processes of biological evolution.
Cassell's Popular Educator, he tells with pride, was 'his only
university.' We may well believe the truth of this statement. That
the great lords of the Mezozoic age did indeed die away completely
and catastrophically, leaving to rise to greatness in the alien
mammalian world their lesser and harried kin, not their own
direct evolving descendants, is an elementary scrap of knowledge
in which the good Cassell had perhaps no space to specialize. Yet
lack of that knowledge has conditioned the being of what purports
to be a 'scientific Socialism' – the creed which was presently foisted
upon the British Labour Party, the creed which presently wrecked
that party completely and disastrously.

In ascribing to Mr MacDonald responsibility for bringing about
(soulfully, with a radio-wide slurring of consonants) that wreckage, one is, of course, personifying many tendencies and many
obscure gospels in the movement itself. Yet this hazy inability to
grasp at the flinty actualities of existence, personal or universal, is
in so many ways characteristically Scots that to Mr MacDonald
more than to any other may be ascribed the major share in this
notable achievement. He is as representationally Scots in his
approach to politics as the late Sir James Arthur Thomson was
in his approach to biology, as Sir Arthur Keith is in his approach to
ethnology. They are as three investigators commissioned to three
minute and elaborate experiments in the weighing and sifting of
chemical constituents: and they approach their tasks uniquely clad
in boxing-gloves and blinkers.

In the case of Mr MacDonald, at least, it is both farcical and
tragic to note how mch his inability to penetrate below words is
caused by the fact that the shape and setting of the words are
racially unfamiliar to him. English remains for him a foreign
language: its terms and expressions, its unique twists of technique,

he has followed and charted laboriously, competently, and unintelligently. Yet, mazed in these pursuits, he has never learned to think like an Englishman, he has never comprehended what Englishmen thought, he has never comprehended essential meanings in English vocabularies or English minds. As a result, he has foisted antique Scotticisms upon quite alien essentials, misapprehended the meaning, origin and intention of a great social movement, and (in ultimate prideful pose) stood aside to watch that movement murdered. . . .

He is supposed to have Norse blood in his veins. It is extremely likely. One of his biographers, a babbling lady greatly given to clothing her expressions in the raggedest of verbal reach-me-downs, tells us that 'his homeland is Morayshire, and Morayshire, north and east of the Grampians, breeds a race in which mingle the blood of the Highlanders and that of the Norse rovers from across the sea.' His grandmother, by whom he was brought up, 'had seen better days, and, even in the poorest circumstances, retained the demeanour of a gentlewoman, a natural grace and dignity of manner.' Oh God, oh Lossiemouth! 'There he made the acquaintance of some of the remarkable men of the country through Samuel Smiles' "Life of a Scottish Naturalist," Thomas Edwards of Banff, "Thomas Dick, the Thurso Baker" – geologist. Above all, Hugh Miller influenced him then. Hugh Miller's "Schools and Schoolmasters" was among the first books he bought. The watchmaker also lent him Scott and Dickens.'

He appears to have flourished greatly in the sipping of this pale scum from the surface of English letters. Young, handsome, genteel, he set out for London.

London for a while was unkind. It employed him as an invoice clerk in a City warehouse at a salary of 12/6 a week. We are assured that this was the foundation of his Socialism and that he never forgot those terrible days. The 1931 cuts in the pay of junior civil servants – cuts in many a case reducing purchasing power to a lower level than 12/6 a week – were authorized during a period of temporary amnesia.

It was 1888. Presently he became secretary to a Liberal Parliamentary candidate; presently he had joined the Social Democratic

Federation. But the Federation had never heard of Samuel Smiles or the dignity of labour or the necessity (they stared, astounded Cockneys) for 'independent *thote.*' Soon their soullessness had vexed the young Mr MacDonald from the ranks. He joined the Fabians, and, about the same time, obtained a footing in journalism.

Meanwhile, Labour representation in the Liberal Party was moulting forth its discontents. Keir Hardie had arisen as the apostle of Independent Labour. The young MacDonald watched this development carefully. At the Bradford Conference of 1893 Keir Hardie was instrumental in founding the Independent Labour Party. A cautious year afterwards Mr MacDonald adhered to the new party.

It was the strangest of parties. Disgruntled Liberal intellectuals with Parliamentary leanings supported it; intelligent workmen supported it; sentimental anarchists supported it. It had all kinds of philosophies, all kinds of codes of action. Round the problems of the class war it revolved like a monkey in a cage, distrustful of the tailnipping propensities of the central axle. In the election of 1895 it put forward twenty-eight candidates. Young Ramsay MacDonald stood for Southampton and was rejected with great unanimity, despite a voice already highly trained in the enunciation, terrifyingly, of those platitudinous nebulosities before which the simple Keir Hardie bowed his head, acknowledging MacDonald Labour's 'greatest intellectual asset.'

For a moment we may let temptation have its way, and turn to the lady biographer for a gem-cut paragraph. She is describing MacDonald of the Southampton election:

'If he appeared a knight in armour, he was hardly, for all his charm and intermittent humour, the glow of his vitality, the Merciful Knight. But at the right hour he met the right woman. A hand was laid upon him that softened the rigidity, mellowed and sweetened the vital strength.'

Predestined the hero of a novelette, Providence had not bungled in her choice. He travelled; he wrote disapprovingly of the un-statesmanlike Boer War; and he had a weekend cottage at Chesham Bois. He was shedding the rougher cut lines of his Scottishness, though the unique accent remained undiluted. Cultured, curving of moustache, he looks out from the photographs of those days. The conviction of continuity of culture became fixed in his mind – the mind which could lump 'Cromwell, Wilton, Hampden, Penn, Burke' as 'the best in the life of England'!

In 1900 the Labour Representation Committee came into being – the embryo Labour Party which returned two men to Parliament in the General Election of that year. MacDonald was elected secretary of the new organization, and worked with a fine assiduity in building it up. In the next election – that of 1906 – he had his reward in two fashions – he himself was returned to Parliament by Leicester and twenty-eight other members of the Labour Party were returned as well. Mr MacDonald became a skilled and outstanding Parliamentatrian; more important, he became the chief theoretician of the Labour Party – of that group of men which claimed, and with some justice, to represent the true commons of Great Britain, the lowly, the oppressed, the Cheated of the Sunlight, the bitter relics of the savagery of the Industrial Revolution. He organized publishing ventures, issues of series of Socialist books and tracts; he engaged and won the attention of a vast audience beyond his immediate ken.

Three quotations from his published works:

'Socialism is no class movement. Socialism is a movement of opinion, not an organization of status. It is not the rule of the working class; it is the organization of the community.'

Surely it was very plain. The stegosaurus was on the move, shedding its vertebrate spikes, abandoning its carnivorous diet, and realizing, appalled, that hitherto its constituent cells had been quite unorganized.

'History is a progression of social stages which have preceded and succeeded each other like the unfolding of life from the amœba to the mammal, or from the bud to the fruit. To-day we are in the economic stage. Yesterday we were in the political stage. To-morrow we shall be in the moral stage.'

It was all so plain. Peace to the Abbé Mendel and his discoveries of violent revolution, from stage to stage, within the sleek skin of evolution. To-day was the economic stage: our fathers lived quite without economic organization, subsisting on sea-kale and mush-rooms. Despite this, they engaged in politics – an abandoned pursuit we have quite outgrown. To-morrow our children will inherit the moral stage – both we and our fathers being entirely without morals. . . . And the day after to-morrow the world would enter on a millenial dotage.

'Intelligence and morality indicate the goal by which the struggle to escape the existing purgatory is guided. Human evolution is a stretching out, not a being pushed forward.'

The much-tried stegosaurus, properly coaxed, would set about elongating its spine . . .

To describe the opinions in such quotations as sub-human maunderings may be natural: it is also profoundly unjust. The Lossiemouth dux was writing good essays: he could, it seems, have written them almost in his sleep, and then stood by with a solemn smirk on his face while the Dominie read them. The Dominie was the British Labour Movement; and it put down each essay and gazed at the writer with a fresh upstirring from the wells of awe . . .

Nevertheless, he was no more than epitome of the movement itself. From 1906 until 1914 there were strikes and disputes and wage-cuts: there were folk who starved to death, folk who lived mean and desperate lives, phthisitic children who gasped out their last breaths in the slums of the Duke of Westminster – but the great trade unions were powerful and comparatively rich. Conditions pressed not too bitterly on the great mass of labouring men and women. There was no direct and brutal tyranny, and this philo-sophy of slow and gradual and easy change, when no blood would be shed and little exertion would be required and the repentant lion would turn to a lamb, suited admirably the temper of the padded times. In Germany, the other country with a great and well-organized labour movement, Marxism, though not definitely repudiated, was watered down to innocuousness, the Day of Change remotely postponed to the era of Germany's grandchildren – those children who have now inherited Hitler.

Then the War came.

The Labour International fell (as Mr MacDonald no doubt said) like a house of cards. Labour leaders lined up in platoons before the

War Ministries of their various countries – not to protest against war, not to threaten sabotage, not to proclaim the General Strike: but to clamour for salaried positions. That unique internationalist, Mr H.+hG. Wells, erupted like an urgent geyser – 'every sword drawn against Germany is a sword drawn for peace.' (Stout, chubby elderly men in comfortable beds could hardly sleep o' nights for dreaming of the gleaming swords.) Mr Arthur Henderson became a Cabinet Minister. Miss Marie Corelli wrote a patriotic pamphlet of great richness and ferocity, *What can we do for England?*, and later was fined for hoarding sugar.

The way was clear for Mr Ramsay MacDonald. He was offered a place in the Cabinet by a muddled Government anxious to conciliate this dangerous Parliamentarian. But the Government did not realize that, Parliamentarian or no Parliamentarian, this Scots Labour Leader, predestined the hero of a novelette, could no more break through the Author's plot than one of his favourite amœba could escape its jelly-film. He refused the offer, proclaimed his opposition to the War, and went into the wilderness, dark, tremendous, and Luciferian.

He was to acquire great kudos with this action. His sincerity in opposing the War is undoubted; his sincerity from those early days in the genteel poverty of Lossiemouth to these modern days as an animated exhibit at the Geological Museum is undoubted. But there can be little doubt that, like Lucifer, he gathered a unique satisfaction from his position – the dauntless tribune (as a Victorian 'historical' novelist would have seen him, in genteel toga and side-whiskers) defying the tyrannical Senate and the brutalized plebs. And there can be as little doubt that (as ever) he quite failed to penetrate behind words to that vile reality that the War was. Addressing a conference in 1918 he spoke of the 'hot and bloody faces on the Somme, only fanned in death by the wings of the angel.' That tumult of fear and filth to Mr MacDonald was no more than excuse for manipulation of the shoddy platitudes of minor poetasters.

In 1917 came the two Russian Revolutions: the first a proper and praiseworthy revolution, the stegosaurus paring its claws and going out to grass; the second – Mr MacDonald looked on the second with an astounded, wurring disapproval. It was a quite different beast, not the old, friendly dinosaur at all – an aggressive, alien, froward beast, biologically unsound. In Great Britain a certain amount of sympathy was manifested for the brute by the Labour Movement. This Mr MacDonald set himself to combat. By 1918, when Leicester refused to re-elect him to Parliament, the battle between Reform and Revolution in the Independent Labour Party was in full swing. By 1920 the revolutionaries had suffered a severe defeat and Mr MacDonald, still in the wilderness, was building up afresh his war-shattered gospel of 'evolutionary Socialism.'

'The patriotism which expresses a share in common life felt and valued is of a totally different quality from that which expresses a share in common power. The latter is the patriotism that "is not enough," that issues is no fine national spirit, and no sane political judgment. It is a blinding pride, not an enlightening dignity. Therefore political education should begin by the cultivation of the tradition of the locality, and democratic government should be founded on the self-government of the local community. "My fathers" graves are there.'

What appeal had Lenin and the sovietism of the Third International compared with this clarion call to upbuild Socialism on the Parish Council heroisms of our fathers – our non-moral, non-economic, but bitterly political fathers?

'In ten years the work of the Bolshevist Government, freed from outside attacks and commanding the necessities of life, will bring Russia to where (and no further) five years of Labour Government in this country, backed by public opinion, would bring us; two years of Bolshevism in this country would bring us where Russia was a dozen years before the Revolution.'

That experiment in Labour Government was unafar. In the 1923 General Election, the Conservatives, though numerically superior to either Labour or Liberal representation, found themselves unable to secure Liberal support. Mr Ramsay MacDonald was summoned to Buckingham Palace; he emerged from it the first Labour Premier. Labour burst into loud pæans.

They were mistimed. Earnest colliers poring over their *Daily Herald* learned astounded of the inclusion of the good and Con-

servative Lord Chelmsford in the Cabinet. There were other as
astonishing personalities. In the Labour Speech from the Throne, a
vague Niagara of bubbling sonorosities, nothing of any moment
was promised. This was but just anticipation. Nothing was done.
The Merciful Knight engaged in nine months' elaborate skirmish-
ing with the Liberals – the radical, undignified, uneasy Liberals
pressing him forward to all kinds and manners of dangerous
experiments with the economic structure of our island. Mr
MacDonald fought them back at every point: he would consent
to the clipping of not a single claw on the stegosaurus' hooves.
Dazed Conservatives realized that here was the most Conservative
Government since Lord Salisbury's; obstreperous Mesopotamians
were bombed with great thoroughness by orders of the Under-
Secretary for Air, the personal friend of the Premier, the pacifistic
Mr Leach. The communists – much the same collection of
irreligious, vigorous blasphemous Cockneys as Mr MacDonald
had turned from in a frayed disgust in the eighteen-nineties –
began to prove quite as obstreperous as the Mesopotamians.
Unfortunately, they could not be bombed. What change was there
in the stegosaurus, they cried – except that it ate more flesh?
Labour cursed them gruffly, turning trusting eyes to its Premier.
He would tell them how the beast was really changing – he knew
about it all, *he* knew, He knew!

Unfortunately, he was rarely visible on the English horizon. He
fled from conference to conference across the European scene; at
rare intervals, returning to Parliament, he uttered profound ap-
peals for national unity to save the peace of the world – a world
injected with a trilling diapason of consonants and false vowels. In
Court dress he displayed an exceptional leg. More and more it was
becoming evident to him how necessary was the slow and gradual
evolution of human society – retaining dignity, tradition, culture.

But evil men conspired. The communists had taken to appealing
directly to soldiers on the subject of the stegosaurus. One of their
propagandists was arrested. Labour – uneasy, moody Labour –
rumbled in protest and Mr MacDonald, bestirred from his sane
and logical immersements in conference-creation, was reminded
that he was a Labour leader. He was prevailed on to have Campbell

released. Thereat the Liberals, soured of his tactics, voted out the first Labour Government.

In the succeeding election the stegosaurus lost all sense of honour – a frightened and unsavoury beast. It produced the famous Red Letter, pleasingly forged in Berlin, and proving that Mr MacDonald took his orders from Moscow. For a moment it seems that Mr MacDonald caught a glimpse of the reality of the beast he had played with and patted so long – the sterile and unlovely beast he had assured the Labour Movement was really a gentle female beast about to give birth to an unique offspring. Then the smashing defeat at the polls came and he abandoned beast and plebs for the wilderness of opposition. And never, during that period of opposition, did he look again on the horror of the dinosaur's countenance. It was merely a dream he had dreamt: the beast was a comely, if occasionally mistaken beast; and he would soon invite him to ride its back again.

Meanwhile wages sank. The hours of the miners were threatened. Labour, long unused to any other general action than the Parliamentary, sprouted a dangerous revolutionism. It proclaimed the General Strike. For Nine Days that strike paralysed and exhilarated Great Britain. There was a blowing up of a sudden comradeship, a sudden and astoundingly Marxian class-consciousness. The Government, appalled, determined to arrest the strike leaders. The strike leaders, appalled, determined to save their skins. They abandoned the strike and abandoned thousands of those they had called out to victimization and intimidation. Mr MacDonald and Mr Baldwin exchanged courtesies and congratulations in the House of Commons, and sent out bulletins to the effect that the dinosaur was itself again.

Labour turned to Parliamentary organization. As the year of the next General Election drew near it flung all its strength into securing a heavy Parliamentary representation – to secure that way to reform and change which Mr Ramsay MacDonald and his colleagues had preached it since the days of the L.R.C. Its hopes were not disappointed. It returned over two hundred and fifty members to Parliament; it returned Mr MacDonald to the premiership; in conjunction with the small and radical group of

Liberal M.P.'s he was free to display to the doubting Stalin – the
abandoned, uncultured, unloquacious Stalin – how a Labour
Government worked swift and efficient change the while a Godless
Bolshevist one did no more than stumble doggedly forward in the
dark.

The stegosaurus' health was far from sound: it complained of
internal pains. Breathlessly each morning the Labour voter opened
his *Daily Herald* to read the news of the beast's safe delivery in the
skilful hands of its midwife, Ramsay MacDonald. But still the news
delayed. Mr MacDonald instead began to issue bulletins – quite
unexpected bulletins – about the beast. Copulation and pregnancy
were indecencies foreign to the dinosaur's nature. It was a cultured, amiable and happy beast – but for those pains. It was the
duty of all men and women of good will to pool their resources to
save the health of this happy, innocent animal. . . . Between whiles,
as in 1924, he sped rapidly about the European scene. He crossed
to America and held a conference with President Hoover. Still the
dinosaur languished. Mr MacDonald laid before his colleagues of
the Labour Cabinet his plan to reduce unemployed relief to
provide fresh rations for the monster's table. He did this with
wrung withers, but the bankers, the dinosaur's physicians, saw no
other way to save its life . . . .

One abandons dinosaur (a very real beast) and simile with
regret. It may be admitted that MacDonald's colleagues, refusing to
agree with this final onslaught on the standard of that dumb,
patient puzzled horde that had elevated them to Parliamentary
position, abandoned the beast with regret as well, in spite of the
feeble flare of revolutionary zeal they displayed when their late
leader appeared – still Premier – at the head of his 'National
Government,' backed by row on row of that enemy against which
so long and so often he had swung his padded mace. But outside
the House of Commons there arose a slow creaking and cracking
and spiralling of dust – it was the Labour Movement crumbling to
dust. At the 1931 General Election, leading the combined Liberals
and Conservatives, Mr Ramsay MacDonald completed his task of
wreckage. On the morning of October the 29th, 1931, the country
awoke to find that the pacifist of the War-time years had for once

abandoned the padded bludgeon and smashed to atoms with a merciless blow that party and group which had raised him to power, which had followed him and his unique philosophy for a long twenty-five years.

The Labour Movement may win again to shadowy triumphs, but the spirit, the faith and the hope have gone from it. Time, impatient, has turned its back on new re-echoings of those thunderous platitudes which once seemed to ring prophet-inspired from a MacDonald platform. New armies are rising, brutal and quick, determined, desperate, mutually destructive, communist and fascist. Mr Ramsay MacDonald has completed to perfection the task set him by the play of historic movements and blind economic forces. He still hastens from conference to conference, solemn and creased; his voice still rings out those rolling periods; he poses, one foot on the step of his aeroplane, for the pressing photographer–

But there is a greyness and chill come upon it all. One realizes that this is hardly a living human being at all, but a hollow simulacrum. One realizes with a start of enlightenment that indeed there was never life here at all, it was a fantasy, a play of the jaded Victorian sense, a materialization of some hazy lady novelist's dreams after reading Samuel Smiles as a bed book. Even so, there are moments when the presence touches raw nerves: this ghost delays so long on the boards of history, unhumorous, unappeasable. There is hardly a Scotsman alive who does not feel a shudder of amused shame as the rolling turgid voice, this evening or that, pours suddenly from his radio. We have, we Scots, (all of us) too much of his quality in our hearts and souls.

Glasgow

Glasgow is one of the few places in Scotland which defy personification. To image Edinburgh as a disappointed spinster, with a
hare-lip and inhibitions, is at least to approximate as closely to the
truth as to image the Prime Mover as a Levantine Semite. So with
Dundee, a frowsy fisher-wife addicted to gin and infanticide,
Aberdeen a thin-lipped peasant-woman who has borne eleven
and buried nine. But no Scottish image of personification may
display, even distortedly, the essential Glasgow. One might go
further afield, to the tortured imaginings of the Asiatic mind, to
find her likeness – many-armed Siva with the waistlet of skulls, or
Xipe of Ancient America, whose priest skinned the victim alive,
and then clad himself in the victim's skin. . . . But one doubts
anthropomorphic representation at all. The monster of Loch Ness
is probably the lost soul of Glasgow, in scales and horns, disporting
itself in the Highlands after evacuating finally and completely its
mother-corpse.

One cannot blame it. My distant cousin, Mr Leslie Mitchell,
once described Glasgow in one of his novels as 'the vomit of a
cataleptic commercialism.' But it is more than that. It may be a
corpse, but the maggot-swarm upon it is very fiercely alive. One
cannot watch and hear the long beat of traffic down Sauchiehall, or
see its eddy and spume where St Vincent Street and Renfield Street
cross, without realizing what excellent grounds the old-fashioned
anthropologist appeared to have for believing that man was by
nature a brutish savage, a herd-beast delighting in vocal discor-
dance and orgiastic aural abandon.

Loch Lomond lies quite near to Glasgow. Nice Glaswegians
motor out there and admire the scenery and calculate its horse-
power and drink whisky and chaff one another on genteelly

Anglicized Glaswegianisms. After a hasty look at Glasgow the investigator would do well to disguise himself as one of like kind, drive down to Loch Lomondside and stare across its waters at the sailing clouds that crown the Ben, at the flooding of colours changing and darkling and miraculously lighting up and down those misty slopes, where night comes over long mountain leagues that know only the paddings of the shy, stray hare, the whirr and cry of the startled pheasant, silences so deep you can hear the moon come up, mornings so greyly coloured they seem stolen from Norse myth. This is the proper land and stance from which to look at Glasgow, to divest oneself of horror or shame or admiration or – very real – fear, and ask: Why? Why did men ever allow themselves to become enslaved to a thing so obscene and so foul when there was *this* awaiting them here – hills and the splendours of freedom and silence, the clean splendours of hunger and woe and dread in the winds and rains and famine-times of the earth, hunting and love and the call of the moon? Nothing endured by the primitives who once roamed those hills – nothing of woe or terror – approximated in degree or kind to that life that festers in the courts and wynds and alleys of Camlachie, Govan, the Gorbals.

In Glasgow there are over a hundred and fifty thousand human beings living in such conditions as the most bitterly pressed primitive in Tierra del Fuego never visioned. They live five or six to the single room. . . . And at this point, sitting and staring at Ben Lomond, it requires a vivid mental jerk to realize the quality of that room. It is not a room in a large and airy building; it is not a single-roomed hut on the verge of a hill; it is not a cave driven into free rock, in the sound of the sea-birds, as that old Azilian cave in Argyll: it is a room that is part of some great sloven of tenement – the tenement itself in a line or a grouping with hundreds of its fellows, its windows grimed with the unceasing wash and drift of coal-dust, its stairs narrow and befouled and steep, its evening breath like that which might issue from the mouth of a lung-diseased beast. The hundred and fifty thousand eat and sleep and copulate and conceive and crawl into childhood in those waste jungles of stench and disease and hopelessness, sub-humans as definitely as the Morlocks of Wells

– and without even the consolation of feeding on their oppres-
sors' flesh.

A hundred and fifty thousand . . . and all very like you or me or
my investigator sitting appalled on the banks of Loch Lomond
(where he and his true love will never meet again). And they live on
food of the quality of offal, ill-cooked, ill-eaten with speedily-
diseased teeth for the tending of which they can afford no fees; they
work – if they have work – in factories or foundries or the roaring
reek of the Docks toilsome and dreary and unimaginative hours –
hour on hour, day on day, frittering away the tissues of their bodies
and the spirit-stuff of their souls; they are workless – great
numbers of them – doomed to long days of staring vacuity, of
shoelessness, of shivering hidings in this and that mean runway
when the landlords' agents come, of mean and desperate beggings
at Labour Exchanges and Public Assistance Committees; their
voices are the voices of men and women robbed of manhood
and womanhood . . .

The investigator on Loch Lomondside shudders and turns to
culture for comfort. He is, of course, a subscriber to *The Modern
Scot*, where culture at three removes – castrated, disembowelled,
and genteelly vulgarized – is served afresh each season; and has
brought his copy with him. Mr. Adam Kennedy is serializing a
novel, *The Mourners*, his technique a genteel objectivity. And one
of his characters has stopped in Glasgow's Kelvingrove, and is
savouring its essence:

'John's eyes savoured the spaciousness of the crescent, the
formal curve of the unbroken line of house façades, the regimenta-
tion of the rows of chimney-pots, the full-length windows, the
unnecessarily broad front steps, the feudal basements – savoured
all these in the shimmering heat of the day just as his nose had
savoured the morning freshness. It was as good for him to walk
round these old terraces as to visit a cathedral. He could imagine
now and then that he had evoked for himself something of the
atmosphere of the grand days of these streets. The world was surer
of itself then, sure of the ultimate perfectability of man, sure of the
ultimate mastery over the forces that surrounded him. And if Atlas
then no longer had the world firm on his shoulder, the world for all

that rested on the same basis of the thus-and-thusness of things. With such a basis you could have that sureness of yourself to do things largely as had been done before. But the modern mind was no longer sure of itself even in a four-roomed bungalow. Its pride was the splitting of its personality into broods of impish devils that spent their time spying one on the other. It could never get properly outside itself, could never achieve the objectivity that was capable of such grandly deliberate planning as in these streets.'

Glasgow speaks. The hundred and fifty thousand are answered. Glasgow has spoken.

This, indeed, is its attitude, not merely the pale whey of intellectualism peculiar to *The Modern Scot*. The bourgeois Glaswegian cultivates æsthetic objectivity as happier men cultivate beards or gardens. Pleasant folk of Kelvingrove point out that those hundred and fifty thousand – how well off they are! Free education, low rents, no rates, State relief – half of them, in fact, State pensioners. Besides, they enjoy life as they are – damn them, or they ought to. Always raising riots about their conditions. Not that they raise the riots themselves – it's the work of the communists – paid agitators from Moscow. But they've long since lost all hold. Or they ought to have –

In those days of Nationalism, of Douglasism, (that ingenious scheme for childbirth without pain and – even more intriguing – without a child), of Socialism, of Fascism, Glasgow, as no other place, moves me to a statement of faith. I have amused myself with many political creeds – the more egregrious the creed the better. I like the thought of a Scots Republic with Scots Border Guards in saffron kilts – the thought of those kilts can awake me to joy in the middle of the night. I like the thought of Miss Wendy Wood leading a Scots Expeditionary Force down to Westminster to reclaim the Scone Stone: I would certainly march with that expedition myself in spite of the risk of dying of laughter by the way. I like the thought of a Scots Catholic kingdom with Mr Compton Mackenzie Prime Minister to some disinterred Jacobite royalty, and all the Scots intellectuals settled out on the land on thirty-acre crofts, or sent to recolonize St. Kilda for the good of their souls and the nation (except the hundreds streaming over the

Border in panic flight at sight of this Scotland of their dreams). I like the thought of the ancient Scots aristocracy revived and set in order by Mr George Blake, that ephor of the people: Mr Blake vetoing the Duke of Montrose is one of my dearest visions. I like the thoughts of the Scottish Fascists evicting all those of Irish blood from Scotland, and so leaving Albyn entirely deserted but for some half-dozen pro-Irish Picts like myself. I like the thought of a Scottish Socialist Republic under Mr Maxton – preferably at war with royalist England, and Mr Maxton summoning the Russian Red Army to his aid (the Red Army digging a secret tunnel from Archangel to Aberdeen). And I like the thought of Mr R. M. Black and his mysterious Free Scots, that modern Mafia, assassinating the Bankers (which is what bankers are for). . . .

But I cannot play with those fantasies when I think of the hundred and fifty thousand in Glasgow. They are a something that stills the parlour chatter. I find I am by way of being an intellectual myself. I meet and talk with many people whose interests are art and letters and music, enthusiasm for this and that aspect of craft and architecture, men and women who have very warm and sincere beliefs indeed regarding the ancient culture of Scotland, people to whom Glasgow is the Hunterian Museum with its fine array of Roman coins, or the Galleries with their equally fine array of pictures. 'Culture' is the motif-word of the conversation: ancient Scots culture, future Scots culture, culture ad lib. and ad nauseam. . . . The patter is as intimate on my tongue as on theirs. And relevant to the fate and being of those hundred and fifty thousand it is no more than the chatter and scratch of a band of apes, seated in a pit on a midden of corpses.

There is nothing in culture or art that is worth the life and elementary happiness of one of those thousands who rot in the Glasgow slums. There is nothing in science or religion. If it came (as it may come) to some fantastic choice between a free and independent Scotland, a centre of culture, a bright flame of artistic and scientific achievement, and providing elementary decencies of food and shelter to the submerged proletariat of Glasgow and Scotland, I at least would have no doubt as to which side of the battle I would range myself. For the cleansing of that horror, if cleanse it they could, I would welcome the English in suzerainty over Scotland till the end of time. I would welcome the end of Braid Scots and Gaelic, our culture, our history, our nationhood under the heels of a Chinese army of occupation if it could cleanse the Glasgow slums, give a surety of food and play – the elementary right of every human being – to those people of the abyss. . . .

I realize (seated on the plump modernity of *The Modern Scot* by the side of my investigator out on Loch Lomond-bank) how completely I am the complete Philistine. I have always liked the Philistines, a commendable and gracious and cleanly race. They built clean cities with wide, airy streets, they delighted in the singing of good, simple songs and hunting and lovemaking and the worshipping of relevant and comprehensible Gods. They were a light in the Ancient East and led simple and happy and carefree lives, with a splendour of trumpets now and again to stir them to amusing orgy. . . . And above, in the hills, in Jerusalem, dwelt the Israelites, unwashed and unashamed, horrified at the clean anarchy which is the essence of life, oppressed by grisly fears of life and death and time, suborning simple human pleasures in living into an insane debating on justice and right, the Good Life, the Soul of Man, artistic canon, the First Cause, National Ethos, the main-springs of conduct, æsthetic approach – and all the rest of the dirty little toys with which dirty little men in dirty little caves love to play, turning with a haughty shudder of repulsion from the cry of the wind and the beat of the sun on the hills outside. . . . One of the greatest tragedies of the ancient world was the killing of Goliath by David – a ghoul-haunted little village squirt who sneaked up and murdered the Philistine while the latter (with a good breakfast below his belt) was admiring the sunrise.

The non-Philistines never admire sunrises. They never admire good breakfasts. Their ideal is the half-starved at sunset, whose actions and appearances they can record with a proper æsthetic detachment. One of the best-loved pictures of an earlier generation of Glasgow intellectuals was Josef Israel's *Frugal Meal* in the Glasgow Galleries. Even yet the modern will halt you to admire the chiaroscuro, the fine shades and attitudes. But you realize he is a liar. He is merely an inhibited little sadist, and his concentrated essence of enjoyment is the hunger and dirt and hopelessness of the two figures in question. He calls this a 'robust acceptance of life.'

Sometime, it is true, the non-Philistine of past days had a qualm of regret, a notion, a thin pale abortion of an idea that life in simplicity was life in essence. So he painted a man or a woman, nude only in the less shameful portions of his or her anatomy (egregious bushes were called in to hide the genital shames) and called it not *Walking* or *Running* or *Staring* or *Sleeping* or *Lusting* (as it generally was) but *Light* or *Realization* or *The Choir* or what not. A Millais in the Glasgow Galleries is an excellent example, which neither you nor my investigator may miss. It is the non-Philistine's wistful idea of (in capitals) Life in Simplicity – a decent young childe in a breech-clout about to play hoop-la with a forked stick. But instead of labelling this truthfully and obviously *Portrait of Shy-Making Intellectual Playing at Boy Scouts* it is called (of course) *The Forerunner*.

The bourgeois returns at evening these days to Kelvingrove, to Woodsidehill, to Hillhead and Dowanhill with heavy and doubting steps. The shipyards are still, with rusting cranes and unbefouled waters nearby, in Springburn the empty factories increase and multiply, there are dead windows and barred factory-gates in Bridgeton and Mile End. Commercialism has returned to its own vomit too often and too long still to find sustenance therein. Determinedly in Glasgow (as elsewhere) they call this condition 'The Crisis', and, in the fashion of a Christian Scientist whose actual need is cascara, invoke Optimism for its cure. But here as nowhere else in the modern world of capitalism does the impartial investigator realize that the remedy lies neither in medicine nor massage, but in surgery. . . . The doctors (he hears) are gathered for the Saturday-Sunday diagnoses on Glasgow Green; and betakes himself there accordingly.

But there (as elsewhere) the physicians disagree – multitudes of physicians, surrounded by anxious groups of the ailing patient's dependents. A brief round of the various physicians convinces the investigator of one thing: the unpopularity of surgery. The single surgeon orating is, of course, the Communist. His gathering is small. A larger following attends Mr Guy Aldred, Non-Parliamentary Anarchocommunist, pledged to use neither knives not pills, but invocation of the Gospels according to St Bakunin. Orthodox Socialism, ruddy and plump, with the spoils from the latest Glasgow Corporation swindle in its pocket, the fee'd physician, popular and pawky, is fervent and optimistic. Pills? – Nonsense! Surgery? – Muscovite savagery! What is needed to remove the sprouting pustules from the fair face of commercialism is merely a light, non-greasy ointment (which will not stain the sheets). Near at hand stands the Fascist: the investigator, with a training which has hitherto led him to debar the Neanderthaler from the direct ancestral line of *Homo Sapiens*, stares at this ethnological note of interrogation. The Fascist diagnosis: Lack of blood. Remedy: Bleeding. A Nationalist holds forth near by. What the patient needs is not more food, fresh air, a decent room of his own and a decent soul of his own – No! What he needs is the air he ceased to breathe two hundred and fifty years ago – specially reclaimed and canned by the National Party of Scotland (and forwarded in plain vans.) . . . A Separatist casts scorn on the Nationalist's case. What the patient requires is: Separation. Separation from England, from English speech, English manners, English food, English clothes, English culinary and English common sense. Then he will recover.

It is coming on dark, as they say in the Scotland that is not Glasgow. And out of the Gorbals arises again that foul breath as of a dying beast.

You turn from Glasgow Green with a determination to inspect this Gorbals on your own. It is incredibly un-Scottish. It is lovably and abominably and delightfully and hideously un-Scottish. It is not even a Scottish slum. Stout men in beards and ringlets and unseemly attire lounge and strut with pointed shoes: Ruth and Naomi go by with downcast Eastern faces, the Lascar rubs shoulder with the Syrian, Harry Lauder is a Baal unkeened to the midnight stars. In the air the stench is of a different quality to Govan's or Camlachie's – a better quality. It is not filth and futility and boredom unrelieved. It is haunted by an ancient ghost of goodness and grossness, sun-warmed and ripened under alien suns. It is the most saving slum in Glasgow, and the most abandoned. Emerging from it, the investigator suddenly realizes why he sought it in such haste from Glasgow Green: it was in order that he might assure himself there were really and actually other races on the earth apart from the Scots!

So long I have wanted to write what I am about to write – but hitherto I have lacked the excuse. Glasgow provides it. . . . About Nationalism. About Small Nations. What a curse to the earth are small nations! Latvia, Lithuania, Poland, Finland, San Salvador, Luxembourg, Manchukuo, the Irish Free State. There are many more: there is an appalling number of disgusting little stretches of the globe claimed, occupied and infected by groupings of babbling little morons – babbling militant on the subjects (unendingly) of their *exclusive* cultures, their *exclusive* languages, their *national* souls, their *national* genius, their unique achievements in throat-cutting in this and that abominable little squabble in the past. Mangy little curs a-yap above their minute hoardings of shrivelled bones, they cease from their yelpings at the passers-by only in such intervals as they devote to civil-war flea-hunts. Of all the accursed progeny of World War, surely the worst was this dwarf mongrel-litter. The South Irish of the middle class were never pleasant persons: since they obtained their Free State the belch of their pride in the accents of their unhygienic patois has given the unfortunate Irish Channel the seeming of a cess-pool. Having blamed their misfortunes on England for centuries, they achieved independence and promptly found themselves incapable of securing that independence by the obvious and necessary operation – social revolution. Instead: revival of Gaelic, bewildering an unhappy world with uncouth spellings and titles and postage-stamps; revival of the blood feud; revival of the decayed literary cultus which (like most products of the Kelt) was an abomination even while actually alive and but poor manure when it died. . . . Or Finland – Com-munist-murdering Finland – ruled by German Generals and the Central European foundries, boasting to its ragged population the return of its ancient literary culture like a senile octogenarian boasting the coming of second childhood. . . . And we are bidden go and do likewise:

'For we are not opposed to English influence only at those points where it expresses itself in political domination and financial and economic over-control, but we are (or ought to be) opposed to English influence at all points. Not only must English governmental control be overthrown, but the English language must go, and English methods of education, English fashions in dress, English models in the arts, English ideals, everything English. Everything English must go.'

This is a Mr Ludovic Grant, writing in *The Free Man.* Note what the Scot is bidden to give up: the English language, that lovely and flexible instrument, so akin to the darker Braid Scots which has been the Scotsman's tool of thought for a thousand years. English methods of education: which are derived from Germano-French-Italian models. English fashions in dress: invented in Paris – London – Edinburgh – Timbuktu – Calcutta – Chichen-Itza – New York. English models in the arts: nude models as well, no doubt – Scots models in future must sprout three pairs of arms and a navel in the likeness of a lion rampant. English ideals: decency, freedom, justice, ideals innate in the mind of man, as common to the Bantu as to the Kentishman – those also he must relinquish. . . . It will profit Glasgow's hundred and fifty thousand slum-dwellers so much to know that they are being starved and brutalized by Labour Exchanges and Public Assistance Committees staffed exclusively by Gaelic-speaking, haggis-eating Scots in saffron kilts and tongued brogues, full of such typical Scottish ideals as those which kept men chained as slaves in the Fifeshire mines a century or so ago. . . .

Glasgow's salvation, Scotland's salvation, the world's salvation lies in neither nationalism nor internationalism, those twin halves of an idiot whole. It lies in ultimate cosmopolitanism, the earth the City of God, the Brahmaputra and Easter Island as free and familiar to the man from Govan as the Molendinar and Bute. A time will come when the self-wrought, prideful differentiations of Scotsman, Englishman, Frenchman, Spaniard will seem as ludicrous as the infantile squabblings of the Heptarchians. A time will come when nationalism, with other cultural aberrations, will have passed from the human spirit, when Man, again free and unchained, has all the earth for his footstool, sings his epics in a language moulded from the best on earth, draws his heroes, his sunrises, his valleys and his mountains from all the crinkles of our lovely planet. . . . And we are bidden to abandon this vision for the delights of an archaic ape-spite, a brosy barbarization!

I am a nationalist only in the sense that the same Heptarchian was a Wessexman or a Mercian or what not: temporarily, opportunistically. I think the Braid Scots may yet give lovely lights and shadows not only to English but to the perfected speech of Cosmopolitan Man: so I cultivate it, for lack of that perfect speech that is yet to be. I think there's the chance that Scotland, especially in its Glasgow, in its bitter straitening of the economic struggle, may win to a freedom preparatory to, and in alignment with, that cosmopolitan freedom, long before England: so, a cosmopolitan opportunist, I am some kind of Nationalist. But I'd rather, any day, be an expatriate writing novels in Persian about the Cape of Good Hope than a member of a homogeneous literary cultus (to quote again the cant phrase of the day) prosing eternally on one plane – the insanitary reactions to death of a Kelvingrove bourgeois, or the owlish gawk (it would speedily have that seeming) of Ben Lomond through its clouds, like a walrus through a fuff of whiskers.

For this Scottish Siva herself, brandishing her many arms of smoke against the coming of the darkness, it is pleasant to remember at least one incident. On a raining night six hundred and fifty years ago a small band of men, selfless and desperate and coolly-led, tramped through the wynds to the assault of the English-garrisoned Bell o' the Brae (which is now the steep upper part of High Street). It was a venture unsupported by priest or patrician, the intellectual or bourgeois of those days. It succeeded: and it lighted a flame of liberty throughout Scotland.

Some day the surgeon-leaders of the hundred and fifty thousand may take that tale of Bell o' the Brae for their text.

Literary Lights

One of the most praiseworthy – praiseworthy in its entertainment value – efforts of the critic has always been his attempt to levitate himself out of himself by the ingenuous method of hauling with great passion upon his own bootlaces. In the words of Mr Alan Porter 'The critic, before he sets down a word, must beat himself on the head and ask a hundred times, each time more bitterly and searchingly, "And is it true? Is it true?" He must analyse his judgment and make sure that it is nowhere stained or tinted with the blood of his heart. And he must search out a table of values from which he can be certain that he has left nothing unconsidered. If, after all these precautions and torments, he is unable to deliver a true judgment, then fate has been too strong for him; he was never meant to be a critic.'

The present writer was assuredly never meant to be a critic. He has attempted no feats of manipulative surgery upon either his personality or his judgment. He confesses with no shame that the dicta of criticism laid down by Mr Porter appear to him analogous to the chest-beating posturings of a righteous baboon prior to its robbing an orchard. Flippancy apart, the researches of Bekhterev and Pavlov should have disposed once and for all of such archaic beliefs as the possibility of inhibiting a reflex by incantation. Indeed, it did not require reflexological research (of which the average critic has never heard – or, if he has, imagines it has something to do with the torturing of dogs and Mr Bernard Shaw) to dispose of this nonsense regarding 'heart' and 'head.' To commit hari-kari may be an admirable and hygienic exercise, but is an operation seldom survived by even the remoter portions of the extra-intestinal anatomy.

Far more serious doubts assail the non-professional critic when he enters upon the study of such a subject as (reputed) Scots letters. If he enters this great library from the open air, not through an underground passage from the book-lined gloom of a study, the piles of stacked volumes are dismaying in their colour and size and plenitude. Only here and there does he recognize a name or a title; the books tower to dim ceilings, are piled in great strata, have the dust of the last few years yet gathered thickly enough upon them. How may he pass judgment? The books he has missed – the books he has never read! What relative importance have the few names and titles in his memory to the hidden values in this great library?

For, in the pressing multitudes of reputedly Scots books which pour from the presses, there may have been a new Melville, a new Typee, a Scots Joyce, a Scots Proust? Nothing impossible in any of those suppositions. The books may have appeared, it failed to be noticed, (as hundreds of good books have failed to be noted,) it was poorly advertised, had inadequate publicity, was overshadowed by the simultaneous publication of a great name – and moulders now its representative copies in two or three libraries while the remainder of the stock – not even 'remaindered' – has returned to the printer for repulping. There is nothing to say that this has not happened very often.

Even if the critic passes a judgment with some fair knowledge of the factors – how of the unpublished books? There may be manuscripts circulating the publishers' offices that sing a new, clear splendid note in letters – sing it so loudly that no publisher's reader can abide the beat of the music in his ears. . . . This is not only possible, but very probable. It was as true of the past as it is of the present, though both gods and machines were of a different order three hundred years ago. Yet even then it is possible that poets dwarfing Shakespeare remained unpublished and unplayed for lack of suitable influences, suitable patronage; and their manuscripts, with the wisdom and delight of the shining minds that begat them, have long mouldered to dust.

The new and unknown Scots writer facing the publishing, printing world has the usual chances and mischances to face in a greater measure than his English compeer. Firstly, in almost every case, he must seek publication in London. Scots publishers are surely amongst the sorriest thing that enter hell: their publicity methods are as antique as their format, their houses are generally staffed by those who in Bengali circles would write after their names, and as their chief qualification, 'failed B.A.' (or slightly worse, 'M.A. (St Andrews)'). He must consign his manuscript to alien publishers and the consideration of largely alien readers.

For, however the average Scots writer believes himself Anglicized, his reaction upon the minds of the intelligent English reader (especially of the professional reader) is curiously similar to that produced by the English poems of Dr Rabindranath Tagore. The prose – or verse – is impeccably correct, the vocabulary is rich and adequate, the English is severe, serene . . . But unfortunately it is not English. The English reader is haunted by a sense of something foreign stumbling and hesitating behind this smooth façade of adequate technique: it is as though the writer did not *write* himself, but *translated* himself.

Often the Scots writer is quite unaware of this essential foreignness in his work; more often, seeking an adequate word or phrase he hears an echo in an alien tongue that would adorn his meaning with a richness, a clarity and a conciseness impossible in orthodox English. That echo is from Braid Scots, from that variation of the Anglo-Saxon speech which was the tongue of the great Scots civilization, the tongue adopted by the basic Pictish strain in Scotland as its chief literary tool.

Further, it is still in most Scots communities, (in one or other Anglicized modification,) the speech of bed and board and street and plough, the speech of emotional ecstasy and emotional stress. But it is not genteel. It is to the bourgeois of Scotland coarse and low and common and loutish, a matter for laughter, well enough for hinds and the like, but for the genteel to be quoted in vocal inverted commas. It is a thing rigorously elided from their serious intercourse – not only with the English, but among themselves. It is seriously believed by such stratum of the Scots populace to be an inadequate and pitiful and blunted implement, so that Mr Eric Linklater delivers *ex cathedra* judgment upon it as 'inadequate to deal with the finer shades of emotion.'

But for the truly Scots writer it remains a real and haunting thing, even while he tries his best to forget its existence and to write as a good Englishman. In this lies his tragedy. He has to *learn* to write in English: he is like a Chinese scholar spending the best years of his life in the mystic mazes of the pictographs, and emerging so exhausted from the travail that originality of research or experiment with his new tool is denied him. Consequently, the free and anarchistic experimentations of the progressive members of a free and homogeneous literary cultus are denied him. Nearly every Scots writer of the past writing in orthodox English has been not only incurably second-rate, but incurably behind the times. The Scots discovery of photographic realism in novel-writing, for example – I refer to *Hatter's Castle*, not the very different *House with the Green Shutters* – post-dated the great French and English realists some thirty or forty years. But to the Scot Dr Cronin's work appeared a very new and terrifying and fascinating thing indeed; to the English public, astounded that anything faintly savouring of accuracy, photographic or otherwise, should come out of Scotland, it was equally amazing. At such rate of progress among the Anglo-Scots one may guess that in another fifty years or so a Scots Virginia Woolf will astound the Scottish scene, a Scots James Joyce electrify it. To expect contemporary experimentation from the Anglo-Scots themselves appears equivalent to expecting a Central African savage in possession of a Brimingham kite to prove capable of inventing a helicopter.

Consciousness of this inferiority of cultural position within the English tradition is a very definite thing among the younger generation of Anglo-Scots writers of to-day. Their most characteristic organ, *The Modern Scot*, is a constant reiteration of protest. Owned and edited by one of those genial Englishmen in search of a revolution who have added to the gaiety of nations from Ireland to Uganda, *The Modern Scot* has set itself, strictly within the English tradition, to out-English the English. As one who on a lonely road doth walk with fear and dread, very conscious of the frightful fiend who close behind doth tread, it marches always a full yard ahead of extremist English opinion – casting the while an anxious backward glance. It decries the children of 'naturalism' with a praiseworthy but unnatural passion, championing in their place, with a commendable care for pathology, the idiot offspring begat on the modern literary scene in such numbers from the incestuous unions of Strindberg and Dr. Freud. It is eclectic to quite an obscure degree, is incapable of an article that does not quote either Proust or Paul Einzig, and raises an approving voice in praise of the joyous, if infantile tauromachic obsessions of Mr Roy Campbell. Its motif-note, indeed, is literary Fascism – to the unimpassioned, if astounded, eye it would seem as if all the Fascist undergraduates of Scotland these days were hastening, in pimples and a passion for sophistication, to relieve themselves of a diarrhoetic Johnsonese in the appropriate privy of *The Modern Scot*. The entire being of the periodical, however, is rather an exhibitory, or sanitary, exercise, than a contributing factor towards authentic experimentation.

With a few exceptions presently to be noted, there is not the remotest reason why the majority of modern Scots writers should be considered Scots at all. The protagonists of the Scots literary Renaissance deny this. They hold, for example, that Norman Douglas or Compton Mackenzie, though they write in English and deal with un-Scottish themes, have nevertheless an essential Scottishness which differentiates them from the native English writer. In exactly the same manner, so had Joseph Conrad an essential Polishness. But few (except for the purpose of exchanging diplomatic courtesies) pretend that Conrad was a Polish writer, to be judged as a Pole. He wrote brilliantly and strangely and beautifully in English; so does Mr Norman Douglas, so does Mr Cunninghame Graham. Mention of the latter is peculiarly to the point. Mr. Graham has, I believe, a large modicum of Spanish blood in his veins, he writes much of Spanish or Spanish-American subjects, and his word-manipulation is most certainly not of the English orthodox. But we have still to hear of Spain acclaiming him one of her great essayists.

The admirable plays of Dr. James Bridie – such as *Tobias and the Angel* or the unforgettable *Jonah and the Whale* – have been hailed in Scotland as examples of modern Scots drama. They are excellent examples – but not of Scots drama. They are examples of how an Englishman, hailing from Scotshire, can write excellent plays. Mr. Edwin Muir writes poems of great loveliness; so does Mr. Roy

Campbell; both are of Scots origin: ergo, great Scots poetry. Dumas père had negro blood in his veins and wrote excellent romances in French: ergo, great negro romance.

That such a position is untenable is obvious. Modern Scotland, the Gaels included, is a nation almost entirely lacking a Scottish literary output. There are innumerable versifiers, ranging from Dr. Charles Murray down-wards to Mr W. H. Hamilton (he of the eldritch glamour); there are hardly more than two poets; and there is no novelist at all. To be oneself a provincial or an alien and to write a book in which the characters infect one's literary medium with a tincture of dialect is not to assist in the creation or continuation of a separate national literature – else Eden Philpotts proves the great, un-English soul of Dartmoor and Tennyson in *The Northern Farmer* was advocating Home Rule for Yorkshire. The chief Literary Lights which modern Scotland claims to light up the scene of her night are in reality no more than the commendable writers of the interesting English county of Scotshire.

Let us consider Mrs. Naomi Mitchison. She is the one writer of the 'historical' novel in modern English who commands respect and enthusiasm. Her pages are aglow with a fine essence of apprehended light. *The Conquered* and *Black Sparta* light up the human spirit very vividly and truly. And they are in no sense Scots books though written by a Scotswoman. Their author once wrote that had she had the command of Scots speech possessed by Lewis Grassic Gibbon she would have written her Spartan books (at least) in Scots. Had she done so they would undoubtedly have been worse novels – but they *would* have been Scots books by a Scots writer, just as the worst of Finnish peasant studies *are* Finnish peasant studies, infinitesimal by the side of Dostoieffski or Tolstoi, but un-Russian in language and content.

Another writer hailed as a great Scots novelist is Mr. Neil Gunn. The acclamation is mistaken. Mr Gunn is a brilliant novelist from Scotshire who chooses his home county as the scene of his tales. His technique is almost unique among the writers of Scotshire in its effortless efficiency: he moulds beauty in unforgettable phrases – there are things in *The Lost Glen* and *Sun Circle* comparable to the best in the imaginative literature of any school or country. He has probably scarcely yet set out on his scaling of the heights. . . . But they are not the heights of Scots literature; they are not even the pedestrian levels. More in Gunn than in any other contemporary Anglo-Scot (with the exception, perhaps, of George Blake, in a very different category from Gunn, and the finest of the Anglo-Scots realists) the reader seems to sense the haunting foreignness in an orthodox English; he is the greatest loss to itself Scottish literature has suffered in this century. Had his language been Gaelic or Scots there is no doubt of the space or place he would have occupied in even such short study as this. Writing in orthodox English, he is merely a brilliantly unorthodox Englishman.

Once again, a writer who has been hailed as distinctively Scots, Mrs Willa Muir. So far she has written only two novels – *Imagined Corners* and *Mrs Ritchie* – and both show a depth and distinction, a sheer and splendidly un-womanly power which stir even the most jaded of enthusiasms. They suffer, perhaps, from the author's learnings and erudition-gatherings in the dull hag-forests of the German psychoanalysts, just as Neil Gunn's *Sun Circle* suffers from a crude and out-dated concept of history and the historical processes. But that psychoanalyst obsession is the common leprosy over all contemporary European imaginative literature, and Mrs Muir's strength of spirit and true integrity of vision may yet transcend it. She has promise of becoming a great artist. But a great English artist. The fact that she is Scots herself and deals with Scots scenes and Scots characters is (to drive home the point ad nauseam) entirely irrelevant from the point of view of Scots literature: if she were a modern Mexican writing in Spanish and her scene was Mexico and her peasants spoke bastardized Nahuatl, would we call it a triumph of Aztec letters?

Mr John Buchan has been called the Dean of Scots letters. Mr Buchan writes mildly exhilarating romances in the vein of the late Rider Haggard (though without either Haggard's magnificent poetic flair or his imaginative grasp), commendable essays on a variety of topics, uninspired if competent biographies of Sir Walter Scott, the Marquis of Montrose, and the like distinguished cadaverlitter on the ancient Scottish scene. He writes it all in a competent, skilful and depressing English: when his characters talk Scots they do it in suitable inverted commas: and such characters as do talk Scots are always the simple, the proletarian, the slightly ludicrous characters.

Mr Buchan represents no more than the great, sound, bourgeois heart of Scotshire. He has written nothing which has the least connection with Scots literature except a few pieces of verse – if verse *has* any connection with literature. In compiling *The Northern Muse*, however, a representative anthology of Scots 'Vernacular' poetry, he turned aside from other pursuits to render a real service to what might have been his native literary language. Yet even in that service he could envisage Braid Scots as being only a 'vernacular,' the tongue of *a home-reared slave.*

Mrs Catherine Carswell is among the most interesting of the Anglo-Scots. Her *Life of Robert Burns* was one of the most unique and innocently mendacious studies of the subject ever attempted; her *Savage Pilgrimage* (which met such a sad fate in the teeth of the enraged Mr Middleton Murry) contributed as little to our knowledge of D. H. Lawrence as it contributed greatly to our knowledge of its author. With such a personality and philosophy much more may be heard of Catherine Carswell: that the philosophy of her school appears a strange and repulsive one, as strange an aberration of the human spirit as history has ever known, merely adds a pathological to a genuine literary interest in her development. Scots letters represses its death-rattle to wave her on with a regretful relief.

Prior to writing *Hatter's Castle, Three Loves*, and *Grand Canary* Dr A. J. Cronin descended five hundred collieries on tours of inspection. As a consequence he is notable for a kind of inky immensity, and an interestingly Latinized barbarization of the English language. While *Hatter's Castle* had a Scots scene its characters were gnomes from the sooty deeps of the less salubrious regions of myth: though acclaimed as great and realistic portraits. In *Three Loves* Dr Cronin showed a disposition to prove uneasy on the Scottish scene; in *Grand Canary* he escaped it entirely, taking his place (probably a permanent place) among the English writers of an order comparable to Miss Mannin or Mr Gilbert Frankau. He is also the author of a history of aneurism.

Sir James George Frazer, a Scotsman by birth, is the author of the immense *Golden Bough*, a collection of anthropological studies. The author's methods of correlation have been as crude and unregulated as his industry and the cultivation of his erudition have been immense. The confusion of savage and primitive states of culture commenced by Tylor and his school has been carried to excess in the works of Sir J. G. Frazer. From the point of view of the social historian attempting to disentangle the story of man's coming and growth upon this planet he is one of the most calamitous phenomena in modern research: he has smashed in the ruin of pre-history with a coal-hammer, collected every brick disclosed when the dust settled on the débris, and then labelled the exhibits with the assiduous industry of a literary ant. His pleasing literary style in that labelling is in orthodox English.

Mr Eric Linklater is a lost Norseman with a disposition to go Berserk amidst the unfamiliar trappings of literary civilization. This disposition came to a head in *The Men of Ness*, a story of the vikings and their raids into the regions of stern guffawdom and unpronunciability. It is a pity that this disposition should be let loose by the author of *Juan in America*, – in the genre of Mark Twain's *Tramp Abroad*, and one of the most acute and amusing picaresque studies ever perpetrated by the literary farceur. It would be even more regrettable if Mr Linklater hampered his genius by an uneasy adherence to a so-called Scots literary Renaissance.[1]

Miss Muriel Stuart is one of the very few great poets writing in non-experimental English. She has a comprehension and a lyric beauty almost unknown to this English day: the deep passion of her poems in *Christ at Carnival* shines the more finely in that they lack the ornate imagery of Francis Thompson. One of the most magic lines in a memory prolific in the waste amusement of collecting magic lines (as is the present writer's) is her '*A thin hail ravened against the doors of dark.*' Miss Stuart, of Scots origin, has been hailed as a great Scots poet. She is as little Scots as Dante.

1. This fear has been pleasingly dispelled with the publication of the excellent *Magnus Merriman*.

Yet Miss Stuart's genius brings us at last to consideration of the two solitary lights in modern Scots Literature. They rise from men who are writers in both Scots and in English – very prolific and controversial writers, men occupied with politics and economic questions, poets in the sense that life, not editors or anthologists, demand of them their poetry. But for the fact that this paper has been devoted largely to an argument that should have needed no enforcing, the work of these two would have occupied almost all the space under such heading as Literary Lights. One of these two is Hugh MacDiarmid and the other Lewis Spence.

MacDiarmid's poetry in Braid Scots came upon a world which had grown accustomed to the belief that written Scots was a vehicle for the more flat-footed sentiments of the bothy only; it came upon a world pale and jaded with the breathing and rebreathing in the same room of the same stagnant air of orthodox English. He demonstrated, richly and completely, and continues to demonstrate, the flexibility and the loveliness of that alien variation of the Anglo-Saxon speech which is Braid Scots. The first of MacDiarmid that the present writer encountered was something which still lingers in his mind (unreasonably, considering the magnificent *To Circumjack Cencrastus* or the sweeping majesty of the *Hymns to Lenin*):

> 'Ae weet forenicht i' the yow-trummle
>   I saw yon antrin thing,
> A watergaw wi' its chitterin' licht
>   Ayont the on-ding;
> An' I thocht o' the last wild look ye gied
>   Afore ye dee'd!
>
> There was nae reek i' the laverock's hoose
>   That nicht – an' nane i' mine;
> But I hae thocht o' that foolish licht
>   Ever sin' syne;
> An' I think that maybe at last I ken
>   What your look meant then.'

This is probably, in Mr MacDiarmid's own view, no more light versification. But it is certainly not English versification; the prisoner behind the polished walls has escaped and engaged himself in the moulding of a curious façade. Mr MacDiarmid, like all great poets, has his in and out moments – some of them disastrous moments; his care to set this planet aright has laid waste some of his finest poems – but, working in that medium of Braid Scots which he calls synthetic Scots, he has brought Scots language into print again as a herald in tabard, not the cap-and-bells clown of romantic versification.

Of an entirely different order, but a genius no less genuine, is Mr Spence in his Scots poetry. To show the width and sweep of Braid Scots from MacDiarmid to Spence, it is necessary to quote only:

> 'Time that has dinged doun castels and hie toures,
> And cast great crouns like tinsel in the fire,
> That halds his hand for palace nor for byre,
> Stands sweir at this, the oe of Venus' boures,
> Not Time himself can dwell withouten floures,
> Though aiks maun fa' the rose shall bide entire;
> So sall this diamant of a queen's desire
> Outflourish all the stanes that Time devours.'

How far these two are isolated phenomena, how far the precursors of a definite school of Scots literature is still uncertain: they have their imitators in full measure: in William Soutar the Elijah of MacDiarmid may yet have an Elisha. When, if ever, the majority of Scots poets – not versifiers – begin to use Braid Scots as a medium that dream of a Scots literary renaissance may tread the *via terrena* of fulfilment, enriching (in company with orthodox English) the literary heritage of that language of Cosmopolis towards which the whole creation moves.

An experiement of quite a different order from MacDiarmid's writing in synthetic Scots, or Spence's in deliberate excavation in the richness of the antique Scots vocabularies, may be noted here. As already stated, there is no novelist, (or, indeed prose writer,) worthy of the name who is writing in Braid Scots. The technique of

Lewis Grassic Gibbon in his trilogy *A Scots Quair* – of which only Parts I and II, *Sunset Song* and *Cloud Howe*, have yet been published – is to mould the English language into the rhythms and cadences of Scots spoken speech, and to inject into the English vocabulary such minimum number of words from Braid Scots as that remodelling requires. His scene so far has been a comparatively uncrowded and simple one – the countryside and village of modern Scotland. Whether his technique is adequate to compass and express the life of an industrialized Scots town in all its complexity is yet to be demonstrated; whether his peculiar style may not become either intolerably mannered or degenerate, in the fashion of Joyce, into the unfortunate unintelligibilities of a literary second childhood, is also in question.

For the Gaels, one cannot do better than quote James Barke, the author of *The World his Pillow* and *The Wild MacRaes*, and himself a remarkable Anglo-Gael:

'In Scotland to-day there exists no body of Gaelic culture. In the realms of imaginative literature – in fiction and drama – there is little or no original work in evidence; and what does exist is of poor quality and vitiated by a spineless sentimentality.

'In verse alone the modern Gaelic writer would seem to find a suitable medium for expression – Donald Sinclair (died recently); Duncan Johnston of Islay; John MacFadyen. MacFadyen, I believe, has it. But here too the output is small and fragmentary and, in quality, perhaps best compared to the Poet's Corner of the provincial press.

'There is no one to-day in any way approaching the stature of the great Gaelic poets: Alasdair MacMhaighistir Alasdair and Duncan Ban MacIntyre – or even Alexander MacDonald or Ewan MacColl.

'The reason for the poverty of contemporary Gaelic culture is not difficult to state.

'When the Young Pretender and his Highland forces were defeated on Culloden Moor in 1746, there followed a ruthless military occupation of the Highland. The clan system was broken up and all forms of Gaelic culture were suppressed. The ownership of partly communal land passed into the hands of a small group of private individuals. The land was soon cleared of its human population. With the exception of a few impoverished crofting communities the native Gael became subservient to the dominant landowning class.

'First military suppression and dictatorship, then economic suppression were the cause of the decay of the Gael and his native Gaelic culture. From the field of Culloden to the first National Government economic, and consequently racial, decay has continued steadily. In the modern capitalist state the Gael finds himself an anachronism – almost an extinct species. The few of them who are articulate turn, therefore, to a hopeless backward looking, backward longing. A decayed race, lingering over-long on a decayed economic system, can produce only a decayed culture.

'The present attempts to revive this culture are necessarily doomed to failure. In its hey-day, Gaelic culture was surprisingly beautiful and vital. As part of Scotland's cultural heritage it will survive for its richness and beauty. But a people can no more live on the glories of the past than it can survive on the memories of its last meal.

'The death rattle of Gaelic culture may be amplified by all sorts of bodies and committees. They delude themselves, however, in thinking that by so doing so they are performing an act of resurrection. . . .

'Fionn MacColla, in English, it may be noted, is far away the finest example of the Gaelic influence. In a very profound sense, his English is the finest Gaelic we have.'

Sic itur ad astra.

Aberdeen

No foreigner can think of that vulgarization of Scots humour and the Scots lyric which Sir Harry Lauder has brought to such pitch of perfection without a bye-thought on a Scots city which would seem to breed, principally, if not entirely, Lauder-imitators. For the benefit of the English-reading public Aberdeen is the home of the typical 'Scotch' joke. In this the Scot is shown as ludicrously mean, he is the victim and perpetrator of a farcical and brainless greed. And most of the material for those tales and fantasies of so-called humour are exported from Aberdeen itself, as the editor of any light-hearted English periodical will confirm.

Now, a tale may be read, quite consciously and knowingly, as humour-fantasy, and yet have curious repercussions on the mind of the reader. So with Aberdeen: it is impossible that its streets can be thronged with reproductions of this odd caricature of humanity who parades in the jokes. Still – and the good Englishman and the good American display a kind of humorous contemptuous care in their dealings with an authentic Aberdonian, set foot in Aberdeen itself with wary grins on their faces. Recently I received a reply-paid envelope from an American publisher. In the course of the accompanying letter the publisher referred to the envelop, (in a business-like fashion, without inverted commas, because the joke in this minor aspect has grown stale and passed into the ordinary vocabulary of American business) as an 'Aberdeen envelope.' Once, in Jerusalem, I struck up acquaintance with an intelligent and interesting Syrian. We talked ethnology; and in the course of the conversation I told him that I was born in Aberdeenshire in Scotland. He was amused and pitiful, though a little hazy. 'Aberdeen – it is the pariah place, is it not?'

These phenomena – Aberdeen's comic reputation and Aberdo-

The Speak of the Mearns

nian humour itself – are worthy of some investigation, just as the man who laughs too loudly and too long stirs curiosities in the mind of the sceptical bystander. Why so much laughter – and why that steely ring in the last guffaw? Here is an Aberdonian 'funny story':

'An Aberdonian died and gave instructions in his will that his body be cremated. This was done. The day after the cremation the widow heard a knock at the door. She opened it and saw a small message-boy standing on the doorstep holding out a package towards her. "What's this?" she enquired. "Your husband, Mem," said the boy, "– his ashes, you know." Slowly the widow took the package in her hand. "His ashes? Oh, ay. *But where's the dripping?*"'

I choose this example deliberately as that of an Aberdonian story insufficiently padded. You laugh, but (if you have any imagination at all) you have a slight qualm. The grisliness below the humour is insufficiently concealed. You can smell the strench of that burning body, you can see the running human fats – with a dish in appropriate position to collect them. . . . You see too closely in this instance the grinning skull behind the large, jolly countenance of the laughing man; you may suspect him, outside the flare of lights in the bar and the help of alcohol, as one solemn and serious enough, uneasy, haunted by an unending apprehension of life as a bleak enough parade.

Bleakness, not meanness or jollity, is the keynote to Aberdonian character, not so much lack of the graces or graciousness of existence as lack of colour in either of these. And this is almost inevitable for anyone passing his nights and days in The Silver City by the Sea. It is comparable to passing one's existence in a refrigerator. Aberdeen is built, largely and incredibly, of one of the most enduring and indestructible and appalling building-materials in use on our planet – grey granite.

It has a flinty shine when new – a grey glimmer like a morning North Sea, a cold steeliness that chills the heart. Even with weathering it acquires no gracious softness, it is merely starkly grim and uncompromising. The architect may plan and build as he will with this material – with its variant, white granite, he may rear the curvetting spires and swooping curlecues and looping whirli-magigs of Marischal College – and not escape that sense of one calamitously in jail. Not only are there no furbelows possible in this architecture, there is amid it, continually, the uneasy sense that you may not rest here, you may not lounge, you cannot stand still and watch the world go by . . . Else presently the warders will come and move you on.

To know that feeling in its full intensity the investigator must disregard the publicity posters and visit Aberdeen in November. Whatever the weather as his train crossed from Kincardineshire into Aberdeenshire, he will arrive at Aberdeen Station in sleet. Not falling sleet or drifting sleet, but *blown* sleet – blown with an infernal and unescapable persistence from all points of the com-pass, from the stretches of the harbour, from the Duthie Park, down Market Street. And through this steely pelt he will see the tower and lour and savage grimace of the grey granite all about him, curdling his nerve centres even as the sleet curdles his extremities. If he holds by Guild Street and Market Street up to the pride of Aberdeen, Union Street, he will discover how really vocal this materialization of an Eskimo's vision of hell may become. Aberdeen is, without exception, the most exasperatingly noisy city in the world. Paris is bad – but one accepts Paris, it is free, it is anarchistic, the cabmen are trying to kill each other – a praiseworthy pursuit – and Citröens were made by devils in hell and manned by chauffeurs from purgatory – and it is all very amusing. But Aberdeen is not amusing in its epitome, Union Street. This street is paved with granite blocks, and over these, through the sleeting downpour, trams rattle, buses thud, and (unescapable) four large iron-wheeled drays hauled by Clydesdale horses are being drawn at break-neck speed. There is no amuse-ment in the thought of the drivers being killed: you can see in each gaunt, drawn face that the driver is doing it not for pleasure or the fun of life or because he is joyously and righteously drunk – he is doing it to support a wife, five children, a blind grandmother, and a sister in the Aberdeen Infirmary.

Aberdeen is the cleanest city in Britain: it makes you long for good, wholesome dirt, littered roadways and ramshackle buildings leaning in all directions, projecting warm brown sins and rich smutty reds through an enticing, grimy smile. Union Street has as much warmth in its face as a dowager duches asked to contribute to the Red International Relief. If you escape the trams and the drays and the inferno where Market Street debouches on Union Street, and hold west up Union Street, you will have the feeling of one caught in a corridor of the hills. To right and left tower the cliffs, scrubbed, immaculate and unforgiving. Where Union Terrace breaks in upon Union Street there is an attempt at a public Garden. But the flowers come up and take one glance at the lour of the solicitors' officers which man Union Terrace, and scramble back into the earth again, seeking the Antipodes.

Union Terrace is beset with statues: the advocates stroll to their windows from plodding through briefs for the Sheriff Court and look out on King Edward to the right, Robert Burns in the middle and William Wallace to the left. Aberdeen may be forgiven much because of those statues. For her flinty granitic heart was moved to wisdom when she commissioned them, giving their subjects that due proportion and appearance which they bore in history: King Edward is merely vulgar, Burns pathetic and Wallace heroic. The investigator may do worse than consider the Wallace with care: round the plinth are written quotations from his speeches to the Army of the Commons of Scotland; lounging upon the plinth, yawning and bored (even in the sleet) are the tired and the old and the unemployed of Aberdeen in great number. Wallace fascinates them, you would say. He belongs to a past they dare not achieve, they have come to such horrific future as he never visioned.

In his right hand is a great sword; his outflung left hand points – to the nearby bulk, cupola'ed and gilded, of His Majesty's Theatre. But I think the gesture is unwarranted, for it is an excellent theatre, there are folk and institutions in Aberdeen far more worthy of gesture and sword. One wonders if the slum landlords of Correction Wynd or the Gallowgate, emerging from their cars to make their way to the padded fauteuils of His Majesty's, ever cast an uneasy glance at the great Guardian.

Probably not – unless some socialist orator is holding forth from the plinth. It is a favourite place of the orator, the communist orator for preference. Unemployed Aberdeen chews tobacco and listens vaguely and smokes vague cigarettes, and you can hear the orator at a great distance, the thin Aberdonian voice in the thin Aberdonian patois – full of long *ee's*, and conversions of *wh's* into *f's*. . . . Agitationally, in spite its unemployed, Aberdeen sleeps these days. A friend of mine once led forth a procession of the unemployed: the mounted police charged: and when they had passed my friend was found clinging far up in the branches of a tree. This is the reality that has succeeded those visions of the barricade that vexed young folk of my ilk in the War-time days: days that distance covers with a fine glamour, when the mob broke up the peace-time meeting in the Music Hall addressed by Ramsay MacDonald: and a party of them made to storm the platform: and a socialist pugilist pacified them, asking for a single representative to come up: and one belligerent young man ascended: and demanded to be led to Ramsay: and the socialist pugilist agreed: and took the young man behind the scenes and socked him in the jaw; and came dragging back the body as an exhibition of what Ramsay did to interrupters. . . . Or another meeting, with locked doors, which a company of the Gordon Highlanders attempted to storm: and broke down the upper half of the door, and climbed in one by one: and as they descended were met by a solemn, six-foot pacifist with the limbs of an aurochs and hands like hams: who solemnly and pitifully knocked each one unconscious: and then revived them and carried them upstairs to the meeting, on the soldiers' tearful promise that they *would* be good. . . . Or the founding of the Aberdeen Soviet when the news of the Bolshevik Revolution came through from Russia; and how I and a cub reporter from another paper attended the foundation meeting; and were elected to the Soviet Council, forgetting we were pressmen; and spent perspiring minutes with our chief reporters afterwards, explaining that we could not report the meeting being ourselves good sovietists. . . . *O tempora! O mores!*

Remote as the banners of the Army of the Commons. Yet (and to presume that the sleet is over, and you are now in your overcoat) if you turn rightwards from Wallace into that grouping and festering of mean streets that lie behind and beyond the Infirmary, surely it is impossible that these things have passed? There are odd little shops here, with revolutionary journals for sale? Instead, odd little shops which sell stockings and shirts and such-like necessitous intimacies on the hire-purchase system: and sue with great savagery the improvident purchasers. Fifteen years ago that young cub reporter who, with myself, had been elected to the Aberdeen Soviet – we were so young and full of dreams we could not sleep o' nights. We prowled Aberdeen all the hours of the night, seeking not amorous adventure, but talking the moon into morning about jolly and heartsome and splendid things: life, death, the Revolution and the great green-cheeseness of the moon. . . . And the years went by, and I journeyed afar; and garnered a little in experience, including a keen distaste for that snarling cry of the machine-gun which sends a man clawing earthwards on his belly; and twelve years went by and I came again to Aberdeen; and for curiosity I wandered into its police court one morning; and a shameful woman had purchased knickers from the owner of a little chain of shops; and had neglected her payments, and was now being sued, poor proletarian with her red-chapped hands and her wrinkled, terrified face, and her poor, shifting eyes and her stammering voice. . . . I turned away my eyes and felt unreasonably sick. But the voice of the owner of the chain of shops brought back my attention as he spoke from the witness-box. And he was—

With me the investigator turns to a thing more pleasant – Allenvale Cemetery, where the dead of Aberdeen lie in serried lines under immense granitic monuments. They move one to a wondering horror. Granite, grey granite, in birth, in puberty, adolescence, grey granite encasing the bridal room, grey granite the rooms of blear-eyed old age. And even in death they are not divided. . . . Lower middle-class Aberdeen comes here of a Sunday in its Sunday blue suit and yellow boots and dickie and bowler: and parades, and admires the monuments, and goes back to Aberdeen high tea.

High tea in Aberdeen is like no other meal on earth. It is the meal of the day, the meal par excellence, and the tired come home to it ravenous, driven by the granite streets, hounded in for energy to stoke against that menace. Tea is drunk with the meal, and the order of it is this: First, one eats a plateful of sausages and eggs and mashed potatoes; then a second plateful to keep down the first. Eating, one assists the second plateful to its final home by mouthfuls of oatcake spread with butter. Then you eat oatcake with cheese. Then there are scones. Then cookies. Then it is really time to begin on tea – tea and bread and butter and crumpets and toasted rolls and cakes. Then some Dundee cake. Then – about half-past seven – someone shakes you out of the coma into which you have fallen and asks you persuasively if you wouldn't like another cup of tea and just *one* more egg and sausage. . . .

And all night long, on top of this supper and one of those immense Aberdonian beds which appear to be made of knotted ship's cable, the investigator, through and transcending the howl of the November sleet-wind, will hear the lorries and the drays, in platoons, clattering up and down Market Street. They do it for no reason or purpose, except to keep you awake. And in the morning when you descend with a grey face and an aching head, they provide you with an immense Aberdeen breakfast; and if you halt and gasp somewhere through the third course they send for the manager who comes and questions you gravely as to why you don't like the food? – should he send for a doctor?

I'm presuming the investigator has taken a room in one of the hotels in Market Street. They are very good and cheap and never advertise, and this is their free advertisement in return for their unostentatious virtues. And their windows look out on Aberdeen Harbour, a wide, dull stretch round which I can never wander these days without a vague feeling that all is not well with the harbour, there is a definite something missing in the ships and shipping. And then I remember: the War-time camouflage when the ships rode bravely bespattered in painted zigzags, and all kinds of odd people came wandering across the North Sea and were landed at Aberdeen from those pantomime vessels. M. Krassin was deported from England by way of Aberdeen and I attempted to interview him as he boarded his boat: he had a little beard and a twisted nose; and I spoke to him in halting Russian and he said kindly that he spoke English when he was allowed to – only he wasn't. And as I came away from that abortive interview I saw a soldier walking along the quays, an elderly man, a sergeant, in full equipment, with rifle and steel helmet. And he stopped and looked into the water, thoughtfully, and laid aside the rifle and helmet, and jumped into the water. There he swam to and fro for a little and some loafers threw him a rope and dragged him out. He shook himself, large, solemn, like a great dog, picked up the rifle and helmet, and departed towards the station without saying a word. . . .

Twice weekly in the summer season the London boat comes into Aberdeen, and twice weekly departs. The Aberdonians are an emotional people: they assemble in great multitudes on the quay where the London boat is leaving. As the syrens hoot they begin to cheer and wave handkerchiefs. About a tenth of the two hundred waving from the shore have friends or relatives on board. The rest are there moved by a curious pity. I have seen an Aberdeen woman in tears as she waved towards the departing boat, though she knew not a soul on board. Some are even more enthusiastic. They pursue the boat from quay to quay, bridge to bridge, waving and weeping, till they can pursue no further. The passengers stand and wave and cheer in return, then light cigars and stroke their tartan ties and tell how they climbed up Lochin-y-Gair.

Leftwards, Footdee sleeps with silent shipyards and factories these days, with great rusting cranes lifting their unmoving chains high in the air, and long cobbled walks silent and nerveless enough. A kind of palsy has fallen here, the investigator will note: the trawlers still come in of a morning in long sweeping lines, with laden creels for the Fish Market, but Footdee smells ill even these salt mornings, even this stinging November morning when the wind has veered a point and it has forgotten to sleet. This assuredly is the morning to survey the Beach.

The Beach, it is at once evident, was constructed by a cretin brought up under the tuition of an imaginative, unreliable, but high-spirited gorilla. Behind it stretch the Links: in front of it, the North Sea. Its buttressed walls rise and swoop with a care admirable for the gambollings of the lesser anthropoids, if somewhat at variance with the needs of a more normal populace. To your right is the Amusements Park; here the gorilla relaxed and scratched and was momentarily human, for here is a lovely scenic railway. The investigator, turning from the horror of the North Sea and the equal horror of the Beach, concludes that if he lived in Aberdeen he would spend his days on that scenic railway.

But this is Aberdeen by day. Aberdeen by night is a different city, thronged with a more subtle, a different folk. The watching granite relaxes on the façades of the great grey buildings, in the manners and customs of the folk in the streets. At eight o'clock on Friday night all Aberdeen assembles and parades in Union Street; and here the investigator stands aside and views with care the high cheek-bones in the brachycephalic heads of the males, that singularly dis-harmonic head that is so singularly Aberdonian. The proletarian wears a cap with a long check peak, the petit bourgeois wears the regulation bowler hat, the bourgeois walks bare-headed, for he is in plus-fours and his domed bald head is browned with the suns of the Links. There is an endless flow and unflow of the thin Aberdeen speech. But the bourgeois speaks English, and, strangely, speaks it successfully, acquiring depths and rhythm as he mislays the false, pale vowels and slurred consonants of his city. The women wear clothes indistinguishable from those of Paris or New York. But a strange fate haunts the Aberdonian woman. She cannot walk. Some go by with a duck-like waddle, some prance on squattering toes, some slouch with laggard steps. It is the granite side-walks responsible, the investigator concludes, as the hours fade and the throngs fade with them, and down over the Town Hall the clocktowers tell it is one o'clock.

But for prostitutes, policemen, and journalists Union Street is deserted now. With a sough and a sigh the night-wind, edged as with a knife, is blowing along Union Terrace: King Edward stands freezing, bald-headed: down in the station a train chugs remotely, with a flying shower of sparks. In the glare of the night lights the tramlines swoop down towards Market Street like great snakes: in a remote shop-front a policeman is flashing his lamp. A young man in a slouch hat goes by, yawning: the *Journal* has been put to bed. Two girls consult the investigator on his needs for the night. He is regretful, with another engagement. They intimate, drifting away, a profound conviction in his illegitimacy. So to bed.

In the days when I first knew Aberdeen two names fascinated me – St. Machar and Kittybrewster. They lie at points remotely one from the other, the St. Machar Cathedral and the Kittybrewster district, but these the investigator (who has now purchased a fresh supply of woolly underwear) may not miss. St. Machar's Cathedral, they tell us, was builded first in the fourteenth century – there are still scraps of fourteenth-century architecture there. But towards the close of the seventeenth century the central tower fell in and smashed and demolished greatly chancel and transept, transforming the building from an active agency in dissemination of a cultural aberration to a seemly haunt for the archæologist. St. Machar sleeps through it all undisturbed. But from youth the notion persists in my mind that he turns in uneasy rememberance now and again of the days when he and Kitty Brewster—

Nor can any tell where Kitty lies. Perhaps beneath the smoke and soot and thundering trains of the Goods Station, lying, like good King Olaf, or Arthur in Avalon, waiting till they call her again and she wake and come forth and free the world. Dreaming below that clatter of an industrialism gone mad, Kitty must yet hear on the early mart mornings sounds more familiar and loved – the lowing of the great cattle herds they drive to the sales there – smell, smell back through the centuries that odour of dust and dung and cowishness that maybe haunted the hills when she and Machar—

But this is incredible romance. From earliest times Aberdeen has engaged itself in eschewing romance. Hardly had Kitty and St. Machar died in each other's arms (after a wild night's orgy on the Beach scenic railway) than Romance blew her trumpets through Aberdeen. It was the year 1411, and Donald of the Isles, gaunt, Highland and hairy, was nearing the city with an army of north-land raiders. The citizens ran and busked themselves, piled into the tramcars at Castlegate and poured out in their thousands to contest the march of Donald. They met him at Harlaw, a misty morning, when the dew was white as hoar or grey granite on the whins, and arrayed themselves in long, dour ranks of spearmen against the usual Highland tactic. Donald flung forward the clansmen in sweeping lines of attack: Aberdeen stood fast through a long and bloody day and at night Donald marched back the remnants of his forces into the hills. This was a great turn of the tide in Scots history – and Aberdeen wrought it.

It was a city that remained incurably and gloriously anti-Highland. Stout business men from Mannofield and Cults may nowadays send their children to the High School in kilts and bonnets: in ancient times they would as soon have thought of sending them forth into the world in dishclouts and tompions. In the '45 the rest of Scotland might go Prince Charlie mad: Aberdeen stared out from its granite doorways with a dour startlement, then turned its back on the whole ill business. Freedom, the winds of romance, the crying of banners marching south – not for it, not for the flinty souls who matched their flinty dwellings. So instead it aided and abetted the men of Hanover, it fêted and feasted the dour butcher Cumberland returning from Culloden field, and made him a guest of the Provost at No. 13 in the Guestrow – and there it stands unto this day to tell you if I lie.

But it is under orders for demolition – great sections of the older streets and wynds stand condemned, streets and wynds with antique names that move the antiquarian to suitable regrets when he considers their fate – the Upper Kirkgate, the Nether Kirkgate, the Gallowgate, the Guestrow. But I have no such regrets. Those gates to kirks and gallows: you think of a fœtid sixteenth-century stench and the staring mobs watching some poor, tormented hind dragged out to the Gallows in Market Square – and you turn, with relief and a new resolve, to face the glinting, flinting structures that tower new-built up Union Street.

For if you cannot come to terms with the grey granite, you must come to an understanding or else escape into Golf and the Conservative Club, if you have the suitable status, or into pub-crawling and the drinking of Red Biddies, that curious Aberdonian stimulant, if you are of the plebs. The understanding is no easy thing. One detests Aberdeen with the detestation of a thwarted lover. It is the one haunting and exasperatingly lovable city in Scotland – its fascination as unescapable as its shining mail.

But is there need to escape? There are moments when I think of it as the essential – something to be apprehended and in its apprehension to uncover new countries of stark and glowing wonder, something lighted and shining with a fine flame, cold and amber and gold, behind the flinty cliffs of Union Street, the flinty cheekbones of the disharmonic faces that press about you in an Aberdeen tram. I prefer to think that the bitterly underpaid and wet and sogging fisherman stumping up from the Fish Market after a night on the reel and drummle of the tides has apprehended that granite-quality and made of it, warmed and kindly, his life quality . . . The investigator looks after him with a warmth and interest in the grey of the sleeting November morning as he peers from the stalactited window of his hotel bedroom and then turns to consult a train time-table.

As for the women of Aberdeen . . . it is strange the vagrant associations the mind hinges on this word and that. About half of the women of Aberdeen appear to rejoice in the name of Grizel – and rejoice with justness, for my saner self tells me it is a lovely and incisive name. But for some strange reason I can never hear it pronounced without thinking of a polar bear eating an Eskimo.

And that is all about Aberdeen.

The Land

I. Winter

I like the story of the helpful Englishman who, when shown a modern Scots Nationalist map with 'Scotland Proper' stretching from John o' Groats to the Tweed, and 'Scotia Irredenta' stretching from the Tweed to the Mersey, suggested 'Scotland Improper' in place of the latter term. The propriety of Northern England to rank as a section of Scotland may have political justice; it certainly has no æsthetic claim. If I look out on the land of Scotland and see it fouled by the smoking slag-heaps of industrialism rightwards and leftwards, a long trailing rift down the eastern coast and a vomiting geyser in Lanarkshire, I feel no stirrings of passion at all to add those tortured wastes of countryside, Northumbria and Lancashire, to the Scottish land. I like the grey glister of sleet in the dark this night, seen through the unblinded window; and I like this idle task of voyaging with a pen through the storm-happed wastes of Scotland in winter; but I balk at reaching beyond the Border, into that chill land of alien geology and deplorable methods of ploughing. This paraffin lamp set beside me on the table was lit for the benefit of myself and Scotland Proper: I shrink from geographical impropriety to-night as my Kailyard literary forerunners shrank from description of the bridal bed.

And now that I bend to the task and the logs are crackling so cheerfully and the wind has veered a point, and there's a fine whoom in the lum, it comes on me with a qualm that perhaps I have no qualifications for the task at all. For if the land is the enumeration of figures and statistics of the yield of wheat in the Merse or the Carse of Gowrie, fruit-harvesting in Coupar-Angus, or how they couple and breed their cattle in Ayrshire, I am quite

lost. And if the land is the lilting of tourist names, Strathmore, Ben
Lomond, Ben Macdhui, Rannoch, Loch Tay and the Sidlaw Hills, I
confess to bored glimpses of this and that stretch of unique
countryside, I confess that once (just such a night as this) I
journeyed up to Oban; and the train was bogged in a snowstorm;
and I spent shivering hours in view of Ben Cruachan; and once an
Anglo-Gaelic novelist took me round Loch Lomond in his car and
we drank good whisky and talked about Lenin; and an uncle once
dragged me, protesting, up Lochnagar, in search of a sunrise that
failed to appear – the sun hid that morning in a diffusion of
peasoup fog; and I've viewed the Caledonian Canal with suitable
commercial enthusiasm and recited (as a small boy at concerts)
verse about the Dee and Don, they still run on (a phenomenon
which elicited complacent clappings of commendation from my
audiences); and I've eaten trout by Loch Levenside. But I refuse the
beetling crags and the spume of Spey; still I think they are not The
Land.

That is The Land out there, under the sleet, churned and pelted
there in the dark, the long rigs upturning their clayey faces to the
spear-onset of the sleet. That is The Land, a dim vision this night of
laggard fences and long stretching rigs. And the voice of it – the
true and unforgettable voice – you can hear even such a night as
this as the dark comes down, the immemorial plaint of the peewit,
flying lost. *That* is The Land – though not quite all. Those folk in
the byre whose lantern light is a glimmer through the sleet as they
muck and bed and tend the kye, and milk the milk into tin pails, in
curling froth – they are The Land in as great a measure. Those two,
a dual power, are the protagonists in this little sketch. They are the
essentials for the title. And besides, quite unfairly, they are all so
intimately mine that I would give them that position though they
had not a shadow of a claim to it.

I like to remember I am of peasant rearing and peasant stock.
Good manners prevail on me not to insist on the fact over-much,
not to boast in the company of those who come from manses and
slums and castles and villas, the folk of the proletariat, the bigger
and lesser bourgeoisies. But I am again and again, as I hear them
talk of their origins and beginnings and begetters, conscious of an

overweening pride that mine was thus and so, that the land was so closely and intimately mine (my mother used to hap me in a plaid in harvest-time and leave me in the lee of a stook while she harvested) that I feel of a strange and antique age in the company and converse of my adult peers – like an adult himself listening to the bright sayings and laughters of callow boys, parvenus on the human scene, while I, a good Venriconian Pict, harken from the shade of my sun circle and look away, bored, in pride of possession at my terraced crops, at the on-ding of rain and snow across my leavened fields. . . .

How much this is merely reaction from the hatreds of my youth I do not know. For once I had a very bitter detestation for all this life of the land and the folk upon it. My view was that of my distant cousin, Mr Leslie Mitchell, writing in his novel *The Thirteenth Disciple*:

'A grey, grey life. Dull and grey in its routine, Spring, Summer, Autumn, Winter, that life the Neolithic men brought from the south, supplanting Azilian hunger and hunting and light-hearted shiftlessness with servitude to seasons and soil and the tending of cattle. A beastly life. With, memory of it and reading those Catholic writers, who, for some obscure reason, champion the peasant and his state as the ideal state, I am moved to unkindly mirth . . . unprintably sceptical as to Mr Chesterton or his chelas ever having grubbed a livelihood from hungry acres of red clay, or regarding the land and its inhabitants with other vision than an obese Victorian astigmatism.'

Not, I think, that I have gone the full circle and have returned among the romantics. As I listen to that sleet-drive I can see the wilting hay-ricks under the fall of the sleet and think of the wind ablow on ungarmented floors, ploughmen in sodden bothies on the farms outbye, old, bent and wrinkled people who have mislaid so much of fun and hope and high endeavour in grey servitude to those rigs curling away, only half-inanimate, into the night. I can still think and see these things with great clarity though I sit in this warm room and write this pleasant essay and find pleasure in the manipulation of words on a blank page. But when I read or hear our new leaders and their plans for making of Scotland a great peasant nation, a land of little farms and little farming communities, I am moved to a bored disgust with those pseudo-literary romantics playing with politics, those refugees from the warm parlours and lights and policemen and theatre-stalls of the Scots cities. They are promising the New Scotland a purgatory that would decimate it. They are promising it narrowness and bitterness and heart-breaking toil in one of the most unkindly agricultural lands in the world. They are promising to make of a young, ricketic man, with the phthisis of Glasgow in his throat, a bewildered labourer in pelting rains and the flares of head-aching suns, they are promising him years of a murderous monotony, poverty and struggle and loss of happy human relationships. They promise that of which they know nothing, except through sipping of the scum of Kailyard romance.

For this life is for no modern man or woman – even the finest of these. It belongs to a different, an alien generation. That winter that is sweeping up the Howe, bending the whins on Auchindreich hill, seeping with pelting blasts through the old walls of Edzell Castle, malagarousing the ploughed lands and swashing about and above the heavy cattle-courts where in darkness the great herds lie cud-chewing and breath-blowing in frosty steam, is a thing for most to be stared at, tourist-wise, endured for a day or a week. This night, the winter on the countryside, the crofter may doze contentedly in the arm-chair in the ingle-neuk and the mistress yawn with an equal content at the clock. For you or I or young Simon who is taking his girl to the pictures it is as alien and unendurable in permanence as the life of the Kamtchatkan.

II. Spring

Going down the rigs this morning, my head full of that unaccustomed smell of the earth, fresh and salty and anciently mouldy, I remembered the psalmist's voice of the turtle and instinctively listened for its Scots equivalent – that far cooing of pigeons that used to greet the coming of Spring mornings when I was a boy. But the woods have gone, their green encirclement replaced by swathes of bog and muck and rank-growing heath, all the land about here is left bare in the North wind's blow. The pigeons have gone and the rabbits and like vermin multiplied – unhappily and to no profit, for the farmers tell me the rabbits are tuberculous, dangerous meat. Unshielded by the woods, the farm-lands are assailed by enemies my youth never knew.

But they are fewer and fewer, the cultivated lands. Half of them are in grass – permanently in grass – and browsed upon by great flocks of sheep, leaving that spider-trail of grey that sheep bring to pastures. We are repeating here what the Border men did in Badenoch and the Highlands – eating away the land and the crofter, killing off the peasant as surely as in Russia – and with no Russian compensation. If the little dykes and the sodden ditches that riveted in the Springs of bygone times with the waters hastening to the Forthie – the ditches that separated this little farm from that – were filled and obliterated by a sovkholz with tractors and high enthusiasm and a great and tremendous agricultural hope, I at least could turn to the hills and the heath – that other and older Land – with no more regret than the sensitive felt in the passing of the windjammers and the coming of the steamboats. But instead there has come here only a brainless greed, a grabbing stupidity, the mean avariciousness and planlessness of our community in epitome. I do not wonder that the rabbits are tuberculous: the wonder is that they are not jaundiced as well.

It was then that I thought what a fine and heartsome smell has rank cow-dung as the childe with the graip hurls it steady heap on heap from the rear of his gurling cart. They sell stuff in Paris in little bottles with just that smell, and charge for it handsomely, as they may well do, for it is the smell that backgrounds existence. And then (having come to the end of the rig and looked at the rabbit-snare and found it empty and found also a stone whereon to sit) I fell into another meditation: this dung that backgrounded existence, this Autumn's crops, meal for the folk of the cities, good heartsome barley alcohol – would never be spread, never be seeded, never gound to bree, but for the aristocracy of the earth,

the ploughmen and the peasants. These are the real rulers of
Scotland: they are the rulers of the earth!

And how patient and genial and ingenuously foul-mouthed and
dourly wary and kindly they are, those selfless aristos of Scotland.
They endure a life of mean and bitter poverty, an order sneered
upon by the little folk of the towns, their gait is a mockery in city
streets, you see little waitresses stare haughtily at their great red,
suncreased hands, plump professors in spectacles and pimples
enunciate theses on their mortality and morality, their habits of
breeding and their shiftlessness – and they endure it all! They
endure the chatter of the city salons, the plannings of this and that
war and blockade, they endure the pretensions of every social class
but their own to be the mainspring and base of human society –
they, the masters, who feed the world! . . . And it came on me that
all over Great Britain, all over Europe this morning, the mean fields
of France and fat pastures of Saxony and the rolling lands of
Roumania those rulers of the earth were out and about, bent-
backed at plodding toil, the world's great Green International
awaiting the coming of its Spartacus.

There are gulls in from the sea this morning, wheeling in comet
tails at the heels of this and that ploughman, a dotting of signatures
against the dark green of the Bervie braes. Here the land is red clay,
sour and dour, but south, by Brechin, you come to that rich loam
land that patterns Scotland like a ragged veil, the lovely land that
even here erupts in sudden patches and brings tall corn while the
surrounding fields wilt in the baking clay. The clay is good for
potatoes in the dry years, however – those dry years that come
every decade or so for no reason that we know of here in the Howe,
for we are beyond the 'mountain-shadow' that makes of Donside
and Braemar the tourist's camping-ground. . . .

In the sunlight, down by Kinneff, the fog-horn has begun its
wail, the sun has drawn great banks of mist out of the North Sea
and now they are billowing over Auchendreich like the soft,
coloured spume from a washing-tub. But leftwards the sun is a
bright, steely glare on the ridged humps of the Grampians,
hastening south into the coming of Summer, crowned with snow
in their upper haughs – much the same mountains, I suppose, as

the Maglemosians looked on that Spring day in the youth of the world and the youth of Scotland when they crossed the low lands of the Dogger Bank and clambered up the rocks of Kinneff into a still and untenanted Scotland. The great bear watched them come, and the eagle from his Grampian eyrie and scattering packs of wolves on the forest fringes saw that migration of the hunters seven thousand years ago. They came over Auchendreich there, through the whins and heath, and halted and stared at the billowing Howe, and laughed and muttered and squatted and stared – dark men, and tall, without gods or kings, classes or culture, writers or artists, free and happy, and all the world theirs. Scotland woke and looked at them from a hundred peaks and stared a shy virgin's amaze.

All winter the cattle were kept to the byres. This morning saw their first deliverance – cows and stirks and stots and calves they grumphed and galumphed from the byre to the park and squat-tered an astounded delight in the mud, and boxed at each other, and stared a bovine surprise at the world, and went mad with delight and raced round the park, and stood still and mooed: they mooed on a long, devilish note, the whole lot of them, for nearly two minutes on end and for no reason at all but delight in hearing their own moo. They are all of mixed breed, except one, a small Jersey cow of a southron coldness, who drops her aitches, haugh-tily, and also her calves. The strains are mostly shorthorn, with a dash of Highland, I suspect: a hundred years of mixed pasturing and crop-rotation weeded out the experimental breeds and left these satisfying mongrels. Presently (after racing a grocer's cart for the length of the field and all but hamstringing themselves on the boundary fence) they abandoned playfulness and took to grazing, remembering their mission was to provide fat carcases for the slaughter-shed—

We balk from such notions, in Spring especially, in especial as the evening comes with that fresh smell all about it, impregnating it, the kind of evening that has growth and youngness and kindliness in its essence – balk from the thought of our strange, unthinking cruelties, the underpit of blood and suffering and intolerable horror on which the most innocent of us build our lives. I feel this evening that never again will I eat a dead animal (or,

I find myself guarding the resolve with the inevitable flippancy, a live one). But that resolve will be gone to-morrow: the Horror is beyond personalism, very old and strange and terrible. Even those hunters all those millenia ago were eaters of flesh.

It is strange to think that, if events never die (as some of the wise have supposed,) but live existence all time in Eternity, back through the time-spirals, still alive and aware in that world seven thousand years ago, the hunters are *now* lying down their first night in Scotland, with their tall, deep-bosomed sinewy mates and their children, tired from trek. . . . Over in the west a long line of lights twinkles against the dark. Whin-burning – or the camps of Maglemose?

III. Summer

I cycled up the Glen of Drumtochty to-day. It was very hot, the heat was caught in the cup of the Howe and spun and stirred there, milkily, by little currents of wind that had come filtering down through the Grampian passes. In the long, dusty stretches of roadway my shadow winked and fluttered perspiringly while I followed in a sympathetic sweat. This till we passed down into Glen itself, when the overshadowing hills flung us a cool shade. There the water sparkled and spun coolly, so coldly, a little burn with deep brown detritus winding amidst the broom and the whins. To the left the reafforested Drumtochty Hill towered up dazzlingly impossible in purple. This Tyrian splendour on Drumtochty Hill is probably unmatched in all Scotland, very breath-taking and strange, alien to Scotland: it is a wonder, a flamboyant flaunting of nature that comes for a month on our dour hill-lands and we stare at it, sober, Presbyterian, from our blacks and browns – much as MacDiarmid visioned the Scots on Judgment Day staring at

> 'God and a' his gang
> O' angels in the lift,
> Thae trashy, bleezin' French-like folk
> Wha garred them shift. . . .'

Beyond the contours of Drumtochty, through the piping of that stillness, snipe were sounding. I got off my bicycle to listen to that and look round. So doing I was aware of a sober fact: that indeed all this was a little disappointing. I would never apprehend its full darkly colourful beauty until I had gone back to England, far from it, down in the smooth pastures of Hertfordshire some night I would remember it and itch to write of it, I would see it without the unessentials – sweat and flies and that hideous gimcrack castle, nestling – (Good God, it even *nestled*!) among the trees. I would see it in simplicity then, even as I would see the people of the land.

This perhaps is the real land; not those furrows that haunt me as animate. This is the land, unstirred and greatly untouched by men, unknowing ploughing or crops or the coming of the scythe. Yet even those hills were not always thus. The Archaic Civilization came here and terraced great sections of those hills and reared Devil Stones, Sun Circles, to the great agricultural gods of ancient times – long ago, before Pytheas sailed these coasts, while Alexander rode his horse across the Jaxartes there were peasants on those hills, on such a day as this, who paused to wipe the sweat from their faces and look with shrewd eyes at the green upspringing of the barley crops. . . . By night they slept in houses dug in the earth, roofed with thatch, and looked out on a wilder and wetter Howe, but still with that passion of purple mantling it in this month. They are so tenuous and yet so real, those folk – and how they haunted me years ago! I had no great interest in the things around me, I remember, the summer dawns that came flecked with saffron over the ricks of my father's farm, the whisper and pelt of the corn-heads, green turning to yellow in the long fields that lay down in front of our front-door, the rattle and creak of the shelvins of a passing box-cart, the chirp and sardonic *Ay*! of the farming childe who squatted unshaven, with twinkling eyes, on the forefront of the shelvin . . . but the ancient men haunted those woods and hills for me, and do so still.

I climbed up the top of Cairn o' Mount with my bicycle and sat and lunched and looked about me: and found it very still, the land of Scotland taking a brief siesta in that midday hour. Down in the north the green parks, miles away, were like plaques of malachite set on the table of some craftsman of ancient Chichen-Itza or Mexico, translucent and gleaming and polished. One understood then, if never before, how that colour – green – obsessed the ancient civilization with its magic virtues. It was one of the colours that marked a Giver of Life – reasonably, for those crops are surely such Givers? It is better land here than in my homeland – darker, streaked with clay, but with a richer sub-soil. Between the green of the corn and barley shone the darker stretches of the tattie-shaws, the turnip tops, and the honey brown of the clover. Bees were humming about me: one came and ate jam from my sandwiches, some discontented apian soul unfulfilled with the natural honey of the heather-bells and longing for the tart, sharp tastes of the artificial.

He is not alone in that. In the days of my youth (I have that odd pleasure that men in the early thirties derive from thinking of themselves as beyond youth: this pleasure fades in the forties) men and women still lived largely on the food-stuffs grown in the districts – kale and cabbage and good oatmeal, they made brose and porridge and crisp oatcakes, and jams from the blackberry bushes in the dour little, sour little gardens. But that is mostly a matter of the past. There are few who bake oatcakes nowadays, fewer still who ever taste kale. Stuff from the grocer's, stuff in bottles and tins, the canned nutriments of Chicago and the ubiquitous Fray Bentos, have supplanted the old-time diets. This dull, feculent stuff is more easy to deal with, not enslaving your whole life as once the cooking and serving did in the little farms and cottars' houses – cooking in the heat of such a day as this on great open fireplaces, without even a range. And though I sit here on this hill and deplore the fusionless foods of the canneries, I have no sympathy at all with those odd souls of the cities who would see the return of that 'rich agricultural life' as the return of something praiseworthy, blessed and rich and generous. Better Fray Bentos and a seat in the pictures with your man of a Saturday night than a grilling baking of piled oatcakes and a headache withal.

They change reluctantly, the men and women of the little crofts and cottar houses; but slowly a quite new orientation of outlook is taking place. There are fewer children now plodding through the black glaur of the wet summer storms to school, fewer in both farm and cottar house. The ancient, strange whirlimagig of the generations that enslaved the Scots peasantry for centuries is broken. In times gone by a ploughman might save and scrape and live meanly and hardly and marry a quean of like mettle. And in time they would have gathered enough to rent a croft, then a little farm; and all the while they saved, and lived austere, sardonic lives; and their savings took them at last to the wide cattle-courts and the great stone-floored kitchen of a large farm. And all the while the woman bred, very efficiently and plentifully and without fuss – twelve or thirteen were the common numberings of a farmer's progeny. And those children grew up, and their father died. And in the division of property at his death each son or daughter gathered as inheritance only a few poor pounds. And perforce they started as ploughmen in the bothies, maids in the kitchens, and set about climbing the rungs again – that their children might do the same.

It kept a kind of democracy on the land that is gone or is going; your halflin or your maid was the son or the daughter of your old friends of High Rigs: your own sons and daughters were in bothies or little crofts: it was a perfect Spenglerian cycle. Yet it was waste effort, it was as foolish as the plod of an ass in a treadmill, innumerable generations of asses. If the clumsy fumblements of contraception have done no more than break the wheel and play of that ancient cycle they have done much. Under these hills – so summer-hazed, so immobile and essentially unchanging – of a hundred years hence I do not know what strange master of the cultivated lands will pass in what strange mechanical contrivance: but he will be outwith that ancient yoke, and I send him my love and the hope that he'll sometime climb up Cairn o' Mount and sit where I'm sitting now, and stray in summery thought – into the sun-hazed mists of the future, into the lives and wistful desirings of forgotten men who begat him.

IV. Autumn

I have a daughter four years old who was born in England and goes to school there, and already has notions on ethnology. Occasionally she and I debate and fall out, and her final triumphant thrust is 'You're only Scotch!'

Autumn of all seasons is when I realize how very Scotch I am, how interwoven with the fibre of my body and personality is this land and its queer, scarce harvests, its hours of reeking sunshine and stifling rain, how much a stranger I am, south, in those seasons of mist and mellow fruitfulness as alien to my Howe as the olive groves of Persia. It is a harder and slower harvest, and lovelier in its austerity, that is gathered here, in September's early coming, in doubtful glances on the sky at dawn, in listening to the sigh of the sea down there by Bervie. Mellow it certainly is not: but it has the most unique of tangs, this season haunted by the laplaplap of the peesie's wings, by great moons that come nowhere as in Scotland, unending moons when the harvesting carts plod through great thickets of fir-shadow to the cornyards deep in glaur.

These are the most magical nights of the land: they endure but a little while, but their smells – sharp and clear, commingled of fresh horse-dung and dusty cornheads – pervade the winter months. The champ and showd of a horse in that moonsprayed dark and the guttural 'Tchkh, min!' of the forker, the great shapes of cattle in the parks as you ride by, the glimmer far away of the lights of some couthy toun on the verge of sleep, the queer shapes of post and gate and stook – Nature unfolds the puppets and theatre pieces year after year, unvaryingly, and they lose their dust, each year uniquely fresh. You can stand and listen as though for the lost trumpet of God in that autumn night silence: but indeed all that you are listening for is a passing peewit.

It is strange how Scotland has no Gilbert White or H. J. Massingham to sing its fields, its birds, such night as this, to chronicle the comings and goings of the swallows in simple, careful prose, ecstasy controlled. But perhaps not so strange. We Scots have little interest in the wild and its world; I realize how compassed and controlled is my own interest, I am vague about sparrows and tits, martins and swallows, I know little of their seasons, and my ignorance lies heavily upon me not at all. I am concerned so much more deeply with men and women, with their nights and days, the things they believe, the things that move them to pain and anger and the callous, idle cruelties that are yet undead. When I hear or read of a dog tortured to death, very vilely and foully, of some old horse driven to a broken back down a hill with an overloaded cart of corn, of rats captured and tormented with red-hot pokers in bothies, I have a shudder of disgust. But these things do not move me too deeply, not as the fate of the old-time Cameronian prisoners over there, three miles away in Dunnottar; not as the face of that ragged tramp who went by this afternoon; not as the crucifixion of the Spartacist slaves along the Appian Way. To me it is inconceivable that sincere and honest men should go outside the range of their own species with gifts of pity and angry compassion and rage when there is horror and dread among humankind. I am unreasonably and mulishly prejudiced in favour of my own biological species. I am a jingo patriot of planet earth: 'Humanity right or wrong!'

Particularly in Autumn. At noon I crossed a field off which the last of the stooks had been lifted and led captive away, the gaping stubble heads pushed through the cricks of clay, the long bouts of the binder wound and wheeled around the park, where the foreman had driven his team three weeks before. And each of those minute stubble stalks grew from seed that men had handled and winnowed and selected and ploughed and harrowed the earth to receive, and sown and tended and watched come up in the rains of Springs and the hot Summer suns – each and all of these – and out and beyond their kindred trillions in the other parks, up to the biggings of Upperhill there, and south through all the chave of the Howe to the black lands that start by Brechin and roll down the coast till they come to the richness of Lothian and the orchards of Blairgowrie . . . This is our power, this the wonder of humankind, our one great victory over nature and time. Three million years hence our descendants out on some tremendous furrowing of the Galaxy, with the Great Bear yoked to The Plough and the wastes of space their fields, will remember this little planet, if at all, for the men who conquered the land and wrung sustenance from it by stealth and shrewdness and a savage and surly endurance. Nothing else at all may endure in those overhuman memories: I do not think there is anything else I want to endure.

The ricks loom tall and white in the moonlight about their yellow bosses: folk are loosening the heavy horses from the carts and leading them tramp, tramp across the cobbles of the close: with a scrape and clatter by the water-trough and a silence and then the sound of a slavering long, enjoyable long suction: I feel thirsty in sympathy with that equine delight of cool, good water in a parched mouth and throat. Then a light blinks through the cobwebs of the stable, an impatient voice says *Wissh!* and harvest is over.

Quiet enough here, because the very young and irresponsible are not here. But elsewhere, nights like this, up and down the great agricultural belts of Scotland, in and about the yards and the ricks, there is still some relic of the ancient fun at the last ingathering of the sheaves – still a genial clowning and drinking and a staring at the moon, and slow, steady childes swinging away to the bothies, their hands deep down in their pouches, their boots striking fire from the cobbles; still maids to wait their lads in the lee of the new-built stacks, and be cuddled and warm and happy against brown, dank chests, and be kissed into wonder on the world, and taste the goodness of the night and the Autumn's end. . . . Before the Winter comes.

To-morrow the potato harvests, of course. But somehow they are not real harvests, they are not truly of Autumn as is the taking in of the corn. It is still an alien plant, the potato, an intruder from that world of wild belief and wilder practice that we call the New, a plant that hides and lairs deep down in the midst of back-breaking drills. The corn is so ancient that its fresh harvesting is no more than the killing of an ancient enemy-friend, ritualistic, that you may eat of the flesh of the God, drink of his blood, and be given salvation and life.

Religion

Definition is the better part of dissertation. Before one sets to a sketch of Religion in Scotland it is well to state what Religion is not. It is not altruism, it is not awe, it is not the exercise of a super-conscious sense. It is not ethics; it is not morality. It is neither the evolution of primitive Fear into civilized Worship nor the deified apprehension of an extra-mundane Terror.

Instead, a Religion is no more than a corpus of archaic science. The origin of Religion was purely utilitarian. Primitives – the food-gatherers, the ancient folk of all the ancient world – knew no religion. Their few and scattered survivors in this and that tiny crinkle of our planet are as happily irreligious as our own remote ancestors. They are without gods or devils, worship or cities, sacrifices or kings, theologies or social classes. Man is naturally irreligious. Religion is no more fundamental to the human char-acter than cancer is fundamental to the human brain.

Man in a Primitive condition is not Man Savage. Confusion of those two distinct cultural phases has led to the ludicrous condi-tion of anthropology and ethnology at the present day – the confusion which produces such eminent Scotsmen as Sir Arthur Keith capable of asserting that racialism is the life-blood of progress. Of a like order and origin are the wordy 'theses' of the various psycho-analyst groups which follow Freud and Jung. Psycho-analysts are our modern supreme specialists in the art of slipshod research. A Viennese Jew has been haunted from early years by the desire (inhibited) to cut his father's throat. The psycho-analyst, excavating details of this laudable, but abortive intention, turns to such gigantic compendiums of irrelevantly-indexed myth and custom as Sir James G. Frazer's *Golden Bough*. Therein he discovers that parricide was common to Bantu, Melanesian, aboriginal Australian. Ergo, common to primitives; ergo, a fundamental human trait. . . . The fact that Bantus, Melanesians and Australians are not primitives, but savages, peoples who have absorbed religious and social details from alien cultures and transformed their economic organization in harmony with that absorption is either unapprehended or dismissed as unimportant: and we reach back to smear the face of Natural Man with the filth of our own disease.

Particularly is this the case with regard to Religion; and particularly is the truly utilitarian nature of Religion manifested in that long life of three centuries which the Scots people led under the ægis of the Presbyterian churches.

Religion for the Scot was essentially a means of assuring himself life in the next world, health in this, prosperity, wealth, fruitful wombs and harvests. The Auld Kirk in Scotland is the greatest example of an armchair scientific Religion known to the world since the decay of the great State cults of Egypt and Mexico. In the case of all three countries the Gods were both unlovely and largely unloved; and in the case of all three definite discomforts of apparel and conduct were undergone in return for definite celestial favours manifested upon the terrestrial scene. One of those innumerable (and generally nauseating) pulpit stories illustrates this:

'A town minister was on holiday in the country, and consented to act one Sabbath in place of the local incumbent. While he was robing himself in the vestry he was approached by some of the elders, farmers all, and tactfully desired to remember in his prayers a supplication for rain – there had been a considerable drouth. Accordingly, he ascended the pulpit, and in the course of the service prayed that "the windows of Heaven might be opened to cheer the thirsty ground, and fulfil the earnest hopes of the husbandman."

'Scarcely had he finished than a flash of lightning was observed through the kirk windows. The growl of thunder followed; and in a few minutes such a downpour of rain as was speedily levelling to the ground the standing crops, and leaving the cornfields ruined and desolate. Ascribing this disastrous phenomenon [very reasonably] to the minister's prayer, one of the farmers remarked as he tramped away through the rain: "That poor fool may be well enough in the town, but God Almighty! the sooner he's out of the country the better for everybody".'

Behind those couthy tales of ministers and kirks, beadles and elders, sessions and sextons, a system operated with a ruthless efficiency for three long centuries. In Scotland the human mind and the human body were in thrall to what the orthodox would call a reign of religion, what the Diffusionist historian recognizes as the reign of a cultural aberration, what the political student might apprehend as a reign of terror. The fears and hopes of long-defunct Levantines, as set forth in the Christian Bible, were accepted as a code of conduct, as a science of life, and foisted upon the Scottish scene without mercy and greatly without favour. This is an attempt at impartial statement, not an expression of anti-Christianity. Had they been the codes of the Korân or the Rig-veda the scene would doubtlessly have been even more farcical objectively, if in subjective essence the same.

Late seventeenth and eighteenth century Scotland saw the domination of the code at its most rigorous. Not only was the Sunday (meticulously then, as still in the meeting-houses of the Free Kirk, misnamed the Sabbath) a day of rigid and inexorable piety, but the week-days as well were under the control and spying activities of kirk-session and minister, beadle – and indeed any odd being with a desire to vex the lives of his fellow-men. The Sunday in particular was sanctified to an exclusive care with the rites and wraths of the Scottish Huitzilopochtli – war-god and maize-god in one. In the *Social Life of Scotland in the Eighteenth Century* a slightly modernized cleric says of the kirk-officers, beadles and deacons:

'There was not a place where one was free from their inquisitorial intrusion. They might enter any house and even pry into the rooms. In towns where the patrol of elders or deacons, beadle and officers, paced with solemnity the deserted causeway eagerly eyeing every door and window,

craning their necks up every close and lane, the people slunk
into the obscurity of shadows and kept hushed silence. So
still, so empty were the streets on a Sunday night that no
lamps were lighted, for no passengers passed by, or if they
did they had no right to walk.'

This was the state of affairs everywhere, not only in small and
obscure parishes. Elders and deacons were empowered to visit
where they liked, to assure themselves that families were engaged
in unsecular interests. If admittance were refused them to a house
they could (and very frequently did) invoke the civil magistrates'
aid for breaking in forcibly. They could impose innumerable fines
and penalties. The power of life and death was in the hands of this
great priesthood, the guardians and functionaries of the science. A
minute of the Edinburgh kirk-session (from *The King's Pious
Proclamation* (1727) says:

'Taking into consideration that the Lord's Day is profaned by
people standing in the streets, vaguing in the fields and
gardens, as also by idly gazing out at windows, and children
and apprentices playing in the streets, warn parents and
threaten to refer to the Civil Magistrates for punishment,
also order each Session to take its turn in watching the streets
on Sabbath, as has been the laudable custom of this city, and
to visit each suspected house in each parish by elders and
deacons, with beadle and officers, and after sermon, when
the day is long, to pass through the streets and reprove such
as transgress, and inform on such as do not refrain'.

During the week the minister might notify any member of his
congregation that he intended to visit him in his own house and
hold a 'catechizing' of his family. This 'catechizing' consisted of a
play of question and answer on knowledge of the Christian
Scriptures, the Christian Code of the Good Life, and the Christian
Code of Eternal Punishment. Everyone was questioned in rote –
the master, the mistress, the children, and all the servants within
the gates. Those who failed to answer according to the code might

be rebuked or punished, according to the nature of the offence; those who failed to put in an appearance at those ceremonies of droned affirmation and incantation might be very bitterly prosecuted. Until well towards the nineties of last century the officials of the Scots priesthood were the real rulers of the Scots scene, they were Spartan ephors, largely elected by the people and keeping the people under a rigorous rule. And then the rank blossomings of Industrialism loosened their hold, weakened their status, and freed Scotland from the nightmare of their power.

It is obvious that any people under the rule of such rigorous and forbidding code – belief in a joyless but necessary agricultural God, belief in a joyless but necessary ceremonial ritual – would develop strange abnormalities of appearance and behaviour. It is evident in the ancient scene in Mexico, for example, where every year thousands of human beings were sacrificed to the Gods of the earth and rain, that a few more hundred years of evolution along the same lines would have wrought a biological deviation from the human norm: the ancient Mexicans, but for the fortunate arrival of Cortes, would have aberrated into a sub-species of *Homo Sapiens*. The same may be said of the Scots. Left alone and uninvaded, they might have passed entirely beyond the orbit of the normally human but for the coming of the Industrial Revolution. This brought Scotland its slums and its Glasgow, its great wens of ironworks and collieries upon the open face of the countryside; but its final efflorescence broke the power of the Church and released the Scot to a strange and terrible and lovely world, the world of science and scepticism and high belief and free valour – emerging into the sunlight of history from a ghoul-haunted cañon.

There is still a Church of Scotland – ostensibly more powerful than ever, having recently amalgamated with its great rival, the United Free Church. There are still innumerable ministers of the Kirk to be met with in the leafy manse walks, the crowded Edinburgh streets, the gatherings of conferences and associations and the like. There is still the trickle of the kirkward folk on a Sabbath morning in summer, when the peewits hold their unending plaint over the greening fields and the young boys linger and kick at the thistles by the wayside, and young girls step daintily down whin-guarded paths and over the cow-dung pats by this and that gate. There is still the yearly Assembly of the Kirk in Edinburgh – the strangest of functions, with the High Commissioner some vague politician generally discreetly unintelligible and inevitably discreetly unintelligent; with elderly clergymen acclaiming War 'for the good of the nation,' the sword the weapon of Christianity, the economic crisis an Apollyon to be moved by prayer. There are still old women and men who find sustenance and ease and comfort in the droned chantings of the risen God, in symbolic cannibal feastings upon the body of the dead God at time of Communion . . .

But it is little more now than a thin and tattered veil upon the face of the Scottish scene. This ostensibly powerful Kirk, twin-headed, is riven with the sorriest of all disputes – a quarrel over meal and milk. For the old United Frees will not give up their own ministers and kirks in favour of the Auld Kirk ministers and kirks; nor vice versa. So in most parishes there are still to be found two churches in close proximity, staffed by ministers preaching exactly the same doctrine, ministers preaching to congregations of twenty or so in buildings erected to house a hundred. But the ministers themselves – of manse and walk and street and conference – are of strangely different quality and calibre to those who manned the Kirk in the mid-eighteenth century.

There are few such pleasant people as the younger ministers of Scotland. Pleasant is the one possible adjective. They are (the most of them) free-hearted and liberal, mild socialists, men with pleasant wives who blush over the books of such writers as myself, but read them nevertheless and say pleasant things about the pleasant passages. But the older generation differs from the younger very greatly. It has run to girth and very often to grossness. It grins with unloosened vest. Its congregation grins dourly in comprehension. It is, in the country parishes, the understood thing that the middle-aged, genial minister generally 'sleeps with' his housekeeper – a proceeding, I remember, which greatly astonished my innocent youth, for why should a man like the minister want to sleep with anyone when he had a big, fine bed of his own? The most luscious of filthy tales (with women the butt and object of each and the sex-act the festering focal point) I have ever heard were from the lips of a highly respected and reputable minister of the Church of Scotland who still preaches to an exclusive congregation in one of the Four Cities. The minister a minister at the beginning of the present century had been greatly freed from the fears and tabus that formerly inhered in the functioning of his office, but had obtained no such measure of mental freedom and enlightenment as his younger colleague of to-day.

And that kirkwards trickle of the folk is delusive as well. Here you behold not the fervid Presbyterian but the bored (if complacent) farmer and his wife attending a mild social function. They are going to church because there is nothing much else to be done on a Sunday; they can meet a neighbour there and ask him to supper; the wife will survey with some interest a neighbouring wife's hat or the advances yet another neighbour is making in exhibition of her stages of pregnancy. The old fires and the old fears are gone. Men and women sit and listen with a placid benignancy to sermons as varied in opinion and scope as are the political reaches between fascism and communism . . . and they are quite unstirred. It is something quite unconcerned with their everyday life of factory and field and hope and fear, it is something to amuse the wife and good for the children. . . . Why good? They are vague.

And though some of those children reluctantly holding kirkwards, reluctantly seated in those unpadded pews and staring with desperate earnestness at the buzzing busyness of a fly seeking to escape through the panes of a glazed window, may indeed have strange fears and dark terrors upon them, fears that awaken them screaming in the nights with this horrific God thrusting them into sizzling pits of fire because of some minor lapse of the previous day, fears that make lonely wood walks a terror, every screech of an owl the cry of some devil or gnome from the pages of Christian myth, yet their numbers are probably few. It is still a terrible and a dreadful thing that the minds of a nation's youth should be twisted and debased by those ancient, obscene beliefs and restraints; yet, good democrats, we may rejoice that it is now only the minds of the minority – the intelligent minority – that so suffer. And they are growing up into habitation of a world that will presently look back upon even the emasculated rites of the Kirk of Scotland as insanely irrelevant to human affairs as the Black Mass.

Nor does the yearly General Assembly resemble (as once) the Sanhedrin of the Jews. To a large extent it is the excuse and occasion for much tea-drinking and the exchange of views on theological scholarship, rose-growing, and the meaner scandals. Its public speeches have an unexciting monotone of supplication and regret: the young are leaving the Kirk, how may they be reclaimed? The tides of irreligion and paganism are flooding in upon us: how may they be stayed? A similar tidal problem once confronted King Canute. It is recorded that he used denunciation with singular lack of success, and modern experience appears to verify the historical precedent. The pedestrian who pauses midway a meadow and seeks to stay a charging bull by alternately denouncing its brutish appearance and calling upon it to forgo its essential bullishness is unlikely to survive the occasion for a sufficient length of time to draw up an unimpassioned monograph on the subject.

Occasionally (as has been noted) the Assembly abandons the pagans and turns to consideration of such pressing matters as unemployment, war, and the economic system. In the case of the first and the last it is, (very naturally and to some extent blamelessly, for it is the assembly of ministers of a State Religion) impotent. More diversity of talent and opinion greets the subject of war. Padded elderly gentlemen with cheerfully carmine cheeks and grey whiskers uphold the Sword as the Weapon of Righteousness, used aforetime by Scotland in defence of her liberties: may not Scotland need the Sword again? A sad commentary on the relation of the Assembly to contemporary military science lies in the fact that no opponent appears to have suggested the archaic character of the sword in modern warfare. Why not the Saw-Toothed Bayonet of Salvation? Why not the Gas of God? . . . Vexed from that humble impartiality which is his aim the investigator toys with a vision of the plump, rosy parson in the dirty grey pallor of a gas attack – Lewisite for preference. He sees the rosy cheeks cave in, the eyes start forth like those of a hamstrung pig, the mouth move vomiting as the gas bites into lung-tissues. He turns with a vagrant sigh from that vision: that sight in actuality would almost be worth another War.

That many of the old and the middle-aged of both sexes find comfort in the Kirk and its ceremonies is undeniable. And this brings us to a fine human essence in the relationship of Kirk and people that may not be abandoned on recognition of the archaic nature of the rites of Communion and the like. That comfort was and is sometimes very real. The bitterly toilworn and the bitterly oppressed have been often sustained and cheered and uplifted for the cheerless life of the day to day by the lovely poetry of the Bible, the kindly and just and angrily righteous things therein. They have found inspiration and hope in the sayings and denunciations of some Jewish prophet long powder and nothing, but one who, like them, had doubted life because of its ills and cried on something beyond himself to redress the sad balance of things, to feed the hungry and put down the oppressor. The humble and the poor have found the Kirk and kirk life not only a grinding and a mean oppressiveness, they have found (and find) ministers who are cheerful and helpful beings, with or without their theology, knowledgeable men in medicine and times of stress, champions against lairds and factors and such-like fauna. They have found in the kirk itself, in the blessed peace and ease of a two hours rest in the pews, listening to the only music they ever hear, refreshment and good feeling. If it has chastised the free and rebellious and wrought many bitter things upon the Scots spirit the Kirk has yet atoned in those little ways.

For they are little ways. A contented helot is not a freeman; a bitterly-oppressed and poverty-stricken serf is still a serf though you tell him tales in an idle hour and bind his worse hurts and sooth his worse fears of night and the dark that comes down on us all. The Kirk of Scotland, the Religion of the Kirk of Scotland, on its credit balance has done no more than that. It has tamed and clipped and sometimes soothed: it has used the sword often enough: after 1600 it used upon the people of Scotland themselves. Its policy and its code in the seventeenth and eighteenth centuries produced that Scot who was our ancestor: the Scot who had mislaid original thought for a dour debating of fine theological points, who was more concerned to applaud the spirited conduct of Elijah with the bears than to guard his

own economic freedom, who at twenty, married, looked on the clean
lusts and desires of the marriage bed as shameful and disgusting
things; who tormented in a pit of weariness his young children,
Sabbath on Sabbath, with the learning by rote of dull and unintelligible theological chatter from a book that can be as painfully
wearying as it can be painfully enthralling; who looked forward to
'catechizings' with a clownish zest or a clownish fear; who mislaid
beauty and tenderness and love of skies and the happy life of beasts
and birds and children for the stern restraints, the droning hymns
and the superhuman endurances demanded of the attendants at Kirk
service; whose social life revolved round the comings and goings,
sayings and preachings, rebukings and praisings of priests who were
often dull and foolish and froward men, often good and dull and
bewildered men; who, a logician, passed a sinner to the grave and
therefore to hell and those zestful burnings beloved of the Presbytery.

Naturally there were sceptics throughout that era, very cautious
but biting sceptics:

> 'There was a Cameronian cat
>   A-seeking for its prey,
> Went ben the hoose and caught a moose
>   Upon the Sabbath day.
>
> The Elders, they were horrified
>   And they were vexed sair,
> Sae straight they took that wicked cat
>   Afore the meenistair.
>
> The meenistair was sairly grieved
>   And much displeased did say:
> 'Oh, bad perverted pussy-cat
>   Tae break the Sabbath day!
>
> 'The Sabbath's been, frae days o' yore,
>   An Institution:
> Saw straichtway tak' this wicked cat
>   Tae Execution!"'

Release from the secular power of the Kirk, or secular enforcement of the Kirk's displeasure, had effects on the Scots similar to those that sunlight and wine might have on a prisoner emerging from long years in a dank cellar. Freedom had been forbidden him: he became the conscienceless anarchist in politics, in commerce, in private affairs. Love of women and the glorying in it had been forbidden him: the modern Scot, escaping that tabu, is still fascinated and horrified by sex. He has seen it swathed in dirty veils of phrase and sentiment so long that now he would expose it for the ludicrous and lewd and ridiculous thing he conceives it must be: Scots in conversation, Scots novelists in their books these modern days are full of details of sex and the sex-act, crude and insanitary details. . . . They have escaped the tabu and sought the reality and stumbled into a midden on the way. An aphasia of the spirit has descended on the Scot so that he can see only the foul in a thing that is neither foul nor fair, that is jolly and necessary and amusing and thrilling and tremendous fun and a deadly bore and exhilarating to the point of making one sing and dreadful to the point of making one weep. . . .

This is where the effects of Presbyterianism join issue with the effects of the other Religions which dwindlingly survived in Reformed Scotland. Catholicism was more mellow and colourful and poetic: it was also darker and older and more oppressed by even more ancient shames. It produced an attitude of mind more soft than the Presbyterian: and also infinitely more servile. Sex has always been a tabu and shameful thing to the Catholic mind, a thing to be *transmuted* – in the fashion of gathering a lovely lily from its cheerful dung and transmuting it into a glassy ornament for a sterile altar. Episcopalianism is in a different category. From the first it was more a matter of social status than of theological conviction; it was rather a grateful bourgeois acknowledgement of Anglicization than dissent with regard to the methods of worshipping a God. A typical Episcopalian was Sir Walter Scott – shallow and sedulous, incurably second-rate, incapable (so had his spirit-stuff been moulded) of either delineating the essentials of human character or of apprehending the essentials of human motivation. The Episcopalian Church in Scotland gave to life and ritual mildly colourful trappings, a sober display: it avoided God with a shudder of genteel distaste.

The modern Free Church member is the ancient Presbyterian who has learned nothing and forgotten nothing. As certain unfortunate children abandon mental development at the cretinaceous age of eight, Free Church doctrine, essentially un-Christian, abandoned development with the coming of the Kelts. It is a strange and disgusting cult of antique fear and antique spite. It looks upon all the gracious and fine things of the human body – particularly the body of woman – with sickened abhorrence, it detests music and light and life and mirth, the God of its passionate conviction is a kind of immortal Peeping Tom, an unsleeping celestial sneak-thief, it seeks to cramp and distort the minds of the young much as the ancient Maya sought to mould the brain-stuff of *their* young by deforming the infants' heads with the aid of tightly-strapped slats of wood. As fantastically irrelevant to contemporary Scottish affairs as the appendix is to the human body, its elimination may be brought about rather by advances in social hygiene than by surgical operation.

Debating those elementary facts with regard to Religion in Scotland the present writer before this time has met with the surprising complaint: 'And what is going to happen now? What are you going to put in the place of Religion?' The question shows some confusion of mind. The present writer had no hand in bringing about the decay of Religion; nor, alas, is he likely to have any hand in planning its succession. That succession lies with great economic and historical movements now in being – movements which may bring to birth the strangest of progeny on which we may look aghast. Of the future of Religion ultimately the historian can have little doubt: he sees its coming in ancient times, in the world of the Simple Men, as a cortical abortion, a misapprehension of the functions and activities of nature interlarded and interwoven with attributes mistakenly applied to human rulers. He sees its passing from the human scene – even the Scots scene – in the processes of change, immutable and unstayable. But—

But there may be long delays in that passing. Another abortion of inactive brains – that of Fascism – looms over a tormented world, a creed of the *must* jungle brute, the cowardly degenerate who fears the fine steely glimmer of the open spaces of the heavens, the winds of change, the flow and cry of strange seas and stars in human conduct and human hope – who would drag men back into economic night, into slavery to the state, into slavery (all slaveries aid his purpose) to the archaic institutions of Religion. What has happened in Italy and Germany may happen in Scotland. The various Scots nationalist parties have large elements of Fascism within them. There is now a definite Fascist Party. If ever such philosophy should reach to power then again we may see deserted streets of a Sabbath, crowded kirks, persecutions and little parish tyrannies, a Free Kirk minister's millenial dream. If such should be the play of chance it is to be hoped that the historian (albeit himself on the way to the scaffold or the pillory) will look on the process with a cool dispassion, seeing it as no more than a temporary deviation, a thing that from its nature cannot endure. Man has survived this disease far too long either to perish in its last bout of fever or permanently retire into delirium tremens.

One sees rise ultimately (in that perfect state that is an ultimate necessity for human survival, for there is no sure half-way house between Utopia and extinction) in place of Religion – Nothing. To return to clinical similes, one does not seek to replace a fever by an attack of jaundice. One seeks the fields and night and the sound of the sea, the warmth of good talk and human companionship, love, wonder in the minute life of a water-drop, exultation in the wheeling Galaxy. All these fine things remain and are made the more gracious and serene and unthreatened as Religion passes. Passing, it takes with it nothing of the good – pity and hope and benevolence. Benevolence is as natural to Natural Man as hunger. It is an elementary thalamic state, a conditioned reflex of mental and physical health.

Yet, because men are not merely the victims, the hapless leaves storm-blown, of historic forces, but may guide if they cannot generate that storm, it might be well to glance at this last at those members of the various Scots priesthoods who affirm their liberalism, their belief in change, their faith that in a purified Christianity is the strait and undeniable way to that necessary Utopia. One cannot but believe that this is a delusion:

> 'Thou, in the day that breaks thy prison,
>   People, though these men take thy name,
> And hail and hymn thee rearisen,
>   Who made songs erewhile of thy shame,
> Give thou not ear; for these are they
>   Whose good day was thine evil day.
>
> Set not thine hand upon their cross.
>   Give not thy soul up sacrificed.
> Change not the gold of faith for dross
>   Of Christian creeds that spit on Christ.
> Let not thy tree of freedom be
>   Regrafted from that rotting tree.'

But, if the investigator should stoop to point a moral, he would do so rather in the tale of the Laird of Udny's fool than in heroic rhyme. Of Jamie Fleeman, the reputed fool of the parish, many a tale is told; and the best is that which relates how, of all kirks in Scotland, Udny suffered the worst from sleepy congregations. Hardly had the sermon begun than heads began to nod. One Sunday the minister – a new minister – looked down in the course of his discourse and saw only one member of the congregation awake, and that Jamie Fleeman.

Halting his sermon the minister exclaimed: 'This sleeping in church is intolerable. There's only one man awake; and that man's a fool!' 'Ay, ay, minister, you're right there,' called up Jamie in reply. 'And if I hadn't been a fool I'd have been sleeping as well.'

SHORT STORIES

Smeddum

Greenden

Sim

Clay

Introduction to three 'English' stories
Jeremy Idle

The Epic

Dienekes' Dream

Revolt

Smeddum

She'd had nine of a family in her time, Mistress Menzies, and brought the nine of them up, forbye – some near by the scruff of the neck, you would say. They were sniftering and weakly, two-three of the bairns, sniftering in their cradles to get into their coffins; but she'd shake them to life and dose them with salts and feed them up till they couldn't but live. And she'd plonk one down – finishing the wiping of the creature's neb or unco dosing of an ill bit stomach or the binding up of a broken head – with a look on her face as much as to say *Die on me now and see what you'll get!*

Big-boned she was by her fortieth year, like a big roan mare, and *If ever she was bonny 'twas in Noah's time*, Jock Menzies, her eldest son, would say. She'd reddish hair and a high, sheugh nose, and a hand that skelped her way through life; and if ever a soul had seen her at rest when the dark was done and the day was come he'd died of the shock and never let on.

For from morn till night she was at it, work, work, on that ill bit croft that sloped to the sea. When there wasn't a mist on the cold, stone parks there was more than likely the wheep of the rain, wheeling and dripping in from the sea that soughed and plashed by the land's stiff edge. Kinneff lay north, and at night in the south, if the sky was clear on the gloaming's edge, you'd see in that sky the Bervie lights come suddenly lit, far and away, with the quiet about you as you stood and looked, nothing to hear but a sea-bird's cry.

But feint the much time to look or to listen had Margaret Menzies of Tocherty toun. Day blinked and Meg did the same and was out, up out of her bed and about the house, making the porridge and rousting the bairns, and out to the byre to milk the three kye, the morning growing out in the east and a wind like a hail of knives from the hills. Syne back to the kitchen again she

would be, and catch Jock, her eldest, a clour in the lug that he
hadn't roused up his sisters and brothers; and rouse them herself,
and feed them and scold, pull up their breeks and straighten their
frocks and polish their shoes and set their caps straight. *Off you get
and see you're not late,* she would cry, *and see you behave yourselves
at the school. And tell the Dominie I'll be down the night to ask him
what the mischief he meant by leathering Jeannie and her not well.*

They'd cry, *Ay, mother,* and go trotting away, a fair flock of the
creatures, their faces red-scoured. Her own as red, like a meikle
roan mare's, Meg'd turn at the door and go prancing in; and then
at last, by the closet-bed, lean over and shake her man half-awake.
Come on, then, Willie, it's time you were up.

And he'd groan and say *Is't?* and crawl out at last, a little bit thing
like a weasel, Will Menzies, though some said that weasels were
decent beside him. He was drinking himself into the grave, folk said,
as coarse a little brute as you'd meet, bonelazy forbye, and as sly as
sin. Rampageous and ill with her tongue though she was, you
couldn't but pity a woman like Meg tied up for life to a thing like
that. But she'd more than a soft side still to the creature, she'd half-
skelp the backside from any of the bairns she found in the telling of a
small bit lie; but when Menzies would come paiching in of a noon
and groan that he fair was tashed with his work, he'd mended all the
ley fence that day and he doubted he'd need to be off to his bed –
when he'd told her that and had ta'en to the blankets, and maybe in
less than the space of an hour she'd hold out for the kye and see that
he'd lied, the fence neither mended nor letten a-be, she'd just purse
up her meikle wide mouth and say nothing, her eyes with a glint as
though she half-laughed. And when he came drunken home from a
mart she'd shoo the children out of the room, and take off his clothes
and put him to bed, with an extra nip to keep off a chill.

She did half his work in the Tocherty parks, she'd yoke up the
horse and the sholtie together, and kilt up her skirts till you'd see
her great legs, and cry *Wissh!* like a man and turn a fair drill, the
sea-gulls cawing in a cloud behind, the wind in her hair and the sea
beyond. And Menzies with his sly-like eyes would be off on some
drunken ploy to Kinneff or Stonehive. Man, you couldn't but think
as you saw that steer it was well that there was a thing like marriage,

folk held together and couldn't get apart; else a black look-out it well would be for the fusionless creature of Tocherty toun.

Well, he drank himself to his grave at last, less smell on the earth if maybe more in it. But she broke down and wept, it was awful to see, Meg Menzies weeping like a stricken horse, her eyes on the dead quiet face of her man. And she ran from the house, she was gone all that night, though the bairns cried and cried her name up and down the parks in the sound of the sea. But next morning they found her back in their midst brisk as ever, like a great-boned mare, ordering here and directing there, and a fine feed set the next day for the folk that came to the funeral of her orra man.

She'd four of the bairns at home when he died, the rest were in kitchen-service or fee'd, she'd seen to the settling of the queans herself; and twice when two of them had come home, complaining-like of their mistresses' ways, she'd thrashen the queans and taken them back – near scared the life from the doctor's wife, her that was mistress to young Jean Menzies. *I've skelped the lassie and brought you her back. But don't you ill-use her, or I'll skelp you as well.*

There was fair a speak about that at the time, Meg Menzies and the vulgar words she had used, folk told that she'd even said what was the place where she'd skelp the bit doctor's wife. And faith! that fair must have been a sore shock, the doctor's wife that was that genteel she'd never believed she'd a place like that.

Be that as it might, her man new dead, Meg wouldn't hear of leaving his toun. It was harvest then and she drove the reaper, up and down the long, clanging clay rings by the sea, she'd jump down smart at the head of a bout and go gathering and binding swift as the wind, syne wheel in the horse to the cutting again. She led the stooks with her bairns to help, you'd see them at night, a drowsing cluster, under the moon on the harvesting cart.

And through that year and into the next and so till the speak died down in the Howe Meg Menzies worked the Tocherty toun; and faith, her crops came none so ill. She rode to the mart at Stonehive when she must, on the old box-cart, the old horse in the shafts, the cart behind with a sheep for sale or a birn of old hens that had finished with laying. And a butcher once tried to make a bit joke, *That's a sheep like yourself, fell long in the tooth.* And Meg answered up, neighing like a horse, and all heard: *Faith, then, if you've got a spite against teeth I've a clucking hen in the cart outbye. It's as toothless and senseless as you are, near.*

Then word got about of her eldest son, Jock Menzies that was fee'd up Allardyce way. The creature of a loon had had fair a conceit since he'd won a prize at a ploughing match – not for his ploughing, but for his good looks; and the queans about were as daft as himself, he'd only to nod and they came to his heel; and the stories told they came further than that. Well, Meg'd heard the stories and paid no heed, till the last one came, she was fell quick then.

Soon's she heard it she hove out the old bit bike that her daughter Kathie had bought for herself, and got on the thing and went cycling away, down through the Bervie braes in that Spring, the sun was out and the land lay green, with a blink of mist that was blue on the hills, as she came to the toun where Jock was fee'd she saw him out in a park by the road, ploughing, the black loam smooth like a ribbon turning and wheeling at the tail of the plough. Another billy came ploughing behind, Meg Menzies watched till they reached the rig-end, her great chest heaving like a meikle roan's, her eyes on the shape of the furrows they made. And they drew to the end and drew the horse out, and Jock cried *Ay*, and she answered back *Ay*, and looked at the drill, and gave a bit snort, *If your looks win prizes, your ploughing never will.*

Jock laughed. *Fegs, then, I'll not greet for that,* and chirked to his horses and turned them about. But she cried him *Just bide you a minute, my lad. What's this that I hear about you and Ag Grant?*

He drew up short then, and turned right red, the other childe as well, and they both gave a laugh, as plough-childes do when you mention a quean they've known over-well in more ways than one. And Meg snapped *It's an answer I want, not a cockerel's cackle: I can hear that at home on my own dunghill. What are you to do about Ag and her pleiter?*

And Jock said *Nothing,* impudent as you like, and next minute Meg was in over the dyke and had hold of his lug and shook him and it till the other childe ran and caught at her hieve. *Faith, mistress, you'll have his lug off!* he cried. But Meg Menzies turned like a mare on new grass, *Keep off or I'll have yours as well!*

So he kept off and watched, fair a story he'd to tell when he rode out that night to go courting his quean. For Meg held to the lug till it near came off and Jock swore that he'd put things right with Ag Grant. She let go the lug then and looked at him grim: *See that you do and get married right quick, you're the like that need loaded with a birn of bairns – to keep you out of the jail, I jaloose. It needs smeddum to be either right coarse or right kind.*

They were wed before the month was well out, Meg found them a cottar house to settle, and gave them a bed and a press she had, and two-three more sticks from Tocherty toun. And she herself led the wedding dance, the minister in her arms, a small bit childe; and 'twas then as she whirled him about the room, he looked like a rat in the teeth of a tyke, that he thanked her for seeing Ag out of her soss, *There's nothing like a marriage for redding things up.* And Meg Menzies said *Eh?* and then she said *Ay,* but queer-like, he supposed she'd no thought on the thing. Syne she slipped off to sprinkle thorns in the bed, and to hang below it the great hand-bell that the bothy-billies took them to every bit marriage.

Well, that was Jock married and at last off her hands. But she'd plenty left still, Dod, Kathleen and Jim that were still at the school, Kathie a limner that alone tongued her mother, Jeannie that next led trouble to her door. She'd been found at her place, the doctor's it was, stealing some money and they sent her home. Syne news of the thing got into Stonehive, the police came out and tormentd her sore, she swore she never had stolen a meck, and Meg swore with her, she was black with rage. And folk laughed right hearty, fegs! that was a clour for meikle Meg Menzies, her daughter a thief!

But it didn't last long, it was only three days when folk saw the doctor drive up in his car. And out he jumped and went striding in through the close and met face to face with Meg at the door. And he cried *Well, mistress, I've come over for Jeannie.* and she glared at him over her high, skeugh nose, *Ay, have you so then? And why, may I speir?*

So he told her why, the money they'd missed had been found at last, in a press by the door; somebody or other had left it there, thoughtless, when paying a grocer or such at the door. And Jeannie – he'd come over to take Jean back.

But Meg glared *Ay, well, you've made another mistake. Out of this you and your thieving suspicions together!* The doctor turned red, *You're making a miserable error* – and Meg said *I'll make you mincemeat in a minute.*

So he didn't wait that, she didn't watch him go, but went ben to the kitchen where Jeannie was sitting, her face chalkwhite as she'd heard them speak. And what happened then a story went round, Jim carried it to school, and it soon spread out. Meg sank in a chair, they thought she was greeting; syne she raised up her head and they saw she was laughing, near as fearsome the one as the other, they thought. *Have you any cigarettes?* she snapped sudden at Jean, and Jean quavered *No*, and Meg glowered at her cold. *Don't sit there and lie. Gang bring them to me.* And Jean brought them, her mother took the pack in her hand. *Give's hold of a match till I light up the thing. Maybe smoke'll do good for the crow that I got in the throat last night by the doctor's house.*

Well, in less than a month she'd got rid of Jean – packed off to Brechin the quean was and soon, got married to a creature that worked down there – some clerk that would have left her sore in the lurch but that Meg went down to the place on her bike, and there, so the story went, kicked the childe so that he couldn't sit down for a fortnight, near. No doubt that was just a bit lie that they told, but faith! Meg Menzies had herself to blame, the reputation she'd gotten in the Howe, folk said *She'll meet with a sore heart yet.* But devil a sore was there to be seen, Jeannie was married and was fair genteel.

Kathleen was next to leave home at the term. She was tall, like Meg, and with red hair as well, but a thin, fine face, long eyes blue-grey like the hills on a hot day, and a mouth with lips you thought over thick. And she cried *Ah well, I'm off then, mother.* And Meg cried *See you behave yourself.* And Kathleen cried *Maybe; I'm not at school now.*

Meg stood and stared after the slip of a quean, you'd have thought her half-angry, half near to laughing, as she watched that figure, so slender and trig, with its shoulders square-set, slide down the hill on the wheeling bike, swallows were dipping and flying by Kinneff, she looked light and free as a swallow herself, the quean as she biked away from her home, she turned at the bend and waved and whistled, she whistled like a loon and as loud, did Kath.

Jim was the next to leave from the school, he bided at home and he took no fee, a quiet-like loon, and he worked the toun, and, wonder of wonders, Meg took a rest. Folk said that age was telling a bit on even Meg Menzies at last. The grocer made hints at that one night, and Meg answered up smart as ever of old. *Damn the age! But I've finished the trauchle of the bairns at last, the most of them married or still over young. I'm as swack as ever I was, my lad. But I've just got the notion to be a bit sweir.*

Well, she'd hardly begun on that notion when faith! ill the news that came up to the place from Seggest. Kathleen, her quean that was fee'd down there, she'd ta'en up with some coarse old childe in a bank, he'd left his wife, they were off together, and she but a bare sixteen years old.

And that proved the truth of what folk were saying, Meg Menzies she hardly paid heed to the news, just gave a bit laugh like a neighing horse and went on with the work of park and byre, cool as you please – ay, getting fell old.

No more was heard of the quean or the man till a two years or more had passed and then word came up to the Tocherty someone had seen Kath Menzies at last – and where do you think? Out on a boat that was coming from Australia. She was working as stewardess on that bit boat, and the childe that saw her was young John Robb, an emigrant back from his uncle's farm, near starved to death he had been down there. She hadn't met in with him near till the end, the boat close to Southampton the evening they met. And she'd known him at once, though he not her, she'd cried *John Robb!* and he'd answered back *Ay?* and looked at her canny in case it might be the creature was looking for a tip from him. Syne she'd laughed, *Don't you know me, then, you gowk? I'm Kathie Menzies you knew long syne – I ran off with the banker from Segget!*

He was clean dumbfoundered, young Robb, and he gaped, and then they shook hands and she spoke some more, though she hadn't much time, they were serving up dinner for the first-class folk, aye dirt that are ready to eat and to drink. *If ever you get near to Tocherty toun, tell Meg I'll get home and see her some time. Ta-ta!*

And then she was off with a smile, young Robb he stood and he stared where she'd been, he thought her the bonniest thing that he'd seen all the weary weeks that he'd been from home.

And this was the tale that he brought to Tocherty, Meg sat and listened and smoked like a tink, forbye herself there was young Jim there, and Jock and his wife and their three bit bairns, he'd fair changed with marriage, had young Jock Menzies. For no sooner had he taken Ag Grant to his bed than he'd started to save, grown mean as dirt, in a three-four years he'd finished with feeing, now he rented a fell big farm for himself, well-stocked it was, and he fee'd two men. Jock himself had grown thin and mean in a way, like his father but worse, his bothy childes said, old Menzies at least could take a bit dram and get lost to the world but the son was that mean he might drink rat-poison and take no harm, 't would feel at home in a stomach like his.

Well, that was Jock and he sat and heard the story of Kath and her say on the boat. *Ay, still a coarse bitch, I have not a doubt. Well, if she never comes back to the Mearns, in Segget you cannot but redden with shame when a body will ask 'Was Kath Menzies your sister?'*

And Ag, she'd grown a great sumph of a woman, she nodded to that, it was only too true, a sore thing it was on decent bit folk that they should have any relations like Kath.

But Meg just sat there and smoked, and said never a word, as though she thought nothing heard worth a yea or a nay. Young Robb had ta'en fair a fancy to Kath, and he near boiled up when he heard Jock speak, him and the wife that he'd married from her shame. So he left them short, and went raging home, and wished for one that Kath would come back, a Summer noon as he cycled home, snipe were calling in the Auchindreich moor where the cattle stood with their tails aswitch, the Grampians rising far and behind, Kinraddie spread like a map for show, its ledges veiled in a mist from the sun. You felt on that day a wild, daft unease, man, beast and bird: as though something were missing and lost from the world, and Kath was the thing that John Robb missed, she'd something in her that minded a man of a house that was builded upon a hill.

Folk thought that that was maybe the last they would ever hear of young Kath Menzies and her ill-getted ways. So fair stammy-gastered they were with the news she'd come back to Mearns, she was down in Stonehive, in a grocer's shop there, as calm as could be, selling out tea and cheese and such-like with no blush of shame on her face at all, to decent women that were properly wed, and had never looked on men but their own, and only on them with their galluses tied.

It just showed you the way that the world was going to allow an ill quean like that in a shop, some folk protested to the creature that owned it, but he just shook his head, *Ah well, she works fine; and what else she does is no business of mine.* So you well might guess there was more than business between the man and Kath Menzies.

And Meg heard the news and went into Stonehive, driving her sholtie, and stopped at the shop. And some in the shop knew who she was, and minded the things she had done long syne to other bit bairns of hers that went wrong; and they waited with their breaths held up with delight. But all that Meg did was to nod to Kath, *Ay, well, then, it's you. . . . Ay, mother, just that. . . . Two pounds of syrup and see that it's good.*

And not another word passed between them, Meg Menzies that once would have ta'en such a quean and skelped her to rights before you could wink. Going home from Stonehive she stopped by the farm where young Robb was fee'd, he was out in the hayfield coling the hay, and she nodded to him, grim, with her high horse face. *What's this that I hear about you and Kath Menzies?*

He turned right red, but he wasn't ashamed. *I've no idea – though I hope it's the worst. . . . It fell near is. . . . Then I wish it was true, she might marry me, then, as I've prigged her to do.*

Oh, have you so, then? said Meg, and drove home, as though the whole matter was a nothing to her.

But next Tuesday the postman brought a bit note, from Kathie it was to her mother at Tocherty. *Dear mother, John Robb's going out to Canada, and wants me to marry him and go with him there. I've told him instead I'll go with him and see what he's like as a man – and then marry him at leisure, if I feel in the mood. But he's hardly any money, and we want to borrow some, so he and I are coming over on Sunday. I hope that you'll have dumpling for tea. Your own daughter, Kath.*

Well, Meg passed that letter over to Jim, he glowered at it dour, *I know – near all the Howe's heard. What are you going to do, now, mother?*

But Meg just lighted a cigarette and said nothing, she'd smoked like a tink since that steer with Jean. There was promise of strange on-goings at Tocherty by the time that the Sabbath day was come. For Jock came there on a visit as well, him and his wife, and besides him was Jeannie, her that had married the clerk down in Brechin, and she brought the bit creature, he fair was a toff; and he stepped like a cat through the sharn in the close; and when he had heard the story of Kath, her and her plan and John Robb and all, he was shocked near to death, and so was his wife. And Jock Menzies gaped and gave a mean laugh. *Ay, coarse to the bone, ill-getted I'd say if it wasn't that we came of the same bit stock. Ah well, she'll fair have to tramp to Canada, eh mother? – if she's looking for money from you.*

And Meg answered quiet, *No, I wouldn't say that. I've the money all ready for them when they come.*

You could hear the sea plashing down soft on the rocks, there was such a dead silence in Tocherty house. And then Jock habbered like a cock with fits, *What, give silver to one who does as she likes, and won't marry as you made the rest of us marry? Give silver to one who's no more than a—*

And he called his sister an ill name enough, and Meg sat and smoked, looking over the parks. *Ay, just that. You see, she takes after myself.*

And Jeannie squeaked *How?* and Meg answered her sudden, a neigh that fair shook the bit walls of the room, *She's fit to be free and to make her own choice, the same as myself and the same kind of choice. There was none of the rest of you fit to do that, you'd to marry or burn, so I married you quick. But Kath and me could afford to find out. It all depends if you're smeddum or not.*

She stood up then and put her cigarette out, and looked at the gaping gowks she had mothered. *I never married your father, you see. I could never make up my mind about Will. But maybe our Kath will find something surer. Here's her and her man coming up the road.*

Greenden

Folk laughed when they heard of the creatures coming to sit them down in the farm of Greenden, that lay west of the Tulloch by Bervie Water. It was a forty-fifty acre place, the Den, wet in the bottom, as well it might be, so low it lay there in its woods. In the midst stood the biggings; they were old and right dark: from the kitchen door you looked round and up at a jungle, near, you would say, lost from the world, so close around and between the trees the broom plants grew, and the whins. But when night came, sometimes over the trees and the rank, wild waste of the moor, you'd see through a narrow pass in the woods the last of the sun as it kindled a light on the Grampian Hills and went off to its bed. And that light in the mirk was near as much as a man would see of the world outby from the kitchen door of Greenden.

Well, old Grant had farmed there till he died, a steady old stock – fair strong in the hands if weak in the head, was the speak of Murdoch of Mains. For a body hardly ever made out what he said; he would whisper and whisper, whispering even as he girned at his horse in the lithe of the woods that watched Greenden. Soon's he'd been ta'en, the old mistress moved her into Drumlithie and took a bit cottage, and lived on his silver; and sometimes she'd say to a crony at night: 'It's fine to be here and with sonsy folk.' They thought at first she would miss her man; the minister came, the Free Kirk loon, he snuffled right godly and said through his nose: 'You'll meet him Above, Mistress Grant.' But at that she gave a kind of a start, near dropped the teapot, she did, when he spoke. 'Will I, then? Ay, fegs, I'll confess that I hadn't reckoned that.'

Well, that was the Grants gone out of Greenden. There the ill place lay as the winter wore on not an offer the factor had for it either; a man could sweat out his guts on a better ploy than

manuring the dour red clay of the Den. Syne the news went round
it was let at last: the factor had let it to no farming body, but a
creature from the town, from Glasgow it was; he'd never handled a
plough or a graip before, and Murdoch at the Mains had a story
about him. For he'd driven the creature and his wife round the
district, and as they went by the parks at Pittendreich they'd seen a
roller of old Pittendreich's there, out in the ley the thing was lying.
And the body of a woman had gleyed at the thing: 'What a shame
to let it get rusty, isn't it?' and looked at Murdoch like a fool of a
bairn.

Folk took that through hand with a laugh here and there; some
said it was surely a lie, though gey witty, for everybody knew that
the Murdoch brute could lie like a tink when the mood was on
him, fell often that was. True or not, you began to think of the
creatures – Simpson the name was – that had taken Greenden and
were moving in there at the February end. Ay, they'd find it a
change from their Glasgow streets; they didn't know what it was to
work, the dirt that came from the towns.

Well, come at last the Simpsons did to Greenden; their gear and
furniture came by Bervie, and the Simpson man went there to hire
two carts for the carting down of the stuff. Webster the grocer had
no rounds that day, and he hired out his carts and drove one
himself, George Simpson the other. It was late at night when they
came to the Den, down through the thick woods, larch it was there,
so close the trunks that the night was dark though the light shone
still out on the high road that walked by the sea. But they saw in the
Den as they wound down there a lantern kindled at last in the
mirk, kindled and shining from the kitchen door. And when the
carts came rumbling into the close there the wife of Simpson was
standing and waiting, the lantern held in her hand.

And Webster took a bit keek at the creature, and half thought
she must be but Simpson's daughter, no wife she looked; she was
thin and slim, bonny in a way, and her eyes were kind. She laughed
up at Simpson coming behind, syne smiled at the grocer, and cried
up in an English-like voice: 'You've been long; I thought I'd have to
spend the night down here – all alone by myself in Greenden.'

Alec Webster said: 'Well, mistress, you'd have ta'en no ill.' And she nodded to that: 'I know that fine. . . . And, of course, the country's lovely to live in.' And she smiled at him like a daft-like quean. He glowered back at her; canny, slow and quiet Alec, he couldn't make head nor tail of her yet, her laugh and that quiver she hid in her laugh.

Syne he loosed and helped them in with their gear, a great clutter of stuff they'd brought up from Glasgow. George Simpson he puffed and paiched right sore, big though he was, with a sappy big face, and a look on that face as though some childe had ta'en him a hard kick in the backside. But his lungs were gey bad, he told to the grocer; he'd come out to the country for his lungs, he said. And when Murdoch at Mains heard of that speak he said: 'Faith, the creature's more like to mislay his anatomy than pick up a bit on the ill clay rigs of the Den.'

So there were the two of them settled in there, Simpson and the little bit snippet of a wife: she looked light enough for a puff of wind to blow her from her kitchen door at night when she opened that door to come out to the grocer as he drove his van down for her orders on Friday. Alec Webster was a kindly stock, and he cried: 'Losh, Mistress, you're not in your Glasgow now, you'll fair need to keep yourself wrapped up.' But she only laughed: 'I'm fine – oh, listen to the trees!' And the grocer listened, and heard them sough, and turned him his head and glowered at the woods: they were just as aye they had been, he thought; why should a man stand still and listen? He asked her, Ellen Simpson, that, and keeked at her white, still stare. And she started again, and smiled at him, queer. 'Oh, nothing. Sorry. But I can't but listen.'

Well, maybe she knew what she meant; he didn't. He sold her her orders – she fair had a lot – and drove away up the February dark; and as he was driving he heard in the dark a hoasting and hacking out there by the barn, and he thought of the Simpson childe and his lungs. Faith, he'd come to the wrong place here for his lungs; it wasn't long likely he would store the kiln.

Mistress Murdoch went down to tea at Greenden. But she couldn't abide George Simpson's mistress, the creature fair got on to her nerves with her flitting here and her tripping there, and her laugh, and the meikle eyes of her in the small doll face that she had. She said it was Simpson she pitied, poor man, with lungs like his and a wife like that, little comfort by day and less in his bed; she herself would rather sleep with a fluff of a feather than depend on *that* on a coldrife night.

And then, as daft-like a blether as ever you heard, the story got about how it was that they'd come to move up from Glasgow to Greenden toun. George Simpson himself it was that told it, one night he dropped in at the Murdoch house – he would go a bit walk there now and again and gley at the daughter, Jeannie. And the way of their moving from Glasgow had been when his lungs took bad it was plain that he wouldn't last out a long while at his clerking work; he was fair for the knackers' yard, you would say. The doctors said he should leave the town, but he'd little fancy for that himself, and his wife had less: she was town-bred, and feared at the country, Ellen; or so he'd aye thought. For next Sunday he'd gone with her to their kirk, and then it was that a hymn was sung, and it fair seemed to change Ellen Simpson's mind. And the hymn was the one that begins with the words:

> *There is a green hill far away,*
>   *Beyond a city wall,*
> *Where the dear Lord was crucified,*
>   *Who died to save us all.*

So when the Simpsons got back to their house Ellen Simpson had kept whispering and remembering that tune, and sudden-like she said they must leave the town; they must find a farm where George could work in the open and mend his ill lungs.

Well, he'd hardly hear of the thing at first, as he told to the Murdochs that night at their house; he thought that work on a farm would kill him. But Ellen had set her mind on the plan, so he set about looking for a place to please her. He'd but little silver to stock up a steading, and land in the south was far over dear, but up in the Mearns he came on Greenden, its rent just inside the reach of his pouch. So he'd ta'en his wife up to see it; she'd stared, down in the hollow, and seemed half ta'en aback. And then she'd said they must take it, and take it they did, and here now they were; and *she* liked it fine.

And fine well she might do, the coarse creature, folk said. It wasn't her had to face up the rains of that year, or the coarse ploughing of the ill red clay of Greenden. Ay, Simpson was a fine bit childe, a bit dour, but faith! he was surely fair a fool as well to let himself be ta'en from a fine town job out to the pleiter and soss of a farm, to pleasure that creature his wife and the fancies she'd got from hearing a hymn in a kirk. Folk with sense knew fine that hymns were just things that you sang at, douce, and then you forgot.

Wet it was that spring: March came flooding in rains down the length and breadth of the guttering Howe; every night you'd hear the swash of the water if your place in the bed was next to the wall; the gulls were up from the Bervie beaches and cawing at all hours over the parks. Down in Greenden it was worse than most, and Simpson with his hoast, poor childe, might well have kept in his bed and blankets, but his creature of a wife wouldn't hear of that, laughing at him, affronting him into a rage. 'Come on, now, George, the day's half dead! And it's fine, a good day for the plough.'

So out he'd to get, and out with his pair, and go slow-stepping up and down the ley haughs that lined the deep Den. His ploughing was fair a sight for sore eyes; of a Sunday the bothy billies would come over, they'd take a bit dander down to the Den and stand and laugh as they looked at the drills, they went this way and that: 'Dam't, man, they've but little sense in the towns!' Syne they'd hear Mistress Simpson crying to her hens, and see her, small, like a snippet of a doll, flit over the close on some errand or another. The poor Simpson childe kept to his bed on the Sundays.

Well, the spring wore on, fine planting weather came, by May the sun was a blaze of heat; up and down the long Howe folk shook their heads. With a spring like this you might well depend that you'd have a summer with sleet, most-like. But it was well enough while it went, and Murdoch of Mains took a dander down to the Den now and then to see how the Simpson man was fairing. And, faith! he'd been kept with his nose at the grind; he'd his parks as well forward as any other place. Murdoch hadn't set eyes on him near for a month, and fair got a shock as he stopped his roller and stood by to speak. He'd grown thicker and bigger, his face filled out; you could hardly see the town in him at all. And Murdoch said: 'Ay, man, you're fair a bit farmer!'

And Simpson smiled wan, right patient-like though, with his sappy red face like an ill-used nout's, and said: 'Maybe,' and paiched to listen at his lungs. And then he told that each night he went to his bed with a back like to break, but Ellen just laughed. She didn't know what an illness was; he wasn't the man to fear her and tell her the truth. So Murdoch saw fine how the thing was going, the Simpson childe working himself to his grave, with his coarse lungs, too, to please his coarse wife. There was nothing he could do in the matter, he thought, but he said they'd aye be pleased to see Simpson at Mains. He said nothing of Ellen, the bit wife, in that; there was damn the pleasure to be had in the creature; with her laugh and her listening and the flutter of her eyes, she fairly got on a body's bit nerves.

What with rain and with heat the Den was green-lush right early that year – the grocer thought it came thicker than ever he minded – the broom stopped up the aisles of the larch that stretched up the braes from the old brown biggings of the Den. Ellen Simpson would come running out to the door as she heard the sound of his wheels on the close, and cry him goodday, and bring him the eggs, and stand still while he counted, a slow, canny childe; but once he raised up his head and said: 'losh, but it's still!'

And the two of them stood there and listened in that quiet, not a sound to be heard or a thing to be seen beyond the green cup that stood listening around. And Ellen Simpson smiled white and said: 'Yes, it is still – and I'll take two loaves and some tea now, please.'

And Webster took a look at her: thinner she'd grown, more a wisp than ever, but still with her smile, and he liked her fine, near the only soul in the district that did. Most said she'd grown thinner with temper, faith! girning at her man to get out and start work, and him no more than an invalid, like.

Just luck she hadn't his death on her hands, and you couldn't blame him that he fell in the habit, nearly every bit evening he would do it now, of taiking away over the brae from the Den to the Mains and the Murdochs; they liked him fine. Jeannie Murdoch

and he would flirt and would fleer – no harm in their fun, folk
'greed about that: the poor stock was no doubt in need of a laugh,
him and that wife with her flutterings that fair set your hackles on
edge. He was better than he'd been, he'd confess, would Simpson;
all the more reason why he wanted some cheer when he came in
about to his own fire at night, not aye to be listening to somebody
cry: 'Oh, George, do you think your lungs are near better?'

And Jeannie Murdoch would say: 'No, I'm sure. Sit you down.
I'll make you a fine cup of tea.' And George Simpson would laugh
out his big, sappy laugh: 'Faith! you're fine as you're bonny, Jean,
lass.'

And Murdoch and his mistress would hear them and gley,
Mistress Murdoch pull down her meikle bit face; maybe she
thought Jeannie went over far with a man that was married –
no more than fun though their speak might be. If it wasn't for that
snippet of a creature, Ellen, you'd think Simpson as fine a goodson
as you'd meet; a bit slow at the uptake, maybe a bit dour, but a
pretty, upstanding childe he was now.

Folk wondered a bit what she thought of those jaunts, Ellen
Simpson down by her lone in Greenden. But she never said a word
to a soul about them, not that she saw a many to speak to; she'd
just smile, and go running and bring you some tea, kind enough
you supposed that the creature was, but you'd never get yourself to
like her, you'd know; she'd set you all unease till you'd sit and
wonder what ailed yourself – till going up home through the dark
you'd be filled with fancies daft as a carrying woman, as though the
trees moved and the broom was whispering, and some beast with
quiet breath came padding in your tracks; and you'd look, and
'twas only a whin that you'd passed. And you'd heave a great
breath, outside of the Den, up in the light of the evening sun,
though the Den below was already in shadow.

But of nights as that summer wore on to its close she took to
standing at her kitchen door, while the light drew in and the dark
came close: now and then some soul would come on her there,
near startle her out of her skin as he cried: 'Ay, mistress, it's a fine
bit night.' And she'd laugh, with her hand at her breast, daft-like,
and then turn her head as though half she'd forgotten you and look

up and away out over the trees, and you'd look the same way and see feint the thing. And then maybe you'd look harder and see what it was; it was from the kitchen door along of Greenden that the swathe of the trees and the broom was broken, and through the hollow that was left in the gloaming the sun struck light on the Grampian slopes, long miles away and across the Mearns, shining immediate, yet distant and blue, their green earth-hazed in the heather-bells. And that was the thing that she stood and watched, as a daftie would, and you'd scrape your feet, and you'd give a bit hoast, and she'd start and switch round, her face gone white, and say: 'Oh, I'm sorry, I'd forgotten you were here. Was it George that you wanted to see?'

Well, that was in June, and the June-end came, as bonny as ever it came in the Howe; folk meeting the Simpson man on the road would cry to him for a joke. 'Ay, man, you're fair smothered away from the world in Greenden.' And, faith! they spoke but the truth, so high was the broom with a mantling of bloom, and the trees were a wall fair blinding the place. George Simpson made out of it every bit night, over to the Mains' new barn they were building; he'd pretend it was the barn he went over to see, but he'd edge away from it soon as he might, taik round to the kitchen, and Jeannie would blush and cry: 'Step away in, Mr Simpson. How are you? I'm sure you are tired.'

Well, that barn it was, Webster was to swear, brought things to an end to that steer at Greenden. He never told the story in a neighbour-like way, he never did that, and he wasn't much liked, for he'd never much news to give to a body when you spoke to him at the tail of his van and would drop a bit hint that you'd like to know why the Gordon quean was getting gey stout, and if Wallace was as coarse as they said to his wife, and such newsy-like bits of an interest to folk. He'd just grunt when you spoke and start counting the eggs, and say he was damned if he knew or he cared. So he told the Greenden tale to none but his wife; he thought her the same as himself, did Alec. But faith! she could claik a tink from a door, and soon it was known up and down the Howe, every bit of the happening that night at Greenden.

For he'd driven down there late, as aye he had done, the grocer, and was coming in by the yard, when he met Ellen Simpson come running up the road; her face was white in the fading light, and twice as she ran he saw her fall; and she picked herself up with blood on her face where a stone had cut as she fell. And Webster stopped his horse and jumped off the van and went running to meet her, and he cried: 'God, mistress, what's ta'en you – what's wrong?'

And she gabbled as he held her, he saw her eyes wild, syne she quieted a minute and covered her eyes, and shivered, hot though the June night was. Then she whispered sudden, he shivered himself: 'They've done something to my hill, they have taken it away! Oh, I can't stand it now, I can't, I can't!'

And Webster said: 'What?' He was clean dumbfoundered; and he thought in a flash of old Grant of Greenden – he also had whispered and whispered like that. But she pointed up across the larch-hill and the broom, and he gowked, did the grocer, and saw nothing for a while. Syne he saw that there rose through that howe in the woods, through which you'd once see the light gleam on the hills, the roof and the girders of Murdoch's new barn. He stared at the thing, and then stared at the woman, and at that she broke down and cried like a bairn; she'd no shame before him, she was surely daft.

'Oh, I can't stand it longer in this hateful place! It's smothering and killing me, down and lost here, I've been frightened, so frightened, since the first hour here. I've tried not to show it, and I *know* that it's nothing, but the trees – they hate me, the fields, and at night. . . . Oh, I can't stand it longer, not even for George, now they've blocked up that sight of the hill that was mine!'

And she cried out more of that stite, and the grocer – he'd aye liked her – was fair in a way. 'Whisht, mistress, go in and lie down,' he said, but she whispered: 'Don't leave me, don't leave me, I'm frightened!' And the dark came then down over the broom, and the horse stood champing and scraping its hooves, and a howlet began to hoot in the larch while Webster sat by her in the kitchen to quiet her. And she whispered once: 'George – he's safe now, he's safe, God died, but I needn't, He saved him, not I.' And what she meant by that Alec neither knew nor could guess, and syne she was

whispering again in her terror: 'The trees and the broom, keep off
the trees; it's growing so dark I can't see it, the green hill. . . .'

But at last she grew quiet; he told her to lie down. She went ben
from the kitchen, and he stood and thought. And he minded her
man might be at the Mains; he went out and drew round his
grocer's van, and got into it and drove up out of the Den, and
whipped his bit beast to a trot as he drew nigh the Mains.

And folk told that when he got there he went stamping in the
kitchen: George Simpson was sitting with Jeannie and her father; the
mistress was off to the pictures at Bervie. And Alec Webster cried:
'Leave your courting until you're a widower; have you no shame at all
to abandon your wife night after night in that hell of a Den?' And
George Simpson stood up and blustered: 'You mucker—', and the
grocer said: 'Away, raise your hand up to me, you big, well-fed
bullock, and I'll crack your jaw where you stand.' Old Murdoch came
in between them then, and he cried: 'What is't? What's wrong?'

So Webster told Simpson his wife was gey queer; was he or was
he not going home? And Simpson scowled and said: 'Yes,' and
went out with the grocer, and that childe swung round his weary
bit horse and lashed it to a trot, and out into the road, and so, in
their time, by the track to the Den. And there it was dark as a
fireless lum, but far off as they neared to the biggings they heard a
voice singing – singing so strange that it raised their hair:

> *There is a green hill far away,*
>   *Beyond a city wall,*
> *Where the dear Lord was crucified,*
>   *Who died to save us all—*

And it suddenly ceased, and Webster swore, and he lashed the
horse, and they came to the close, and Webster jumped down and
ran into the house. Behind him went Simpson, more slow – he was
feared. In the kitchen it was dark and still as they came. Then the
grocer slipped, there was something slippery and wet on the floor.
So he kindled a match, and they both looked up, and they saw what
it was, and it turned them sick. And a waft of wind came in from
the door, and the Shape from the beam swung to and fro.

And Webster turned round and went blundering out, as though he couldn't see, and he called to Simpson: 'Take her down and I'll go for the doctor, man.'

But he knew right well that that would help nothing, and the thought went with him as he drove through the woods, up out of the Den, to the road that walked by the sea, and the green hills that stood to peer with quiet faces in the blow of the wind from the sunset's place.

Sim

What profit hath a man of all his labour which he taketh under the sun? – Ecclesiastes i., 4.

Sim Wilson came of a fell queer stock, his mother a spinner at the Segget Mills, his father a soldier killed by the Boers. When news of that killing came up to Segget the wife just laughed – 'Worse folk than the Boers' – and went on with the tink-like life that she led. In time that fair grew a scandal in Segget, a body wasn't safe to let her man out of her sight for a minute, in case he met in with that Wilson creature, and was led all agley with her coarse green glower.

Sim was no more than five years old when at last things came to a head in Segget, his mother went off on a moonflight flit with the widow Grant's son and half of her silver. Folks wondered which of the two would last longest. Young Sim was left in an emptied house, till his auntie that bade in a house by Drumlithie took pity on the loon and had him down there. She came all a-fuss and a-pant with pity, the aunty, a meikle big creash of a woman, and she said to Sim, 'You're my dawtie now.' And Sim said, 'Maybe – if you'll leave me a-be.'

Faith, that was his only care from the first, as sweir a nickum as you'd meet, folk said, sweir at the school as he was at his home, it was a fair disease with the ill-getted loon. And an impudent creature he was, forbye, with his glinting black hair and his glinting green eyes, he'd truant from school more often than not and be off in the summer to sleep in the sun, under the lithe of a whin or a stook. And once, he was then about ten years old, his auntie came on him high on the brae, in the heat, his chin in his hands as he keeked down through the veils of broom at the teams, steaming at work in the parks below. She cried, 'You coarse brute, why aren't you at school? Aren't you fair black affronted to lie there and stink?'

Well, Sim just sneered, not feered a wee bit, 'No, I'm not. I was watching those fools in that park. You won't find me sossing and chaving like that when I'm a man with a fee of my own. The dafties – not to take a bit rest! . . . Lessons? Away, do you think I am soft?'

And he stuck out his tongue and slipped under her arm, his auntie near greeting with rage as he ran. But she couldn't catch up, loaded down with her creash. Sim was soon out of sight on his way up the hill. He spent the whole day lying flat on his back, the only sweir soul in the hash of the Howe.

Folk said that he'd come to an ill-like end, his sweirty would eat to his bones and they'd rot. But then, near the middle of his thirteenth year, he heard the news in his class at the school that the prize for dux that year was a pound; and all of a jiffy he started to work, like mad, near blinded himself of a night with reading and writing and learning his lessons, the hills hardly saw him except back of a book. And he'd cleverness in him, sweir though he'd been, he was dux for that year and the dominie delighted.

He said to the loon, 'You'll do even better,' but Sim just sneered in his impudent way, 'I'm finished with chaving at lessons and dirt. I've tried, and I know that they're not worth the sweat.' The dominie was fair took aback to hear that. 'You'll gang a hard gait through the world, I fear.' And Sim said, 'Maybe; but I'll gang it myself. And I'll know what I'm getting ere I gang it at all.'

He fee'd his first fee at Upperhill in Kinraddie. Big-boned he had grown, and supple and swack, but as sweir as ever and an ill-liked brute. He'd sneer at his elders and betters in the bothy, 'What, work my guts out for that red-headed rat? Whatever for, can you tell me that? Show me a thing that is worth my trauchle, and I'll work you all off the face of the earth!'

The foreman there was a canny-like childe, and the only one that could bear with Sim. They both stayed on for a four-five years, Sim sweir as ever, with his glinting green eyes, he'd a bigger power for lazing around than a pig in a ree, was the speak of the bothy. And young and buirdly, well-happed like a hog, he'd doze through the work of the Upperhill parks, goodnatured enough were he letten alone. But sometimes he'd stop from making his brose, of a night, when the bothy was lit by the fire, 'And to think that the morn we'll be doing the same!' The billies in the bothy would maybe say 'What?' and he'd say, 'Why, making more brose to eat! And the night after that and the night after that. And we'll get up the morn and slave and chave for that red-headed rat – and go to our beds and get up again. Whatever for, can you tell me that?'

And the brute, in one of those unco-like moods, would go off on a jaunting down to Segget; and take a dram or so in the Arms; and look round about for a spinner to spite. And if there were such Sim would swagger up to him, 'Ay, man, you've a look on your face I don't like. And I don't much like your face the look's on.' The spinner would maybe look Sim up and down, with a sneer, and call him a clod-hopping clown, and Sim would take him a bash in the face, and next minute the spinners would pile in on Sim; and when he got back to Upperhill bothy he'd look as though he'd been fed through the teeth of a mill. But he'd say as he got in his bed, 'That was fine. Man, I fairly stirred up that dirt down in Segget!' And next day he'd be sleepy and sweir as before.

Syne he met with Kate Duthie at a dance down in Segget, she was narrow and red-haired, with a pointed chin and hard grey eyes you could strike a spunk on, a quean that worked as maid at the Manse. Well, Sim took a look at her, she one at him; and he fair went daft that minute about her. He waited till that dance was over and said, 'Can I have the next?' and Kate Duthie said, 'Maybe. Who might you be?' And Sim Wilson told her, and Kate gave a laugh, 'Oh, only a ploughman.'

As the Upperhill lads walked back that night in a bunch from the dance they had been to in Segget, Sim told them the speak of the grey-eyed quean. The foreman said, 'And who might she think that she is? A joskin's as good as any damned maid.' Sim shook his head, 'Most, maybe; not her. Faith, man, but she's bonny, and I wish that I had her.'

Well, that was only the beginning of the stir, his sweirty went like a mist in June, he was out nearly every bit night after that, down at the Manse or hanging round Segget. Kate sometimes saw him and sometimes she didn't, she kept as cool as a clayed-up coulter. At last it came to a night Sim said, 'I'm thinking of marrying'; Kate Duthie said, 'Oh, well, I wish you joy.' And Sim said, 'Ay, I'll get that fine – if you'll come and provide it.'

Kate laughed in his face and told him plain she wasn't cut out for a ploughman's wife, to drag through her days in a cottar house. Sim said there would maybe be no need to cottar, though he'd never thought of the thing before, he spent every meck he ever had made on drink and coarse queans, any coarseness at all that didn't trouble his sweirty too much. But now with the grey-eyed quean in his arms he felt as he'd done that time when a loon and he made up his mind he would win the school prize. 'I get a bit place of my own. You'll wait?'

Kate shrugged and said, 'Maybe, you'll have to risk that.' Sim held her and looked at her, suddenly cuddled her, daft and tight till she nearly screamed, just for a minute, and syne finished with that. 'You needn't be feered, I'll wait for my turn. That's just a taste of what I'll yet take. What about a kiss?' And she gave him one, cold, like a peck, but he thought it fine, and lapped it in and put her away, and went swinging away home the Kinraddie road; you could hear him nearly a mile from the bothy, singing as he climbed up the road in the dark.

Well, God! there fair was a change in him then. It was brose and then brose and syne brose to his meat. The other billies in the bothy would laugh, and mock at Sim, and cry, 'What's it all for?' But Sim didn't heed, he saved every penny, he worked extra work, and afore two years, what with saving and scraping, he'd enough silver saved for the rent of Haughgreen.

It lies low down by the Segget burn. The clay of the Mearns has thickened down there till in a dry season a man might well think he stood in the yard of a milk-jar potter, the drills just hillocks and slivers of clay. Its rent was low, in spite of its size, the most of the biggings just held together, disheartened-like, as though waiting the time to fall in a rickle on somebody's head. But Sim gave a swagger, 'I'll manage them fine,' the daft-like glaze on his queer green eyes; and was off every night from the Upperhill bothy, not down as afore to Kate Duthie in Segget, but down to Haughgreen with a saw and an axe, pliers and planes, and the Lord knows what. In the last week afore he was due to move in, the Upperhill foreman went down for a look, and he found Haughgreen all shored-up and trig, the house all new-papered, with furniture in it, the stable fit to take horses again, the stalls in the byre set well for nout – he'd worked like a nigger had that sweir brute, Sim.

The foreman said 'twas a miracle, just; he was glad that Sim had wakened at last. Sim gave him a clap that near couped him at that, 'Ay, man, and for why? Because I'll soon have the best quean in the Howe. What think you of that? In my house and my bed!'

That night he tramped to his quean down in Segget, and knocked at the kitchen door of the Manse, and Kate came to it and said, 'Oh, it's you?' And Sim said 'Ay,' with his eyes fit to eat her, 'You mind what I asked you near two years back?'

Kate said, 'What was that?' She thought little of him, and knew nothing of his slaving to save for Haughgreen. But he started to tell her, as he stood in the door, that he was a farmer, with a farm of his own, and ready to take her there when she liked.

She gaped and said, 'Sim, it's not true, is it now?' And he said, 'Ay, it is.' And she fair seemed to thaw, and speired him up hill and down dale all about it, Sim standing and staring at the white of her neck, white, like cream, and he felt like a cat, and licked his lips with a hungry tongue.

Well, she soon said, 'Aye,' she needed no prigging, foreseeing herself a braw farmer's wife. At the end of the term the two of them married. Sim looked that day as though wedding an angel, not just a quean with a warm, white skin and close grey eyes and a mouth like a mule. Not but that the creature had smiles for the hour, and was awful kind to the ploughmen that came. She danced with the foreman and said, 'You're a joskin? Maybe my husband will give you a fee?' And the foreman spat, 'Well, would he now, then? But you see I'm particular-like about the mistress.'

She would try to put Sim against him for that, the foreman knew, and keeked over at Sim; and he saw his eyes as they fixed on Kate, hungry and daft, more a glare than a glower. And he suddenly minded Sim back in the bothy, in the days before he had met with this quean, and that speak of his, 'Trauchle the day just to trauchle the morn! But show me a thing that is worth my chave and I'll work you all off the face of the earth!'

Well, he'd gotten the thing, good luck go with him, the foreman thought as he tramped away home, up through the grey of the morning mists, with the bothy lightless and grey in the dawn, leaving Sim with his hard-eyed quean; you hoped he'd not eat her, that's what he'd looked like.

But faith! she survived, fair the kind to do that. Folk gave a bit laugh at the news from Haughgreen, and shook their heads when they heard that Sim, no sooner married, was as sweir as before, taking life cool as ever he had done, in spite of the nagging and prigging of Kate. The ploughing was on; but Sim Wilson's was not, the parks were lucky did they see him by nine, instead of six, when other childes yoked. Even then he'd do little but stand up and gant, or weeber out loud as he sat on a gate.

Now and then a body would cry to him, 'Ay, your ploughing's far back for the season, is't not?' and he'd say, 'Damn the doubt. What o't though it is?' And he'd whistle and stare at the clouds in the Howe, his cat-like eyes a-blink in the sun.

The foreman at last took a taik in about, and Sim was as pleased to see him as though he wasn't new-married, new-buried instead. Kate snapped from the room like an ill-ta'en rat; she didn't like the foreman, he didn't like her. And he thought as he sat and waited his dram it was more than likely that she wore the breeks.

But right soon he was changing his mind about that. As they sat at their dram, him and Sim, she came back. 'It's dark, and it's time you went for the kye.' 'Gang for them yourself,' Sim said, and never turned. 'You enjoy trauchle; well, enjoy some more.'

Kate's face blazed up like a fire with rage, she choked and went out and banged the door. The foreman felt a bit shamed for the quean. Damn't, you could see it wasn't so easy to be married to a sweir, queer brute like Sim; it wouldn't be long that these two together would store the kiln in Haughgreen, you knew.

There were more stammy-gastered than him at the change. For all of a sudden, as the May came in, Sim seemed to wake up and his sweirty went, he was out at all hours at the work of the parks, chaving like daft at his weed-choked drills. The land had lain fallow, he wasn't too late, and afore folk had well gotten over their gape they saw Sim Wilson was having fine crops, manured with the sweat of his own meikle hams. He snored no more in the lithe of a whin and he stopped from ganting by every bit gate.

The reason for that was soon plain to be seen, Kate with a bairn, and the creature soon due. The Upperhill foreman met in with Sim one night as he drove from the mart at Stonehive, and the foreman cried up, 'Ay, man, and how are you?' Sim stopped and cried back, 'Oh, it's you is it, then? Fine, man, I'm aye fine; I get what I want. Have you heard the news of what's coming to Haughgreen?'

And he told the foreman of the bairn that was coming, as if half the Howe didn't know about that, his green, glazed eyes all glinting and shining. You'd have thought by the way that Sim Wilson spoke 'twas the first bit bairn that had waited for birth in all the windy Howe of the Mearns. He was daft on it, as daft as he had been a wee while before to marry its mother. And the foreman thought, as he wished him luck, there were some that had aye to be looking ahead, and others looked back, and it made little odds, looked you east, looked you west, you'd to work or to die.

Kate had a sore time and let every soul know, but the midwife said that the queer-like thing was the way that that meikle Sim Wilson behaved, not like most of the fathers she ever had known, and she'd known a fell few; they went into three classes – fools, poor fools, and just plain damn fools. Well, the last were mostly the fathers of first-born, they'd wabble at the knees and whiten at the gills and pay no heed to aught but the wife. Sim Wilson was different, with his unco green eyes, 'twas the bairn that took him his first minute in the room. He had it in his arms as ready as you please, and cuddled it, chuckled to it – the great silly sumph – till Kate whined out from the bed where she lay, 'And have you got nothing to say to me now?' And Sim Wilson said, 'Eh? Damn't, Kate, I'd forgotten you!'

An ill-like thing, that, to say to a wife, but that was the way that the brute now behaved; there was nothing he thought on earth worth the price of daddling his bairn up and down in his arms, and swearing she'd winked, and wasn't she a topper? The Upperhill foreman came down for a look, and keeked at the creature, an ordinary bairn, like an ill-boiled swede; but Sim sat and glowered at her, the look in his eyes he'd once turned on Kate ere he'd money to marry. 'Man, but I'll make a braw life for this lass – I'll give her education and make her a lady.'

The foreman said that he thought education was dirt; if ever he had bairns he'd set them to work. Sim laughed in a way that he didn't much like. 'You? Maybe. I was kittled on a different day.'

So the foreman left him, fair angered at that. 'Twas nearly five years ere he saw Sim again, for he moved down the Howe and took a fresh fee, and got married himself, and had bairns of his own. And sometimes he'd mind of that sweir brute, Sim, and the speaks of his in the bothy long syne: 'Well, what's it all for, all your chaving and care?' And when he'd mind that the foreman would laugh, and know that most likely his stomach was wrong.

Though he didn't see Sim he heard now and then of him and his capers down at Haughgreen. Folk told that he'd turned to a slaver, just, he'd fee'd two men and near worked them to death, and himself as well, and long Kate forbye – faith, if she'd thought she did herself well, marrying a farmer and setting up braw, she'd got many a sore heart since her marriagemorn. Sim gave her no help, he wouldn't fee a maid, he was up and out at the blink of dawn, crying his men from their beds to work. He spared neither man nor beast, did Sim; in his four-five years he'd made a fair pile. But he was as ready as ever he had been to blab what he thought, a sneer or a boast. And he'd tell any soul that would care to listen the why and the wherefore he moiled like a mole. 'It's that lass of mine, Jean – faith, man, she's a topper! I'm to send her to college, away from this soss, and she'll lack for nothing that money can bring.'

And neither she did. It fair was a scandal, folk said, that plain though they are at Haughgreen the bairn was fed on this dainty and that. Sim had bought the were wretch the finest of beds, and he'd have her aye dressed like the bairns of gentry. You'd heard afore this of folk daft on a bairn, but he was surely the worst in the Howe. Folk shook their heads, he had better look out, 'twas fell unchancy to show over-plain that you thought over-much of any bit bairn.

And faith! folk weren't far wrong in their speak – the bairn didn't die, she was healthy enough, but just when it came for the time of her schooling, they seemed to wake up to the fact at Haughgreen. She was unco backward and couldn't speak well, and had funny-like ways; she would croon a bit song all the hours of the day, staring up at the hills of the Howe, not caring a fig what she ate or what she wore, only caring to lie in the sun and to sleep.

Sim sent for a specialist out from Dundon and had the bit bairn taken away south, and treated and tested and God knows what. That went on a six months and the cost was a ruin, a time of sore hearts and black looks at Haughgreen. And he well might have spared his time and his silver, she came back just the same – the bairn was a daftie, and the doctors said that so she'd remain, a bairn of three, all the years of her life.

Folk thought it awful, but they gave a bit snicker, 'Ay, what will that fool at the Haugh say now?' Well, he went in a kind of a daze for weeks, but his work didn't slacken as the foreman had thought – when he heard of the thing he had minded long back how Sim had behaved when he married his Kate and found that angel of common enough clay. But slaving was deep in his bones now, and he couldn't well stop though he wished, you supposed. The foreman met him one day at a roup, sneering and boasting as loudly as ever. But there was a look in the queer green eyes as though he were watching for something he'd tint.

He made no mention of the daftie, Jean, that had answered his question, 'What's it all for?' Sun, wind, and the batter of rain in his face – well, he'd settle now as others had done, and take it all for the riddle it was, not a race to be run with a prize at the end.

Then the news got about and you knew in a blink why he'd acted so calm with his firstborn, Jean. His wife had brought another bit bairn in the world, a lassie as well, and fine and strong. And soon's it was born Sim Wilson was crying, 'Is it right in the head, is it right in the head?' The doctor knew neither one way nor the other, but he said, 'Ay, it's fine,' to quieten the fool.

Sim doted on Jess from the day of her birth, promising her all as he'd done with Jean – Jean that now he could hardly bear to look upon, any more than on Kate, his wife, thin and old. She'd fair withered up, had the thin-flanked Kate, except her big tongue, it could scoriate your skin. But it didn't vex Sim with his daughter Jess, he would stride in the kitchen when he loosened at night, 'Where's ma wee quean?' and Jess would cry 'Here!' Bonny and trig, like a princess dressed, nothing soft about her like that thing in the corner, hunched up and crooning, aye half-way in sleep. She was clever and bright and a favourite at college, Jess, and Sim swore she should have what she liked, she never need soss with the land and its pleiter, she would marry no joskin, a lady she'd be.

He bled the red clay of Haughgreen near to white, to wring silver from it for Jess and her life, to send her to college and give her brave clothes. Fegs, he was fair a long gait from the days when he'd mock at the land – 'Ay, come and get me – get me if you can – I'm not such a fool!'

The foreman had clean forgot him for years, Sim Wilson the sweir and the fairlies he chased; and when next he did hear he could hardly believe one thing in the tale that came swift up the Howe. That thing was the age of the daughter, Jess. 'Why, the lassie is only a bairn,' he said. But the childe that stopped to pass him the tale said, 'Faith no, man, eighteen if a day. Ay, a real coarse quean, and you cannot but laugh at the nasty whack it is in the mouth for that meikle fool that farms Haughgreen!'

There was nothing unco in the tale when told, the kind of thing had been known to the world since the coming of men – and afore that, no doubt, else all the ill pleiter would have never begun. But for that to happen to the dawtie of Sim! – Jess, the student, so haughty and neat, the maid that had led his question so on, up out of the years: 'What's it all for?'

It seems that she carried her shame a long time, and the creature that found her out was the daftie, Jean. One night when old Sim came home the daftie pointed at her sister, Jess, and giggled and moved and made slabbering sounds. Sim had paid her no heed a good twenty years, but something in the wrigglings of the creature took him. He cried, 'What's that?' and glowered at his wife, old Kate, with her thinning face and greyed hair.

But Kate knew nothing, like himself she stared at Jess that sat red-faced by the fire. And then while they stared Jess jumped to her feet, weeping, and ran from the room, and they saw – plain enough, the way she was in; they'd been blind.

Old Sim gave a groan as an old horse groans when you drive him his last bit bout up a hill, and stood and stared at the daftie, Jean, that was giggling and fleering there like a bairn, like something tint from his life long syne, in the kitchen quiet as the daylight waned.

Clay

The Galts were so thick on the land around Segget folk said if you went for a walk at night and you trod on something and it gave a squiggle, it was ten to one you would find it a Galt. And if you were a newcomer up in the Howe and you stopped a man and asked him the way, the chances were he'd be one of the brood. Like as not, before he had finished with you, he'd have sold you a horse or else stolen your watch, found out everything that you ever had done, recognised your mother and had doubts of your father. Syne off home he'd go and spread the news round, from Galt of Catcraig that lay high in the hills to Galt of Drumbogs that lay low by Mondynes, all your doings were known and what you had said, what you wore next your skin what you had to your breakfast, what you whispered to your wife in the dead of the night. And the Galts would snigger *Ay, gentry, no doubt*, and spit in the vulgar way that they had: the average Galt knew less of politeness than a broody hen knows of Bible exegesis.

They farmed here and they farmed there, brothers and cousins and half-brothers and uncles, your head would reel as you tried to make out if Sarah were daughter to Ake of Catcraig or only a relation through marrying a nephew of Sim of High Rigs that was cousin to Will. But the Galts knew all their relationships fine, more especially if anything had gone a bit wrong, they'd tell you how twenty-five years or so back, when the daughter of Redleaf had married her cousin, old Alec that now was the farmer of Kirn, the first bit bairn that came of that marriage – ay, faith, that bairn had come unco soon! And they'd lick at their chops as they minded of that and sneer at each other and fair have a time. But if you were strange and would chance to agree, they'd close up quick, with a look on their faces as much as to say *And who are you would say ill of the Galts?*

They made silver like dirt wherever they sat, there was hardly a toun that they sat in for long. So soon's they moved in to some fresh bit farm they'd rive up the earth, manure it with fish, work the land to death in the space of their lease, syne flit to the other side of the Howe, with the land left dry as a ratsucked swede. And often enough, as he neared his lease-end, a Galt would break and be rouped from his place, he'd say that farming was just infernal, and his wife would weep as she watched her bit things sold here and there to cover their debts. And if you didn't know much of the Galts you would be right sorry and would bid fell high. Syne you'd hear in less than a six months' time that the childe that went broke had bought a new farm and had stocked it up to the hilt with the silver he'd laid cannily by before he went broke.

Well, the best of the bunch was Rob Galt of Drumbogs, lightsome and hearty, not mean like the rest, he'd worked for nearly twenty-five years as his father's foreman up at Drumbogs. Old Galt, the father, seemed nearly immortal, the older he grew the coarser he was, Rob stuck the brute as a good son should, though aye he had wanted land of his own. When they fell out at last Rob Galt gave a laugh, *You can keep Drumbogs and all things that are on it, I'll soon get a place of my own, old man.* His father sneered *You?* and Rob Galt said *Ay, a place of my own and parks that are MINE.*

He was lanky and long like all of the Galts, his mouser twisted up at the ends, with a chinny Galt face and a long, thin nose, and eyes pale-blue in a red-weathered face, a fine, frank childe that was kindness itself, though his notion of taking a rest from the plough was to loosen his horses and start in to harrow. He didn't look long for a toun of his own, Pittaulds by Segget he leased in a wink, it stood high up on the edge of the Mounth, you could see the clutter of Segget below, wet, with the glint of its roofs at dawn. The rent was low, for the land was coarse, red clay that sucked with a hungry mouth at your feet as you passed through the evening fields.

Well, he moved to Pittaulds in the autumn term, folk watched his flitting come down by Mondynes, and turn at the corner and trudge up the brae to the big house poised on the edge of the hill. He brought his wife, she was long as himself, with a dark-like face, quiet, as though gentry – faith, that was funny, a Galt wedded decent! But he fair was fond of the creature, folk said, queer in a man with a wife that had managed to bring but one bairn into the world. That bairn was now near a twelve years old, dark, like her mother, solemn and slim, Rob spoiled them both, the wife and the quean, you'd have thought them sugar he was feared would melt.

But they'd hardly sat down a week in Pittaulds when Rachel that would trot at the rear of Rob, like a collie dog, saw a queer-like change. Now and then her father would give her a pat, and she'd think that he was to play as of old. But instead he would cry *Losh, run to the house, and see if your mother will let you come out, we've two loads of turnips to pull afore dinner.* Rachel, the quean, would chirp out *Ay, father,* and go blithe to the shed for her tailer and his, and out they would wade through the cling of the clay and pull side by side down the long, swede rows, the rain in a drifting seep from the hills, below them the Howe in its garment of mist. And the little, dark quean would work by his side, say never a word though she fair was soaked; and at last go home; and her mother would stare, whatever in the world had happened to Rob? She would ask him that as he came into dinner – *the quean'll fair have her death of cold.* He would blink with his pale-blue eyes, impatient, *Hoots, lassie, she'll take no harm from the rain. And we fair must clear the swedes from the land, I'm a good three weeks behind with the work.*

The best of the Galts? Then God keep off the rest! For, as that year wore on to its winter, while he'd rise at five, as most other folk did, he wouldn't be into his bed till near morning, it was chave, chave, chave till at last you would think he'd turn himself into an earthworm, near. In the blink of the light from the lanterns of dawn he would snap short-tempered at his dark-faced wife, she would stare and wonder and give a bit laugh, and eat up his porridge as though he was feared he would lose his appetite halfway through, and muck out the byre and the stable as fast as though he were paid for the job by the hour, with a scowl of ill-nature behind his long nose. And then, while the dark still lay on the land, and through the low mist that slept on the fields, not a bird was cheeping and not a thing showing but the waving lanterns in the Segget wynds, he'd harness his horses and lead out the first, its hooves striking fire from the stones of the close, and cry to the second, and it would come after, and the two of them drink at the trough while Rob would button up his collar against the sharp drive of the frozen dew as the north wind woke. Then he'd jump on the back of the meikle roan, Jim, and go swaying and jangling down by the hedge, in the dark, the world on the morning's edge, wet, the smell of the parks in his face, the squelch of the horses soft in the clay.

Syne, as the light came grey in a tide, wan and slow, from the Bervie Braes, and a hare would scuttle away through the grass, and the peesies waken and cry and wheep, Rob Galt would jump from the back of Jim, and back the pair up against the plough, and unloose the chains from the horses' britchens and hook them up to the swiveltrees. Then he'd spit on his hands and cry *Wissh, Jim!* no longer ill-natured, but high-out and pleased, and swink the plough into the red, soaked land; and the horses would strain and snort and move canny, and the clay wheel back in the coulter's trace, Rob swaying slow in the rear of the plough, one foot in the drill and one on the rig. The bothy billies on Arbuthnott's bents, riding their pairs to start on some park, would cry one to the other, *Ay, Rob's on the go*, seeing him then as the light grew strong, wheeling, him and his horses and plough, a ranging of dots on the park that sloped by its long clay rigs to the edge of the moor.

By eight, as Rachel set out for school, a slim, dark thing with her well-tacked boots, she would hear the whistle of her father, Rob, deep, a wheeber, up on the hill; and she'd see him come swinging to the end of a rig, and mind how he once would stop and would joke, and tease her for lads that she had at the school. And she'd cry *Hello, father!* but Rob would say nothing till he'd drawn his horse out and looked back at the rig, and given his mouser a twist and a wipe. Syne he'd peek at his daughter as though he'd new woke, *Ay, then, so you're off*, and cry *Wissh!* to his horses and turn them about, and set to again, while Rachel went on, quiet, with the wonder clouding her face that had altered so since she came to Pittaulds.

He'd the place all ploughed ere December was out, folk said that he'd follow the usual Galt course, he'd showed up mean as the rest of them did, he'd be off to the marts and a dealing in horses, or a buying of this or a stealing of that, if there were silver in the selling of frogs the Galts would puddockhunt in their parks. But instead he began on the daftest-like ploy, between the hill of Pittaulds and the house a stretch of the moor thrust in a thin tongue, three or four acre, deep-pitted with holes and as rank with whins as a haddock with scales, not a tenant yet who had farmed Pittaulds but had had the sense to leave it a-be. But Rob Galt set in to break up the land, he said it fair cried to have a man at it, he carted great stones to fill up the holes, and would lever out the roots when he could with a pick, when he couldn't he'd bring out his horses and yoke them, and tear them out from the ground that way. Working that Spring to break in the moor, by April's end he was all behind, folk took a laugh, it served the fool fine.

Once in a blue moon or so he'd come round, he fair was a deave as he sat by your fire, he and your man would start in on the crops, and the lie of the land, and how you should drain it, the best kind of turnips to plant in the clay, the manure that would bring the best yield a dry year. Your man would be keen enough on all that, but not like Rob Galt, he would kittle up daft, and start in to tell you tales of the land that were just plain stite, of this park and that as though they were women you'd to prig and to pat afore they'd come on. And your man would go ganting wide as a gate, and the clock would be hirpling the hours on to morn, and still Rob Galt would sit there and habber, *Man, she's fairly a bitch, is that park, sly and sleeked, you can feel it as soon as you start in on her, she'll take corn with the meikle husk, not with the little. But I'll kittle her up with some phosphate, I think.* Your man would say *Ay, well, well, is that so? What do you think of this business of Tariffs?* and Rob would say *Well, man, I just couldn't say. What worries me's that park where I've put in the tares. It's fair on the sulk about something or other.*

And what could you think of a fool like that? Though he'd fallen behind with his chave on the moor, he soon made it up with his working at night, he fair had a fine bit crop the next year, the wife and the quean both out at the cutting, binding and stooking as he reapered the fields, Rachel had shot up all of a sudden, you looked at her in a kind of surprise as you saw the creature go by to the school. It was said that she fair was a scholar, the quean – no better than your own bit Johnnie, you knew, the teachers were coarse to your Johnnie, the tinks. Well, Rachel brought home to Pittaulds some news the night that Rob came back from the mart, he'd sold his corn at a fair bit price. For once he had finished pleitering outside, he sat in the kitchen, his feet to the fire, puffing at his pipe, his eye on the window, watching the ley rise up outside and peer in the house as though looking for him. It was Rachel thought that, as she sat at her supper, dark, quiet, a bit queer, over thin to be bonny, you like a lass with a good bit of beef. Well, she finished her meat and syne started to tell the message the Dominie had sent her home with; and maybe if she was sent to the college she'd win a bursary or something to help.

Her mother said *Well, Rob, what say you to that?* and Rob asked *What?* and they told him again, and Rob skeughed his face round, *What, money for school? And where do you think that I'll manage to get that?*

Mrs Galt said *Out of the corn you've just sold*, and Rob gave a laugh as though speaking to a daftie – *I've my seed to get, and my drains to dig, and what about the ley for the next year's corn? Damn't, it's just crying aloud for manure, it'll hardly leave me a penny-piece over.*

Rachel sat still and looked out at the ley, sitting so, still, with her face in the dark. Then they heard her sniff and Rob swung round, fair astonished-like at the sound she made. *What ails you?* he asked, and her mother said *Ails her? You would greet yourself if you saw your life ruined.* Rob got to his feet and gave Rachel a pat. *Well, well, I'm right sorry that your taking't like that. But losh, it's a small bit thing to greet over. Come out and we'll go for a walk round the parks.*

So Rachel went with him, half-hoping he thought to change his mind on this business of college. But all that he did on the walk was to stand now and then and stare at the flow of the stubble, or laugh queer-like as they came to a patch where the grass was bare and the crop had failed. *Ay, see that, Rachel, the wretch wouldn't take. She'll want a deep drill, this park, the next season.* And he bent down and picked up a handful of earth, and trickled the stuff through his fingers, slow, then dusted it back on the park, not the path, careful, as though it were gold-dust, not dirt. So they came at last to the moor he had broken, he smoked his pipe and he stood and looked at it, *Ay, quean, I've got you in fettle at last*. He was speaking to the park, not his daughter, but Rachel hated Pittaulds from that moment, she thought, quiet, watching her father and thinking how much he'd changed since he first set foot on its clay.

He worked from dawn until dark, and still later, he hove great harvests out of the land, he was mean as dirt with the silver he made; but in five years' time of his farming there he'd but hardly a penny he could call his own. Every meck that he got from the crops of one year seemed to cry to go back to the crops of the next. The coarse bit moor that lay north of the biggings he coddled as though 'twas his own blood and bone, he fed it manure and cross-ploughed twice-thrice, and would harrow it, tend it, and roll the damn thing till the Segget joke seemed more than a joke, that he'd take it to bed with him if he could. For all that his wife saw of him in hers he might well have done that, Mrs Galt, that was tall and dark and so quiet, came to look at him queer as he came in by, you could hardly believe it still was the Rob that once wouldn't blush to call you his jewel, that had many a time said all he wanted on earth was a wife like he had and land of his own. But that was before he had gotten the land.

One night she said as they sat at their meat *Rob, I've still that queer pain in my breast. I've had it for long and I doubt that it's worse. We'll need to send for the doctor, I think.* Rob said *Eh?* and gleyed at her dull, *Well, well, that's fine, I'll need to be stepping, I must put in a two-three hours the night on the weeds that are coming so thick in the swedes, it's fair pestered with the dirt, that poor bit of a park.* Mrs Galt said *Rob, will you leave your parks, just for a minute, and consider me? I'm ill and I want a doctor at last.*

Late the next afternoon he set off for Stonehive, and the light came low and the hours went by, Mrs Galt saw nothing of her man or the doctor, and near went daft with the worry and pain. But at last as it grew fell black on the fields she heard the step of Rob on the close, and she ran out and cried *What's keep you so long?* and he said *What's that? Why, what but my work?* He'd come back and he'd seen his swedes waiting the hoe, so he'd got off his bike and held into the hoeing, what sense would there have been in wasting his time going up to the house to tell the news that the doctor wouldn't be till the morn?

Well, the doctor came in his long brown car, he cried to Rob as he hoed the swedes, *I'll need you up at the house with me.* And Rob cried *Why? I've no time to waste.* But he got at last into the doctor's car, and drove to the house, and waited impatient; and the doctor came ben, and was stroking his lips; and he said *Well, Galt, I'm feared I've bad news. Your wife has a cancer in the breast, I think.*

She'd to take to her bed and was there a good month while Rob Galt worked the Pittaulds on his own. Syne she wrote a letter to her daughter Rachel that was fee'd in Segget, and Rachel came home. And she said, quiet, *Mother, has he never looked near you? I'll get the police on the beast for this,* she meant her own father that was out with the hay, through the window she could see him scything a bout, hear the skirl of the stone as he'd whet the wet blade, the sun a still lowe on the drowsing Howe, the dying woman in the littered bed, But Mrs Galt whispered. *He just doesn't think, it's not that he's cruel, he's just made on Pittaulds.*

But Rachel was nearly a woman by then, dark, quiet, with a temper that all the lads knew, and she hardly waited for her father to come home to tell him how much he might well be ashamed, he had nearly killed her mother with neglect, was he just a beast and with no heart at all? But Rob hardly looked at the quean in his hurry, *Hoots, lassie, your stomach's gone sour with the heat. Could I leave my parks to get covered with weeds?* And he gave her a pat, as to quieten a bairn, and ate up his dinner, all in a fash to be coling the hay. Rachel cried *Aren't you going to look in on mother?* and he said *Oh, ay,* and went ben in a hurry, *Well, lass, you'll be pleased that the hay's done fine. – Damn't there's a cloud coming up from the sea!* And the next that they saw he was out of the house, staring at the cloud as at Judgment Day.

Mrs Galt was dead ere September's end, on the day of the funeral as folk came up they met Rob Galt in his old cord breeks, with a hoe in his hand, and he said he'd been out loosening up the potato drills a wee bit. He changed to his black and he helped with his brothers to carry the coffin out to the hearse. There were three bit carriages, he got in the first, and the horses went jangling slow to the road. The folk in the carriage kept solemn and long-faced, they thought Rob the same because of his wife. But he suddenly woke, *Damn't man, but I've got it! It's LIME that I should have given the yavil. It's been greeting for the stuff, that park on the brae.*

Rachel took on the housekeeping job at Pittaulds, quiet, dark as her mother, aye reading in books, she would stand of a winter night and listen to the suck and slob of the rain on the clay, and hated the sound as she tried to hate Rob. And sometimes he'd say as they sat at their meat *What's wrong with you, lass, that you're glowering like that?* and the quean would look down, and remember her mother, while Rob rose cheery and went to his work.

And yet, as she told to one of the lads that came cycling up from Segget to see her, she just couldn't hate him, hard though she tried. There was something in him that tugged at herself, daft-like, a feeling with him that the fields mattered and mattered, nothing else at all. And the lad said *What, not even me, Rachel?* and she laughed and gave him that which he sought, but half-absent like, she thought little of lads.

Well, that winter Rob Galt made up his mind that he'd break in another bit stretch of the moor, beyond the bit he already had broke, there the land rose steep in a birn of wee braes, folk told him he fair would be daft to break that. It was land had lain wild and unfed since the Flood. Rob Galt said *Maybe, but they're queer-like, those braes, as though some childe had once shored them tight up.* And he set to the trauchle as he'd done before, he'd come sweating in like a bull at night, and Rachel would ask him *Why don't you rest?* and he'd stare at her dumbfoundered a moment, *What, rest, and me with my new bit park? What would I do but get on with my work?*

And then, as the next day wore to its close, she heard him crying her name outbye, and went through the close, and he waved from the moor. So she closed the door and went up by the track through the schlorich of the wet November moor, a windy day on the winter's edge, the hills a-cower from the bite of the wind, the whins in that wind had a moan as they moved, not a day for a dog to be out, you would say. But she found her father near tirred to the skin, he'd been heaving a great root up from its hold, *Come in by and look on this fairely, lass, I knew that some childe had once farmed up here.*

And Rachel looked at the hole in the clay, and the chamber behind it, dim in the light, where there gleamed a rickle of stone-grey sticks, the bones of a man of antique time. Amid the bones was a litter of flints and a crumbling stick in the shape of a heuch.

She knew it as an eirde of olden time, an earth-house built by the early folk, Rob nodded, *Ay, he was more than that. Look at that heuch, it once scythed Pittaulds. Losh, lass I'd have liked to have kenned that childe, what a crack together we'd have had on the crops!*

Well, that night Rob started to splutter and hoast, next morning was over stiff to move, fair clean amazed at his own condition. Rachel got a neighbour to go for the doctor, Rob had taken a cold while he stood and looked at the hole and the bones in the old-time grave. There was nothing in that and it fair was a shock when folk heard the news in a two-three days Rob Galt was dead of the cold he had took. He'd worked all his go in the ground, nought left to fight the black hoast that took hold of his lungs.

He'd said hardly a word, once whispered *The Ley*, the last hour as he lay and looked out at that park, red-white, with a tremor of its earthen face as the evening glow came over the Howe. Then he said to Rachel *You'll take on the land, you and some childe, I've a notion for that?* But she couldn't lie even to please him just then, she'd no fancy for either the land or a lad, she shook her head and Rob's gley grew dim.

When the doctor came in he found Rob dead, with his face to the wall and the blinds down-drawn. He asked the quean if she'd stay there alone, all the night with her father's corpse? She nodded, *Oh, yes*, and watched him go, standing at the door as he drove off to Segget. Then she turned her about and went up through the parks, quiet, in the wet, quiet gloaming's coming, up through the hill to the old earth-house.

There the wind came sudden in a gust in her hair as she looked at the place and the way she had come, and thought of the things the minister would say when she told him she planned her father be buried up here by the bones of the man of old time. And she shivered sudden as she looked round about, at the bare clay slopes that slept in the dusk, the whistle of the whins seemed to rise in a voice, the parks below to whisper and listen as the wind came up them out of the east.

All life – just clay that awoke and strove to return again to its mother's breast. And she thought of the men who had made these rigs, and the windy days of their toil and years, the daftness of toil that had been Rob Galt's, that had been that of many men long on the land, though seldom seen now, was it good, was it bad? What power had that been that woke once on this brae and was gone at last from the parks of Pittaulds?

For she knew in that moment that no other would come to tend the ill rigs in the north wind's blow. This was finished and ended, a thing put by, and the whins and the broom creep down once again, and only the peesies wheep and be still when she'd gone to the life that was hers, that was different, and the earth turn sleeping, unquieted no longer, her hungry bairns in her hungry breast, where sleep and death and the earth were one.

Introduction to three 'English' stories
'The Epic', 'Dienekes' Dream' 'Revolt'

Mitchell looks back on himself at the age of eighteen 'in charge of a provision barge which every fortnight journeyed up and down the Tigris, between Baghdad and Basra during the Arab revolt' [. . .] What he saw of the fighting was not of his liking.

Ian Munro, *Leslie Mitchell: Lewis Grassic Gibbon*[1]

Orientalism is not a mere political subject matter that is reflected passively by culture [. . .] nor is it a large collection of texts about the Orient, nor is it expressive of some 'Western' imperialist plot to hold down the 'Oriental' world. It is rather a distribution of geopolitical awareness into aesthetic, scholarly, economic, sociological, historical and philological texts.

Edward Said, *Orientalism*[2]

I

Leslie Mitchell got out of Iraq quickly, but although his writing career saw repeated reworkings of his interest in the land and people of North-East Scotland, he also remained obsessed with overseas travel and the 'Orient'. His first published work, 'Siva plays the game', is a tale of 'oriental cunning'[3] set in the Sahara in which Arabs outwit an Englishman. He went on to write over

1 Ian Munro, *Leslie Mitchell: Lewis Grassic Gibbon* (Edinburgh, 1966) p.32.
2 Edward Said, *Orientalism* (Harmondsworth, 1991) p.12.
3 Munro, p.41.

twenty stories set in the Middle East, inspired by his stay as a soldier in places such as Egypt, Iraq, Persia and Palestine. These were originally published individually in the *Cornhill* and *Macmillan's Magazine* before being collected into *The Calends of Cairo* (1931) and *Persian Dawns, Egyptian Nights* (1932). The latter's narrator reappears in a whole novel set in Cairo, *The Lost Trumpet* (1932). The cumulative effect of these three books is a panorama of Cairo, complicit with, yet questioning of Orientalist clichés.

Each story in *The Calends of Cairo* is narrated by Anton Saloney, a Russian ex-professor and ex-soldier but now a Cairo tourist guide. His style is marked by a foreign syntax, making it irritating yet memorable. Eastern colour dominates the book, most markedly in 'The Epic', in which its protagonist John Connan fantasises about the 'Spirit of the East':

> Could [. . .] Cairo be anything else but a woman? Oh, she'll look a princess and a dream, fair and wild and dark and splendid, robed and crowned, with jewelled feet and jewelled hands. Age-old and very young, evil and dear and desirable . . .

The fact that the woman embodying Cairo comes in a dream of a madman may serve as an interpretation-warning. However, Mitchell is not entirely in control of his stereotypes. The ending can be read in different ways, one of them favourable to Connan's vision, and the narrator certainly rhapsodises over Connan's work when it is produced. It is

> The epic of Cairo's soul – of her who was life and more than life, Purpose and desire and achievement. Out of the dreams and changing fantasies she came, veiled and singing, lovely and alien, she who was love divine itself – and yet had known no lover.

Here, then, is 'the East' of Western fantasy: feminine, illicit, exotic, alien. It is the fantasy complained about by Edward Said in *Orientalism*, who tracks over two centuries of writing which produces and fixes an 'Orient' from the heterogeneous complexity of different ethnicities, cultures and political systems in the 'Middle East', associating it with so much that is 'other' to Western culture.

Moving on to modern-day representations, Said also observes that 'in newsreels and news photos, the Arab is always shown in large numbers'.[4] Crowds, of course, are often threatening, often irrational and sometimes compared to the sea. The story 'Revolt' delivers all this. Mitchell might be excused his big crowd of Egyptian revolutionaries as it suggests unanimity against British oppression. It does, though, certainly involve 'massing insurrectionists' in a 'frenzy', and 'wave upon wave of faces' – plus an analogue in the shape of a 'horde of native children'. The story does foreground the feelings of both British and Egyptian communities before the revolt, the ambivalence of a British–Egyptian hybrid, and the problem of individuals' rights in relation to community ones, but its picture of a mob brings to mind George Orwell (quoted by Said) on colonial indifference to the humanity of the colonised:

> When you walk through [a large colonial town with thousands of inhabitants] it is always difficult to believe you are walking among human beings. All colonial empires are founded on that fact. The people have brown faces – besides, there are so many of them! Are they really the same flesh as yourself? Do they even have names? Or are they merely a handful of undifferentiated brown stuff, about as individual as bees or coral insects?[5]

Individuals and masses are high on Mitchell's agenda, though he failed to explore the issues at book length in his Eastern fiction. *A Scots Quair*, of course, shows passion for the rights of the masses even as his central character continues to scorn them and pursue her 'Mania for self-reliance', as one critic puts it.[6] The tension is

4 Said, p.287.
5 George Orwell, qt. in Said, p.251–2.
6 Angus Calder, 'A Mania for Self-reliance' in Douglas Jefferson and Graham Martin (eds), *The Uses of Fiction* (Milton Keynes, 1982) pp.99–113.

productive and never resolved. The use of Chris as a personification of Scotland may be handy for teachers who write explanatory notes for schoolchildren but makes one wonder if Chris is supposed to be worth a million or so average Scots. Her son certainly decides that he is worth lots of Scots as he and a trade union leader are the bearers of history, 'THE WORKERS'. Complexity is added in that they acknowledge that they may be trampled over and made unimportant in future revolutions but other workers are still clearly less heroic and less capitalisable.[7]

II

While *Orientalism* attracted glowing reviews on publication for its wide scholarship and moral passion, Said's work has suffered critical attacks more recently from left, right and centre. The charge is that Said is too dependent on aesthetic and geographical texts, has insufficient focus on historical fact and makes too much of a distinction between East and West. The Marxist Aijaz Ahmad refuses the East versus West formulation point-blank.[8] Imperialism is about trade, the argument goes, and trade does not oppose East and West. A crucial way to look at imperialist power, he contends, is to identify the who, the where and the how of the possession, use and transfer of money and goods. (Apologists for imperialism such as Ernest Gellner, some of whose other arguments are poor, have also made this valid point.)[9]

To be fair to Said, *Orientalism*'s introduction does warn readers that his focus is a bookish one, and it is indubitable that from 1700 onwards a mass of Western writing produces and fixes an 'East' without an equivalent mass of texts working the other way. However, Said could have done with including what he himself recommended to others: narrative. By *Orientalism*'s conclusion, Said leaves readers not much the wiser about the actual history of

7 Lewis Grassic Gibbon, *Grey Granite* (Edinburgh, 1990) p.181.
8 Aijaz Ahmad, *In Theory: Classes, Nations, Literatures* (London, 1992)
9 Ernest Gellner, 'The Mightier Pen? Edward Said and the Double Standards of Inside-out Colonialism', review of *Culture and Imperialism*, Edward Said, *Times Literary Supplement*, 19 February 1993: 3–4.

the Middle East, despite this inspirational paragraph on why (accurate) stories are a good idea:

> Narrative is the specific form taken by written history to counter the permanence of vision. Narrative asserts the power of men to be born, develop and die, the tendency of institutions and actualities to change, the likelihood that modernity and contemporaneity will finally overtake 'classical civilisations'; above all, it asserts that the domination of reality by vision is no more than a will to power, a will to truth and interpretation, and not an objective condition of history. Narrative, in short, introduces and opposing point of view, perspective, consciousness, to the unitary web of vision; it violates the serene [. . .] fictions asserted by vision.[10]

If 'The Epic' gives us basically a static Eastern tableau, 'Dienekes' Dream' involves narrative in Said's sense, following the progress of weavers in Sparta who leave their homeland due to impending financial ruin. In Cairo they find nowhere to settle and work, until their attention turns to a derelict site used as a rubbish dump. They move in, and begin to die from disease until an enormous removal project, carried out entirely by themselves, rids the place of all the infectious garbage and sewage. The land is cleared, renovated and planted. The Greeks begin to prosper, but the 1920s bring trouble with them:

> Cairo was advancing in Westernisation in great strides. Site-prices had doubled and trebled since the war. New buildings were springing up in every ward in the ancient city of the Mamelukes. Nor were effects unforeseen and numerous enough slow to erupt from all that causal activity. Title-deeds and land-rights were everywhere being questioned and overhauled.

10 Said, p.240.

A Parisian Egyptian emerges with rights to their land and wishes to evict them without paying them anything. They are desperate to stay put until a bill gets through the Egyptian chamber of Deputies, and violent conflict results when they resist the eviction order and then the police. Here, then, East–West differences mean little, despite contrived references to Thermopylae as the Greeks defend their patch of ground against the overwhelming force of invaders. The details of class struggle while Cairo lurches into modernity give this story its edge. How do new societies come into being? Said never gets round to telling us, but Mitchell has at least a try.

Why read these three stories? 'The Epic' compels attention because of its outrageous concentration of Oriental colour and its nod to perspectives such as Said's that 'The East' as the West knows it is very in the mind. 'Revolt' shows Mitchell's powerful sympathy for Egyptians who want to end British rule (despite, or because of, his time spent there as a soldier in the occupying army) and his interest in those of mixed-race caught up in anti-imperialist struggle. 'Dienekes' Dream' is the closest Mitchell gets to the material realities of survival among the working poor in a changing Cairo cityscape, demonstrating that he spent his time there looking as well as dreaming. Despite the uncertainties of style and melodramatic elements, those who come to these stories with an interest in Mitchell's concerns with archetypes, individuals versus masses, and ordinary people under threat from massive social change will be rewarded.

Jeremy Idle has published articles on Scottish writers including Leslie Mitchell/Grassic Gibbon, Spark, McIlvanney and Buchan.

The Epic

I

But you are of the moderns, my friend, and therefore primitive. In the squatting-places of the dawnmen also was the telling the story. They honoured the stylist long before there was the written style. Art was of art, not of life. But to me the tale without theme, the poem without purpose – it is salt without meat. The theme is the man. . . . God mine, as Connan proved!

Here, under the night-sky, above the Khalig, where once Connan sat and planned to snare the immortals – who may believe that all the tales are told? Our Cairo – she pens such plot and theme through every hour as makes of all recorded tale a ghostly script, a story writ in water.

Mother of aliens, alien to us all! Yet what city is like to her? In the scents and smells of her, her days and nights, colours and chance voices there are that wring the heart. Unreasonably. Unforgettably. Her very street-names cry in our ears like bugles: Ismailia, El Musky, El Manakh, Maghrabi, Shiekh Rihan. They ring beyond their meaning. . . .

Surely no language like the English in which to tell the Cairene tale! Only this wayward, featureless, fatherless tongue may sing our Poly-chromata. Not even the Arabic, I think, comes near to English for him who seeks to interpret Cairo's soul.

As Connan sought to do.

II

He came to Cairo, this Englishman – though I think he had perhaps the Irish blood – John Connan, early one July, when there were but few tourists and the khamsin blew every morning as a furnace back-blows upon a stoker. I met him outside the Hotel Continental and he engaged me as his guide because I did not call him Mister nor say that I would take him to the place of the genuine antiques.

He was a wit. 'Russian? Good God! Do any survive outside Dostoievsky?' And he regarded me with amazement and sadness, then selected one driver of arabiyeh from the smellsome horde that surrounded us.

'We will go to the Pyramids,' he said. I assumed surprise.

'Do they exist outside the little Hichens?'

Thereafter we became the more friendly, though he did not cease to yawn. He was a man whose soul and mind yawned; me he reminded of those bull-men of Assyria whose faces are curved and cruel, yet stamped with an awful weariness in their stone. Then I remembered the frontispiece of a little book.

'You are Connan the poet,' I said. 'I read your poems in Kazan.'

He closed his eyes and mimicked this book-English of mine – for I have never made to learn your speech argots – still wearily.

'I was Connan the poet. But now I am Connan the lost. I write no poetry, because there is no poetry left in the world. I know, for I have heard men screaming on wire entanglements, and known a woman who sold her body and taunted the buyer.'

'These things have been,' I said. 'Always they have been. They are old as the world is old.'

'I also am old,' he said, 'and every minute I listen to moralists – especially moralists out of Dostoievsky – I age an hour.'

He followed me amidst the Pyramids, Kheops, Khefren, and Menkaura, yawning. Only the Sphinx amused him. He said of it disrespectful things in that fashion I cannot imitate, with the humorous no-humour of the Englishman or American, comparing its face to that of a notable pugilist. The next fortnight I took him exploring the Cairene bazaars.

And slowly in that fortnight, in the hours we tramped the Khan Khalil or the Suq el Fahlamin – where the little artists of Europe pursue the local colour and the wood-workers of Egypt pursue their art – I came to know that his indifference was no pose. He was a sick man. Mentally. He wrote no poetry. He never read in books. Some thing in life there had been that blinded the windows of his soul. Perhaps that woman who had taunted the buyer.

Once he had been a poet of note in your English world. But that time was long past. He had written nothing for many years.

You must see him, a bull of a man, this Connan – great, with the black-blue hair and the blue eyes and ruddy face. His was no bodily sickness. Never I learned the story of the wanderings that had brought him to Cairo or that thing which had shocked the assurance from his heart. Perhaps the woman I imagined was not all to blame: such the idea that grew on me. Yet I liked him. . . .

The English 'like!' So English a word, the word of a-little-cold-love!

He had been the ruthless individualist, with a little courage and a little splendour, one who could sing of passion but not of pity. And he had found no pity. He might have been a genius but that he was a brute.

III

And then, towards the end of that fortnight, came the change upon him. He yawned not so much. He walked and looked with a stirred interest, a dawning wonder. All unknown to me, some Cairene colour there had been, piercing his darkness, and he had awakened. In a little while I saw in him grow, dimly yet, a purpose and desire.

For evening after evening he turned, though we were far in El Katal or El Fostat, and led back to this place where I had once brought him – here to this table in front of the cafe of Simon Papadrapoulnakophitos.

Then I understood that the Sharia Khalig had gripped him also, though I knew not to what ends, and I told him the history of it – this street young in Cairo, this street where once was a canal and one may still see the tide-markings of the waters. Young though it be, it is somehow Cairo itself, and immemorably ancient, as though the city had awaited this street since the first of its years. If you sit long enough in the Khalig all Cairo will sometime pass by

– boyar and beggar, brown man and black, and the men of the
shades of white, and all the women of the history of the world, the
vile and the fair and the pitiful. And you will hear the drifts of all
speech and all passion, all hope and all desire if you sit and listen in
the Street of All Egypt, that is older in soul than the Ramesids and
so young that it rides the electric tram-car. . . .

Perhaps I told him these things, perhaps I told him more. He
listened, but the last night of the fortnight it was he who talked.
And he invented a little childgame, as I thought it. We would sit
and scrutinise the Khalig's throngs, looking for the face that
symbolised the Khalig's – the soul of Cairo herself passing by.

'If we sit long enough we may – who knows? – look on Cairo
herself. Eh, colonel? And we'll know her at once. A face will rise
from the crowd-drifts and haunt us, and be gone in a minute, and
we'll know we've looked on the Khalig. And all our lives we'll
remember that face.'

I took up the jest and played with it, for I also have been a poet.
'Why a woman? And what will she look like?'

'Could the Khalig or Cairo be anything else but a woman? Oh,
she'll look a princess and a dream, fair and wild and dark and
splendid, robed and crowned, with jewelled feet and jewelled
hands. Age-old and very young, evil and dear and desirable, she'll
go by. . . . With the pride of all her days and all her blood and all
the colours of Moqattam.'

But there had come on me the irritation. This bullman un-
wearied I found I liked less. The Nietzsche, the fascist, the
bolshevik – how may any one of them ever reach to the heart
of a maid or a sunset? 'Perhaps like the Christ she will pass, poor
and despised, with hidden face, without splendour or sin, this
Cairo's soul you dream.'

And I can still hear the roar of his bass-laughter.

IV

For a week or so I did not see him at all. He knew his Cairo by then,
and could heed to himself. But I had to live and seek out other
employers.

Just then came another my way, and for some days I forgot Connan. He was a so-rich Egyptian millionaire, my new client, and had made much money putting the cattle into tins in Argentina. Now he had returned and built a great house in Heliopolis, and me he chartered to compile his family tree. At the end of three days I had proved his descent from Akhnaton, Cleopatra, and de Lesseps, but he was still unsatisfied. But also he paid well, so I took no ease, but spent another three days creating and allying his ancestors to Moses, Mohammed, and the Mamelukes. When I had run out of ancestors I remembered Solga Yon, the Tartar who burned the monks in Kiev, He was my own ancestor, but I take no pride in him. So I brought him on a raid into Egypt and married him into the millionaire's family, thereby ridding my family history of unpleasantness and adding fresh valour to the blood that had tinned the good bullocks of Argentina.

This work kept me away from the Khalig, and to the café of the little Simon I came not. But the evening I returned again, there, where you now sit, great and black against the sunset, like an Assyrian bull-god, was Connan. He was very drunk.

'I will have beer,' I said, 'English beer.'

He shook his head, calling me Fedor, for it was still his jest that I came out of Dostoievsky. 'A man who will drink beer in the Khalig will crack monkey nuts on Mount Olympus.'

'It is a kindlier drink than Greek brandy. I would drink but little of the good Simon's cellar, my friend.'

'I am very certainly drunk, Fedor. But it's a celebration.' He ordered beer for me. 'For I am no longer homeless. I am a citizen of Cairo, and the rat-like Simon boards me by the month, brandy and all.'

He had rented a bare room in the Khalig and bought himself a table and chair and an Indian string-bed. Simon Papadrapoulna-kophitos sent him his meals, and he spent his days in sleep and his nights in wandering the streets.

'Down in the Gozi quarter, my room, and above where the metal-smiths chink their tools in early dawn. High up it is, Colonel, and you can hear the rustle of Cairo awake and watch the morning come down the streets like – oh, like Wilde's girl with silver-sandalled feet. And the wind comes from the early Nile, across the Cairene roofs. . . . Must come and see me there. Sometime. Moralise to your heart's content, and I'll show you the ugliest nigger that ever salaamed outside a Beardsley grotesque.

'A decadent place, the Gozi.

'Rented the room from an old Jew who takes the precaution of being an absentee landlord. The house has canal tidemarks on it still, is five stories high, and rocks in the traffic. Like a tomb inside – a greasy tomb full of the unease of the unquiet dead – what a phrase! A warren where pallid things live like worms cut off from the sunlight. When I am not listening to the Khalig itself, I lie abed listening to the house up there in my garret – as God probably lies and listens to the attenuated whisperings of terrestrial life. . . . When you come, look out for the stairs, Colonel. They're of stone and have no banisters, and they sweat in the night-time.'

'How long are you to stay there?' I asked.

'Eh? Till I die or Simon's cellars empty.' He brooded for a little and was not drunk. The Khalig cried below us. I heard his voice come in the halfwhisper. '. . . Or I turn poet again.'

So, only for a moment, then he moved his glass of brandy, and laughed his bass-laugh, and was the ruddy animal.

'What a street! Even its ugliness is as nowhere else. Should see the new femme de chambre in the Gozi house. She came three days ago – brings up my food from Simon's waiter and cleans out the room. A Sudanese I think she is, and as hideous as a harpy. Kinky and clumsy, with a plague-pitted face; a body and soul both embryonic. . . . Ugly as sin, though willing enough. Hangs round unnecessarily, as though she had something to say and had forgotten the way to say it.'

'A slave, perhaps,' I said. 'There are still slaves.'

'Are there?' He had forgotten me again. So intent did he sit that I turned to look at that which drew his eyes. But it was only the Khalig. Then he spoke again in a whisper.

'Oh, it'll come to me yet. Some day it'll come to me, and I'll write it all – stuff that'll blind and drown the Georgian poetasters.'

'Eh?' I said. 'What stuff?'

'God, man, haven't you eyes? The Khalig – the Epic of the Khalig!'

V

Next night, though I came here to the usual table, there was no Connan. Nor the night after that, nor the next. Perhaps he had gone from Cairo, grown wearied, I thought, or wandered in some other part of our Many-Coloured. I asked of him from the little Simon. He still sent meals to the Gozi quarter, but himself had seen nothing of the Lord.

By this he did not refer to divine revelation, but to Connan, whom he believed a noble, being English, and it being a proper thing for Englishmen to be lords. Just as we of Russia who are neither bolsheviki nor boyars are incomprehensible to English minds.

But the fourth evening the waiter told me a woman awaited me with a message. I went down to the Khalig and the woman who waited came out of shadow and gave me an envelope. Then I saw her face and knew she must be the Sudanese slave.

I turned my eyes quickly from that poor, hideous face, so alien and unlovely. She stood silent, looking at the Khalig, the while I broke open the envelope. It held an unsigned note.

'Come with the messenger, colonel. I have something to show you.'

'This is from the Khawaja Connan?' I asked, not looking upon the face I knew was turned towards me. But she said nothing, and I raised my eyes to her. She was making motions with her fingers, As she did so, set in that so-grotesque mask of a face I saw her eyes, deep and brown and sad, infinitely patient and beautiful eyes. I made foolish noises before I understood.

She was dumb.

VI

The Sudanese left me to climb alone, and in the darkness I found that the stairs did verily sweat, as Connan had made avow. The

stairs were without the rail, and far down, as in a well, was the lamp
of the street doorway. I spread my fingers against the wall and so
climbed to the ultimate attic, where was Connan's room.

I knocked and went in, and Connan, sitting in his chair, wheeled
round. For a moment I thought him again drunk. He sat with hair
like feathers, and his ruddy face as one sleepless. He read my
thoughts and laughed aloud, and at that his laughter echoed down
and down into the silence of the house. Not until I heard the echo
had I ever noted how cruel was that laugh of his.

'Drunk as a mujik, Fedor. But not with brandy. There was never
yet man drunk what I've been drinking.'

He waved his hand to the room, and then I saw. It was littered
with the scrawled sheets of paper. On the table in front of Connan
was a disordered pile and on the string-bed another. He thrust a
bundle upon me.

'Sit down, man, sit down and read. Not all of it – it would take
you hours. Only that. Read it.'

I sat on the bed with the pile of pages on my knee, and for the
little while the so-dim light of the oil-lamp and the English script
vexed me; also it was a chance page, and much had gone before.
But almost at once a line leapt to my eyes and rang in my brain. In
a minute I had forgotten Connan and his room, and was far on the
wings of Connan's genius.

For I had lied. He was a genius, and I knew that this century
might never see his like. Once I was the Professor of English
Literature, and I have read much in the language, but nothing to
compare with those sheets that lived and sang in Connan's garret
of the Gozi.

For it was the song of the Khalig he had written, the song of all
Cairo, the song of Egypt and the world and the days unnumbered
since first the brown Stone Men drifted their dusk hordes across
the Nile. In the Khalig's colours and voices he had found the tale of
all humanity and told it as I had never read it told before – not even
in the songs of your Shelley. Of the dædal wars and love and death
and the birth was his tale; sunset and morning and the travail of
heat and the lash; the battle-song ringing across the waiting lines at
dawn; the bridal song and the birthnight agony, and all the quests

and fulfilments of men. All the voices that Cairo has ever known cried from his pages – the emir's voice and the voice of kings and the love-song of the slave outside his wattle hut. . . . God mine! I can but remember it now as one remembers the faint chords of music once heard and lost. . . .

And I sat and read on and on, till presently, out of the Khalig's colour and clamour I heard arise a new note, faint at first, but clearer growing till it dominated. And I understood with sudden flash of memory of Connan's child-game at Simon's café. What I had read was but background and scene, and this was the Epic of Cairo's soul – of her who was life and more than life, Purpose and Desire and Achievement. Out of the dreams and changing fantasies she came, veiled and singing, lonely and alien, she who was love divine itself – and yet had known no lover. . . .

I knew of a great silence. I had finished the last page. I looked at Connan, great, a bull-god in the black shadows from the little lamp. But in the dimness his eyes were bright-shining.

'Well?'

'You are a genius, friend Connan,' I said, and could think of no more.

'Genius? I have achieved the impossible, colonel.' His voice rang with arrogance. 'I've done what every Cairene poet has dreamt of since the days of Harun – found the Soul of the Khalig, as I swore I'd do. One by one I draw the veils from her face.' His cruel laughter boomed again. 'To her first bridal I bring the Spirit of the Khalig.'

I cannot explain it, but a strange shiver passed through me then. I made ready to go. 'If you do not rest and sleep you will have the breakdown.'

But he did not hear me. He had pulled more paper towards him and had begun to write, and when I said good night I might have been to him but one of the murmurs that ever haunted that room.

Then I passed down through the dank darkness, and so into the midnight Khalig, with the music of Connan's lines still ringing in my head. Out in the night-quietened way it was cool and sweet, and I stopped and looked up at the stars. . . .

And suddenly a great desolation came on me, under those bright

stars. For I could not doubt the truth of Connan's vision. Life –
beauty and splendour, blood and strife and colour – and nothing
more. Pity and faith and hope – the foolish whispers drowned in
the roar of the Khalig. . . .

I remember standing with that foolish, wistful ache at heart,
looking up at the light-glow from Connan's room.

VII

From dawn the next day I was followed and haunted by a
premonition – the foolish thought uprising urgent and crying:
This happens, this is Fear. It wheeled through my brain as I worked
in a room of the millionaire's house at Heliopolis. Somehow its
concern was Connan. All day it haunted me, and in the evening
when I returned to change, before taking the millionaire and his
family on a moonlight excursion to Gizeh and the tombs of their
ancestors, I made a determination. I would go down the Khalig and
call at the Gozi house.

But opposite the little Simon's I was seen and a letter brought to
me. It had been awaiting me since midday.

I looked at Connan's writing. 'For God's sake come to me. I am
afraid.'

That shock that follows a premonition justified was mine. In
minutes I was in the Gozi, had climbed the stair, and knocked on
Connan's door.

He bade me come in, but in the dark doorway I stood hesitant, I
remember, till he lit a match, and so the lamp, and we looked at
each other. . . . And I looked upon the face of a man who had seen
terror.

His black-blue hair above the temples was patterned in crisp-
grey. I stared at that hair of his, and it seemed to me that the
markings were in shape like the impress of fingers. Then I looked
round the room. The papers were gone, but in a corner – there was
no fireplace – were heaped great piles of charred pages.

'Yes, that's the Epic, that's the song of Cairo's own soul that the
world will never hear.'

I turned back to him. He laughed dreadfully and covered his face with his hands. So doing, his fingers covered the greyed lines on his hair, and I stood frozen with understanding.

'God mine, but why?'

'Why? If I hadn't burned it, man, hadn't sent for you, I'd have gone mad. Do you hear? He stood up and his voice rose to the scream. 'Mad. Look at me. . . . God, say it – say I'm not mad! . . .'

And then, in a burst of remembered fear and horror, he told me of the happenings of the night and morning. He had written all through the night, leading the Epic triumphant to its triumphant conclusion, but with the coming of dawn he had stopped exhausted. The lightening of the East roused him a little. He went to the window, and opened it, and leaned out into the air. The false dawn had passed from the sky, and it seemed to him quieter than the first morning of creation. Down below, far off in the quarter, he heard the tinkling tools of some Gozi smith. Something else also he heard, but thought it a delusion, and still leant there, leaning with closed eyes.

He thought he had heard a footstep. The delusion persisted. He opened his eyes and turned round. . . .

'My God, don't look at me like that, colonel! She was real, I tell you. She stood not three feet away from me, arms outstretched – *The Spirit of the Khalig, the woman I created*!'

He covered his face again, then jumped up and raved at my silence.

'She was real, I tell you, real. Veiled and unearthly, but real. I think I cried out, for I knew I was mad. And then, my God, she was in my arms, her arms around my neck, and we kissed each other, and there was such magic and wonder in the kiss as my Epic had never known. . . . A ghost, a dream, a symbol – she kissed my lips, colonel! – and called me the one lover for whom she had waited throughout ages.'

I tried to laugh at him, but the laughter choked in my throat. He was staring blindly in front of him, and suddenly he broke into a whispered chant.

'*Oh my beloved! you for whom I have sought so long! So weary and never-ending they've seemed, the years in their suns and shadows. . . . Tonight, at midnight, I come to our bridal.*'

'I think I fainted then. When I awoke the Khalig was stirring below, I was alone in the room.'

VIII

So, in that early dawn, he had taken the Epic of the Khalig, the thing of beauty which he had created, and burned it. Page by page he had burned it, then spent rest of the day fighting wave after wave of madness which rose up out of his heart to engulf him.

But the exhaustion he had held off crept on him now. He had sat down on the bed, and, while I talked, his head began to nod in weariness.

I talked on, and he lay back with closed eyes. Of anything and everything I talked, except poetry and the Khalig. I talked of autumn and stars and his English fields, and smell of ploughed lands, and kindly peasant song. Of all the quiet secure things I talked, and in a little I looked at him and saw he was asleep.

I spoke on, dropping my voice to the whisper, then stopped, and tip-toed over to him, and listened to his breathing. Nature had come to his help and he was safe from dream and delusion. . . . I remember his face turned from the light, and of how I thought it, in despite its cruelty and wan strength, the face of a child, pitiful and uncomprehending. . . .

I closed the door of his room and crept down the stairs of that unquiet house. The darkness moved as if alive. There was no lamp and I had to feel for each step. In the entrance doorway, in the radiance of the street, I stopped and listened, hesitating, then shrugged at the foolishness which had come upon me also.

For it had seemed to me that I heard, far in the depths of the house, the sound of a woman weeping, desolately, as one in despair.

IX

The stuff of dreams that we are! How might I have known – I who do not know even yet?

For the next morning Connan was discovered dead in his room.

Somewhere near midnight he had shot himself through the heart with the second chamber of his revolver.

In the doorway, also shot through the heart, lay the Sudanese slave. . . .

Accident? Coincidence? *God mine, she was clad in the bridal robes of a Cairo maiden!*

Dienekes' Dream

I

To see the face that launched a thousand ships peep from below a poke-bonnet at a street-corner confessional induces a sense of shock that speedily passes into irritation. Such face, you feel, no doubt had once its appropriate function and setting; but in the twentieth century it is fantastic. Horatius kept his bridge well enough for the purpose of inspiring later ages to juvenile recitation; reincarnated as a gangster with a machine-gun in a Chicagoan alley he loses charm. Leonidas and his Spartans, holding liberty and Thermopylæ against the hosts of Asia, were heroes, but —

And you stand, a strayed tourist in the unfrequented warrens of Cairo, and stare at that wall and inscription in the Sharia el Ghoraib.

It rises high, this street-wall that girds the rear of some ancient khan. It glimmers dour and brown and unremarkable, all the length of it – except at this one spot. For here, from a distance of three feet upwards, the dried mud is pitted and flaked as though, in its liquid state, it had been pelted with pebbles. Below those marks of an incomprehensible hail-storm, a great red stain is a dull blotch in the sun-shimmer, and carved into that blotch, in letters Greek and gigantic, is the single word

ΘΕΡΜΟΠΥΛΑΙ

You stare at it and transliterate Thermopylæ; you go closer and see a line of smaller lettering. A quotation – a familiar enough quotation.

A misascribed quotation.

Who really spoke it? You wander back in thought to forgotten

pages of a forgotten history-lesson. Of course! Not Rhizos –
whoever he was – but Dienekes of Sparta when they told him
the Persian arrow-hail would darken the sun. . . .

Fantastic thing to find inscribed on the wall of a Cairene khan!

II

It stood a wall still uninscribed that night seventeen years ago when
the weavers of Selitsa – over thirty of them, men, women, and
children, clinging to pathetic and parlous packages wherein were
shrouded their dismembered looms – tumbled out of the Alexandria train into the dark inhospitality of Cairo Central Station.

'Are you all here?' roared Georgios Londos, a trifle mechanically,
when they grouped round him outside the station gates. They
chorused a tried and optimistic yes. Londos ran his eye over them,
scratched his head, considered the flowing darknesses and jaundiced lightings that were Cairo, and seemed a little at a loss.

'Then – we're here, then.'

Here indeed at last they were – Sina, with his wife and mother and
two daughters; the Latas; the Vasos; the little thin widower with a
single son and a name like a battle-cry, Kolocrotoni; these, the others,
and the two who were the group's actual, if unnominated, leaders,
little Trikoupi and the giant Londos. Here in Cairo at last. . . .

'What shall we do now, Big Londos?' piped ten-years-old Rhizos
Trikoupi from the side of his father, Elia. He voiced the silent
questionings of the party.

The giant of Selitsa yawned, ear-achingly, and found solution in
the yawn. His silhouette vanished, materialising to view again as a
dim recumbency.

'We'll sleep. I haven't had a wink since we left Dourale. . . .'

III

There was no moon that night, but presently the coming of a fine
frostiness of stars. In that starlight the Greek weavers huddled in an
uneasy rhythm of sleep beneath the bland bass snorings of giant
Londos.

The winter nights are cold in Cairo – as you may have noticed from the terrace of the Continental. And long – when you lie on damp cobblestones and your body exudes heat and inhales rheumatism in enthusiastic accord with some mystic law of physics. Young Rhizos Trikoupi was never to forget the feel of those cobblestones under his insufficiently-padded hip: it was so bad he thought the cobbles must ache almost as much as he did. . . .

A late train chugged out of Cairo. He raised himself on his elbow and watched its wavering comet-tail of sparks grow dim and disappear. Perhaps on board it was some Greek returning to Greece – Cairo to Alexandria, Alexandria by unending discomforts of the trading boat to Dourale, Dourale to – perhaps someone on board that train would even journey up from Dourale to Mother Selitsa in the eparchy of Oitylos!

Once Spartic of the Spartans, Selitsa town. But its weaving community had fallen on evil days and were near to starving when Londos, a lumbering Moses, knocked from door to door and at each delivered his ultimatum.

'Stay here – and starve; abroad – we may eat. Greece buys but the goods of the American machines; Mother Selitsa has no need of us – but she's sent our reputation abroad. Such cloths as ours still sell well in Egypt. Let us go there.'

And here the most of them were – the last of their money gone in fares for their varied and uneaseful journeyings – sleeping on the Cairene cobblestones, waiting for the dawn.

Rhizos laid his head down again, and again sought sleep. But, with a pallor upon the stars, the night had grown colder than ever. He found young Kolocrotoni awake near him, and they conversed in whispers, looking at a sky that grew darker and darker in the moment before morning, and then was suddenly aflaunt, all along the flat roof-spaces, with the blown streamers of a host of crimson banners. The boys stared raptly, the cold forgotten.

'When we've beds,' averred young Kolocrotoni, cautiously, 'it mayn't be so bad to live here.'

Rhizos remembered giant Londos's promise. 'Our Mother has a fortune waiting us here.'

IV

And then—

Were this still no more than prelude I might sing you a very pretty Odyssey indeed of the wanderings of those Selitsa weavers in search of a place in Cairo wherein to lay their heads. Penniless, full of hope, and much be-cursed by the Greek consul, Londos and Elia Trikoupi tramped the streets while the other males guarded the women and looms and grew hungry and thirsty and were evicted by carbine'd gendarmes now from one squatting-place, now another. For Cairo declared itself overcrowded and poverty-stricken already. 'Go back to Selitsa,' said Cairo, literally and in effect. Whereat Londos, an uncultured man, cursed it forcibly. 'We'll stay in Cairo and set up our looms,' said he, 'on a midden – if need be.'

Not that they might not have found employment. But they had learnt, they and generations before them, tenacity in the bitter Peloponnesus. They were determined, with an altogether regrettable archaic obstinacy, to erect their own looms, not to work for others. They found an archway under which they were allowed to camp, and there endured existence for three days until on the third midnight giant Londos returned to them in some excitement and shot the sleepers out of sleep, and some of them nearly out of their wits, with his shout:

'I've found it!'

Dazed and drowsy, they packed up and set out after him, tramping through the dark Cairene streets for hours, a grotesque procession enough. Until beyond the Bab el Zuweiya, and at the foot of the Sharia el Ghoraib, Londos halted and pointed. And the place to which he had brought them was the cul-de-sac wherein the sharia terminated, a waste space of half an acre amid the high walls of the surrounding khans. Once it had been a rubbish depository, but had been long abandoned for even that purpose. Yet still from the ancient buried offal arose a sickening odour.

It troubled even the nostrils of the gentle Elia Trikoupi, no æsthete. 'Has it not – a little perfume?' he asked, turning diffident eyes on the giant. Whereat Londos's immense laugh boomed out over the sleeping Warrens, startlingly. The other Greeks took it up.

They stood and rocked with laughter in that Cairene midnight, hungry, forsaken, light-hearted. The giant of Selitsa wiped his eyes.

'Little Perfume – what a name for our midden! You have christened it, Elia!'

V

They set to building sheds on the edge of it next day – the waste and odoriferous piece of land claimed by no one, the seeming haunt of half the pariah dogs and all the amorous cats of Cairo. They tramped to the edge of the town, to Nile-bank, to the Greek quarter, begging, borrowing and stealing stray pieces of timber and canvas. They delved out foundations at the edge of the waste – the smells that arose were dreadful – and drew up the huts at an angle fronting towards the Sharia el Ghoraib. In three days the huts were almost habitable. And then Londos procured a slab of wood and a piece of charcoal and, grinningly, scrawled a legend on the slab, and nailed it up above the angle hut:

'Little Perfume.'

They were on an island, the Selitsa settlers – an exceedingly dry island. There was no water nearer at hand than that in the public fountain at the far end of the Sharia el Ghoraib. From this fountain water had to be fetched – a task which fell to the children, for the older settlers from Selitsa, men and women, betook themselves to the looms as soon as these were erected. On an advance of yarn and silk they set to weaving the mantles that had already won them reputation in Egypt, and the straggling, hourly procession of children making towards the fountain would hear the thump and boom, rise and fall, behind them in every hut of Little Perfume.

It seemed to them the only friendly sound in Cairo. The sharia looked on them sourly, and at the fountain itself they would find the Arab hosts marshalled to give battle – children who threw stones and dirt, and spat with some venom. Ringleader of this Asiatic opposition was a small, ferocious and underclad girl whose favourite amusement was to drop dust-bricks into the fountain just prior to the arrival of Rhizos and his companions. Rhizos bided his opportunity, found it one afternoon, dropped his bucket, pursued the damsel, tucked her head under his arm in a businesslike if unchivalrous fashion, and proceeded to punch her with great heartiness. . . . But such satisfactions were few enough, and wilted in retrospect on the painful return march to Little Perfume, with small arms aching and small back breaking and the conviction deep in one's heart that some meddler had elongated the sharia in one's absence. . . .

That was in late winter and for a time the locality was endurable. But the summer drew on. Desperately engrossed as they were in the attempt to find an opening for their wares in the Egyptian markets, the Selitsa settlers had borne with their strangely-odoured habitat uncomplainingly. They rose with the first blink of daylight, into those fervid Cairene mornings when the air is unthinkably pure and the day for an hour has the hesitating loveliness of a lovely woman, and cooked their scanty breakfasts and set to work at their looms. They ceased not even at the failing of the light, but took to the coarser work under the glimmer of great tallow candles, giant Londos and the gentle Elia leading in feats of endurance. Sometimes it was midnight before the humming of the looms would cease, and Londos, a little unsteady, would lumber out of doors to look up at the splendour of the Cairene moon and chuckle tiredly as he caught the glitter of moonlight on the notice-board of the settlement.

But the summer drew on, and with it each morning arose from the waste of Little Perfume, as though a foul beast hibernated underfoot, a malodorous breath of a vileness unendurable. With it came clouds of mosquitoes – insects rare enough in Cairo – and hordes of flies. By midday the ancient dunghill had a faint mist. In a fortnight two of the Greek children were dead and half of the community was sick in bed.

The evening of the day on which they buried the children Londos stalked to the door of the hut where Trikoupi leant pallidly over his loom and little Rhizos knelt by the heap of sacking on which his mother slept uneasily.

'Come out, Elia.'

So Elia went out, and waited. Londos strode up and down in the evening light, debating with himself, once stopping and throwing out his arms hopelessly. Then he halted in front of the gentle Trikoupi.

'There is only one thing we can do, Elia.'

'Leave Little Perfume?' Elia had guessed this was coming.

'No, remove it.' Londos pointed to the waste hillock towering away behind the huts. 'We must shift that, and quickly.'

Trikoupi stared at him as though he had gone mad. 'Remove it? But how? And where?'

Londos indicated the louring of the Moqattam Hills in the sunset. 'There. It is two miles away, beyond the town boundaries.'

'But move this hill – It is a month's work for scores of men.'

Londos nodded. 'And we must do it in a fortnight – if our children are to live.'

VI

They did it. It turned in the telling of later years into an epic of struggle, a thing of heroism and great feats, intermingled with shouted laughter. The fatigue and horror and weariness the years came to cover with the tapestry of legend: how Londos, stripped to a breech-clout, dug and excavated and filled every one of the sacks and baskets for four days on end, the while the others bore them on their two-mile journey – Londos, gigantic, unsleeping, pausing now and then to drink the coffee brought him, and vomit up that coffee at the next nest of dreadful stenches and even more dreadful refuse his shovel uncovered; how the gentle Trikoupi bore loads without ceasing, day or night, till he was found walking in his sleep, a babbling automaton; how the women, laughed at and pelted by the Cairenes, bore load for load with the men; how three died in that Iliad – one of them, the Vasos mother, by the pits beyond the walls – and there was no time to bury their corpses; how the police descended on the excavators and gave them a time-limit in which to finish the work; how in desperation the weaver Gemadios went to Citadel in the dark hours of one night and stole a great English Army handcart, and worked with it for two days (doing feats in the removal of offal) and then returned it, the theft still undiscovered; how—

They did it. It was cleared at last. The burning Cairene sunshine smote down on ragged floors, once the floors of some Mameluke's palace, perhaps, in the days of Cairo's greatness. Underneath those floors was plentitude of bricks and stonework. And the odours died and passed, and the weavers, men and women, reeled to their huts and flung themselves down beside their looms and slept and slept, and woke and groaned with aching muscles, and slept again.

Little Rhizos Trikoupi, staggering to the fountain alone that night with an endrapement of pitchers, found seated on the coping the ferocious little female whose head he had once punched. She sat and regarded him without apparent hostility. He disregarded her, ostentatiously.

But as he lifted up the laden jars she came to his side.

'I'll help,' she said, friendly of voice.

She bore a jar to the confines of Little Perfume. There she set it down and smiled at Rhizos. 'My name is Zara,' she said, inconsequently. Then told him disastrous tidings, casually. 'They are not to allow any more of your people to carry water from the fountain to the Place of Stinks.'

VII

It was a crushing blow. Londos and Elia Trikoupi went and argued with the ward-masters. But they refused to be moved. All of them except Muslih, a Nationalist and father of that advanced feminist Zara, were quite openly hostile to the Greeks. The fountain was intended to supply the streets which surrounded it, not such carrion-grubbers as might settle in abandoned middens . . .

That evening Londos himself, bidding the children stay at home, went for water with two great buckets. He came back hatless and bleeding, but grinning, with a jeering, stone-pelting crowd behind him. But the buckets were full. He put them down, emptied them into the settlement's jars, and started out again. By the fountain-coping three men still lay and groaned where he had left them. He refilled the buckets.

But next morning Rhizos and young Kolocrotoni, scouting, came back to tell that there was a policeman on guard at the fountain. Giant Londos swore at that information and scratched his head. It was one thing to crack the cranium of the stray and obstreperous Cairene, another to do the same to a gendarme. The Greeks collected to debate the matter, Elia Trikoupi, dust-covered from exploring the uncovered floors of Little Perfume, arriving last.

'Abandon Little Perfume now we will not,' swore Londos. 'Not though we have to carry water from the Nile itself. Those lawyers! Elia, we'll rear that son of yours to be one and defend our interests. Then we may drink in peace.'

'We may drink before that,' said Trikoupi, gently. 'If you will all come with me—'

They went with him. He led them to the middle of the waste of Little Perfume. In the ground was a circular depression filled with earth and building rubbish. Londos stared at it and then embraced Trikoupi.

'A well – once a well. And we'll make it one again.' He threw off his coat, groaned like a bull at an ache that leapt to fiery being between his shoulder-blades, and called for a spade. 'This will clinch for ever our right. We can start building. We can start making gardens.' He sighed, almost regretfully. 'The great tale of Little Perfume is over.'

VIII

But indeed, could he have known it, they had lived no more than its prelude. Almost unnoticed, yet weaving assiduously into the web and woof of Cairene life stray threads of story-plot from Little Perfume, the War years passed over Egypt. Demand for the products of the looms that had once hummed in Selitsa grew in volume and value. Nor did the aftermath bring any slump. The settlers flourished.

Yet out of its profits the little community succeeded in banking scarcely a piastre. Replacing the saving instinct of generations a new habit had grown upon the weavers – the enrichment and embellishment of Little Perfume. Its gardens grew famous throughout the Warrens. They even planted trees – quick-growing Australian trees procured by Rhizos Trikoupi when he learnt of those plants in botany lessons. A great shed, built of mud-bricks, airy and cool and flat-roofed, gradually rose to being in the centre of the one-time rubbish depository. This was the communal loom-shed. Round it, one by one, were built the houses of the weavers – twelve houses with much space and garden-room. Those houses at night were lighted no longer by candles, but by electricity. The long-tapped well brought water to each. . . . Londos, gigantic still, but bulkier, slower, than of yore, would sometimes walk away down the Sharia el Ghoraib and then wheel round abruptly, in order to shock himself into fresh surprise over the miracle of Little Perfume. He would stand and stare at it fascinatedly, and so was standing one evening in October when young Rhizos Trikoupi, the law-student returning from his studies in Cairo, hailed him as he came down the sharia.

'Dreaming again, *papakes?*'

'Eh?' The giant started. 'Ah, you, Rhizos. And how much have you learned to-day?' He chuckled. 'Apart from the shape of the ear of Zara Muslih, I mean.'

Rhizos coloured a trifle, and attractively. Daily, almost, he and Zara, both students at the University, travelled into Cairo together. Her father, the fervid progressive and friend of the Greeks, had determined to give her such education as would shock her mother and every other veiled woman east of the Bab el Zuweiya. . . . She had certainly lovely ears.

Londos chuckled again, clapping an ungentle hand on the law-student's shoulder.

'And why not? But remember you are our Samson, and there must be no Delilahs.'

'There are no Philistines,' said Rhizos, tolerantly, and then nodded back towards the Sharia el Ghoraib, the street which had stood decaying ever since that midnight when the Selitsa settlers passed through it to the conquest of the ancient offal-heap. 'At least, not nearer than the sharia! What is happening there?'

'Eh? Oh, the house-breaking in the upper half?' Londos shrugged indifferently, his eyes on the night-shadowed peace of

Little Perfume. 'Its owner following our lead at last – it has taken him ten years. Clearing away the huts and building houses, I hear. Site-prices are soaring high in Cairo.'

IX

Cairo, indeed, was advancing in Westernisation in great strides. Site-prices had doubled and trebled since the War. New buildings were springing up in every ward of the ancient city of the Mamelukes. Nor were effects unforeseen and numerous enough slow to erupt from all that causal activity. Title-deeds and land-rights were everywhere being questioned and overhauled, claim and counter-claim jostled one the other in every lawyer's office. And presently, from the midst of this maelstrom of modernisation, a long wave reached out and burst like a thunder-clap against the shores of Little Perfume.

Twenty-four hours after that talk with Londos, Rhizos returned to find his father, the giant, Vasos, and old Sina in anxious consultation over a long tri-lingual typescript. They cried out their relief at sight of him, and Londos handed over the document.

'It was wise to train this son of yours, Elia,' he said, and wiped his forehead. '*He* will deal with it.'

Rhizos took the crinkling sheets of paper and sat down and read them, and presently was aware of a deafening, sickening beat of blood around his ears.

It was a notice to the effect that the site-property of El Ghoraib, 'commonly known as Little Perfume,' was required by its owner for building purposes, and that the Greek squatters at present in occupation must vacate it within a month's time.

X

The Greeks took the case to the courts, Rhizos engaging a lawyer on behalf of the settlement. But even with this development Londos and the older weavers refused to treat the claim seriously.

'An owner for Little Perfume?' said Londos. 'It must be the man in the moon. Or of a certainty a lunatic.'

He proved less unharmful. They caught their first glimpse of him as the case was being tried – a *rentier*, a Parisian Egyptian of the new generation, suave, sleek, and bored. His lawyers submitted the claim with a casualness which was deceptive. It covered certainty. El Ghoraib, together with the nearby Sharia el Ghoraib, had been the property of the Falih family from time immemorial. The title-deeds were impeccable.

'Why did you not evict the squatters before?' demanded the Greeks' lawyer.

Falih smiled. 'Because until recently I'd forgotten El Ghoraib's existence.' He added cooly: 'And I make no claim on the squatters now, provided they leave the site undamaged.'

It was as heartless a case as had come within his province, said the Egyptian judge in a curt summary. Nevertheless, there could be no disputing the claim of Falih.

Judgment was entered accordingly, and Londos and Trikoupi, acting for the settlers, allowed to appeal.

The appeal was quashed.

XI

The news was brought to Little Perfume. Giant Londos, shrunken, rheumatism-crippled, stared from Rhizos to his father, then around the circle gathered to hear the news – all old men, bent with toil at their looms. Rhizos could not meet that stricken look in the eyes of the giant whose labours in clearing the rubbish-waste were already legendary.

'But – it means we go out of here as we came! It is impossible,' said Londos, and burst into tears. . . . The old men sat silent, but Rhizos slipped out of the gathering and walked the Cairene evening in a red passion of anger. He found himself at length outside the door of the Muslih house, at the other end of the Sharia el Ghoraib. It was a familiar enough door to him and in a moment it was closing behind him the while he made his way to the room where Zara sat over books and lecture-notes. At sight of him she rose eagerly.

'The appeal?'

He laughed. 'Quashed. Falih can evict us when he chooses.'

She kindled from his own anger. 'It's a shame – oh, a damned shame! Those old men and women who have worked such a miracle. . . . Can't they claim compensation?'

'They can take away nothing but the looms they brought. We're liable to prosecution if we damage the very houses we've built.'

She looked at him in helpless pity. 'Surely something can be done? If only that Bill were passed in the Chamber!'

'What Bill?' he asked, indifferently.

He had been too busy heeding to the court cases to know of outside events that might affect them. He listened half-unlistening, until meaning of what she was saying penetrated the cloud of his anger.

'A Bill enforcing value-compensation for improved sites – to become law as soon as passed! That would mean Falih would never dare evict us from Little Perfume. It would cost him too much. . . . But when will it pass?'

'They are fighting it, my father says, but it is bound to pass. When? Within the next week or so, perhaps.'

'Too late. If only—'

He began to walk up and down the room, Zara looking at him. He stopped and started at her, absently. They had each the same thought.

'If we could keep off Falih till then—'

XII

That was on the Monday. Next day the Greeks of Little Perfume received a notice from Falih's agent to vacate the site within twenty-four hours.

They made no attempt to comply. Instead, Rhizos went and argued with the agents. Reluctantly, those agents extended the time-limit another forty-eight hours. But they were insistent that at the end of that period the site be left vacant. Later in the day they sent a note curtailing the extra forty-eight hours to twenty-four. The growth of support for the new Bill in the Chamber had alarmed Falih.

Meantime, Rhizos organised the inhabitants of Little Perfume. At a meeting they voted him to control the situation, with young

Kolocrotoni his assistant. Then they retired to uneasy beds, wondering what the next day would bring.

It brought Falih's bailiffs, four of them, knocking at the door of Trikoupi's house. The Greeks gathered round the arrivals quickly enough, while a crowd of curious Egyptians flocked in from the far end of the sharia. Nor were they hostile to the Greeks, those Egyptians. The Greeks had won their place. Here were thieves come to disposses them. . . . The bailiffs grew angry and frightened, beating upon Trikoupi's door. The gentle Elia opened it.

'This house must be cleared,' said the leader. He motioned forward one of the others. 'Carry out the furniture.'

Londos, who had been waiting for this, as instructed by the absent Rhizos, rose from a chair. They saw a tipsy giant behind a table littered with full and empty bottles. 'Drink first,' he invited, swayingly. 'Drink to our leaving this place of stinks. Sit down and drink.'

The bailiffs hesitated, but a growl came from the crowd pressing round the open door. Falih's men sat down and, not unwillingly, filled glasses from the bottles indicated. . . .

They passed down the Sharia el Ghoraib late that evening in two arabiyehs hired by Rhizos; they passed down it drunk and roisterous and singing improper songs. They had fallen mysteriously asleep after the first drinks, had slept until afternoon and had awakened to be again forcibly regaled with draughts of the potent Greek brandy. . . . Listening to their drunken brawling receding into the evening, Rhizos turned to Zara, who had come to see the day's *dénouement*. She was flushed and laughing at the strategem's success, and he stared at the shapeliness of her ears.

'We've won the first skirmish, but to-morrow—' and his face grew dark.

She suddenly kissed him. 'Luck for tomorrow!' And was gone, leaving him staring after her breathlessly, with flushed face.

XIII

To-morrow—

The papers bore news of the Bill. It had passed, after a fierce struggle, into the Egyptian equivalent of the committee stage. From there it had still to emerge, still to receive the King's sanction. Rhizos read the news from the sheets of *El Ahram*, he and young Kolocrotoni together.

'Falih's men will return long before then,' said Kolocrotoni.

'They'll return to-day,' said Rhizos, 'unless we go to them instead.' He had already planned his next move. Within half an hour, after canvassing from house to house in Little Perfume, he went down into Cairo with notes to the value of three thousand piastres in his wallet. Of what he accomplished on that journey he never told. But he returned with an empty wallet and Falih's agents did not come that day. Falih himself, indeed, had gone to Alexandria.

But Rhizos knew it was only a respite, that to buy off subsidiary agents was not to buy off Falih's lawyers. He read the news about the Bill with growing anxiety. There were difficulties in the committee stage.

'It's hopeless to wait for it,' said Kolocrotoni, dark and young and fierce. They stood together in the sunset, looking at Little Perfume from Londos' ancient stance at the mouth of the sharia. 'Better that we leave it so that this Falih will wish it were a midden again.'

'How?' asked Rhizos.

'Burn it, blow it up.'

'Blow it up? Where are you to get the explosives?'

Kolocrotoni laughed. 'That would be easy.' And he told of a warehouse in Cairo where arms were stored before being smuggled through to the Senussi. 'It is from there that the Nationalist students get their arms.'

'Could we?' asked Rhizos.

Kolocrotoni stared. He had hardly meant to be taken so seriously. 'Revolvers?'

'Yes.' Young Trikoupi seemed to be calculating rapidly. 'Or automatics. Thirteen revolvers and ammunition.'

XIV

Now, as I've told, there was only one street which led into the square of Little Perfume. Down this street the next morning came a body of men, labourers and carpenters. With them was Falih's own lawyer. Gemadios's youngest son brought to the Greeks news of the invaders' approach. Giant Londos, bending over the garden-patch in front of his house, with a great hose in his hand, nodded.

The lawyer halted his host, glanced at Londos, and then walked past him. Or rather, he prepared to do so.

'I would not pass,' said Londos, in friendly tone. And added, as an anxious afterthought, 'This is the first time I have used a garden hose and I am still inexpert.'

The little lawyer turned on him angrily, and at that moment was lifted off his feet by a stream of water hitting him in the chest. He rolled out of Londos's garden, rose, and was promptly knocked down again. The hose appeared to have gone mad in the hands of Londos. He stabbed a beam of water to and fro amid the heads of a lawyer's following. They broke and ran for the sharia, and, running, found themselves objects of suspicion to the Egyptians of the sharia's hovels.

Cries rose: 'Who are they?'

The answering cry came quickly. 'Thieves! Stop them!'

Thereat, apparently in a passion for justice, the Sharia el Ghoraib emptied a multitude of pursuers and assailants upon the followers of Falih's lawyer. They were pelted with refuse, kicked, cuffed, and finally driven ignominiously from the street. The little lawyer, beyond the reach of the last missile, turned and shouted. Zara Muslih, standing listening at the door of her father's house, heard him and went up through the laughing, excited street towards Little Perfume. Beyond the inhabited quarter, towards where the sharia terminated in the strange settlement of the Selitsa weavers, she found Rhizos Trikoupi staring up and down the two hundred yards of high, blank-faced street-wall.

'The lawyer has gone for the police.'

Rhizos nodded. 'I expected he would. But he'll take some time to change his clothes and get there. By then the police chief will be having his siesta. They'll not dare to disturb him very early in the afternoon. When they do, the lawyer will find that my father has arrived simultaneously with himself, lodging a counter-complaint for assault and damage.'

Zara's eyes sparkled. 'This is generalship. Oh, splendid!' Then her face fell. 'But how long can you keep it up – playing them off by tricks?'

'This is the last of the tricks.'

'And father says the King is almost bound to sign the Bill the day after to-morrow.'

Rhizos's eyes turned to the high, ravine-like walls about them. 'We shall keep Little Perfume until then.'

And then some realisation came to Zara of what he intended. She stared at him, sick at heart. 'But – it will be the gendarmes who will come tomorrow.'

He nodded. 'I know. And you must not come again until – after. Not down into Little Perfume, I mean. I don't want other people implicated or arrested.'

'Am I "other people"?'

He could smile at that. 'Always, for me. Apart and adorable, my dear.'

But her momentary flippancy had passed. 'Oh, it'll be madness.' Her eyes widened. 'And it's not just a scuffle you intend. *That* is why Kolocrotoni has been buying revolvers – I heard of it. . . . Rhizos – you who've always hated fighting and laughed at the dark little melodramatics of history!'

His look almost frightened her. 'Do you think I haven't hated the trickeries and treacheries of the last few days? Do you think I don't hate the dirty little pantomime we're staging now? But I'd rather mime in the dark than crawl like a coward in the sunlight.' He shuddered and passed his hands across his eyes. His voice fell to a dull flatness. 'And there'll be no fighting. Look here, Zara, I must go back.'

They touched hands, not looking at each other. She did not kiss him this time. Her eyes were suddenly blind with tears.

XV

That evening the Greeks – thirteen of them, young men between the ages of eighteen and thirty, and all unmarried – moved out from Little Perfume with pickaxes and shovels, and, a hundred yards along the

Sharia el Ghoraib, began to dig up the roadway. It was very quiet, in that hushed Cairene semi-darkness, and Rhizos Trikoupi, with knit brows and a tape-line, went from side to side of the street, measuring and calculating. It might have seemed to the casual onlooker like an ordinary gang of street workmen but for the silence that went with its operations. Young men from the representative families of the settlement – Kolocrotoni, Vasos, Sina, the two young Latas, Gemadios, Zalakosta and the others – they dug and hewed through the dried mud and were presently excavating the ancient paving-stones. From behind them there was silence also in all the locked and shuttered houses of Little Perfume. Even the looms had ceased to hum.

For a battle had been fought there over the paper Rhizos had prepared and forced the Greek house-holders – his father among them – to sign. This was a document disowning Rhizos and his followers as 'young hotheads' whom the elders of the community were unable to restrain. Little Perfume, it declared, entirely dissociated itself from them.

'I will not sign it,' swore Londos, in bed with rheumatism, and groaning as he stirred indignantly. But, like all the others, sign he did at last, and held Rhizos's hand, peering up into his face. 'If only I could come with you!'

'You'll be less bored in bed, *papakes*,' Rhizos assured him lightly. 'Probably we'll all catch damnable colds. But our bluff will keep them off for a time – and they can only give a few of us a week or so in prison when it's over.'

But midnight saw a barricade, business-like enough and breast-high, spanning the sharia from side to side. Then, leaving the Latas, armed with cudgels, to look after it, Rhizos and his companions went back and slept in Little Perfume, a sleep that was broken in early dawn by one of the Latas coming panting to the door of the Trikoupi house with the news that Falih's lawyer was approaching with his gang of labourers. Evidently he expected to take the settlement by surprise.

Rhizos dressed hurriedly and went to the barricade. With the lawyer he saw two Egyptian policemen.

The party was evidently staggered at sight of the barricade. What happened then is not quite clear. For a little, while his young men ran up, Rhizos stood and parleyed with the lawyer, the gendarmes at first laughing and then losing their tempers in the quick, Egyptian way. One of them unslung his carbine – it was in the days when they still carried carbines – and, levelling it at Rhizos, ordered him to start demolishing the barricade. For answer Kolocrotoni, looking over the barricade, at some distance from Rhizos, called out:

'Drop that carbine!'

The gendarme looked up and found himself covered by a dozen revolvers. His carbine clattered to the ground. At the order of Kolocrotoni the other policeman also disarmed. Sina climbed over the barricade, and, in the midst of a queer silence, went and collected the weapons. Then he returned and the two parties looked at each other undecidedly. Suddenly the first gendarme turned round and hastened down the Sharia el Ghoraib. His companion trudged stolidly after him. Falih's lawyer, after a moment of hesitation, followed suit, his gang behind him in straggling retreat. The young Greeks at the barricade avoided each other's eyes and beat their hands together in the chill morning air. Somewhere a cock began to crow, shrilly.

At ten o'clock a policeman came down the sharia, surveyed the barricade and its defenders, and then retired. Kolocrotoni brought Rhizos a cup of coffee, and while the latter drank it, himself mounted to highest point of the defences and watched. Suddenly he drew a breath like a long sigh.

'Here they come.'

XVI

How far those thirteen young Greeks had imagined the affair would go it is impossible to say. In the subsequent enquiry the police affirmed that the Greeks fired the first shot. There can, at least, be little doubt that the police at the beginning made no attempt to shoot. The squad of twenty men marched to within ten yards or so of the barricade, and Rhizos called them to halt. For answer the officer in command ostentatiously turned his back on the barricade, ordered his men to club their carbines and charge, himself turned round again – and came forward at a rapid run, swinging a loaded stick in his hand. The attackers were greeted with a hail of stones. Carbine and revolver shots rang out. The officer pitched forward into the dust, and for a moment the policemen wavered. But only for a moment. They came on again. And then Rhizos committed himself openly. He leant over the barricade and shot three of them in rapid succession. Thereat the survivors broke and ran. The Greeks did not fire, but glanced, white-faced, at their leader. Rhizos, white himself, calmly ejected the spent rounds from his revolver, and re-loaded it.

Then, with a glance down the empty sharia, he climbed the barricade and inspected the four uniformed figures lying in the dust. The officer and one other were dead. Two of them lived, one with a broken arm, the other with his skull slightly grazed. Rhizos bandaged the last one, helped the man with the wounded arm to his feet, and pointed down the sharia. Holding to the wall, like a sick dog, the policeman shambled out of sight. Rhizos was turning in perplexity to the other bodies when his companions called to him urgently. . . . He gained shelter just as the rifle-fire opened.

None of the defenders had any experience of warfare, and it says much for the skill with which the barricade was constructed that in the first few minutes only two of them were killed. Kolocrotoni was shot through the shoulder. Rhizos, calling to the others to keep their places, crawled to him and bandaged him. Presently the rifle-fire ceased for a moment, but after another abortive charge opened again. . . .

By evening there were eight Greeks, including Rhizos, left alive. In spite of threats and entreaties on the part of those who held the barricade, non-combatants – the gentle Elia among them – crawled out from Little Perfume and took away the bodies of the dead. But with the evening the gendarmes withdrew (in futile search of a way over the khan walls, as was afterwards told), the stretch of street in front of the barricade was left deserted, and, staring at each other unbelievingly, the young men ate the food brought them from Little Perfume.

They seemed unending those evening hours. Rhizos had two bonfires lighted at a distance of fifty yards or so down the sharia, so that there might be no surprise attack. A tarpaulin had been brought from the settlement and erected behind the barricade in the form of a hut, and what dark thoughts assailed the outlaws till they dropped exhausted in its shelter no one will ever know. But long after midnight some of them awoke and heard Rhizos, alone wakeful and guarding the barricade, singing in a strange, shrill voice snatches of a song they had never heard before. It was a frightening thing to hear in the listening silence of the sharia, and Kolocrotoni prevailed on him to go and lie down. Utterly weary, he swayed to the shelter, staggered – and was asleep before Kolocrotoni's arm caught him and lowered him to the ground.

Near three in the morning, eluding somehow the police-picket at the upper end of the Sharia Ghoraib, Zara Muslih reached the barricade and whispered the news to Kolocrotoni: the Bill was to be signed and issued in the morning. The story of the affray in the Warrens had hastened the signing.

'And you must all get away at once,' she urged. 'Throw up rope-ladders over the khan walls.'

Kolocrotoni shook his head. 'We cannot leave here until the Bill is definitely signed, Rhizos says. If we abandon the barricade now the police may be in possession of Little Perfume before morning.'

'Rhizos – he doesn't know what he's done! You people were in a searchlight of sympathy before he started this resistance – no one has a scrap of pity for you now. . . . Oh, tell him I *must* see him!'

The young Greek shook his head again, looking at her with narrowed eyes. 'He's asleep. This isn't a woman's business.'

A moment they looked at each other, Kolocrotoni implacable, Zara desperately pleading. Then she glanced at that tragic barricade for the last time, and went back through the dying light of the bonfires and never saw either Rhizos or Kolocrotoni again.

For at starset, in the lowering darkness that precedes the Egyptian morning, they shook Rhizos awake. The police were approaching again, and in considerable force. He started up as he felt their hands on his shoulder, and looked at them, Kolocrotoni and the younger Latas, remotely, alertly.

'*What is it? The Persians?*'

They stared at him, stumblingly attempting to follow strange rhythms and accentuations in his speech. 'It's the gendarmes,' said Kolocrotoni. 'And we'll hardly be able to make them out. There's not a gleam of sun yet.'

Rhizos laughed, jumping to his feet, speaking again in words they barely understood – albeit they might have been direct answer to Zara's passionate denunciation. . . . Then he shuddered and passed his hands across his eyes, as though awakening from an inner sleep.

'What is it? What have I been saying? I had a dream. . . . The gendarmes?'

Far down the sharia came the steady tramp of disciplined feet.

XVII

They sent an armoured car against it eventually, that flimsy erection behind which a dwindling band of Greeks defied the hosts of the Orient. It crashed through, indifferently, half an hour after the promulgation of the Bill, and it was then that Rhizos and Kolocrotoni were killed. Three of the defenders, Sina and the two Latas, escaped back into Little Perfume, their ammunition exhausted. There they managed to scale the khan walls and were seen never again in Cairo. But before they went they told the tale of those last few hours. . . .

The historian pauses, his theme in diminuendo, himself standing in the bright Cairene sunshine, lost in fantastic speculation as he sees again that misascribed quotation graved below the word ΘΕΡΜΟΠΥΛΑΙ on the dusty wall of the Sharia el Ghoraib:

'*So much the better. We shall fight in the shade.*
— RHIZOS OF SPARTA.'

Revolt

I

Boom!

Hardly had the distant reverberations ceased before the sunset wind blew in the greenery of the city palms. It was as if Cairo sighed audibly. Day was officially dead. Crowned in red, squatting in the colours of the west, the Moqattam Hills peered down, perhaps to glimpse a miraculous moment on the surface of the Nile.

The Nile flowed red like a river of blood.

Rejeb ibn Saud, squatting in the Bulaq hut by the Nile bank, looked at his wrist-watch, at the face of the unconscious boy on the string-bed, at the fall of light on Gezireh across the river. But for one insistent whisper, the startling sunset was now a thing woven of silence.

'*The sea! The sea!*'

It was the whisper of the homing Nile. Gathering, hastening to fulfilment and freedom, joining its thousand voices, all the yearnings of its leagues of desert wandering, in that passionately whispered under-cry: '*The sea!*'

All that afternoon the cry had haunted him. Now, as the boy on the bed tossed and moaned, ibn Saud shook himself, stood up, and bent over the bed.

'Oh, Hassan . . .'

The hut door opened of a sudden. Out of the sunset glare, into the dimness of the hut, Sayyiya, ibn Saud's sister-in-law, entered. She was a Sudanese, young, full-faced, thick-lipped. At the tall figure of ibn Saud she glanced enquiringly, then also went to the bed and bent over it. The boy Hassan seemed scarce to breathe.

'In an hour we shall know, master.'

'In an hour I shall not be here.' The man looked away from the string-bed. The chill on his heart had chilled his voice. Even at that moment, only by an effort could he keep from listening to the insistent whisper of the river.

'You go to the Khan Khalil to lead the Jihad? It is to-night?'

Ibn Saud nodded. It was to-night. An hour after the fall of darkness the Warren hordes, poured into the Khan il Khalil, were to be mustered and armed. Police and gendarmes, half of them active adherents of the insurrection, would have withdrawn from all western and central Cairo. The two native regiments had been seduced from allegiance to the puppet Nationalist Government: were enthusiastically for the rising: themselves awaited only the signal from the Khan il Khalil, the lighting of the torch.

And it would be lit. That was to be Rejeb ibn Saud's part. Golden-tongued, first in popularity of the rising's masters, he was to be the last to address the brown battalions in the Khan. For them he was to strike fire to the torch that would, ere another morning, light the flames of vengeance and revolution across the European city from Bulaq to Heliopolis.

The song of the Nile – such the cry – of fulfilment, of freedom attained – that would to-night rise on the welling tide of the Black Warrens, from thousands of throats, from all the pitiful Cohorts of the Lost, the Cheated of the Sunlight . . .

'Master, if you come not back—'

Ibn Saud started. In his cold ecstasy he had forgotten the hut, Sayyiya, even Hassan.

'That is with God. But if Hassan – Listen, woman. You will come to me at the Khan. When the change, one way or another, has passed upon my son, come to the Shoemakers' Bazaar, by the south side of the Khan, and send word to me. You will find your way?'

'I will come.'

Something in her glance touched him, stirred him from his abstraction.

'The time has been weary for you since Edei died, Sayyiya. If I live through this night—'

Suddenly the woman was crouching at his feet on the mud floor. Passionately, scaredly, she caught at the long cloak he had wrapped about him.

'Master Rejeb. . . . Those English whom you lead against to-night – they are ever strong, ever cunning. If you die, what will happen to Hassan and to me? Master—'

Ibn Saud's cold eyes blazed. He flung the woman from him, flung open the hut door. Beyond, seen from the elevation of the Bulaq bank, the Cairene roofs lay chequered in shadows.

'And what of the folk – our brothers, our sisters – who die out there in their hovels and hunger? Thousands every year.' He blazed with the sudden, white-hot anger of the fanatic. 'What matters your miserable life – Hassan's – mine – if we can show the sun to those who rot their lives away in the kennels of the Warrens? We miserable "natives" – unclean things with unclean souls – to-night we shall light such a candle in Egypt as no man—'

He halted abruptly. The fire fell from him. Speaking in Arabic, he had yet thought in a famous alien phrase. Under his dark skin there spread a slow flush. Without further speech he bent and kissed his son, and then walked out of the hut into the wine-red gloaming.

Sayyiya crouched dazed upon the floor. Then a sound disturbed her. From the throat of the boy Hassan came a strange, strangled moan.

The small, fevered body tossed for a little, then lay very still.

II

Darkness was still an hour distant. European Cairo thronged her streets, cried her wares, wore her gayest frocks, set forth on evening excursions to Saqqara and the Sphinx. John Caldon, seated on the terrace of the Continental, awoke from a sunset dream and turned towards his brother-in-law, Robert Sidgwick.

'Eh?'

'. . . the edge of a volcano.'

'Where?'

'There.' Sidgwick waved his hand to the brown driftage in the street below them. 'The political situation's the worst it has been for months. The Cairenes have been propaganda'ed for months by Nationalist extremists. Trade and employment are bad. The native quarters ate seething.'

'Very proper of them.'

Caldon smiled into the lighting of a cigarette. An artist, he was making a westward world-tour from England. Together with his wife and daughter, he had arrived from India, via Suez, only the day before. Sidgwick's statement left him unimpressed. He had never yet encountered a white man, settled amongst brown, who was not living on the edge of a volcano. It was the correct place to live, just as it was the correct thing for a volcano to seethe pleasingly upon occasion.

Sidgwick had the monologue habit. Through the quiet air and the blue cloud from his own cigarette Caldon caught at a number of phrases.

'This damn self-government foolishness began it all . . . Treat a native as a native.'

'Why not as a human being?'

'That's what we've done here. Look at the result.'

Caldon was boredly ironical. 'Self-government – with an army of occupation! An alarum-clock with the alarum taken away!'

'It's advisable – if you give it to a native. . . . Take it my sister's never told you about young Thomas O'Donnell?'

Caldon shook his head. Sidgwick nodded, without pleasantness.

'Well, the telling won't hurt you. He was a half-caste – an Irish-Sudanese, of all grotesque mixtures. His father had had him sent to a school in Alexandria; some kind of irrigation engineer out here the father was, and pious to boot. He died when his son was seventeen, leaving instructions for the latter to be sent to a theological college in England to train as a missionary. All very right and proper. To England young Thomas O'Donnell came. To Bleckingham.'

Caldon, with some little show of interest, nodded. Sidgwick resumed.

'You know – though your people didn't settle in Bleckingham till about a year after the time of O'Donnell – the lost tribes the

Theological College spates over the country-side to tea and tennis on spare afternoons? One of these tennis-do's I met O'Donnell. He was a tall, personable nigger – not black, of course. Cream-colour. But it wouldn't have worried me in those days if charcoal had made a white mark on him. He was interesting. I liked him, invited him to tea. Clare was young also, in those days, you'll have to remember.'

'Why?' A tinge of red had come on the artist's cheekbones.

'Oh, Cæsar's wife is stainless enough. But a young girl hardly knows herself – or the stuff she handles. Had it been a white man, of course . . .

'Yes, Clare became fairly intimate with O'Donnell. Flirted with him, no doubt. Mother was then the same invalid as you knew; I was supposed to be my sister's protector. But I suffered from attempting the assimilation of indigestible theories on the brotherhood of man. I admired O'Donnell. Oh, he fascinated.'

The light all down the Sharia Kamil had softened. Caldon sat rigid. It was Sidgwick who dreamt now.

'The outcome of it all was what I'd expect now. O'Donnell and Clare went picnicking on Bewlay Tor. . . . The nigger attempted to act according to his nature. Clare's screams saved her – attracted some students mountaineering. O'Donnell went berserk amongst them. You see, he wasn't a white man.'

'What happened to him?'

'God knows. He didn't wait to be kicked out of the College. They traced him as far as Southampton, where it was supposed he'd managed to get a job on board some ship. . . . Hallo, here's Clare. Good Lord, what's the—'

A woman was running up the steps from the taxi which had stopped below the terrace – a woman with a white, scared face. Behind her, weeping, came trailingly the ayah of Caldon's daughter.

'Jack, Jack! . . . Little Clare – we lost her down in the bazaars, in the horrible Warrens. Jack – they stoned us when we tried to find her. . . .'

III

Never had it all seemed so secure.

But Rejeb ibn Saud, far out of the direct route from Bulaq to the Khan il Khalil, and striding down the Maghrabi with his 'aba pulled close about his face, saw signs enough that were not of the olden times. Few native vendors were about; no desert folk, sightseers of the sightseers from foreign lands, lingered by the hotels. Here and there, making way for the strolling foreigner, some dark Arab face would grow the darker.

Ibn Saud had sudden vision: Fire in the Maghrabi, massacre and loot; the screamings of rape, crackle of revolver fire, knives in brown hands . . .

In three hours – at the most.

Ibn Saud half stopped in his stride; the Maghrabi blurred before his eyes. Slave of the faith which had bound him these many years, he was yet compounded of so many warring hopes and pities that his imagination could suddenly sway him, to gladness or to despair, from a long mapped-out path. . . . The Green Republic of Islam – attained by those means – was it justified?

A stout Frenchman and his wife moved off the sidewalk in order to pass the crazed native who had suddenly stopped in their path, muttering. Looking curiously back at him, they saw him move on slowly, dully, with bent head.

So, with none of his former pace and purposefulness, he went, in a little turning northwards into the deeper dusk of the Sharia Kamil. The whimsical intent that had originally led him to diverge through the European quarter still drew him on, but he followed it in a brooding daze. At the entrance to the bookshop of Zarkeilo he was jarred with realisation of his quest.

Nevertheless, he entered, and, disregarding the assistant's question, passed down into the interior of the shop to the section that housed Continental editions of English fiction and verse. With an almost feverish eagerness he began to scan the titles. About, the walls were here and there decorated with sham antiques – bronzes, paintings of Coptic Virgins, and the like. To a small red volume ibn Saud at length outreached an unsteady hand.

Rememberingly he turned the leaves. Ten years since this book had lain in his hands, but he had remembered it – remembered because of those lines which haunted him, which had inspired him since, a homeless vagrant, he had landed at Suez to his dream of Egyptian Renaissance, to the years of toil and persecution in which he had built up this night's insurrection. . . . With their music and their magic, haunting as ever, the words leapt at him from the printed page:

> 'One man with a dream, at pleasure
>   Shall go forth and conquer a crown;
> And three with a new song's measure
>   Shall trample a kingdom down.'

Rejeb ibn Saud replaced the book, straightened, stood upright with shining eyes. Doubts fell from him. Outside, in the night, his dream went forth to conquer. . . .

His eyes fell musingly on a sham antique crucifix. Last of the gloaming light upon it, the tortured Christ fell forward from the cross. Upon his head, each carven point a-glitter, shone the crown of thorns.

IV

'Stone her! Stone her!'

Nightfall; in the fastnesses of the native quarter – the maze of the streets that radiate around the eastern sector of the Sharia el Muski; a girl running – a child of nine, English, with a flushed, scared face; behind, peltingly, laughingly, dirt and stone hurling, a horde of native children.

Such adults as were about turned amused glances to follow the chase. The hunt was up!

Ibn Saud halted and watched. Nearer drew the child, casting terrified glances to right and left. Then she caught his eye. Straight as an arrow towards him she came, clutched his cloak, and clung to him, panting.

The pursuing children surrounded them. One, a ranged hunch-back, caught at the girl's dress. Ibn Saud spoke.

'Let be.'

'Why? She is English. We are to kill them all to-night.'

Hate and curiosity in their eyes, the children drew closer. Two loafers joined them, and one addressed ibn Saud.

'It is so, brother. Let the children have their sport. Who are you to stop it?'

'I am ibn Saud.'

At that name the children, cruel no longer, but shy and worshipping, drew away. The loafers, whose hatred of the English had apparently not induced in them any desire to join the army of the insurrection in the Khan il Khalil, slunk aside. Ibn Saud touched the girl's head. She had lost her hat.

'How did this happen?' he asked in English.

'Mother and nurse took me to the bazaars. I saw a shop I liked, and went into it. It had lots of doors. Perhaps I came out at the wrong one. When I did I couldn't see either mother or nurse. Then I walked and walked. And those children struck me and cried things and chased me. I ran. Then I saw you.'

Thus, succinctly, the little maid. Ibn Saud stared down at her, a wonder in his eyes.

'But why did you think I would help you?'

The girl raised clear, confident eyes. 'Oh, I knew you would because – because you are different.'

An odd flush came on the face of the insurrectionist. He stood thoughtful. Folly, in any case. He was only saving the child for—

Oh, inevitable. He glanced impatiently round the dusking street. Then:

'What is your name?'

'Clare.'

He stood very still and then bent and stared into her face. For so long did he remain in that posture that the child's lips began to quiver. As in a dream ibn Saud heard himself question her.

'Where is your mother staying in Cairo?'

'At the Continental. If I could get a taxi—'

She was calm and methodical and very grown-up now. Ibn Saud took her hand.

'Come.'

He hurried. Through a maze of odoriferous alleys and walled-in corridors – the kennels of the Cheated of the Sunlight – he led her till on the dusk blazed a long sword of light. It was the Sharia el Muski, strangely bereft of traffic. With difficulty ibn Saud found an *'arabiyeh*. When directed to take the child to the Continental, the driver blankly refused. Not to-night. Then ibn Saud drew aside the folds of his head-dress and spoke his name, and the driver saluted to head and heart. In Cairo that night that name was more powerful than the Prophet's.

What would it be by dawn?

'Thank you very much.' The earnest eyes of the child looked up into ibn Saud's dark face. With a sudden thought: 'Please, what is your name? – so that I can tell mother.'

Child though she was, she was never to forget him, standing there in the lamplight as he answered her:

'I am Thomas O'Donnell.'

V

Brugh! Boom! Brugh!

In a great square space, ringed about by the bulking of the bazaars, three bonfires burned, shedding a red light on the massing hundreds of the Black Warrens. Against the Khalil wall was upraised a giant platform. At the other side of the square, curious, antique, a thing of the ages and with the passion of all Man's sweated travail in its beat, was mounted a gigantic drum. Out into the night and the lowe, over the heads of the massing insurrectionists, over the hastening chains of Cairenes converging on the Khan from alley and gutter, its challenge boomed, menacing, stifled, a gathering frenzy.

Already, eastwards and northwards, curtains of scouting insurrectionists, awaiting the final word, hung as self-deputed guards upon the heart of the revolt. But there was little need of guard. The gendarme had laid aside his uniform, kept his rifle, and was now mingling with the mobs of the Khan il Khalil. The petty official, long European-clad, was in burnous and kaftan, uplifting his voice in the wail of chanting which ever and anon rose to drown even the clamour of the drum. Spearhead of the revolt, the Cairene Labour Union massed its scores of rail and tramway strikers.

The hour was at hand.

'Brothers—'

From amidst the notables on the platform, one had stepped forth. High and dim above the Cheated of the Sunlight he upraised his hand.

Es-Saif of El Azhar. An echo and an interpretation of the savage drumming, his voice beat over the silenced square. He had the marvellous elocutionary powers of the trained Egyptian, the passion of the fanatic, the gift of welding a mob into a Jihad.

Presently, at the words rained upon them, long Eastern wails of approbation began to arise. Other speakers followed Es-Saif. The great bonfires, heaped anew, splashed the throngs and the grisly walls with ruddy colour. Quicker began to beat the blood in heart and head. Clearer and louder arose the pack bayings of applause.

Jammed in the midst of the vast concourse below the platform, Rejeb ibn Saud stood listening to the voices of his lieutenants. As if deafness had crept upon him, they sounded incredibly remote. . . .

That child . . . By now she would be safe. And to-morrow, somewhere amidst charred beams and smoking rafters, he might stumble over her bones. . . .

Surely the square and the bodies around him steamed with heat? What was Es-Saif saying? 'Our starved children who have died, who have cried in the darkness and held out their dying hands—'

Children crying in the darkness. . . . What was all history but a record of that? Hundreds, this night. Clare weeping in terror, the terror-filled mites of the Warrens, Hassan . . .

'Ibn Saud!'

In a long lane that was closing behind him, a man had forced his way from the foot of the giant platform.

'We thought you lost or captured. We would have torn down your prison with our bare hands. Come, it is near your time to speak.'

He spoke in the commanding voice of a worshipping disciple, and then turned back towards the platform. Through the opening throng ibn Saud followed him . . . Near his time. In a few minutes now he would stand forth on that platform and fire the blood-lust in the maddened horde whose wrongs he had stressed and nourished all those long years.

He found himself climbing to the platform. Dim hands guided him on either side, faces, red-lit, grotesque, profiled and vanished in the bonfires' glare. Abayyad was speaking now. At sight of ibn Saud, Es-Saif leapt up, and kissed him and led him to a seat, wondering a little at his lack of greeting, and the brooding intentness of the dark, still face.

Wave upon wave, a sea of faces below him. As one looking out upon his kingdom ibn Saud stood a moment, and suddenly his eyes blazed, aweing to silence the murmured questionings of Es-Saif.

Clare – Hassan – all the children of the Warrens and of all the warring races of men – *With them lay the world.* Not with his generation – white and brown alike, they had failed. He sought to poison the unguessable future that was not his: he sought to murder it now in death for the hearts and hands that might save the world. Never his generation, but some time, it might be, *theirs*, would yet win a wide path through all the tangles of breed and creed and race, reach even to that dream that might yet be no dream – the Brotherhood of Man. . . .

Below him the mist that was the mustering insurrection quivered. What was that?

He stared across to the far side of the Khan. Through the throngs, from the direction of the Shoemakers' Bazaar, a Sudanese was slowly forcing his way towards the platform. With the force of an utter certainty, Rejeb ibn Saud knew him for what he was.

He was Sayyiya's messenger.

VI

Abayyad's voice rose and fell in penultimate peroration. Behind him, ibn Saud, watching the approach of the messenger, stood with a sudden fire alight in his chilled heart.

For the sake of that his vision of the World of Youth, he would stake all on Chance and the mercy of God. If Sayyiya's note told of

Hassan's recovery, he would violate every enthusiasm of his life in the Warrens, would speak peace to the mobs, cry on them to desist, preach to them the vision of the world that had arisen before his eyes. So, if there was a God, if he had but spared Hassan, he would speak. . . .

The lights in the Khan il Khalil flung a glow upon the heavens. Ibn Saud looked up. Beyond the glow, clear and cold, shone the stars. Infinitely remote, infinitely impersonal. . . .

Clare-Hassan – the saving of the near and dear to one – how pitiful!

'Ibn Saud! ibn Saud!'

The shouting of his name beat in his ears. Urgently upon his sleeve he felt the hand of Es-Saif. Abayyad had finished. Following the shout, upon the Khan fell a vast hush, broken only by the sound of a throaty breathing as Sayyiya's messenger reached the platform.

Ibn Saud took the note that was handed up to him, unfolded it, and read.

VII

Then a strange thing happened. About him, on the platform of the insurrectionists, they heard him. Ibn Saud laughed – a low, clear laugh, and glanced up again at the stars.

Infinitely remote.

The note slipped from his hand. To the edge of the platform he stepped forward and spoke.

For a full minute, sonorous, golden, the voice beloved of the dim brown multitudes of the Warrens rang clear. Then, obscuring it, began to rise murmurs of astonishment, counter-murmurs for silence. The stillness that had held the massed insurrection vanished. The crowds wavered and shook.

'Traitor!'

A single voice spoke from the heart of the mob. A hundred voices took it up, a hundred others – those of ibn Saud's personal following – shouted to drown the word. Pandemonium broke loose. Men screamed and argued, and over the whole Khan swung and wavered the hand of an incredible fear.

'Infidel! Englishman!'

Face distorted, Abayyad sprang forward upon ibn Saud. As at the touch of frost, the hand of that fear stilled for a moment the tumult below.

In that moment Abayyad, with gleaming knife, struck home.

Ibn Saud shook him off. Crowned in his purpose, infinitely humble, he outreached both arms to the mob. . . .

With a roar as of the sea, the hordes rose in a wave and poured upon the platform.

VIII

Es-Saif wanders an exile in the land of the Senussi. The secret history of that night in the Cairene Warrens – that night which saw the insurrection fall like a house of cards in the wreckage of the stormed platform of the Khan, which saw the rebel battalions, heart-broken and in despair, break up and scatter to hut and hovel – is as dim to him as to any who heard the traitorous speech for which Rejeb ibn Saud paid with his life.

Yet from the platform Es-Saif salved a curious relic – the crumpled note sent by Sayyiya to the leader of the insurrection. Reading it, who can guess the dream for which ibn Saud cheated himself of his bargain with God, or what crown he went forth to conquer?

'To my master, Rejeb ibn Saud. The mercy of God the Compassionate be with you. Thy son Hassan died at the fall of darkness. – SAYYIYA.'

Select Bibliography

James Leslie Mitchell's early death in 1935 meant that little was reissued by publishers who preferred to have an author available to
publicise new work: the situation was worsened by loss of copies
through bomb damage in World War II. Early editions are scarce:
there was sporaidc reprinting of some titles, particularly *A Scots
Quair* in the 1960s and 1970s, though hitherto the most available and
illuminating copies of the *Quair* and its three constituent novels
(*Sunset Song, Cloud Howe* and *Grey Granite*) have been those
introduced by Tom Crawford for Canongate Classics, issued both
as individual volumens (1988, 1989 and 1990) and as a trilogy
(Edinburgh, Canongate, 1995); they have been supplemented by
Valentina Bold's anthology of poems and short prose pieces, *Smeddum* (Canongate, 2001). One of the pieces reprinted in *Smeddum* is
The Speak of the Mearns, first published by the Ramsay Head Press,
1982; and enlarged version, with short stories prefaced by Jeremy
Idle, was published by Polygon in 1994 and is revised (still with
Jeremy Idle's valuable introduction) in this edition. The short stories
and essays came from a volume Grassic Gibbon wrote in collaboration with Hugh MacDiarmid in 1934, *Scottish Scene*, long out of print
but occassionally reissued and available second-hand.

Polygon published editions of *Sunset Song* and the whole *Scots
Quair* in 2006, and has also republished individual titles other than
the *Quair* including *Spartacus* (republished Scottish Academic
Press, 1990: Scottish Classics Series no. 14: updated version by
Polygon 2001 and reprints; new version 2005)

Gay Hunter (Edinburgh, Polygon, 19??)
Persian Dawns, Egyptian Nights (Edinburgh, Polygon, 1998)
Stained Radiance, (Edinburgh, Polygon, 2000)

Nine Against the Unknown (Edinburgh, Polygon, 2000)
Three Go Back (Edinburgh, Polygon, 2000)
The Lost Trumpet (Edinburgh, Polygon, 2001)

Ian S Munro, Grassic Gibbon's first biographer (Edinburgh, Oliver & Boyd, 1966) also produced a selection of essays and short stories *A Scots Hairst* (London, Hutchinson, 1967) but serious criticism began with Douglas Young, *Beyond the Sunset* (Aberdeen, Impulse, 1973) and William K Malcolm, *A Blasphemer and Reformer* (Aberdeen University Press, 1984). Douglas Gifford's *Neil M Gunn/Lewis Grassic Gibbon* was published (Edinburgh, Ramsay Head, 1983). and Ian Campbell's *Lewis Grassic Gibbon* appeard in the Scottish Writers series (Edinburgh, Scottish Academic Press 1985). There have been important postgraduate dissertations, unfortunately not yet extensively published, by Michael McGrath (Edinburgh, 1983) and Keith Dixon (Grenoble, 1983); Daniel Grader has a ground-breaking thesis on the classics and *Spartacus* (Edinburgh, 2004). Important work has been appearing in Germany: Uwe Zagratzki, *Libertäre und utopische Tendenzen im Erzählwerk James Leslie Mitchells (Lewis Grassic Gibbons)* (Frankfurt, Lang, 1991: Studien zur Germanistik und Anglistick 8) and Christoph Ehland, *Picaresque Perspectives – Exiled Identities* (Heidelberg, Universitätsverlag Winter, 20030, the latter "A Structural and Methodoligical Analysis of the Picaresque as a Literary Archetype in the Works of James Leslie Mitchell". A regular newsletter appears from the Grassic Gibbon Centre Arbuthnott Parish Hall, Arbuthnott, Laurencekirk AB30 1YB) with criticism and announcements of forthcoming publication www.grassicgibbon.com. A recent critical collection, with a good bibliography, has appeared, *A Flame in the Mearns: Lewis Grassic Gibbon, a Centenary Celebration* ed. M.P. McCulloch ans Sarah M. Dunnigan (Glasgow, Association for Scottish Literary Studies, 2003), and further work is in progress.

Further Work by the present editor can be consulted: on the letters in "Lewis Grassic Gibbon Correspondence: A Background and Check-list", *The Bibliotheck* 12/2 (1984), 46–57; on the short stories and essays in "Gibbon and MacDiarmid at Play: The Evolution of *Scottish Scene*", *The Blibiotheck* 13/3 (1986), 44–52; on the topography of the novels in "The Grassic Gibbon Country" in *A Sence of Place: Studies in Scottish Local History in Memory of Eric Forbes* ed. Gramae Cruickshank (Edinburgh: Scotland's Cultural Heritage Unit, 1988), 15–26; and on their literary qualities in "The Grassic Gibbon Style" in eds. J. Schwend and H.W. Drescher, *Studies in Scottish Fiction: Twentieith Century* (Scottish Studies no. 10) (Frankfurt and Bern, Peter Lang, 1990), 271–87. His schooling is treated in "Looking Back and Looking Forward: the Schooling of Lewis Grassic Gibbon" in ed. D. Northcroft, *North-East Identities and Scottish Schooling* (Aberdeen, Elphinstone Institute, 2005), 56–65, which contains much interesting material on the North-East. *Sunset Song* has been adapted for television, and more recently for stage and published as SUNSET SONG, Dramatised by Alastair Cording (London, Nick Hern Books, 2004) The topography of the *Sunset Song* country, and much interesting secondary detail, is in *Grassic Gibbon and his World* ed. Peter Whitfield (Aberdeen, Aberdeen Journals Ltd., 1994).

Works appearing under the name of James Leslie Mitchell

Hanno, or The Future of Exploration (London, 1928)
Stained Radiance: A Fictionist's Prelude (London, 1930)
The Thirteenth Disciple (London, 1931)
The Calends of Cairo (London, 1931)
Three Go Back (London, 1932)
Persian Dawns, Egyptian Nights (London, 1932)
The Lost Trumpet (London, 1932)
Image and Superscription (London, 1933)
Gay Hunter (London, 1934)
The Conquest of the Maya (London, 1934)

Appearing under the name of Lewis Grassic Gibbon

Sunset Song (London, 1932)
Cloud Howe (London, 1933)
Grey Granite (London, 1934)
A Scots Quair (London, 1946) [with Hugh MacDiarmid] *Scottish Scene: or, The Intelligent Man's Guide to Albyn* (London, 1934)
Niger: The Life of Mungo Park (London, 1934)
A Scots Hairst: Essays and Short Stories, ed. Ian Sherwood Munro (London, 1967)
Smeddum: Short Stories and Essays, ed. Donald MacAllister Budge (London, 1980)
The Speak of the Mearns, ed. Ian Campbell (Edinburgh, 1982)

Appearing under the name of JLM and LGG combined

Nine Against The Unknown: A Record of Geographical Exploration (London, 1934)

Among Recent Reprints/New Editions:

The Thirteenth Disciple (Edinburgh, 1981)
Sunset Song (Edinburgh, 1988)
Cloud Howe (Edinburgh, 1989)
Grey Granite (Edinburgh, 1990)
Gay Hunter (Edinburgh, 1990)
Spartacus (Edinburgh, 1990)
Stained Radiance (Edinburgh, 1993)

Criticism – Books/unpublished theses with substantial material or useful sections on LGG

Anderson, Carol, *The Representation of Women in Scottish Fiction: Image and Symbol* (unpublished doctoral thesis, University of Edinburgh, 1985)
Campbell, Ian, *Lewis Grassic Gibbon* (Edinburgh, 1985)
Gifford, Douglas, *Neil Gunn and Lewis Grassic Gibbon* (Edinburgh, 1983)
Hart, Francis Russell, *The Scottish Novel: A Critical Survey* (London, 1978)
McGrath, Michael, *JLM/LGG: A Study in Politics and Ideas in Relation to his Life and Work* (unpublished doctoral thesis, University of Edinburgh, 1983)
Malcolm, William K., *A Blasphemer and Reformer: A Study of JLM/LGG* (Aberdeen, 1984)
Munro, Ian Sherwood, *Lewis Grassic Gibbon* (Edinburgh, 1966)
Murray, Isobel and Tait, Bob, *Ten Modern Scottish Novels* (Aberdeen, 1984)
Young, Douglas, *Beyond the Sunset* (Aberdeen, 1973)
Zagratzki, Uwe, *Libertäre und Utopische Tendenzen in Erzählwerk JLMs/LGGs* (Frankfurt, 1992)

Criticism – Articles

Campbell, Ian, 'Lewis Grassic Gibbon and the Mearns', in *A Sense of Place: Studies in Scottish Local History* ed. Graeme Cruikshank (Edinburgh, 1988), pp. 15–26
Craig, Cairns, 'Fearful Selves: Character, Community and the Scottish Imagination', in *Cencrastus* (Winter, 1980–81), pp.29–32
Dixon, Keith, 'Letting the Side Down: Some Remarks on JLM's Vision of History', in *Études Écossaises no. 1: Écosse: Regards d'Histoire: Actes du Congrès international d'études écossaises, Grenoble, 1991* (Grenoble, 1992), pp.273–81
MacDiarmid, Hugh, 'Lewis Grassic Gibbon', in *The Uncanny Scot* (London, 1968), pp.154–63; article first published 1946
Ortega, Ramon Lopez, 'Language and Point of View in LGG's *A Scots Quair*', in *Studies in Scottish Literature* (1981) vol.XVI, pp.148–159
Trengove, Graham, 'Who is You? Grammar and Grassic Gibbon' *Scottish Literary Journal* (No. 1, 1974), pp.47–62